# TRICKED INTO IT

## WAR OF THE MYTH
## BOOK THREE

MIRANDA GRANT

# BY MIRANDA GRANT

---

# TRICKED INTO IT

This is entirely a work of fiction. Names, characters, places, and incidents are all products of my imagination and should not be seen as having any more credibility on reality than fake news does. Any resemblance to actual events, locales, organizations, or persons, living, dead, or stuck in purgatory, is entirely coincidental.

https://www.facebook.com/warofthemyth/
https://www.instagram.com/authormirandagrant/
https://www.tiktok.com/@authormirandagrant
authormirandagrant@gmail.com
www.mirandagrant.co.uk

ISBN: 978-1-914464-55-3

Cover, header, and breaks designed by MiblArt.
Map designed by Writing Evolution.
Edited by Writing Evolution.

### To you, dear reader:

It's a 'bit' late, but better than never, right?
*Right???*

### And a huge thanks to:

*Mary Reilly*
*Awesome Forensic Scientist*

I said it was research for the book, but I really just
wanted to talk about dead bodies without being
recommended a therapist. Haha. JK. Not all the scenes
made it, just enough to not call the cops.

I hope...

# TERMS

**Amazon** – An organization of female assassins. Trained from when they were children, they have no morals and they will take any job from anyone as long as their fees are met.

**Angel** – A winged creature of 'purity'. They can tell when someone is lying, cannot lie themselves, and can shoot a blinding light from their palms that has the power to burn the souls of demons.

**Archangel** – Six black-winged angels who are tasked with policing the gods and holding order and justice in the Seven Planes. Light cannot exist without darkness.

**Ascension** – "Puberty" for creatures of the Myth. This is when they get their powers and their bodies become capable of healing themselves.

**Atlantian** – The ancestors of humans. Illegally created by Prometheus, they were then hunted down like animals by the gods. They were believed to be extinct before Charlie was discovered.

**Berserker** – There is only one family of berserkers and Tegan Jólfrson's family, which consists of him, seven older sisters, and his parents, is it. Once they enter a Rage, they will kill anything and everything they see.

**Blood Moon** – A dark red moon that rises on the plane of Blódyrió and forces werewolves to undergo their change under the power of the Craving. The blood moon's cycle can't be tracked, and can appear at anytime of the moon's cycle. It doesn't have to be full. Anyone caught outside during this time, has a high chance of being slaughtered by werewolves.

**Craving** – Severe bloodlust that makes one mindless with the need to hunt. Made vampires broken during their change and werewolves under the blood moons are the most at risk into falling under the power of the Craving.

**Descendant** – A child whose parents are both gods, but is not a god themselves. They were made infertile by the archangels.

**Drazic Demon** – A red-skinned demon with horns and fangs, both of which grow as they age. They're reckless and stubborn but hold loyalty above all.

**Deusychosis Plague** – A deadly disease that wiped out almost everyone on Perspic, causing the plane's portals to be permanently closed. It only targets persapics, but it can give them the power of a god, allowing them to bend reality...for a week anyway. Then they'll die. It's highly transferrable.

**Echidna** – A monster/killing machine that speaks using a mode of telepathy. Due to this, their human forms are mute.

**Elementalist** – A person with the ability to control one of the four elements: water, earth, air, or fire. If strong enough, a person can control their element in all its forms, but there isn't a single person that can wield more than one element.

**Elv've'Norc** – A mythical special ops organization tasked with protecting the Seven Planes. It was founded by Tegan Jólfrson three and a half thousand years ago, when Sebastian the Ancient Destroyer and Rakian the Call of Ragnarok had started their war. A member of the Elv've'Norc is called an Elv've'Nor.

**Hel's Exit** – The backdoor to Niflhel. Souls continuously try to escape back into the world of the living here. It's guarded by the Heldron royal family and will ring anytime there's a breach.

**Incubus** – A male creature who survives through sex, their power and 'food' coming from the act. Other races are also subconsciously hesitant to attack them, giving them the illusion of being 'extremely lucky' when slicing through an army of warriors. A female of this creature is called a succubus.

**Kultara** – A massive pain in the ass. A thorn in one's side.

Someone you want to kill because of how much they annoy you.

**Phasing** – Teleporting, regardless of distance. A person must either know the place they're phasing to or be told of it in great detail. Other people can be taken with them, though they suffer side effects such as headaches, nausea, and occasionally death. Most people with this ability can only phase from inside a plane, but those strong enough can phase from one plane to another.

**Primordial** – The first created person of a species of the Myth.

**Pulsing** – When a powerful creature undergoes their ascension, their powers lash out uncontrollably at random intervals. For a short time after pulsing, they become vulnerable.

**Telepath** – One with the ability to communicate through their mind. They can also force people to do as they command, as well as create bleeds in the brain.

**Trickster** – A creature capable of creating illusions and shapeshifting. Their objects of illusions are just that – illusions. They mimic an object in every sense, but they do not have a physical body.

**Scrolls of Atlantis** – A book of unspeakable power, written by Prometheus, who stole the wisdom from the well of

Mimir, the same well Odin sacrificed his eye to in exchange for knowledge. Its pages don't just hold the secrets of life. They *are* the secrets of life. It can only be read by Atlantians.

**Seven Planes** – The seven worlds where creatures created by the gods live. They are: Earth, Gaera, Halzaja, Persic, Blódyrió, Konistra, and Alazul.

**Shadow Walkers** – Creatures with the ability to morph into and control shadows. They cannot be harmed while in shadow form, but they can consume shadows, which will kill their victims given the soul is attached to the shadow.

**Skinwalker** – Born from the shadows of titans, these monstrous creatures have the ability to skin their victims alive and then don it like clothing. They will then look and sound exactly like their victims.

**Vampire** – There are two types: born or sired. A born vampire is able to walk in direct sunlight with only mild discomfort and has the ability to phase. They are also stronger and faster. Sired vampires are created by born vampires through a biting and exchanging of blood ritual. They are infertile and their bodies 'freeze in time' at their point of rebirth. They awake in a frenzy and will kill whoever is nearby in their need to feed.

**Werewolf** – A bipolar monster roughly resembling a wolf.

Their bite is poisonous to vampires. Their ability to follow a scent is unmatched.

# CHARACTERS

**Adriel** – Heldron king mourning his dead wife and family. Rules over Heldron and helps protect Hel's Exit. A drazic demon.

**Aisla** – A hotheaded fey princess and member of the Elv've'Norc. Teammate to Rico and Dominix.

**Cariad** – An incubus and the last member of his team. They were all slaughtered at Xi'aghn by Elizabeth when she retrieved the *Scrolls of Atlantis.*

**Charlie** – The only known person who can read the *Scrolls of Atlantis.* Jack's lifemate and mother to Tony. She is currently being held prisoner by Sebastian.

**Delentia** – A meddling, sightseeing goddess who may or may not be mad. Her plans are known only to herself.

**Dominix** – An echidna, mute as all her kind is. Teammate to Rico and Aisla.

**Elizabeth** – A descendant, daughter to Aphrodite and Hades. Controlled by Sebastian due to her curse, she is forced to obey his every command. She has the power to kill with a single touch, to raise the dead, and manipulate emotions. Emma's younger twin sister.

**Emma** – A descendant, daughter of Hades and Aphrodite, with the power to kill with a single touch, control the dead, and can force people to do whatever she wants. Rogan's lifemate. Elizabeth's older twin sister.

**Gabriel** – An archangel who's in love with Xeno. They have a rocky history, and it's because of that that he's helping the Elv've'Norc more than he should. He did something to Xeno to help her stop her fall.

**Galvanor** – A secret child of three: someone with the abilities of a telepath, astralist, and telekinetic. Everyone but Tegan believes him to be a telepath only. Matakyli's lifemate. Member of Rogan's team.

**Hunter** – A tech whizz curious about everything. Member of Rogan's team. Human.

**Jack** – A half-trickster with a deadly secret. He's being hunted by the gods and is much older than his team thinks. Member of Rogan's team.

**Kaide** – An Elv've'Nor Reaper. He and his twin brother, Kasem, go in when things are too fucked up to send anyone else. A teleporting swordsman.

**Kasem** – An Elv've'Nor Reaper. He and his twin brother, Kaide, go in when things are too fucked up to send anyone else. A teleporting swordsman.

**Lamia** – Sebastian's only remaining blood relative. A born vampire devoted to his cause.

**Lucille** – A young sired vampire. Sebastian is believed to have created her. Currently imprisoned in the Heldron dungeons.

**Lycra** – Head of the Amazon compound in Heldon. She is often hired by Sebastian. A shadow walker and Jack's lifemate.

**Matakyli** – Fourth in line to the Heldron throne and a guardian to the backdoor of Niflhel. A drazic demon and lifemate to Galvanor.

**Nivan** – One of Matakyli's best friends. Despite being fourth in line to the Zaknad throne, he was being trained by Adriel to take his place as Heldron king. But then he was taken by Sebastian. Infected with the Deusychosis Plague, he is a danger to everyone. A drazic demon. Currently missing.

**Pyro** – Second in line to the Heldron throne. A drazic demon and guardian to Hel's Exit.

**Rahu** – Third in line to the Heldron throne. A drazic demon and guardian to Hel's Exit.

**Rakian** – A descendant killed three and a half thousand

years ago by Sebastian.

**Rico** – An alpha werewolf and Elv've'Nor. Teammate to Aisla and Dominix.

**Rogan** – Head of the Retrieval Elv've'Norc team. A water elementalist and Emma's lifemate.

**Sebastian** – A sadistic, clever vampire who wants to destroy the Seven Planes and reshape them in his image. He tried once three and a half thousand years ago, but his plans were thwarted by Delentia.

**Tegan** – Head of the Elv've'Norc. A berserker..

**Tony** – A four year old traumatized boy. He is being held captive and tortured by Sebastian. He is Charlie's son.

**Xeno** – An angel in the midst of her fall. Once she loses her wings, she'll never get them back. Member of Rogan's team.

CAVE
PORTALED TO

VENTRA VENTRANIMUS RIVER

HIMPITI RIVER

KOIPINSA RIVER

 MOUNTAIN    TOWN

WOODS

RIVER

CAVE   CASTLE

CRYSTALCAVE

30 MILES

48 KILOMETRES

# ONE

*LOCATION UNKNOWN*

Every click of Charlie's shoes pierced her ears like a knife to the stomach. Every breath she stole from the putrid cold air burned its way down her throat. Every closed door she passed in the empty castle mocked her with the reality of her imprisonment.

The bastard had summoned her.

It killed her to walk at a normal pace when all Charlie wanted to do was run. The suspense was tearing into her heart, ripping out huge chunks of her soul. She needed to know what Sebastian had done to her child more than she needed her pride. But it wasn't her dignity that kept her legs steady and slow.

It was knowing that whatever she did now wouldn't matter. Sebastian had already played his hand. Whatever sick action he had taken against her son couldn't be reversed. Charlie would rather rot in hell than give the bastard the additional satisfaction of breaking her.

So she ignored the sharp pains in her heart that every footfall brought. She ignored the tightening of her throat as sobs lodged there along with the contents of her stomach. She ignored the motherly voice inside her as it begged with constant screams for her to pick up the pace, for her to end the nightmare haunting her imagination.

As much as she wanted to pay it heed, Charlie ignored it all.

She had to.

For if she lost her spirit and weakened her spine, she lost Anthony. Once Charlie was broken, there would be no reason for Sebastian to keep her child alive. So she would take everything that bastard threw at her with her head held high and her shoulders back.

And when she finally had the opening to kill him, she would take it with the utmost satisfaction.

It might not be today. It might not even be in this lifetime. But one day Charlie would find a way to rip the bastard's heart from his chest and toss it into the Eternal Flames. He would never be reborn again.

She held onto her anger as she walked the halls, desperate to keep her pace steady. With every step, she cursed the vampire's mind games. Sebastian had the ability to teleport to her exact location. Instead, he had sent a bitch with a letter. There was only one word scribbled upon it, but it was enough.

Written in blood, it demanded obedience.

*Come.*

At first she had shaken with rage and fear. Then she'd stilled with cold determination. Fighting the tears and sobs that threatened to break her, Charlie had carefully folded the paper and placed it on her desk. Under the heedful gaze of Sebastian's minion, she'd refused to look at the severed finger hanging above her.

As frail as her mind was, looking at Anthony's pinkie would have destroyed her.

But now, as she'd had the chance to build up her strength, envisioning it only brought anger.

The bastard had harmed her child. She was going to kill him.

One day.

Over and over she promised this to herself.

But all too soon she was greeted by the menacing door of the throne room. As if doused by a fire extinguisher, her spirit diminished. Shakily, Charlie collected her breath and gathered up the jagged pieces of her soul. After binding them together with tape that did not stick, she shoved her way inside.

"Charlie, my love. How nice of you to bless us with your presence."

Sebastian's tone was warm and friendly. Yet it carried the icy touch of death. He grinned just as warmly, just as coldly, as Charlie stepped into the room. His tongue darted out to lick a bloody fang. At her hard swallow, his smile widened.

Holding his gaze, Charlie forced herself to shut the door. She told herself that it didn't matter, that even with it open she wouldn't be able to escape. It didn't help.

Fear danced erratically inside her veins. Her legs merged with the stone of the floor. Only her breath escaped, leaving her cruelly behind. But her life had never been easy. Charlie had long ago perfected the art of walking on deadened legs.

So with a false bravado, she moved between a double row of obsidian pillars. Each one was carved into a spiral of flocking ravens. They petered out at the top, morphing into the face of a prominent vampire. Ancient mythical lords and ladies stared down at her from both sides and Charlie couldn't help but flick her gaze between them.

Oddly, they were soothing, offering strength where her

heart and soul could not.

As she neared the end, her eyes dropped to the throne. Sebastian lounged across it, a leg lazily sprawled over an arm. Dressed in his usual aristocratic wear, the bastard looked as if he actually belonged there. Like an arrogant prince about to be redeemed in a fairytale – if not for the bruised and battered soul tossed at his feet.

The man's face was heavily disfigured. His skin was pale beneath the marks of Sebastian's rage. His clothes had been ripped from his body. His pride had been shattered so fiercely that he no longer tried to cover himself.

Curled up in a ball, he was undoubtedly wishing for the nightmare to be over.

Charlie, however, had learned the futility of such a wish long ago. Holding the bastard's gaze, she stopped at the bottom of the steps leading up to the throne and waited for her nightmare to continue.

With a small grin, Sebastian lifted his bloodied wrist to his mouth. After sniffing it like one might a luxurious meal, he gave it a leisurely lick. As he slowly cleaned the stains from his skin, his eyes never left hers. It was a game he delighted in playing, one she would never let him win.

He might be able to hear her rapid heartbeat and smell her terror, but Charlie would die before she let him see it.

Chuckling, Sebastian finally dropped his hand to his side. Rising with the grace of a king, he descended the few steps to her, stopping only a handspan away.

A moment of silence strained between them.

Seconds ticked into minutes, but still he said nothing.

She clenched her fists for strength.

He stared at her without a word.

Her throat tightened to the point of strangulation.

And still the bastard stayed silent.

Charlie's urge to look away, to speak, was becoming unbearable. Her mind screamed to be heard, demanding that she ask what he had done to Anthony. Her heart wailed in agony, pleading that she drop to her knees and beg for his forgiveness.

But she did nothing.

She would not break.

Not now.

Not ever.

Tilting his head, Sebastian used it to point at the man behind him. "You remember Kevin."

She flicked her eyes to him, but came up blank. With her photographic memory, Charlie normally didn't need more than a few seconds to recognize something familiar. Though given the man's current state, he could have been her deadbeat father and she wouldn't have known.

"No," she answered calmly. "Should I?"

Sebastian shrugged. "Doesn't really matter. He died months ago."

A strangled noise sounded from behind the vampire. Whether it was one of fear or relief that the pain would soon be over, only the man could say.

Not that it mattered. As Sebastian had said, the guy was already dead. Any of his pleas would go unheard.

Just as hers did. Just as Tony's did.

Ignoring the memory of her son's screams, Charlie bit out, "So is there something you actually wanted me for or am I free to go?"

He grinned like a superstar, his two dimples appearing with a warmth that mimicked the sun. "I love that about you. Always so willing to take off your clothes for me."

Her jaw tightened as she dug her nails into her palms. His eyes dipped to them and she knew he scented her blood.

If she could lace it with poison, she'd do it in a heartbeat. Unfortunately, the bastard would smell it before he sank his teeth into her flesh.

Striving for an air of boredom, Charlie asked, "Is that what the note was for?"

He gave a half-hearted shrug as he began circling around her. She stifled the urge to turn with him. He might now be at her back, but it wasn't like she could have stopped him had he attacked from the front. Still, as Sebastian continued his slow perusal, Charlie had the instinctive urge to run.

He stopped right outside of her peripheral vision and her entire body cranked alive. She was intensely aware of the monster beside her. Her skin crawled. Her breath hitched. Her pulse painfully slowed in suspense.

When he leaned in to whisper, his breath hot across her neck, she couldn't help but shiver.

"I called you here, love, because Kevin there told me a little secret about the *Scrolls.*" He trailed a finger down her shoulder, her back. Cupping her ass, he purred, "Imagine my joy when I learned that what's inside your head could be in mine."

Charlie did swirl around then, her eyes wide and her fists tight. Her heart thumped wildly as she feared what would happen if the claim was true. Sebastian had told her never to disappoint him – not if she wanted her child to stay safe.

"Bullshit," she growled as she jerked backward out of his touch.

"You calling me a liar?" Sebastian asked with a raise of the brow and an oh-too-smug look on his face. His eyes, however, were deadly.

"No," she spat as she jerked her head to the pathetic

man behind her. "I'm calling that dick one."

Sebastian cocked his head to look at the guy over her shoulder and then gave a casual shrug. "Maybe. I did torture him a bit before he told me. At that point the bastard probably would have said anything." He sighed heavily in disappointment. "They just don't make them like they used to. One little session and your kind breaks."

He stepped past her, his pace slow and uncaring. There was so much carnage around him, caused by him, and yet he didn't care. Charlie cringed with the knowledge that whatever she claimed, he would not believe her.

"Then again," Sebastian drawled as he turned back around to face her. "You didn't finish reading all of the *Scrolls*, did you, love?"

Charlie swallowed hard. She had no refute against that. Still, she had to try. "I can't even vocalize its secrets and you really believe there's a method for me to give them to you telepathically? Come on, you sick fuck, you're smarter than that."

Sebastian smiled in amusement as he reached out to toy with the golden strands of her hair. If this exact moment was taken out of context, captured in its own still frame, Charlie had no doubt that people would find it lovely. It was only her own disgust that would hint at something more vile, and unfortunately, people were all too willing to overlook that.

Though it's not like anyone could actually help her if they noticed anyway. As always, Charlie would have to save herself.

"If you truly believe his claims," she countered, "then why not kill me and use him?"

Her heart danced frantically from her question, but she couldn't do anything to take it back. Even if she had the power to command time, she would still leave her words hanging heavily in the air.

Sebastian didn't want another weak puppet at his command. He was finding pleasure in her strength and it was because of her entertainment value that she was still alive.

He stepped forward, closing the distance between them. Almost tenderly, he gripped her hips and pulled her the remainder of the way. He lowered his face to a scant inch above hers. The way he looked at her lyingly spoke of a man in worship.

"Because, my love, I live for the day you will break. The day when you're down on your knees in front of me and doing whatever I desire. Anthony will already be dead, sucked dry as you watched, and yet you will never leave me." He trailed his fingers along her cheek before cupping the back of her head. As if drugged by an immobilizer, Charlie couldn't break away.

"The doors will all be open," he continued softly. "The sunshine will be lighting your way to freedom. And yet, you will never feel its warmth."

Struggling just to breathe, Charlie wasn't sure where she found the strength to snarl, "And you'll grow bored within the hour."

He shrugged, then dropped his hand from her face and crossed over to Kevin. Despite being half the man's size, Sebastian lifted him easily with one hand. He held him by the throat, of course, and raised him until his feet no longer touched the floor.

"Maybe, but after the ritual, you'll turn into a vegetable. I might as well have a little bit of fun with what remains of you."

He flicked her a godly grin before jerking his prey down to his face and biting deep into his vein.

Charlie's stomach revolted, but she kept her voice

strong. "You're really going to risk going after the *Scrolls* on a deadman's tale?"

Tossing said deadman to the floor, Sebastian phased in front of her. "No, I'm going to do that for fun." With his bloodied tongue, he licked her face, smearing death from her chin to her forehead.

In little more than a whisper, the vampire vowed, "The Elv've'Norc stole from me and they will pay with their lives. I will wipe the entire organization from every plane and every history book. People will be so horrified over their downfall that not a single word of them will ever be uttered in fear of my wrath."

Gripping her chin, Sebastian jerked her forward for a hard, rough kiss. He released her just as quickly, his eyes dancing with an honesty that chilled her bones.

"And you, my love, are going to help me do it."

# TWO

*HELDRON CASTLE,*
*HALZAJA UNDERGROUND*

Jack leaned against the wall of the study, his mouth twisted into a wry grin. The room was taut with tension as the two demons glared at Tegan, the head of the Elv've'Norc. Their king was as close to death as he'd ever been and their sister was currently in the upper skies of Halzaja, a place better known as Heaven.

To a demon that was as good as dead.

And not in the good, happy, puppy's now on the farm way either.

The Heldrons were on the verge of declaring war, and as much as Jack understood the consequences of such a thing, he couldn't help but be excited over the prospect. For even though he was an Elv've'Nor, an agent that had dedicated his life to upholding the peace of the Seven Planes, he was still a trickster.

The desire for chaos was in his blood.

"Bring her back," Pyro demanded as his eyes heated a deadly red. He was on the cusp of changing into full demon mode where his horns and claws would lengthen, his bulk would double, and all sense would fly out the window. The time for talk was nearly over.

And thank the gods for that. Politics, even devious, scheming politics, was not Jack's idea of a fun time.

"I promise you she's there of her own will," Tegan began. "When she's ready –"

"A demon in Heaven by her own will!" Rahu, the younger brother, erupted. "You insult us with such a half-assed lie!" His eyes blazed with anger. With one challenging step, he destroyed the distance Tegan had left between them. Snarling, he reached forward with a thick hand. His intent to wrap it around the man's throat until death was obvious.

Like a viper about to strike, Jack stilled instantly. His fingers tingled with magic as his grin widened. Finally, things might start to get interesting.

But as much as he itched for a quick fight, Jack still flicked his eyes to Tegan first. The man had a slight tightness around his mouth, a definite clenching of the teeth, but no true anger. Sighing in disappointment, Jack relaxed in an instant. He might've been brought here as backup, but it wasn't to safeguard the head of the Elv've'Norc.

Blindfolded and on fire, Tegan could still take on an army if he went into a Rage. Gifted with the strength of Thor, the speed of Loki, and the bloodthirstiness of Odin, even the weakest berserker could take on a hundred men. But being the eldest son of a Primordial, the direct descendant of the very first of his kind, Tegan could do much more damage than that. Within a few days, he would annihilate every man, woman, child, and their pet lizard in all of Heldron if he went unchecked.

Stopping him was the whole reason Jack was here. As a trickster, he had a damn good chance of curbing the berserker's rage if he could trap him in an illusion. As one gifted with the power of transforming others, though, Jack could guarantee it. Of course, doing so would really fuck over his life. For as funny as it would be to turn his boss into a harmless little toad, going on the run again, would not.

Because it wouldn't matter if Jack saved millions of innocent people with his little trick. It wouldn't matter if Tegan gave him a golden star, a raise, and two thumbs up afterwards. For to change another was a power reserved only for the gods, and once word got around about Jack's little secret... There would be no less than half a dozen deities jumping on the fastest train to come and kill him.

Then again, Jack thought dryly as he eyed the two demons. As unfortunate as the true death might be, it had to be better than playing fucking politics. They had been here for a good quarter of an hour and Tegan still hadn't managed to get to the bloody point.

"She followed Galvanor there," Tegan said. As if he'd spoken an enchantment, Rahu stopped in his approach. Whipping his head around, he narrowed his eyes at his brother. What he saw there caused him to growl.

"Kaz-ij!" Rahu snapped in their native tongue, his eyes mad in anger.

Immediately, Jack's easy smile disappeared, replaced by the sly, devious grin his enemies had learned to fear. A friendly brawl he would have enjoyed more than most people did chocolate. An actual threat to his friends, however, and things got serious fast.

Shifting his weight off the wall, he was about to call upon his magic when he noticed the amused look on Pyro's face. Flicking a glance at Rahu, Jack rolled his eyes when he noticed what he had originally missed.

The demon's teeth weren't bared.

Though that, in itself, wouldn't mean much in most tongues given Rahu's aggressive tone and narrowed eyes, it changed everything in drazic.

Rahu hadn't said 'kill him' as in 'Let's kill Galvanor now,' but rather 'kill him' as in 'Dammit! We should've killed him when we had the chance, but we can't now because our sister's in love with him. Urgh!'

Ah yes, Jack had forgotten how overly complicated this language was. Which was ironic really given its elementary sentence structure and extremely limited word bank.

Muttering a string of curses, Rahu turned back around. "And what is Galvanor doing up there?" he gritted out.

When the berserker simply dipped his eyes to the hand hovering around his neck and back up again, the demon flashed his teeth.

There was a second of tense silence before Rahu dropped his hand.

"Do you know what the Deusychosis Plague is?" Tegan questioned, causing Rahu's eyes to narrow in contemplation as Pyro's widened in alarm. Jack on the other hand, rolled his in utter boredom. By the gods, a new born babe could converse faster than this. Tegan needed to come out and say it already.

*Oh hey, we're bringing an angel down here to check if anyone else has been infected. Yes, I know that you and their kind have been warring since the dawn of creation. Yes, I am aware an angel has never been down here before and her very presence will probably start a war. But tough.*

See, simple. And Tegan said he didn't know politics.

But before Jack could provide such generous help, Pyro asked, "The same one that wiped out half the Persic plane?"

"Yes," Tegan replied. "The demon that threw the grenade at your king had it and passed it on."

"Nivan!" they both exclaimed.

"But how? He's not a persapic."

The berserker's eyes narrowed shrewdly. Even Jack's boredom faded as he too caught what was not said.

In a calm that forewarned of a storm, Jack drawled, "Aren't you going to ask where he got it? Considering it hasn't been around for millennia, I mean."

The two demons shared a humorous look and the last of Jack's patience slid away.

"You fucking morons."

It was one thing for him to root for a war between the Elv've'Norc and Heldron royals. It was quite another to celebrate over an outbreak of the Deusychosis Plague.

"Jack," Tegan warned.

Fighting his urge to continue, Jack acknowledged his boss with an irritated glance. With only a look, Tegan reminded him that he was here as backup, not as an instigator. Had Rogan or Hunter been able to come down, he wouldn't even be here as that.

With a roll of the eyes, Jack mimed the locking of his lips. By the gods, he was seriously tempted to throw an illusion up in his place while he wandered down to the drazic market. Their kebabs were bloody amazing. Then again, he'd happily eat dragon turd to get out of this.

"Where did Nivan enter Persic?" Tegan asked calmly despite the angry tic in his jaw.

"Wouldn't know," Pyro said with a nonchalant shrug as Rahu grinned like the devil.

Jack didn't need to be a telepath, an angel, nor even a genius to know that they were lying through their teeth. Drazics never had learned to mask their tell signs well. When strength was everything, it didn't matter if you were claiming that pigs could fly as long as those you told were too afraid to call you out on it.

But Jack wasn't afraid. There were very few people he feared and not one of them was a creature of the Myth.

But again, he hadn't been brought here to instigate shit. Calling the demons straight out on their lie would bring the tension back into the room. Best to let Tegan tip toe his way around this as Jack had two left feet and was proud of it.

"What might you have heard on the grapevine then?" the berserker asked slowly.

As if they had rehearsed it, the two brothers crossed their arms in synchronization. Though they undoubtedly knew that the Elv've'Norc knew they were lying, their grins only widened.

"What we heard was that Nivan was heading to Persic via the portal in Volskera."

"Shit," Tegan swore just as Jack perked up with a grin. The one thing he loved more than chaos was a challenge that tested his skills.

Volskera was an infamous wasteland on the outskirts of the Heldron kingdom. Despite its massive size and deadly terrain, however, the real challenge would be sneaking an angelic cleanup crew into it. There was only one known way into the wasteland and that was through the heart of the biggest, busiest city of the Halzaja Underground.

Though bringing Xeno down here would require Jack to deceive more demons, the route wouldn't be so packed as to necessitate him clouding their sense of touch. Tricking one's eyesight was much easier as people saw what they expected to see. And no demon would expect to see an angel in the heart of their home.

But to get to Volskera, Jack would have to get her into

Volskera's Head, an infamous club that was constantly packed with demons. It would be impossible for anyone to step inside without getting mashed against three others. Maybe more. If a single person slipped outside of Jack's illusions, it would be game over. First would come an immediate riot and then a declaration of war.

*Oh, this is going to be good.*

But before Jack could volunteer his services, Rahu cut in with a snicker.

"Whoever managed to send him down there without being spotted by a single one of the Elv've'Norc spies was quite clever, don't you think?" he asked, completely oblivious to the consequence of Nivan's journey.

"No," Tegan snapped as his blue eyes turned red. His muscles rippled beneath his skin as the berserker rage finally began to rear from his frustration. "You see, I have to send a team there to make sure the disease hasn't spread to anyone else."

Rahu snorted an easy dismissal. "There aren't any persapics in Volskera."

Jack rolled his eyes. That was it. He had put up with this nonsense long enough.

"Nivan isn't a persapic," Tegan stiffly pointed out just as Jack helpfully added, "It'll be a team of angels, you know. They're the only ones that can contain it."

He hadn't even finished his sentence before the two demons exploded.

"Angels in the Underground! There will be war!"

"Try it! We'll slaughter them as soon as they step into our domain! And then all thirty-eight million of us will take to the skies on dragons!"

As the demons carried on with their threats, Jack met Tegan's glare with a wide grin and a two thumbs up. "Look at that. We finally got to the part that we've been trying to get to for the last half hour. You're welcome."

But though Jack didn't get a word of thanks nor did he get reprimanded for stepping out of line. It seemed Tegan too had been getting fed up with these negotiations.

"Look," the head of the Elv've'Norc said. "You can either risk having your enemies get this power or you can let us do our job!"

Rahu opened his mouth to counter that, then snapped it shut with a growl. Flinging his gaze to his brother, he started a conversation that was too quick for Jack to follow.

But though he didn't understand half the words, he could still make a damn good guess about what was being said. The Heldrons were in an extremely precarious position. They couldn't afford to be attacked right now, especially not by anyone with supernatural powers. For though they were the strongest of the demon kingdoms, they were also the guardians to the back door of Niflhel. Their attention was divided at the best of times.

Normally they had a castle full of soldiers to stand guard while they dealt with the undead, but they had recently sacked them all to keep Galvanor's kidnapping as quiet as possible. Even their slaves were gone.

To top that all off, their king had stopped healing, something was driving souls out of Niflhel at an alarming rate, Rahu and Pyro were both still recovering from fighting human-angel hybrids, and their sister was soon to be joining the Elv've'Norc thanks to the fatal prophecy hanging over her head.

It didn't take a foreseer to know that they were going to agree to Tegan's terms. They had no other choice to make.

"One angel," Pyro finally growled as he held out his hand. When it was taken without pause, he yanked the berserker to him and vowed, "And if anyone can link it to us, I'll kill it myself."

Tegan smiled tightly. "I'm sure it won't come to that. Will it, Jack?"

The berserker's hard glare warned him not to come back with a half-assed remark.

"Of course it won't," Jack replied. Shoving off the wall, he waited just long enough for Tegan to relax, then added, "He couldn't take on an archangel even if he tried."

As Pyro erupted again behind him, Jack tossed a two fingered wave and a lolling smile at his captain. Leaving Tegan with the Herculean task of convincing them it'd be a regular angel visiting and not one that could wipe out their entire kingdom within minutes, Jack slipped into the hallway.

Three steps later he was joined by Rahu. The demon cast him a long, uneasy glance and Jack's body hummed with the anticipation of a fight. Though he knew he needed to conserve his energy so he could bring Xeno down here unseen, properly weighing the consequences had never been Jack's strong point.

But in the end Rahu merely shook his head and carried on down the hallway. Huffing in disappointment, Jack followed behind him.

"We exit through the west," he informed the demon once they had made it through the maze-like castle and neared the front door of the castle.

Rahu shook his head as he replied, "There has been an increase of harenae activity near there. The east –"

Jack cut him off with a laugh. "I know. That's why we're going up that way. Have you ever had a harenae burger? They're absolutely delicious."

He pulled open the front door, stepping with it so Rahu could exit first. But the demon was frozen a few paces behind him, his mouth slack and his eyes wide.

"Well, are you coming or not?" Jack teased, well aware of what had startled the demon.

Harenae flesh was poisonous enough to grant the first death if consumed. Even the tiniest bite could kill an adult giant and it was common knowledge that a human merely had to touch it before they would keel over in an agonizing death.

But on the plus side, they really were delicious. And given Jack had a father whom could bring him back to life with a snap of his fingers, as he had done many times before, eating one was damn well worth it.

With a slow blink, the demon finally broke out of his stupor. "I know you're joking about the burger part."

He wasn't.

"But tell me you're also joking about exiting on the west end."

Jack flashed him a warm smile that conveyed he was. But immediately after the demon sighed in relief, Jack snickered. "I wasn't joking. With the harenae there that means the tunnels will be the clearest. You can, however, always stay here."

The glare he received told him exactly where he could shove that thought. As Rahu passed him, the demon muttered a phrase in his native tongue. Though it wasn't something Jack understood, he knew a prayer when he heard one.

Grinning, the trickster eased the door shut behind them and then sent up a prayer of his own.

*Please let there be at least one harenae up there. Also, answer your goddamn phone already, dad. What's the point of having me spy for you if you never take my bloody calls?*

Distracted by truly frivolous matters, neither god nor

goddess bothered to listen.

# THREE

"*That's* your plan?" Rahu snorted as they took the final turn to the surface. His face was a mixture of 'you're crazy' and 'that's insane' and his tone didn't speak of anything different.

Pretending to be offended, the trickster scoffed. "It's a good plan."

Well, depending on one's definition of good, anyway. Was this someone a crazy, reckless, brainless idiot with a devil-may-care attitude? Yes? Then it was a brilliant plan. No? Well –

"It's a horrible plan!" Rahu shouted as if he'd pulled the words right out of Jack's mind.

Grinning, Jack waved away the demon's concerns. "Nonsense. It'll work."

"So will setting your house on fire to get rid of bed bugs! Yes, the bugs will all be gone, but it'd still be a horrible plan."

Jack opened his mouth, then shut it again. The demon made a good point.

But still.

What was the point of saving the world if he couldn't have a little fun while doing it? He sure as hell didn't do it for the pay.

"Aren't drazics supposed to be the bravest of us all?" Jack goaded as they caught the first light of the Surface.

It was common knowledge that Rahu's kind was quick to anger. If Jack couldn't win the argument with logic, then he'd have to revert to more primitive tactics like name calling and insults. Of course, there was the minor risk of being ripped apart if Rahu erupted into full demon mode, but hey, no plan was perfect.

"There's no if about it," the Heldron prince growled through clenched teeth. It was obvious that he'd caught on to Jack's plan, but it was in a drazic's nature to always meet a challenge.

After all, it's what they had been designed for. The desire for victory had been woven into their blood, as it had been with every champion race of the myth. The angels, the drazic demons, the tricksters, the fae, the succubi, the elementalists, hell, even the atlanteans, all had that instinctive drive to win at all costs programmed into their DNA.

Not that anyone but the angels and the gods knew about it. For as immortal as everyone was, ten thousand years was still a hell of a long time in which to survive. Most beings barely made it past the five thousand year mark. And unlike the humans, no other race was really bothered about history. Either you had lived through it so you didn't need to read about it or you knew someone who had. Anything past that had happened too long ago to be of any concern.

Which was foolish really, Jack had always thought, given what happened every ten thousand years. But hey, who was he to lecture about foolishness?

Flicking his eyes to the demon, he snorted. "So then stop acting like an eknor and get on with it. It's not like you'll be riding one of the damn things."

"No," Rahu replied dryly. "I'll just be running for my life as they randomly pop out of the ground to chase me."

Jack rolled his eyes. "It won't be random. Wherever you last stepped, that's where they'll most likely be."

"Gee, thanks."

Jack gave him a friendly, infuriating swat on the back. "You're welcome. Always happy to help."

"You can help by getting eaten by one of those damn things," the demon muttered as they stopped a few feet from the exit.

Staring out at the vast expanse of crimson sand, Jack's blood spiked with adrenaline. Though he couldn't see any signs of the monstrous harenae being in the area, his sixth sense told him that they were out there, burrowed beneath the dunes.

With a wicked grin, Jack cranked his neck from one side to the other. As the popping of his bones echoed through the tunnel, he loosened his shoulders with a quick roll.

"I'm wounded, Rahu. Truly, I am." Ignoring the demon's snort, he added, "Now, how do you want to do this? Shall we run for it like headless chickens or walk out all slow and badass like, pretending an explosion has just gone off behind us?"

With a quick flex of his fingers, Rahu summoned a black ball of fire into his palm. "You know," he said calmly, having now fully accepted Jack's ridiculous plan. Not that he had been given another choice. "When I'm the sane one, that's when my brothers know things have gone to shit."

A crazy gleam sparkled in the trickster's eyes. "Oh, you ain't seen nothing yet."

Bending down, he scooped up a few stones, careful to only pick up those inside the mouth of the cave. Harenae didn't have any eyes, ears, or noses, but they had a keen sense of vibration. A single brush of Jack's pinkie across the sand would have alerted the beasts to their presence. And though they would know of them soon enough, it would be suicide to have the harenae crashing up at the mouth of the cave.

If Jack got stuck inside, then he would have to use his magic to cloak the descent of his team instead of using a convenient cloud of dust. Though he probably did have enough magic to do that *and* sneak them into the Heldron Castle, it wasn't something he would bet on. For if he miscalculated and ran out of magic halfway to the castle, they were royally screwed. Xeno might be most of the way to becoming a fallen angel, but she wasn't anywhere near enough to put the demons at ease. With 'near enough' being full on turned and hunted by her own kind.

Or ex kind. Whatever.

"Wait until I say and then leg it," Jack ordered as he rotated the rocks in his hand. After he'd settled them into a comfortable position, he raised his arm. Casting a sly glance at the demon, he sagely added, "And once out there, I would highly recommend not stopping."

"No shit," Rahu barked as he tensed his legs. His all black eyes spoke heavily of the cursing going on in his head, but beneath all that was the slightest sliver of excitement.

With a cocky smile, Jack reared his arm back and threw the rocks with all his strength. They sailed through the air like little missiles, their impact just as deadly. For as soon as they touched the ground, it rumbled with the force of a giant, then erupted in terrifying glory.

At the heart of the explosion of sand twisted a worm-like creature as thick as a train. Its head was shapeless, marked only by the cavernous hole of teeth that snapped and snarled in its hunger. An acidic waterfall of drool dripped from its mouth, burrowing a hole in the ground as it vaporized everything it touched.

But as impossible as it seemed, the most dangerous thing was its tongue. Six sharp barbs lined the end, able to open like the delicate bloom of a flower. And like a frog or a chameleon, a harenae could wield it like a whip. Once it latched onto its prey, only the severing of it could release them.

With the speed of Hermes, Jack bent down for another handful of rocks. In one smooth motion, he launched the pebbles through the air, and when they hit the ground, another explosion erupted. This time, two harenae fought for the same trickery of food.

"Now!" Jack yelled as he lunged into a sprint. After a muttered prayer to Hel, Rahu darted out behind him.

They had only a few seconds of safety before the harenae crashed back to the ground. As soon as the monster's heads were under the sand, they'd be able to sense the vibrations of their run.

Before that happened, Jack and Rahu needed to be within touching distance of their chosen harenae. As fast and agile as the monsters were, it was near impossible for them to sink back into the sand and erupt in the exact same place. Of course, that didn't stop the other harenae from trying to eat them, but one less animal able to grab them was definitely a good thing.

Adrenaline burning in his lungs, Jack darted to the side. His quick side step morphed into a rolling dive to avoid being crushed by the massive bulk of the harenae.

Back on his feet, the trickster made a mad dash for Rahu.

Without the aid of a strong wind, Jack was relying solely on the harenaes eruptions to dispel the sand into the air. So the closer he and the demon stayed together, the more focused the dust cloud would be and the faster it would rise up to block out the sun.

As Rahu's roar of surprise ruptured the air, Jack's eyes gleamed with laughter. Somehow the lucky bastard had ended up directly on top of a harenae's neck, and as it reared from the surface, it had taken the demon with it.

Unable to pause long enough to watch, Jack swiveled to the left. He'd caught a ripple of sand out of the corner of his eye, that tell tale sign a harenae was about to erupt. If he didn't reach the side of another beast soon, he was as good as dead.

With a burst of speed, he raced for his life. The ground shook beneath his feet. A curse rang out in his head as he did the math and came up short. Another few seconds and he would have made it.

Unfortunately, he didn't have even half of one to spare.

Skidding to a halt, Jack braced himself for the feel of pain. The harenae erupted with a blaze of teeth, its acidic saliva burning deep into his skin.

It shoved him upwards on a rapidly deteriorating pile of sand. Before he could lose his footing entirely, Jack lunged for the tongue. In a mad play for survival, he grabbed hold of the smooth area beneath its barbed tip with both hands. Yanking with all of his might, he slammed the barbs deep into its own flesh.

The harenae shook with a scream of agony. Its sudden bellow of breath shot Jack out of its mouth like a cannon.

*Thor's balls, that actually worked!*

He hit the ground hard and rolled. Well, 'rolled' was a bit of a stretch if he was being honest. It was more like he underwent a series of jarring cartwheels he had no power to stop. By the end of it, his eyes were crossed and stars floated in his head.

But as dizzy as he was, he still had a clear enough mind to think, *Oh shit.*

As the sand vibrated beneath him, he cursed further in annoyance. Fuck, if he'd survived, that would have been so cool.

But instead of the harenae erupting beneath him, it shot up a few feet to the left. Jack's eyes squinted in confusion as he staggered to his feet. Normally, the beasts were more accurate than a missile with GPS coordinates.

He had definitely been saved by a third party, but he couldn't think of by whom. Though his dad would always bring him back from the dead, the god thought it was absolutely fucking hilarious to watch him die. Especially if it was painful. The bloody asshole.

Rahu could have tricked the harenae by throwing a fireball there, but one glance his way told Jack the demon was way too occupied with saving his own hide to have done so.

*The cover is adequate.*

*Ah*, Jack thought as Galvanor's calm, controlled voice sounded inside his head. *That explained it.*

Though the persapic would never mention it, the trickster knew he had played with the mind of the harenae. As a telepath, Galvanor was able to manipulate the mind of every living thing. It would be no mean feat for him to trick the primitive mind of a harenae.

Or it normally wouldn't have been.

But Galvanor had recently contacted the Deusychosis Plague and was still recovering from the infection. Who knew how much that had taken out of him?

Nodding his head to the sky, Jack sent his comrade a

mental thanks and then legged it back to the cave. Though the harenae could still sense them moving inside the tunnels, the rock was far too thick for them to bust through.

Jack skidded to a halt as soon as he was safe inside and Rahu soon stopped hard beside him. They both breathed heavily, their hair a wild mess of sand and sweat.

Wiping at his brow, Jack flicked his eyes to the demon. Between deep huffs, he cackled, "You enjoyed that. Admit it."

Rahu's grin was bright enough to scorch the sun. "It was fun, true. But it was still a horrible plan."

Shaking his head, Jack turned to look up at the sky. He tried to peer through the swirling dust to spot his descending teammates, but the cloud was too thick for him to see more than a foot away.

Admitting defeat, he leaned against the rock wall and waited for them to arrive. It didn't take long. Within the space of a few seconds ten newcomers dropped inside the mouth of the cave, five of which were angels.

Immediately, Rahu's easy mien disappeared under an avalanche of aggression.

"We agreed to one," he growled.

Jerking away from the one that had carried her down, Matakyli saddled up to her lifemate. "Oh stop it, Rahu. How do you think we were going to get here? They were going to toss us out of the sky?"

But his sister's attempt at reason couldn't penetrate the sudden fog that had wrapped around Rahu's brain.

For the angel Matakyli had stepped away from wasn't the average winged warrior of justice. Their wings were white or gray, sometimes a light brown. But never were they black. That ominous color was only reserved for an archangel. Or a *kazul*, 'bringer of death', as the demons called them.

"No way in Niflhel is that *thing* coming into our our castle," Rahu growled. His nostrils flared and his eyes brightened into the crimson red that foretold of a change. Though the archangel could easily take him even in full demon mode, Jack couldn't fault the guy for trying.

He too was nervous in the man's presence.

As an archangel Gabriel was tasked with policing the gods. Though Jack didn't quite fall into that category, he was the son of one of the major players. That, in itself, wouldn't mean much (for unlike the Elv've'Norc and High Council, the archangels didn't damn someone simply because of their heritage), but what Jack had done five thousand years ago, sure as hell would.

As nonchalantly as he could, Jack eyed his path to the exit. There were a few angels in his way, not to mention Rogan and Emma, but he could probably shove past them before they recovered from their surprise. Because if Gabriel did know about his little role in Kyravic, Jack would definitely be better off getting eaten by a harenae.

"He's not," Xeno said as she stepped forward. "I am."

Reluctantly, Rahu tore his gaze away from Gabriel to give her an assessing glance. The fierce glare he pinned her with quickly gave way to shock. Though the Heldron Underground was home to the occasional fallen angel, it was unlikely the drazic prince had ever seen one in the midst of their fall.

Holding the demon's gaze, Xeno slowly turned around so he could have a clear view of her wings. Though they looked better than the last time Jack had seen them, they still resembled the gruesome remains of a bird that had been savaged by a wolf.

Open wounds oozed black puss and dulled blood. The knots in her bones were clear signs of breakages that for some reason hadn't healed. And then there were her feathers. Though the patches, once horribly raw and bare, were now all filled in, it looked as if they had been done so by a child. Like one had simply grabbed a pile of them off the floor and shoved them against a wall of glue.

Turning back around, Xeno held the demon's gaze without flinching. "I'm as good as fallen."

Despite the delight in Rahu's eyes and the smirk of his lips, he wasn't stupid enough to say anything. He simply gave a jerky nod to Gabriel and then turned on his heels to make his way back home.

As one, all of the angels par Xeno launched out of the cave. Gabriel shot her a look that Jack couldn't read and then, he too, took to the skies.

Letting out a silent breath of relief, the trickster finally relaxed.

"So shall we get going?" Jack asked as he gestured down the tunnel. "I kinda left Tegan in a bit of a bind and he may or may not be dead already."

Rogan shook his head in disapproval as Emma's eyes widened in concern. The water elementalist murmured something in her ear that brought a bit of color back to her cheeks. Then he slipped his hand in hers and led her down the tunnel. Hunter went next with a roll of his eyes, followed by Galvanor and Matakyli. The telepath, as always, didn't even register that he'd made a joke. The demoness, however, shot him a toothy grin and Jack replied with a wink.

How those two had ever ended up together was beyond him. They were as different as night and day, as far apart as heaven and hell. But as Jack watched the two lifemates walking side by side, he couldn't miss the obvious love radiating between them. Even though they didn't touch like Emma and Rogan did, their love was just as bright.

By the gods, it hurt his eyes just to look at them.

"If I ever get like that," Jack drawled as he and Xeno fell into step behind them. "Do me a favor and shoot me."

## FOUR

# FOUR

The trek through the exit tunnels had gone better than Jack had expected. Not many people were willing to risk a trip to the Surface in the first place and of those that were, it seemed none were willing to use a route guarded by a nest of harenae.

With another mile to go before they came upon the outskirts of Dirk, Jack sneaked a glance at Xeno. Once he was certain she wasn't paying him any attention, he twirled his fingers down at his side. In an instant he was concealed by a basic illusion, granting him the freedom to do what he needed to without revealing a damning secret.

He raised his hand until it was level with his chest, his knuckles down and fingers flat. A sudden rush of power surged through his veins and he concentrated it into his open palm. As the first green wisp of magic seeped out of his skin, Jack flicked his eyes back to Xeno.

He was certain she couldn't see through his illusion, but that didn't do anything to soothe his paranoia. If anyone saw him using the magic he currently was and word got around, then Jack would be struck down by the gods.

Literally.

But as the power kept building in his palm, the green wisp growing into a tornado of activity, Xeno never once looked over at him.

The magic built up for a bit longer, searing hot in his hand before suddenly vanishing as if it'd never been. Left in its wake was an intricate slice of metal, similar in design to an over-the-ear earphone but without the wire. A runic concealment spell was etched onto both sides of it, so powerful that not even Odin's Eye could eavesdrop on their conversation.

The weight was solid; the device was real. Jack hadn't merely created an illusion. He'd conjured an actual item from out of thin air. Or, if you wanted to be a Hunter about it (Jack's favorite way of saying 'technical'), he'd summoned an item from the other side of the universe, directly out of Odin's Vault. And tricksters, no matter how long they studied, couldn't do that.

They could create an illusion that seemed so real that those caught inside it would never know the difference. They could kill their enemies by making them believe they were in such agony, it tricked them into having a heart attack. But not a single one could solidify an illusion and bring it over into reality.

Jack, however, wasn't *just* a trickster. Although, what else he was, he wasn't entirely sure. In truth, he knew more about what he wasn't than what he was.

He wasn't *just* a trickster because he had powers they could only dream of. He wasn't a descendant, a child of the gods, because despite having a deity for a parent, he only had one of them. Descendants always had two; demi-gods only had one. But he wasn't a demi-god either because those came from the union of a god *and* a mortal (or immortal as the humans called them). Jack, on the other hand, had been born by the power, not seed, of only one god.

Placed in the womb of a mortal, he had been taken immediately after birth and raised by his godly father. Although 'raised' was giving the guy more credit than was due, Jack thought dryly.

For the better part of a century Jack had been left to fend for himself. It was only when his father had come back from his fishing trip and found him to still be alive that he'd decided to actually raise him. Not that he knew what he was doing in the slightest.

But he had tried and somewhere along the way the two had ended up bonding. Their relationship might not be the easiest to understand, but it was solid.

Curving *Sannurthogn,* the enchanted device, around his ear, Jack rang his father with only a thought. His skin broke out in goosebumps as he waited for the call to be connected. Though Odin shouldn't be able to see him using it, if Jack was somehow caught, he'd end up with a fate worse than Prometheus'.

*Come on,* the trickster urged as the first ring buzzed inside his head. It went on for only two seconds, but to Jack it rang for an eternity. As all went silent when it finally faded, the hairs on his neck rose with a shiver.

And then the second ring sounded.

*Come on. Come on. Answer the goddamn phone.*

But that one too went unanswered.

A cold chill swept through Jack's body and it took everything he had not to snatch *Sannurthogn* off his ear and send it back to where it belonged.

The gods did not take kindly to being robbed and Odin was the most bloodthirsty of them all. If a single one of the god's guards noticed the device was missing from the vault, then Jack might as well hang himself now. He might have thousands of years of experience hiding and running from the gods, but that was only because his father had always been there alongside him. Take their communication away and...

"Jack, my boy!"

On a flood of relief, Jack closed his eyes. *About damn time.*

But before he could get in a hello, his father rattled on. "I'm not here right now. I might be off doing important god things or I might've looked at caller ID and decided to ignore you. Either way, leave a message if you must, but unless it's in dance form, I ain't gonna listen to it."

*Mother. Fucker.*

Locking his jaw, Jack exhaled sharply in irritation. Though really, he didn't know why he was surprised. He'd been trying to get ahold of his dad for weeks now and every time, he'd been met with a voicemail.

"I'll call you when I can," the god promised. He said it sincerely with just the right amount of regret in his tone. It was as if he really was upset over having missed his son's call.

But Jack knew better than to buy it.

"Not think of anything else to do instead," his dad added with a chuckle. "I hear watching rocks evolve is nice. Oooh, or maybe I'll wait until the galaxy explodes. That's more up my –"

"Fuck you," Jack growled as he disconnected the call. Yanking *Sannurthogn* off his ear, he sent it away with his magic. Seriously, what was the fucking point of having him act as a spy if his dad never answered the bloody phone?

Closing his eyes in an attempt to combat his irritation, ·

Jack breathed deep. If Xeno caught on that something had upset him, she'd start digging until she figured out what. And if that happened, he'd have to kill her. For though Xeno had promised her loyalty to the Elv've'Norc years ago, he knew that she also reported back to the archangels.

From there all it would take was one little birdie in the wrong ear and then Jack would be shark chum.

Exhaling, the trickster covered his emotions in a mask of boredom and then stepped out of his illusion. The transition was smooth, flawless, leaving Xeno none the wiser to what he had done.

Estimating they had another half a mile to go before reaching Dirk, Jack turned his head to his comrade and asked, "So what's up with your wings?"

Her jaw didn't tick in irritation. Her nostrils didn't flare in anger. Her eyes didn't widen in fear that he dared ask her secret. She simply stared silently ahead, not doing a single thing that conveyed she had heard him.

But he knew she had. He also knew she wouldn't answer. Angels were as secretive as they came and Xeno was even more tight lipped than most these days.

She hadn't always been like this, but eleven years ago, everything had changed. That joyous woman Jack had once known, the one whom would crack jokes with him in the dead of night, was dead. She had died in that castle and not one of them could revive her.

Nevertheless, Jack was too curious to let it go. Ever since they had saved her from her torture, Xeno had been consistently turning into a fallen angel. Not even two weeks ago, she had barely been able to fly given the ragged mess of her wings. Now, all of a sudden, over a single night, she was healing? It didn't make any sense.

In all of his years alive, Jack had never come across a

single angel who had managed to reverse their transition into a fallen. It had always been a done deal with the only variable being the length of time it took. Some fell within days, others it took years, decades even. Jack had been certain that Xeno wouldn't last much longer.

*But now...*

"What happened, Xeno? What'd Gabriel do to you?"

At this, she did look at him. Her eyes were as dead and empty as always, but there was something in her face, something shielded. Whatever her secret was, Jack had guessed right. Gabriel was at the heart of it.

"Drop it, Jack," she said calmly. "Or it won't be just my secret that's bared."

The shock hit him like a solid blow to the chest. She didn't know. She couldn't. But her steely eyes said she did.

Shrugging casually, Jack ignored the hammering of his heart and the cold chill running down his back. "If you're talking about telling them I'm bi, I doubt that'll come as a surprise."

She didn't say anything, just turned her attention back ahead. Her threat had been made and Xeno never uttered them twice. She never needed to.

Cursing violently in his head, Jack tried to ignore the dark whispers rising inside him. That deep, menacing voice that warned him Xeno hadn't merely been bluffing to throw him off her trail. That monster who urged him to protect their secret at all costs.

In another few minutes, they would be entering the outskirts of Dirk. The city was home to over a quarter million demons and twice that many convicts. Even the most quiet of alleyways would have someone all too willing to kill an angel. Especially one that doubled as an Elv've'Nor.

For despite how far the Underground of Halzaja had

progressed over the years, it was still a land of barbarians. They lived by their own code and they policed by their own code. Anyone who tried to regulate that was as unwelcome as a cannibal at a blow job fest.

It would be so easy for Jack to 'run out of magic' at just the wrong moment. Even with everyone falling back to protect her, Xeno wouldn't survive an outing in the middle of a drazic city. His comrades would fight as well as they could; Hunter would even helplessly sacrifice himself in an attempt to save her.

And yet, Xeno would still fall, torn apart by teeth and claws until only her blood remained.

*She's my friend,* Jack reminded himself even as that dark part of him latched onto the idea of her death as a welcome solution. With every step he took toward the city, those whispers rose in volume until his head pounded with the force of their screams. And then that *thing* shifted inside him, its movements a physical slither across his ribcage.

*But our secret will be safe.*

The *thing* made it sound so easy, so desirous that Jack almost found himself agreeing. After all, he'd done a lot of callous shit over the years; what was one more?

*Nothing,* it whispered. *Her death will mean nothing.*

An image flashed inside Jack's head. A beast as black as death and as large as a dragon crouched behind silver bars. Luminescent runes were carved into the metal, their power so strong that Jack could feel them pulsing in his veins.

And then suddenly, there he was, appearing in the image as if it was his right. He stood outside of the cage staring into the bright, eerie eyes of the beast. They weren't amber like he had, for some reason, expected but a deep dark red that burned with intelligence. And hatred.

As Jack looked into those eerily familiar eyes, his skin crawled as if it was home to a million spiders. With sudden clarity, he realized that this wasn't a random image that had popped into his head. It was a peephole into his very soul. And that *thing* in front of him wasn't just a blood-curdling monster. It was that dark other half of him that terrified even his father.

But though Jack heard the warning bells and wanted desperately to listen to them, he still saw himself reaching out a hand. His fingers had just slipped through the bars of the cage when Galvanor's calm voice ruptured the *thing's* spell.

*Demons in sight. We've reached the outskirt of Dirk.*

Blinking rapidly, Jack watched as the scene inside his head disappeared on a plume of smoke. One more blink and it was gone completely.

Swallowing hard, he flicked his eyes to Xeno. She didn't look as if she'd noticed his mini trip down the rabbit hole and Jack was too unsettled to dig any deeper than that. With a wave of his hand, he placed her under the cover of his magic.

A moment later the demons Galvanor mentioned came into view. Jack forced his lips to part in an easy smile as he fought to stay calm.

He hadn't touched that *thing*, hadn't released it from its cage to wreck death and destruction across the Planes. He had denied its wishes yet again. He was not about to uncover his friend and watch as she was ripped apart by her mortal enemies. Reminding himself of all this helped, but then –

*Give it time. I will be free.*

Swallowing hard, Jack did his best to ignore it.

Only it wasn't that easy to dismiss something that, he too, believed in. He had been fighting the *thing* for too long and where he'd been growing tired, the *thing* had only grown stronger. It was only a matter of time before it finally broke free.

Jack could feel it in his bones. Everything was about to change.

# FIVE

*CHARLIE'S LAB,*
*LOCATION UNKNOWN*

Charlie shook with rage as she stared at the corpse on her table.

*Goddammit!*

She had told Sebastian she hadn't read about this in the *Scrolls*. How the fuck did he expect her to be able to do this? If he was setting her up for failure so he could have an excuse to hurt Tony, she would –

What? Smack him across the face while he laughed?

"Goddammit!" she yelled as she spun on her heels. Grabbing the item closest, Charlie launched the beaker at the wall. Her chest heaved from frustration as her eyes stung with the painful fear of a cornered mother. She had to figure out a way to do this.

For Tony's sake, she could not fail.

Closing her eyes, Charlie lifted her chin and breathed deep. Except she struggled to find strength amongst the chasm of hopelessness inside her. Bracing her arms on the counter, Charlie took another deep breath and prayed.

To whom she prayed to she wasn't sure. To what she

asked she couldn't say. All she could think was 'please.'

Just '*please.*'

Everything else got jumbled in the knot at her throat.

With her eyes squeezed tight, she waited in silence, hoping against hope that her mother had been right. That there was an actual god out there. Someone who would protect her from the monsters of the world. Someone just and someone kind. Someone who actually gave a damn about saving a four year old boy from a fate worse than death.

But there was nothing.

With an angry scream, Charlie flung an arm across the counter. Beakers and jars holding things she could not name crashed onto the floor.

The sound of broken glass created an angry symphony that was building up to the release of a primal scream. She could feel her frustration rising as if it was a physical thing, tearing through her lungs and up her esophagus like a raging bull. Her lips parted to allow it free, desperate to release some of the terrible rage threatening to bring her to her knees.

But life had other plans.

The deafening turn of the handle silenced her scream. Her mouth still open, Charlie's head snapped to the entrance like a whip. Her eyes grew steadily wider as the pounding of her heart crescendoed until all she could hear was the rapid beat of her fear.

It was only when the door parted from the frame, that she finally snapped out of her faze. Dropping to her knees, she scrambled madly for a piece of broken glass. Though it would be suicide to attack Sebastian, his minions were all fair game.

Rising, Charlie tucked the jagged piece against the inside of her wrist. As she stepped quickly to the left, she placed herself directly in the middle of the gurney. From here if she braced her hands on the counter behind her and kicked out strong enough, she could send the table slamming into her opponent.

She wasn't as fast as a vampire, but she'd quickly learned that if she waited until they lunged, it'd even out the playing field a little.

Gripping the makeshift blade tight against her wrist, Charlie forced it deeper until she felt the sharp bite of its edge. The smell of fresh blood would make any vampire crazed to taste. They'd gain a bit more power, a bit more speed, but in their hunger they'd also be more prone to making mistakes.

*Come on, you bastard*, Charlie mentally taunted as her legs tensed in preparation for a jump.

But instead of the door banging open like Charlie had expected, it parted in a gentle ease. Whoever was behind it almost seemed timid to come in, as if they were afraid of her. Her, a mere human.

*It has to be a trap.*

Charlie's pulse raced as she swung the blade around. She held it like a kitchen knife down at her side and the drop of blood that had gathered on its edge fell onto the floor.

By the time the door opened all the way, it felt as if the whole world had slowed down. As if every existing particle was invested in what was about to happen.

The first thing Charlie saw was a long swish of black hair. It was soon followed by a haggard face, severely indented by hollow cheekbones and sunken eyes. The woman that entered looked as if she regularly bathed in death and despair and lived in a world far, far worse than Charlie's.

But looks could be deceiving. Charlie had known that

long before she'd met Sebastian with his angelic face and smooth words. Her time here had only reinforced that lesson.

"What do you want?" she demanded. The question came out harsh, but Charlie didn't bother apologizing. Whatever the lady wanted, it couldn't be anything good. She was Sebastian's right hand lady, his personal little bodyguard who killed as easily as he did. The woman's eyes might dull each time she took a life, but that never stopped her from doing it. It never even slowed her down. She was the perfect little puppet.

Whatever Sebastian was holding over this person to keep her here, it was powerful enough to garner him her complete and utter loyalty. Charlie would be a fool to trust her with anything. Sister prisoners be damned.

The newcomer shut the door softly behind her and Charlie's pulse spiked with another heavy dose of adrenaline. Raising her arm, she brandished the weapon in warning.

Dark brown eyes dropped to the piece of glass, but not a speck of fear flashed inside them. Lifting her gaze back up, the woman murmured, "To escape."

Charlie blinked in genuine surprise. It wasn't the words themselves that had thrown her off guard nor the agonizing honesty they had been spoken with. It was the fire behind them, a raging inferno that Charlie'd assumed had been extinguished long ago.

With a lift of her chin, the woman added on a sneer, "To kill him."

Faced with such brutal honesty it took everything Charlie had not to lower her guard and find kinship with this woman. They might share the same hopes and dreams, the same anger where a certain bastard was concerned, but this woman was still the enemy. She was still Sebastian's puppet and Charlie would be a fool to forget that.

"But it doesn't matter what I want," the enemy softly added, her words turning bitter. "He controls everything I do. If he tells me to kill my own twin sister, I'll do it. I wouldn't even hesitate."

Her eyes locked on Charlie's, giving her an insight into the broken, crushed soul inside her. But deep, deep down, beneath the woman's fear and frustration, beneath her overwhelming agony and incapacitating helplessness, burned a strength that mirrored Charlie's own.

"Why are you telling me this?" Charlie asked. As much as she wanted to hate this woman, to keep her at arm's length, she simply couldn't do it. She always had been a sucker for people in need.

"Because he sent me down here to work with you and I thought you should know that." She hesitated as a brief flash of pain seared her eyes. But as quick as her regret had come, it vanished. "Don't trust me," she advised. "I will kill you if he tells me to."

Charlie swallowed hard, but eventually she lowered the knife. If Sebastian had sent the woman, neither of them had a choice about whether they worked together or not anyway. Best to just get on with it in case he popped down to see how they were doing.

For though Sebastian had never upheld his end of the bargain about letting her see Tony if she pleased him, he'd always kept his vow to harm him if she didn't.

"What's your name?" Charlie asked as she placed the shard on the counter behind her. She pivoted to grab some paper towels and pressed them firmly to her open wound. Though it wasn't a deep cut, she didn't want to get blood on her clothes and tempt Sebastian into taking a bite out of her. Not that not having a reason would stop him, but he hadn't done it yet and Charlie didn't want to test her luck.

"I need to know your name," she said as she yanked open a drawer. "I talk to myself when I work and you need to know when I'm doing that or actually talking to you," she explained as she rummaged for some tape.

"My name's Elizabeth."

Nodding, Charlie turned around. She taped the bit of paper towel to her wrist and then gestured at the mess on the floor. "So you know what any of that is?"

Elizabeth flicked a glance at the pile, but her eyes didn't skirt around each individual item. Charlie almost groaned in frustration. If Sebastian had sent Elizabeth to piss her off with the woman's uselessness, Charlie was going to stab him in the throat. Right after she kicked him in the balls and saved her child.

"No. I won't be able to help you with any of that," Elizabeth said. Taking a deep, shuddering breath, she added, "I'm only here to raise the dead."

"Holy shit." The words escaped before Charlie even realized they'd formed. "That's, that's..."

"Yeah," Elizabeth sighed. "My sister has the ability to make Sebastian claw at his own throat and I can raise the dead. Pretty useless, huh?"

Charlie's jaw might as well have dislocated with the distance it fell. "You're saying your sister did that, when he...?" She raised a hand to her throat.

Elizabeth nodded without her having to continue. The memory of Sebastian grabbing hold of each of them as a stream of blood gushed from his neck was not something anyone could forget. The fact that his spine had been clearly visible wasn't what kept the memory sharp and in focus either, at least not for Charlie. It was his bone chilling laugh of amusement, a deep, warm rumble that should never have been matched with someone so cold.

"Damn, I wish I could have seen how he got that."

Elizabeth broke her gaze as she looked off in the distance. "I wish I hadn't been there. If I hadn't, he'd be dead."

Charlie's stomach knotted as the hairs on the back of her neck rose in trepidation. "What do you mean?"

Elizabeth swallowed hard as she squeezed her eyes shut. A second passed and then another before she opened them and looked back at Charlie. "He told me to kill her."

*I will kill you if he tells me to.* Elizabeth's earlier warning sounded shrill in Charlie's head. Reaching her hand behind her, she slowly inched back toward the blade she had dropped, cursing herself for having dropped it in the first place.

"I didn't, though," Elizabeth said and for a second Charlie breathed a sigh of relief. Then she saw the pain and guilt in those dark brown eyes and her stress levels rocketed once more.

"But I tried to," Elizabeth murmured, her voice strained. "I had no choice. Anything he says, I'm bound to do." She flicked her gaze at the piece of glass Charlie was inching toward. "Pick it up. I meant what I said about not trusting me. You'll be safe until he tells me otherwise, but don't ever let your guard down around me. Your friendship, as much as I would welcome it, will mean nothing."

Charlie looked at the shard calling to her. She wanted the comfort of having it in her hand, itched for the false sense of security it would give her. But this woman was screaming for help even as she was warning her away. Charlie couldn't turn her back on that, couldn't ignore that desperate cry that mimicked her own. If the roles had been reversed, Charlie would have given anything to have a friend.

So with a deep breath, she wrenched her eyes away from the shard. Stepping to the edge of the gurney, she kept her gaze fastened on Elizabeth.

"Thanks for the heads up, but we both know that if he tells you to kill me, there'll be nothing I can do about it. A small piece of glass isn't going to make a difference." Taking a deep breath, she steeled herself for her next words. "Just when that happens, do me a favor and make it quick."

Elizabeth nodded jerkily. "I promise."

Ignoring the cold chill of that vow, Charlie gave a sharp nod of her head. "Good. Now let's get to work."

She dropped her eyes to the corpse on her table, focusing on her task completely. Her heart raced at the idea of it reanimating in front of her, but she quickly locked down that fear. Anthony was counting on her to bring this guy back to life exactly how he'd been before he died. She didn't have time to give herself a moment to gather her strength. She needed it now.

Glancing up at Elizabeth, Charlie calmly said, "I want you to raise him so I have a control to compare things to."

"A control?"

"Yeah, a control. How else do you expect me to know if there's a change?"

Seeing the shame on Elizabeth's face, Charlie bit back a wince. "Sorry. I've been told I can be a right bitch when it comes to the sciences."

"It's okay," the woman mumbled.

She opened her mouth to argue, but in the end, Charlie dropped it. They couldn't be friends here. Not with that bastard pulling their strings.

"A control is the baseline in any experiment," she explained. "By seeing how the corpse reacts without anything done to it, then I'll be able to see what effects things have on it. For instance, if it can already talk, then I won't think that something I did caused it to say, 'Fuck off, you bitch. Leave me alone.'"

Instead of smiling, Elizabeth merely stepped froward and raised both of her hands. She placed them a few inches over the man's chest and instantly, there was a crackle of power around them. The very air shimmered with energy, replacing Charlie's fear with a scientist's curiosity.

Though she had been a stripper in her old life, Charlie had been in love with biology ever since she had taken her first lesson. Tony's birth was the only reason she'd never gone to college to pursue it professionally. With no supporting family and the death of Tony's father before he'd been born, Charlie had no other choice but to keep her job at the club. It was the only way she could afford to feed the both of them.

As weird as it seemed to everyone that judged her for her profession, Charlie much preferred being a stripper than a waitress. Where she'd grown up, waitresses got their asses and breasts grabbed just as much. At least in a club, she had the protection of the bouncers during work and afterwards when they walked her to her car.

It wasn't a great job, but it provided and that was enough. Kind of like this one. Except instead of getting paid with cash, she was now given insurance for Tony's health.

"Talk me through what you're doing," Charlie said. "I want to be able to understand the process."

"Um...I'm calling him? I don't know. It just works."

Before Charlie could bombard Elizabeth with all the questions in her head, the corpse jerked upright with a bellow. Her skin broke out in goosebumps as she jumped back. She fell against the counter on a silent scream, but then she quickly shook her head.

She did not have the luxury to panic.

Grabbing the piece of glass on the counter, Charlie swiped at the corpse trying to get off the table. It didn't make a noise when the blade cut into its skin, nor did it jerk in response. And though it still bled, it didn't seem to feel pain. Could it feel any sensation at all?

Before she could test for that, it reached out with a retaliating swipe of its hand. The speed was incredible, much faster than a vampire's. One second Charlie was out of reach and the next thing she knew she was being dragged toward him by the arm.

As she stared into those merciless eyes of death, her every missed moment with Tony stampeded inside her head. "Turn it back off!" she screamed.

Elizabeth's right hand snaked around the thing's bicep and it immediately collapsed. Charlie jumped out of the way as it crumbled, rubbing her arms as she breathed deep to recollect herself.

Only once she was certain it wasn't going to move anymore, did she lift her gaze to Elizabeth. The woman stood pale and frozen on the other side of the gurney. Pain laced her face as she stared at the ground and seeing that, Charlie was hit with a sudden blow to the chest.

But as much as she admired Elizabeth for still having a hold on her humanity, Charlie couldn't let her own come back to life. Not in this. The corpse had to stay an it.

Even when she brought it back with all its memories and emotions intact, Charlie couldn't afford to see it as anything other than an experiment. If she saw it like Elizabeth obviously did, as a person who deserved her pity and concern, then this job would break her.

And Charlie had vowed never to break.

"Ropes," she snapped firmly. She needed Elizabeth's

attention whether the woman was done mourning or not. "We need ropes."

After a hard swallow, the woman gave a weak nod, then rushed out of the room. This time she didn't ease the door open, but slammed it in her hurry to escape.

Charlie looked up at the ceiling as she fought her own desire to follow. Then with a return of her resolve, she bent down to look at the corpse. With a shaky hand, she reached out to touch it, feeling the temperature of its skin. It was warmer than she had expected and with a leap to her feet, she rushed to get a thermometer.

"Temperature is thirty-seven degrees Celsius," she said to herself. "That's within the normal healthy range for a human. I suspect the corpse had been dead for at least a few hours before its revival, leading me to conclude its temperature did rise upon reanimation."

She reached down to pull back an eyelid, swallowing hard when she stared into death itself. But as off putting as all this was, Sebastian expected her to bring this thing fully back to life and Charlie would not fail him.

"Eyes are bloodshot. However, I am unsure if that's a side effect of the experiment or of the original cause of death. I will need to check over the rest of the body before coming to a conclusion."

She examined the corpse slowly, moving from its head down to its feet. Though she was only giving it a physical examination, she didn't want to miss anything that might later be important. She'd never done anything like this before and though Sebastian had promised to get her some books, at the moment all she had guiding her were free online courses from edX and documentaries on YouTube.

And though a few weeks ago Charlie would've sworn that it was possible to learn everything on the latter, now it wasn't filling her with much confidence.

Pushing to her feet, Charlie swiped at the wayward hairs tickling her face. She placed her hands on her hips, trying to be brave when all she wanted to do was break down and scream. Inhaling sharply through her nose, she turned her head to the wall, to that damning spot that housed her child's finger.

Tony's pinkie hung pristine by magic, never decaying nor smelling despite having been cut off days ago. At first Charlie had refused to believe it was his. She had tried to convince herself that it was the wrong color or shape or size – anything to believe that her son hadn't been tortured because of her.

But then Sebastian had showed her the video of its removal.

That day, after the last cry had been wrung from her, Charlie had vowed she would do the same to Sebastian. One beautiful day she would cut his digits off one by one, then move up his body a joint at a time.

Recalling her promise, she kept her eyes latched onto the only piece of her son she was ever allowed to see. As her raw anger surged through her veins with each beat of her heart, Charlie prayed again. Except this time she didn't plead to a merciful god.

She bargained with the devil himself.

# SIX

*HELDRON, HALZAJA*

Something wasn't right.

Jack didn't need his sixth sense to know that. He saw it in the unanimous tensing of the crowd. He heard it in the sudden, all consuming silence and smelled it when the scent of unease and trepidation smothered the rich, spicy aromas of the nearby drazic market. But mostly he felt it inside him, a dark cloud of death that was on the verge of being released.

Though the *thing* hadn't moved nor spoken since the outskirts of Dirk seven cities back, it still sat heavily in his chest. Coiled with all the power and deadliness of a viper, it was merely waiting for the perfect chance to strike.

And given they were currently pinned in an alleyway only a few streets over from one of the biggest markets in the Heldron kingdom, now was a damn good time to do it. Xeno wouldn't make it a step before she was ripped apart by the thousands or so demons ahead of them.

*Stop it*, Jack ordered, but of course the *thing* didn't listen. It had been slowly draining his powers since the outskirts of Dirk and now, eight cities later, Jack was nearly depleted. Sweat beaded at his temples as he peered out of the alley and latched onto the front door of the castle.

It wasn't far, maybe a couple hundred or so yards, but it might as well have been a million. He was already struggling to keep Xeno's heat under wraps, it irritating the thousands of drazics before them. If she brushed up against a single person, the whole underground would hone in on her like a missile.

As two demons, both seven foot tall beasts of rippling muscle, passed close by, Jack was immediately slammed by the dark lure of temptation. It would be so easy to claim he was fine, then lure her out in the middle of that throng.

Hunter wasn't strong enough, Galvanor was on the verge of collapse, and Matakyli would run to her lifemate's aid, not that of an angel's. Only Rogan and himself would be left to cover Xeno. From there a single flare of Jack's fingers and the water elementalist would turn his full power to protecting Emma.

Xeno would be dead within minutes.

Tempted, the trickster's fingers twitched from an unconscious demand. Adrenaline surged through him as the *thing* reared its monstrous head with a demanding growl. It practically drooled in its anticipation, its muscles rippling from excitement. Jack's gut squeezed as his heart rate tripled. A cold sweat formed on the back of his neck and his body buzzed from a burst of power.

All it would take was one little wave of his hand.

*One little wave and our secret will be safe.*

*Pull it together, Jack. We're almost there.* Galvanor's calm voice snapped him out of his dark musings and with a sharp shake of his head, the trickster flicked his eyes to

Xeno. She held his gaze with knowing eyes and Jack swallowed in both shame and guilt.

Turning away, he directed his thoughts to Matakyli. *We need a secret entrance. I won't make it to that castle.*

There was a moment of silence, but Jack knew the demoness' answer long before she spoke. He could feel her reluctance as strongly as he felt the anticipation of his *thing.*

*No can do.*

Knowing he wouldn't get anywhere with someone so stubborn, Jack addressed Galvanor. *Just peek inside her head and tell me where to go, will you?*

Though his tone was carefree, almost joking even, Jack's body was coiled tight with fear. As if they could sense his rising panic, the demons closest turned their heads in his direction. With a lazy stretch of its powerful body, the *thing* stood up inside him, kicking Jack's heart into overdrive. When its tongue lolled out of its mouth in a devilish grin, Jack knew he only had minutes left to act.

Clenching his teeth, the trickster pressed, *Dammit, Matakyli, I can't keep this up much longer!*

With a snicker, she replied, *Tell all the girls that, do you or am I just that special?*

Jack heard Galvanor's cough of surprise and had he not been so irritated, he would've broken into a smile. He and Hunter had been trying to break the persapic's calm for years now, making jokes far dirtier than that one.

As if sensing just how close Jack was to falling apart, Rogan cut in on his behalf. *Galvanor –*

But before the elementalist could give a direct order, the telepath said, *Do not ask of me what you would not do to Emma.*

With a heavy sigh, Jack closed his eyes in defeat. Dear gods, how could it be that only two weeks ago this team had operated with smooth efficiency? And now, with the addition of just two more people, they'd broken down into this quibbling mess?

*I'm not joking, Xeno,* Jack claimed. *If I ever get like these two, please shoot me dead.*

*Hey!* Hunter complained with feigned hurt. *Why does she get that honor? I thought I was your best friend.*

Despite the *thing* rising inside him, Jack couldn't help but smile. His world might be turning to shit, but at least he could always count on Hunter – a pathetic, squishable human. What more could he possibly ask for?

Oh yeah, sanity from his other professional teammates.

As if answering his prayer, Xeno stepped away from the wall and spread her wings. Eyes focused on the castle, she said, *Tegan, I'm coming in through the second floor. Open the window above the front door.*

Before anyone could argue about the state of Xeno's wings, she launched into the air. She struggled with the first few flaps and Hunter sucked in his breath, terrified she'd crash back to the ground. Though Jack shared the man's sentiment, he didn't dare express it so brazenly. Only Hunter was ever allowed to do so and still walk away with all of his limbs intact.

As soon as the team was certain Xeno wasn't about to fall on top of the throng of demons, they hurried to the castle. Though it was far less effort for Jack to cloak his comrades' faces, he was still running dangerously close to empty. If any one of them were identified, trouble of one kind or another would begin almost immediately.

Rogan was like a celebrity in these parts. Hunter was easy prey. Emma was a descendant, a forbidden child of the gods that any warlord would pay top dollar for. And Galvanor, well he was the Heldrons' recent prisoner. The fact that he was free would've prompted a hundred faces to be pressed against the windows of the castle as everyone tried to get a peek inside.

But even after the Elv've'Norc entered the Heldron home, the tension in their shoulders didn't ease.

Rushing up to the second floor, they found Pyro and Rahu standing aggressively in the middle of the hall. Though the two demons faced away from them it was obvious that their arms were crossed and their eyes burned a dangerous red. Every inch of the stand-in king was screaming of his desire to attack and Rahu was eager to back him.

Xeno and Tegan stood united further along, their backs up against the wall. Though the window was still open, allowing for an easy escape, to leave through it was suicide. Jack didn't have any more magic left inside him and for Tegan to protect his comrade, he would have to go into a Rage. Out of the two choices, Xeno would be less at risk if she stayed where she was.

"Kaz-ik!" Matakyli snapped as she shoved her way past the Elv've'Norc to confront her brothers.

Jack slipped a knife out of its sheath before he realized he'd misheard her.

*Kaz-ij* meant to kill her. Kaz-*ik* meant to kill yourself. *Aka: how dare you. Aka: you should be ashamed of yourself.*

Rolling his eyes, Jack put his knife away. He could live another fifteen thousand years and still not come to grips with this ridiculous language.

"Loiek-ij," Matakyli continued, this time managing to pull a reaction from both of her brothers. Rahu dropped his head on a groan and Pyro's arms swung wide as he gesticulated feverishly in his reply.

With a raise of the brow, Jack looked over at his comrade. But if Galvanor was touched by Matakyli's claim that he was family and her brothers' acceptance of that, he wasn't showing it. As masked as always, the persapic stared silently ahead and waited until he was needed.

"Loieka-ij," Pyro countered and though that phrase could mean he refused to accept Galvanor as family, Jack was certain he had been talking about Xeno. Gods, this language made his head hurt.

Matakyli crossed her arms, her chin stubbornly set and Jack felt immediate pity for the demon prince.

As if he too realized that his defeat was imminent, Pyro threw up his hands in exasperation. The demon muttered something in drazic, Matakyli snapped back, and then he exhaled strongly in surrender. Rahu groaned beside him, but he too nodded his head in forced agreement.

Grinning, Matakyli made her way back to Galvanor's side. "Don't ever let them save her," she said cryptically.

Hunter frowned in confusion. Before anyone could request clarification, Xeno demanded, "That vampire you have in your dungeons. Take me to her."

Pyro's eyes narrowed as he crossed his arms and glared at her. "There is no vampire."

As Xeno marched right up to him, her eyes blazing with pure hatred, Jack and the rest of the team stood still in shock. It wasn't because of her sudden demand but because of her rare show of emotion.

"You want to protect your sister from Sebastian," Xeno said, "then you'll take me to her."

Pyro's teeth ground loudly in the silence. His eyes burned bright red. Then with a snarl, he turned on his heels and led the way to the dungeons.

Jack flicked a quizzical eye at Galvanor, but whatever the telepath knew, he wasn't about to share. Not even his lifemate was privy to his findings judging by the look on her face, and if that wasn't enough to make Jack worried, then Rogan's mien damn well was. That wasn't a look of confusion on his face; it was the look of a coldblooded killer.

Whoever this vampire was, she wasn't about to live much longer.

Halfway up the stairwell, Hunter ground to a stop. His face turned multiple shades lighter and his eyes widened in horror. Though he didn't say a word, Jack knew him well enough to know something had finally clicked inside that brilliant mind of his.

Before he could ask about his findings, Hunter croaked, "I need to go to Hel's Exit." When none of the demons turned around to take him, he said a bit more forcibly, "It's about your king."

Immediately, Rahu was by his side, and a split second later, they disappeared back down the stairs. Pyro shared a concerned look with Matakyli. After a nervous nod, she took the lead as her brother took off after them.

"She won't talk, you know," Matakyli said as they continued up the stairs. Her desire to follow her brothers was as evident in her quick pace as it was in her worried tone.

"Yes she will." Xeno didn't elaborate and the demon princess didn't press.

Two floors away from their destination, the demoness yelled up the stairs. "Let these people pass, Malphas! And don't panic when you see the blonde. I'll be right back!" And with that she turned tail and fled back down the stairs. After a nod of permission from Rogan, Galvanor turned to follow his lifemate.

As they neared the entrance to the dungeons, Jack's curiosity peaked so high even the *thing* was captivated for once.

With shaky hands, a tall demon pup – Malphas, Jack presumed – stood on a stairway landing. Stepping aside, he swallowed hard as Xeno passed, and Jack was certain that if she so much as looked at him, the poor boy would pass out in a heartbeat.

Her eyes straight ahead, she led them up the rest of the stairs, then through the maze of cells. He wasn't surprised when they stopped outside of one that looked almost as empty as all of the others. Though he couldn't see its occupant, he could smell her stench of piss and sweat.

"Hello, Lucille," Xeno said softly with no trace of her earlier hatred. "I want to ask you a few questions."

In a streak of white, a woman slammed into the bars of the cage. She was a tiny little thing, young too given her fangs barely poked past her lips. And yet, something about her caused goosebumps to break out on Jack's skin.

"Go for it!" the vampire giggled, her red hair a mess of massive proportions. Her eyes were just as crazed, just as crimson and fucked up as her hair. But though it was obvious the demons had tortured and starved her for however long they'd had her, Jack doubted that was the only reason for her insanity.

As if determined to prove him right, Lucille gripped the bars of her cage and cooed, "And oh, I hope they're about Sebastian, love. That dick left me here; can you believe it! He sent his new bitch all the way here, but instead of releasing me she came to pick up a collar! Arrrrgh! Thirteen fucking years I've stayed loyal to him and what do I get for that? Nothing! I hope he rots in heaven, that bastard. No, hell. No, heaven. No, wait, which one has all the dogs? Sebastian hates dogs."

"Lucille."

"What?" she shrieked as she snapped her gaze back to Xeno. Then with a slow blink, she sat down with a sweet smile. "Oh yes, you wanted to ask me some questions. Well, what would you like to know? Where his hiding spots are? What his grand bloody plan is? How he likes to fuck? I'll tell you anything you want."

"Xeno, ye don–"

As if she hadn't heard him, Xeno stepped right up to the bars. Her face was carved from stone as she peered into the deranged eyes of the vampire.

"Name your price then," she murmured.

"Well," Lucille said as she stretched her smile as wide as it would go. "Angel blood is so delicious and, oh, look at that, you're an angel."

A flash of fear crossed Xeno's face, so faint and brief that Jack almost believed he'd imagined it. But then it hit him, the bloodsucker's identity, and he knew his eyes hadn't played any tricks.

His blood chilled as Lucille scrambled back onto her hands and knees. She gripped the steel of her cage with her bony fingers and pressed her haggard face against the bars. As her eyes scattered wildly, Jack had the sudden urge to kill her where she knelt.

The *thing*, on the other hand, wanted to release her in hopes that she would finish what she and Sebastian had started. Fourteen years ago, Lucille had tormented Xeno so much she'd pushed her down the path of a fallen angel. Maybe this time she'd actually kill her.

*Shut up.* Jack tried to ignore the dark whispers of the *thing*, but even in the few hours since it had first grasped onto the idea of killing Xeno, its power over him had grown measurably. Something was changing inside him, and Jack couldn't do a damn thing to stop it.

"Xeno," Rogan tried again, this time grabbing the angel by the arm. "Don–"

But again she cut him off. "It is my decision," she said

as she jerked out of his hold and rolled up a sleeve.

Cursing, Rogan yelled for Malphas to bring them a cup. The order had barely passed his lips when Lucille cut in with a mad shriek. "No! I want it raw! Not in a cup or in a bowl or even drizzled on a delicious meal made of steak! I want it directly from the vein and for thirty seconds! That or no deal!"

With a speed Jack hadn't thought possible given her young age and tortured state, the vampire reached out and snagged Xeno's arm. Her bloodshot eyes peered up at the angel she craved. Smiling deliriously, Lucille bared her teeth and sank them deep into Xeno's flesh.

Although his friend didn't make a sound, Jack could hear her scream all the same. He saw it in her glazed eyes, in the awful tensing of her body. She was in sheer agony, both physically and mentally. Instead of stumbling back in pain, though, Xeno reached through the bars with her other arm and pinned the vampire to her.

Lucille giggled as she reached up to grab the hand tangled in her hair. A crude joke passed her lips as she rolled her hips forward.

But then she tensed.

Her eyes widened.

Her body jerked.

Her giggle turned into a muffled scream.

Clawing at Xeno's grip, Lucille thrashed frantically. Her nails scratched into the angel's arms, her torso, her stomach, her legs, revealing pitch-black blood from every wound.

*What the fuck?*

Her lips in a tight line, her eyes firmly on Lucille's tears, Xeno stayed rigid in her attack.

In his thousands years of life, Jack had seen many torture sessions, had been at the heart of a good few, but as he watched Lucille convulse violently from the pain, even his twisted old self felt a tiny flurry of unease. Xeno, however, never even flinched. Even after the vampire fell limp in her grasp, her hands dropping to her side, her screams turning into helpless whimpers, the angel held her upright until her thirty seconds was up.

When Xeno finally released her, the wretched thing fell to the floor with a sob. Coughing and wheezing, Lucille convulsed in the blood of her tears.

Without as a hint of remorse, Xeno bent down and grasped the dirty red hair of her target. She dragged the poor girl back to the edge of the cage and looked her dead in the eye.

And in that moment, Jack didn't see an angel coming back from her descent as a fallen. He saw a monster embracing the darkness with open arms.

In a voice as cold as her heart, Xeno murmured, "Now tell us where Sebastian is."

# SEVEN

## *STEREGOI CASTLE, BLÓDYRIÓ*

*Blood red moon, bright and full,
Never venture past your door.
Blood red moon, not yet full,
Fear the days of three or more.*

Sebastian stared at the moon from the living room balcony, a glass of spiked blood in his hand. He frowned as Blódyrió's most famous rhyme crept into his head. How many times had he ventured out on the full moon for a bit of fun? How many werewolves had he tracked down and killed when they were at their most powerful? That childish rhyme of caution should have been wiped from his memory long ago.

Irritated, the vampire raised the glass to his lips. He was no longer the pathetic little boy that had been hunted in these woods, under this red sky, along with his adopted brother and sisters. He was no longer helpless and afraid, concerned about the monstrous, mindless werewolves that had closed in around them. Nor did he fear his hated, vicious bloodkin who had chased them until his feet were raw and his heart was shredded over the death of his adopted parents.

His lips curled. He took another sip.

No, he wasn't afraid of them at all. It was hard to fear the dead, even harder to fear those he, himself, had killed. It might have taken him decades to build up his strength, but he had showed them in the end. He had taught them all what it meant to be afraid.

*If only you had stopped there...*

Turning sharply, Sebastian headed back inside. It had been a risk coming here after all these years. For nearly four millennia, he had avoided this castle, this place he'd once called home. Long before he'd changed his name from the Kind Hearted to the Ancient Destroyer, he'd played in these halls, had learned what it meant to love in these halls.

His bloodkin had 'gifted' him to the Steregoi royal family as a sign of their loyalty after the civil war. But his real purpose had been to spy on them, to discover their weaknesses and fears so that one day, the Movradi family could take the throne they believed was rightfully theirs.

His lips tight, Sebastian raised his glass to his lips as his eyes swept around the familiar hall. He could see all the blood, hear the screams of that fateful night. He could feel the small hand of his brother's grip as he'd dragged him, barefoot and terrified, into the woods with the blood red moon shining above them.

He never should've spied for the Movradi's. He never should've believed his blood mother when the bitch had looked him straight in the eye and promised she would put aside their feud. That his marriage to Sophina was a good alternative to them taking the throne by force.

Irritated at the naive little boy he had once been, Sebastian tossed back the contents of his glass. As soon as he stepped onto the plush navy carpet of the living room, his bare feet sank into the fine strands and sent up small clouds of dust.

*Father would have a fit if he –*

Abruptly, Sebastian cut off his thoughts. He looked down at his glass with a scowl, blaming the cocktail for the rise of his unwanted memories. His family was dead, killed by his own bloodkin four and a half thousand years ago. There was no changing that, no fixing that. There sure as hell wasn't any point thinking about that.

He was too close to the finish line to be slipping up now. He had destroyed Perspic for the gods, had traded his heart to the gods, and had abandoned his love for the gods. Soon, he would become a god.

There would be no changing that, no failing that.

Dropping the glass at his feet, Sebastian walked over to his bloodkin. Lamia was the only one of his left and though humans would call her his sister, he never would. Abba was his sister. Sophina was his sister. She, on the other hand, was not. They might share a sperm and egg donor and a bloodline that could be traced back to the dawn of time, but they would never share the bonds that made them family.

"Have you found Nivan?" he asked.

"No."

"Then what are you doing here?"

His blatant threat didn't scare her, but Sebastian hadn't expected it would. Lamia might have been born weak, but against all odds, she'd grown strong. Now there was nothing he, nor anyone, could do that would make her cower.

"I found this."

She held out her hand, showing him the trinket of a dark blue bird. In an instant Sebastian snatched it from her and wrapped his other hand around her throat.

"Where?"

Though her lips moved, no sound came out.

Fighting control over his wrath, Sebastian released his grip just enough for her to speak.

"In a Heldron club called Headmistress' Brothel."

Cursing, Sebastian released her. Marching over to the balcony, he rolled the bird in his hand. He didn't need to study it to know that it was made from ciera, a rare stone found only in the treacherous mountain ranges of Lyr. He didn't need to examine it to know that it had the Steregoi crest on its breast. It had been the first gift he'd ever received, crafted by his father, the then king of these lands.

It had also been lost in these very woods, dropped by a panicking boy who didn't have the strength to save his family.

His heart clenched; his hand clenched tighter.

Staring into the darkness, Sebastian sneered with rage. The trinket cut into his hand. Lamia stared in blatant curiosity, like a shark wheedling out the weak. But he didn't care. All of his thoughts were focused on one thing and one thing only.

The bitch was back.

The amount of rage he was feeling was ineffable. She had destroyed his plans once before, had set him back thousands of years in pursuing his goal. She would not do so again.

Sebastian was not the gullible man he'd once been. She had no idea, no fucking idea of the monster he'd become. Her sight would not save her, not this time. For not even the gods could sense a godslayer, and Sebastian now knew exactly where to find one.

Delentia would regret playing him this time. Would regret everything.

Sneering, the vampire glanced down at the bird in his hand. He forced himself to look at it, to overcome all the fears and regrets holding him back. The end result was all that mattered and nothing Delentia could remind him of would make him forget that.

But though he'd expected it to be hard, the memories still hit him like the knockout blow from a boxer. With a gasp, his lungs emptied of all air and his brain filled with scenes best left forgotten.

Sophina, his lifemate and adopted sister, stared at him with warm hazel eyes. She'd seen how much the gift had meant to him, had smiled in encouragement for him to accept it. She had been his lifeline since the very beginning – right up until the moment she'd betrayed him.

Erin, his brother, came next. He'd scrambled over the couch, desperate to see what Sebastian had been given. One look and he'd begged to play with it. He'd offered to trade his playing cards and his drum kit, but Sebastian had refused.

Abba, his youngest sister, had yet to be born, but she was still there. In the womb of their mother, his smiling, loving mother who –

*Enough!*

Angrily, Sebastian shook his head. He would not fall for that bitch's tricks. He was exactly where he wanted to be, exactly who he wanted to be. He was strong and he was powerful and he had no regrets over how he'd become so. Remembering his old family, their morals and codes, wouldn't change that.

Curling his lips, Sebastian tossed the trinket off the

balcony. He watched it sail through the air for a moment, his chest tight, before turning sharply on his heels. He marched back inside, poured another glass. His hands shook in the barest of tremors. It wasn't enough to upset the liquid, but it was enough for him to know he was failing.

Clenching the glass tightly, Sebastian raised the drink to his lips. The memories started slower this time, drifting in only as fragments of voices. Sophina, Erin, Abba, his parents – happy, excited, loving...screaming, terrified, ashamed. Unrelenting. A crescendo of voices that wouldn't stop, wouldn't wan.

Desperate, Sebastian poured another glass. She would not win. That crazy bitch and her meddling ways, she would need more than a forgotten trinket to tip him over the edge.

*I shouldn't be here.* He should be in Merlin's Dimensio. He *would* be in Merlin's Dimensio if it wasn't for the fucking Elv've'Norc. They'd been a pain in his ass ever since he'd kidnapped Tegan's wife.

Shaking his head, Sebastian looked up with bleary eyes. He was both pleased and pissed to see that Lamia had dismissed herself. On the one hand, he wanted to hurt the messenger. On the other, he didn't want anyone seeing his vulnerability.

Scowling, Sebastian poured another glass.

He wasn't vulnerable. He was strong and in control. He'd planned for everything, had prepared for even more. Everything was finally coming together and his time was coming. There was nothing anyone could do to stop that – not even Delentia.

Shakily, Sebastian poured another glass. When only a drop came out, he blinked once in surprise, then again in rage. With a feral scream, he threw the bottle at the wall and phased.

He was not weak.

By the gods, he was not.

Elizabeth stared at herself in the bedroom mirror, hoping that the bulge of her stomach was just her getting fat. Ever since she'd started working with Charlie, she'd seen the return of her appetite. She knew it was foolish to hope that the two of them could end up as friends, but she couldn't help it. For months she had been alone with only Sebastian for sick, twisted company. She wanted someone to lean on, to talk to, to cry with. She wanted some stability and comfort, no matter how fragile it would be.

What she didn't want, though, was a child.

Pressing her fingers to her stomach, Elizabeth tried to decide if it was bigger than it was yesterday. She cocked her head to the side as if a new angle would show her the truth. It was weird how calm her heart was, given how terrified she was about being pregnant. As she turned for a better look, a touch of evil shivered down her spine.

*Sebastian.*

Eyes bulging with terror, Elizabeth dropped her shirt and sprang as far away from the bed as she could. The distance wouldn't stop him from raping her, but it would keep the bed clean.

Never once had he bothered to take her anywhere 'comfortable.' Wherever she was at the time, whether it be curled up on the floor or backed into a corner, that was good enough for him. And though Elizabeth knew it was stupid to pin her strength and sanity on something so easily stained, she couldn't survive if she didn't.

By keeping the bed pure, not only did it give her a sense of control (however false), but it also gave her hope.

Hope that if she thought hard enough and worked slyly enough, then one day she could best him.

But that day would not be today.

In the blink of an eye, Sebastian stood in front of her in all of his terrifying glory. This time his eyes weren't bright with cruel merriment. Rather they burned with a ragged torment. His handsome face was twisted in agony and his words came out slurred by grief.

Had Sebastian come to her like this three months ago, Elizabeth would have embraced him with open arms. Young and foolish, she would have stupidly believed that she could soothe away all his aches and pains with only the blossoming love in her heart.

But now, as he stared at her with a silent plea for help, Elizabeth saw his pain for what it was.

Something new to fear.

Terrified, she took a step back. Only there wasn't anywhere left for her to go.

As soon as Jack stepped foot on Blódyrió, he cursed like a drunken sailor. He didn't need to exit the portal's cave to know that the moon was red and almost full. He could feel the power of it tugging in his veins. Its feverish desires for him to change, to run, to feast were near impossible to ignore. It wanted him to hunt every bloodsucker around, to rip their hearts from their chests or their heads from their necks. It wanted him to bathe in their blood and frolic in the gruesome aftermath of their bodies. But what it truly wanted, above all else, was to be a right pain in the mother fucking ass.

Thor's balls, he did not have time for this.

Harsh laughter rose up inside him, a deep bark of amusement that pissed him off even as it gave him the chills.

*For this?* the thing mocked as it paced around its cage. *The moon empowers me, fool, and you have grown weak. Already you have seen me and we both know what that means. My time is coming and soon Leyding will hold me no longer.*

*Blah, blah, blah,* Jack replied with a roll of his eyes. *You're as dramatic as my father. Now be a good boy and shut the fuck up.*

Ignoring the rising snarls of outrage, the truth behind the *thing's* words, and the goosebumps crawling down his spine, Jack forced an easy smile. Galvanor and Rogan were soon to be behind him and he would be a fool if he gave them anything to suspect. He might have been able to stop the *thing* from killing Xeno, but there was no way he'd be able to protect everyone.

Luckily, Jack was a huge believer in not worrying about tomorrow's problems.

Stepping out of the mouth of the portal, the trickster tugged off his shirt and then his boots. Their destination was a good three days walk away. The full moon rose in two. If he didn't trans into his teammate's transportation and get them there tonight, they wouldn't live long enough to see the castle.

Already the blood moon would have claimed the weaker wolves, forcing them into a mindless frenzy of bloodlust. Soon, their demented howls would fill the night sky, mixing with the screams of their victims. By the end of the night, thousands upon thousands would be dead, or worse, infected. For unlike the full moon's, the blood moon's cycle could not be tracked. With the whole plane caught off guard, tonight was to be a bloodbath.

And tomorrow would be something worse.

Working quickly, Jack slipped his fingers under his

waistband, then pulled down his pants. The portal glowed softly behind him, painting the cave's walls with the warm colors of a moonset. By the time the various pinks faded, Jack was standing butt naked with his two teammates and Matakyli beside him.

As this was only a RECON mission, everyone else had stayed behind on Halzaja. The need to find Nivan was more pressing than scouting out a castle that was most likely to be empty. Though Lucille had sworn up and down that Sebastian was here, information gathered by torture was rarely proven to be correct. Not to mention, the young vampire hadn't seen nor spoken to Sebastian in years.

But orders were orders and Tegan wasn't keen on ignoring any possible lead.

As Jack stepped out of the cave, he rolled his shoulders and spread his arms wide. Within seconds he had transed into a magnificent illyra eagle, a bird native to this plane. They towered near fifteen feet tall, weighed surprisingly little, and their feathers were a warm golden, each tipped with a fiery red. They burned like the sunset, a ripple of color that would sparkle in the night sky whenever they caught the light of the moon. Believed to be omens of good luck, the birds were wished upon like shooting stars. And though Jack didn't believe in such things, tonight they could all use a bit of luck.

"Hel's fire, you're beautiful," Matakyli breathed as she stepped out alongside Galvanor.

Her words were those of worship; her gaze was full of awe. Only behind all of that lurked a devilish glint.

Eyes narrowing, Jack flexed his talons.

He knew he should have argued harder against her tagging along. The demoness didn't know their rhythm. She was unpredictable and too controlled by her emotions.

One look at Sebastian and she'd probably rush to her death, killing Galvanor in the process.

But though Tegan had agreed with most of his points, the berserker had also decided it would be beneficial for them if she tagged along. It would show her brothers that the Elv've'Norc was serious about working together and given this was just a RECON mission...Jack hadn't stood a chance.

But bloody hell, if she plucked one of his feathers, she wasn't going to make it back to this portal. Politics be damned.

*We need to move quickly,* Galvanor warned as he stepped out beside Matakyli. He halted her mischief with just a look. It wasn't a withering, don't-you-fucking-dare one like Jack was giving her. Rather, it was one full of love and devotion and a promise to get her something just as pretty afterwards.

Dear gods, he was going to be sick.

*Yes, best not to linger,* Jack offered dryly as he looked away from the nauseating love birds. *Wouldn't want to make Rogan jealous that Emma isn't here.*

*Nay, having her safe elsewhere is my preference,* the elementalist claimed. He scanned the tree line as he spoke. It didn't matter that Galvanor would be alerted to any minds nearby, Rogan never relaxed when on a mission. *But aye, we need to move quickly. Galvanor, Matakyli, then –*

*No time,* Galvanor interrupted. *Four wolves changing twenty miles out.*

*Fuck.* Though Jack had expected them to have company eventually, he hadn't expected it to be so soon. Seeing others under the power of the Craving was going to tempt the *thing* like no other.

*Can ye take the two together?* Rogan asked as he

reached inside his jacket for a vial of liquid silver.

*Looks like we're about to find out.*

Launching into the air, Jack grabbed Matakyli and Galvanor with his talons. Though their combined weight was well over what he could safely carry, there wasn't any other choice.

When one changed into a werewolf, their senses heightened to the point of near godlike powers. They could track a month old scent across an entire plane. A fresh trail twenty miles out wouldn't even be a challenge.

As the first howl shattered the peace of the night, Jack rose that first bit off the ground. The strain on his body was near overwhelming and it was only by some miracle that he managed to stay in the air.

*Do you smell that?* The *thing* stood up in its curiosity, its nose pointed into the wind.

*Bit busy here,* Jack replied as he focused on finding a thermal. The rising hot air would help to ease his load immensely and with luck he would be able to ride it high enough to then coast to the castle.

When he hit rough air three thousand feet off the ground, Matakyli's grip on his talons tightened.

*If you drop Galvanor, I swear to Hel I will carve my name in your ass using your eye as an ink jug.*

*Relax,* Jack said as he tightened his circle. *It was only a bit of rotor. Besides, if I have to drop anyone, it's going to be you.*

Ignoring what was surely a scathing reply, Jack returned his attention to feeling the wind on his wings. He adjusted his path until he was riding the strongest part of the thermal. Within minutes, the castle appeared below them.

*They've caught Rogan's scent,* Galvanor informed them just as Jack was about to descend. *We'll prepare for a drop landing.*

*A what?* Matakyli asked.

Grinning, Jack didn't wait for Galvanor to explain. The castle was well within sight. The surrounding trees had been cleared. The ground looked soft enough – well, as long as they missed the boulders. And really from this height, they didn't look that big.

With a joyful chuckle, Jack opened his talons and listened to Matakyli scream.

A pity though that the demoness was shrieking more from excitement than fear, the fucking lunatic.

Veering back around, Jack made a beeline for the portal. He was still a mile out when he spotted the wolves up ahead. Though undoubtedly young, there was no way Rogan would be able to fend them off. One or two, maybe. But four? Not under a blood moon when they still had enough sense to work together.

Swearing, Jack considered wasting precious energy on another trans. If he changed into a dragon, he could shoot fire from afar. Of course, there was a good chance he burned Rogan and everything in these woods along with them, but what was life without a bit of risk?

Smirking in amusement, Jack prepared to change. He had just called upon his magic when he caught sight of a blue jacket being waved on his left.

*You clever bastard.* Cancelling his trans, Jack dropped into a dive toward the tree Rogan was standing on.

*Grabbing on the count of three,* he said.

*Aye,* Rogan confirmed, raising his arms.

*One. Two. Three!*

Jack reached out with his talons. He snagged Rogan by the wrist. The grab was flawless, a perfect ten.

With a hard flap of his wings, he rose high above the trees. A few minutes later and he was back at the hill.

*There are four werewolves already on our tail,* Rogan said as soon as his feet touched the ground. *We need to make this quick.*

Although Jack had already taken the liberty of cloaking their scent, that wouldn't fool the wolves for long. They had a sixth sense with it came to tracking, and after Rogan's little trick back there, they wouldn't be keen to lose him. No one did vengeance better than a crazed werewolf, except maybe a certain sightseeing fury named Delentia.

*On second thought,* Jack mused to himself as he transed back into his usual self. *There's no maybe about it. That chick can hold one hell of a grudge.*

*That might not be possible,* Galvanor said calmly across their link. *Target's inside.*

When Rogan didn't reply immediately and Galvanor didn't continue, Jack turned toward them warily. He took in the heavy silence, the unsaid words. His eyes narrowed. Godsdammit, he knew pauses like this, was well versed in them thanks to his dramatic-ass father. It didn't matter the culture or the species, a tension filled pause like this one – it only ever meant trouble.

*And he still has access to the* Scrolls.

Yep, trouble with a capital fucking T. Exactly what Jack needed on a blood moon when the *thing* was determined to wrestle for control.

*How?* Rogan demanded.

Another pause. Another raise of Jack's hairs.

*One of the hostiles has discovered a way to retain its knowledge.*

On a silent swear, Jack angled toward the treeline. He didn't need to look at his captain to know Rogan's eyes had hardened into focus and his jawline had tightened with determination. The man was sacrilegious about finishing his missions and if there was even a hint of Sebastian still having the *Scrolls*, then his previous one wasn't done. Throw in his raging desire to protect the Seven Planes and Jack figured those words had probably given Rogan an orgasm.

Which meant there was no bloody way they were only going to be here a few hours.

And though Jack knew it was impossible for what Galvanor had said to be true, it wasn't something he could explain without ruining his cover. He was supposed to be a less-than-a-hundred-years-old trickster, not the fifteen-thousand-year-old ancient god-child he was. And given no one but the gods knew about the Readers of the Scrolls and they had personally seen to that race's extinction long ago, Jack had only one option if he wanted to get off this plane quickly: lift the cloaking spell just enough for the werewolves hunting them to catch their scent.

They'd force them to abandon the mission and come back once the blood moon was over, so it's not like it would really jeopardize anything. And given Galvanor's recent infection, the telepath wasn't strong enough to keep track of both the werewolves and the vampires at the same time, so no one would even know Jack was at fault.

But just as he started to lift the spell, a sharp prickle of awareness crawled down his spine. Goosebumps broke out across his skin as the *thing* grew increasingly restless. It paced as if with a fever. Mouth foaming, eyes bright with madness, the *thing* rammed against its cage so hard Jack winced in pain.

He shot a quick glance to his teammates. When it was clear no one had noticed, he snapped, *Cut it out.*

*I want what's in that castle.*

*Seriously? No way am I going to let you anywhere near a potential combat zone tonight.*

Jack had expected a growl in reply. It was the *thing's* usual reaction when it didn't get what it wanted. So when it started to chuckle in a bone chilling, goosebumps raising way, Jack experienced a horrible sense of unease.

*Why are you laughing?* he demanded.

But it wasn't the *thing* that spoke. It was Rogan.

*Galvanor, ye said ye can breach Sebastian's blocks?*

*Yes. They're lower than normal.*

*Then inform any teams nearby that we'll need backup and send a message to Tegan if ye can. Matakyli, stay here with Galvanor. He'll need a watcher as he controls Sebastian. Jack –*

*Oh shit*, Jack thought privately. *Please don't say it.*

He needed the werewolves to get here immediately. They had to blow their cover and force them to retreat before Rogan finished that sentence. Jack might not know why the *thing* was desperate to get inside this castle, but he was determined to never find out.

Delentia hadn't told him his future for nothing. Jack's whole purpose in life was to keep the *thing* from having whatever it was it wanted, and given all it ever wanted was to escape its magical cage, entering that castle would damn them all.

*Fuck me, please don't say it.*

But as the *thing* laughed and Rogan looked him in the eye, Jack knew that luck was not on his side tonight.

Ignorant to the consequences, his captain said the one thing he didn't want to hear. "We're going in."

# EIGHT

Through bloodshot eyes, Sebastian peered around the room. The walls were a bit worn. The furniture was covered in a thick layer of dust. A disgusting descendant stood in the corner, pressed against the wall like a sacrificial lamb. But despite the harsh wearing of time, to him the room looked exactly how it used to be.

Sebastian didn't notice pristine sheets or a glistening mirror. What he saw was a room of childhood innocence. He heard the beautiful laughter of his beloved, her joyful cries as he chased her around the room. He recalled her sweet, sweet voice as they cuddled on the bed simply talking about the mundane.

He felt her warmth. That bright light she was always radiating. The touch of her fingers as she held his hand. The feel of her love as she slipped into his arms. Always sharing, always giving. Always easing away his troubles. Always except for now.

Now her sweet voice sounded like tar. Her lovely warmth burned a hole in his heart.

With a feral growl, Sebastian headed for Elizabeth. He needed to taint the room, to cover it in violence before his drunken memories of Sophina could get to him.

He'd made it only two steps before her pain erupted inside him, before her screams brought him to his knees.

*No!*

*Please!*

*I beg of you, have mercy!*

*Stop!*

*He's just a boy!*

*You're hurting me! Sebastian, stop!*

His deceased wife's shrill and painful cries were a brutal companion to the alcohol coursing through his system. Together they were all too much. Squeezing his eyes shut, Sebastian gave a feral growl. He was desperate to silence the ghosts of his past, but they didn't stop and they didn't wane. They just grew louder and louder as every life he had taken, as every pain he had inflicted, joined the cries of his loved ones.

Sophina's bloodied face gazed up at him, broken yet still defiant. At the time of her deaths, Sebastian had been consumed by anger, overwhelmed by her betrayal. He had brought her back to life only to kill her again and again, never once hesitating to torture the woman he loved. Blinded by his twisted path of justice, Sebastian hadn't been able to see his wife's pain. But now, all these years later, her tears left him crippled, her cries left him broken. Her pain was his pain and for the first time in millennia, Sebastian felt the agony of guilt.

But before he could beg for forgiveness, Sophina was swept away in a sea of more faces, of more regret. They came in bright, piercing flashes of accusation. First Erin, a brother he could not protect. Then Abba, a sister he had betrayed. A mother and father whom he had failed.

Faceless victims he could not remember. All screaming, all crying, all driving him insane.

*My dear brother, what have you become?*

*I'm so sorry we failed you, Seb.*

*Listen, boy. You must remember who you are. My son, the Kind Hearted. The loving brother who stayed at Abba's side all day when she was sick. The one who coached Erin through his ascension. The man who –*

"Enough!" Sebastian roared. "You will be silent!"

Immune to his rage, the voices did not cease. They didn't even falter. Instead, they grew louder and louder, becoming more frantic and tangled in their attempts to get him to listen.

But he would not be swayed.

Angrily, Sebastian opened his eyes and staggered to his feet. The bright light pierced his brain like flaming daggers. The crumbling walls spun like a carousel on crack. Already, his focus was dissipating, evaporating like precious water in a desert.

His lack of control was as embarrassing as it was enraging. Unable to walk in a straight line, Sebastian stumbled to the bed. As the vampire continued to be consumed by guilt, he turned to Elizabeth in desperation.

Her eyes were wide with frozen horror. Her mouth was agape in sheer torment. In all the time he'd had her, she'd only looked like this twice. The first had been when she had walked in on him eating her friend. The second had been after he'd ordered her to kill her sister.

Even as mad and unstable as he now seemed, it didn't warrant that devastating look. But whereas an hour ago he would have found pleasure in her pain, all he felt now was guilt.

"Smile, love."

Slowly, a smile etched onto her face.

"Now come here."

Without the slightest of hesitations, Elizabeth walked over to the bed. He gripped her wrist and just that small contact helped him focus back on reality. He could still hear the cries of his wife, but everyone else was muffled.

Unfortunately, it was Sophina's screams that killed him the most.

Tormented, Sebastian's grip on Elizabeth tightened. As she whimpered, the vampire sat up and purred, "Now, Liz, my love. I need you to scream."

"*Goddammit*!" Charlie slammed a fist onto her desk. "God-fucking-dammit!"

On a scream of frustration, she lashed out with her arm. Beakers and vials went flying. Papers were tossed about the room. Her heart and soul were ripped to pieces, then buried under an avalanche of fear.

She had failed. Despite staying up all night, despite reading until her eyes were raw, Charlie had failed. She was no closer to finding a way to grant her subject all its memories than she had been the night before. She didn't even know where to start. Test after test she'd feverishly tried, but not a single one had made a difference. If anything, her subject's mentality had started to deteriorate faster.

"God-*fucking*-dammit!"

Sebastian was going to be here within the hour. Despite her failings, she couldn't give him nothing. That bastard had her child and had already proven he wouldn't hesitate to hurt him. She couldn't give up.

Goddammit, she wouldn't. She would not die in this fucking place without making the bastard pay.

First, she would cut off his finger just as he had

Anthony's. Then she'd gouge out Sebastian's eyes with a molten spoon. She wouldn't use dragon fire to heat it nor any of the flames from the Underworlds. No, she would use regular fire so that they would regenerate, giving her the continuous pleasure of removing them as he screamed.

The only thing she would leave alone would be his ears. Though vampires could easily hunt via hearing alone, Charlie would never harm them. She wanted him to hear every buzz of a chainsaw, every scrape of a blade, every fucking crackle of a fire. She wanted him afraid, piss-shitting terrified, about what she was going to do to him next.

But as pleasurable as torturing him this way would be, it wouldn't be enough to sate her. It wouldn't be nearly enough. She would want to do it over and over again. Kill him a hundred times, a thousand, until he understood the agony of her pain.

Slowly, Charlie turned to the mess on the floor and eyed the only unbroken flask. It would be the perfect solution to her rage. With a cruel smile, she picked it up with renewed determination.

"I'll figure this out," she swore to herself. Because killing Sebastian wouldn't be enough. She wanted to bring him back with him knowing she had already ended him once. And when the light faded from his eyes a second time, Charlie would revive him once more. And then again and again and again until her burning heart was finally content.

But that wouldn't be the end for him. Oh hell no, not after all he'd put her through. She'd pass him over to Elizabeth. Open up the queue to every one of his victims. Then she wouldn't have to imagine him in Hell. She would be the mother fucking queen of it.

High on her rage, Charlie returned to her desk. She placed the empty flask in front of her, took a deep breath, and froze.

Standing in the doorway of her lab, with his beautiful green eyes puffy from tears, was her little boy. Her sweet, sweet little boy.

"Mummy?"

His lonely voice broke her. Three weeks at the mercy of Sebastian and she'd never once given him the satisfaction. But hearing her little boy, whose voice she'd thought she'd never hear again...

Her heart couldn't take it. With an uncontrollable sob, Charlie broke into a million pieces. She dropped her head onto her desk. The agony inside her was so consuming she didn't even realize she'd cracked the flask and cut her forehead in the process. She simply collapsed, depleted of all her strength.

"Mummy?"

That little voice, that trembling little voice –

Charlie cried from the very pit of her soul.

He wasn't real. She knew he wasn't real. That the only reason she was seeing him, hearing him, was because she'd finally gone crazy. She'd wanted this for so long and now she was hallucinating in an attempt to cope with her despair.

That bastard had actually done it. He'd finally found a way to bulldoze over every defensive wall she'd erected. She was never going to kill him. Hell, she was never going to escape this nightmare. Sebastian had won and there was nothing she could do to change that.

"Mummy, I wanna go home."

On a wail of torment, Charlie started to shake. She squeezed her eyes shut, begging her mind to stop torturing her with Tony's apparition.

But then she felt him. His little hand on her leg.

*Jesus Christ, he's real.*

"Pumpkin?"

"Mummy, I wanna go home."

"Pumpkin, oh dear God!" She snatched him off the ground and cuddled him tight to her chest. Her vision was still blurred from her tears, so she used her hands to check him over and make sure he was okay. Satisfied he wasn't about to die in her arms, she covered him in kisses. Sobbing with happiness, she could barely speak.

*Charlie.*

Freezing with her lips still pressed to Tony's temple, Charlie held her boy tighter. Her name had been spoken inside her head, but not by her voice. Terrified, her heart squeezed painfully and her lungs stopped working.

*No.*

*No, no, no, no, no! This has to be real.* Dear God, she couldn't take it if this wasn't real.

*It's okay,* the voice said calmly. *We're here to help. We have Sebastian distracted, but he won't be tricked for long. We need you to get outside through any means necessary. Understand?*

No. No, she did not fucking understand. *Who are you?* Charlie demanded.

She would not be tricked by another one of Sebastian's games. Though the vampire had never used her child like this before, he had tempted her with escape. Once, he'd dangled Tony's keys in front of her and dared her to take them. Later, when he'd left the lab, having 'accidentally forgotten' them on the counter, Charlie had been stupid enough to grab them.

For her recklessness, Sebastian had told her he'd heat the keys until they glowed. Then he'd force Tony to hold them until they were branded into his skin. Terrified, she'd grabbed hold of his hand and dropped to her knees. She'd begged him for nearly an hour to reconsider, to give her the punishment instead. She swore up and down she'd never attempt to save her boy again. Miraculously, she'd eventually convinced him.

But Sebastian hadn't placed the keys in her hand. He hadn't wanted to hinder her work. Instead, he'd pressed them against her breast and laughed as she screamed.

The pain from that moment still lingered. She could feel the heat of those keys as if they were still pressed against her skin. And yet, that unbearable agony would be nothing compared to how she would feel if her little boy wasn't real.

*I know you want answers,* the voice replied. *But it's taking all of my strength to hold Sebastian. Now I need you to get up and move.*

*But –*

*Go!*

On a jump of panic, Charlie crushed Tony to her chest and bolted out the door. But she could only take two steps before grinding to a halt. Gritting her teeth, she tried to will herself to keep going, but it was no use. She couldn't leave without Tony's finger. There would be no part of him left behind for Sebastian's twisted pleasure. For him to track them through.

Swearing, Charlie spun on her heels and dashed back inside the room.

"Mummy?"

"It's okay, pumpkin. Mummy needs to get something and then we're going. I promise, okay? We're going home."

She planted a soothing kiss on Tony's forehead as she rushed over to her desk. Ripping the framed finger off the wall, Charlie tucked it between her and her child, then raced again for the door. This time she made it halfway down the hall.

Blocking her way was a woman. Her shoulders were relaxed, her hands down at her side. Her brown eyes were empty, more indifferent than threatening, but there was something about her, something dark and vicious that caused Charlie to take a step back.

Her heart thudded like a little boy's percussion kit. Her grip on Tony started to slip from sweat. But this was her best, and most likely only, chance of getting out of here. She had to try.

Swallowing hard, Charlie took a deep breath and stood her ground.

On a chuckle of amusement, Lamia advanced. "Don't be naive," she purred. "This was never a rescue mission. It was an ambush and you, my dear, were the bait."

Sinking his teeth into Elizabeth's neck, Sebastian fed on the ambrosia-tasting liquid of her blood. She didn't taste like Sophina. She wasn't as sweet. She was guarded and bitter, but her power hummed with an essence that was ground shaking. He could feel her parent's magic running through her veins: the cold hand of Hades, the warm embrace of Aphrodite's. Life and death balanced on the tip of his tongue, coming in strong and hot with an aftertaste of cool refreshment.

As their screams reverberated in his ears, Sebastian tightened his grip on Elizabeth and drank faster.

*Stop! You're hurting me!* Sophina's words burned into his mind, his lips.

He closed his eyes.

But she was still there inside him. Accusing. Disgusted. Growling, Sebastian lifted his fangs and sank them into

Elizabeth's neck again. And again. And again.

He wanted her to hurt like he was hurting.

On the fifth bite, she spasmed in his arms.

Her scream turned into a whimper.

Then silence.

*Sophina laid so cold in front of him, her eyes lifeless, her hands fallen to her sides, her swollen belly –*

*Enough!*

Dropping Elizabeth, Sebastian took a sharp step back. He brushed his hand across his mouth, closed his eyes, and breathed.

Something was wrong. He never lost control like this.

He would never risk killing Elizabeth when so much of his plans banked on having her by his side.

And although Aphrodite had no love for her daughter, jealous over the love Hades gave to her, Freya would crush his heart and take back the powers she had given him. The power to never be weakened by his heart again.

*It's not weak to remember who you are.*

Stumbling back, Sebastian shook his head. He fought through the haze of his memories, his own desire to hear his lifemate again. It wasn't real.

None of this was real.

Which meant someone was messing with him.

His eyes narrowing, he looked out the window. He couldn't see anything lurking in the darkness, but his sixth sense flared like he was being watched, like he was being hunted.

*The fucking Elv've'Norc.*

Created just to spite him and Rakian during the Great Binding three and a half thousand years ago, they'd been a right pain in his ass ever sense. Not even kidnapping Tegan's wife had gotten them to back the Hades' off. They had stalked him, harassed him, and had now stolen the

*Scrolls of Atlantis* from him.

Oh, he was going to enjoy finding them and making them pay.

A smile curling his lips, Sebastian phased to his room.

"Galvanor, get down!"

Matakyli slammed into her lifemate as an arrow cut the air above them. Pure adrenaline rushed through her as her sixth sense skyrocketed with fear. She twisted as they fell, making sure to take the brunt of the force as they hit the ground.

Rolling, she deposited the telepath on the floor and leaped back to her feet. Her knives glistened in her hand as she stood protectively over her lifemate.

Though she couldn't see the vampire yet, she knew he was nearby. She would never forget the nauseating, near painful clenching of her stomach she'd felt for the first and only time thirteen years ago. Sebastian had triggered more than a bad taste in her mouth and a shiver down her spine. He had a certain darkness to him, a violent curtain of death and despair that clung to him like a jilted lover.

"I've been waiting for this my whole life!" Matakyli shouted into the darkness. "Come at me, you coward, and I'll show you what I've learned!"

The demoness was strung tighter than a high-walker's rope, but she refused to back down. She would meet death head on or not at all.

With a low chuckle, Sebastian appeared out of the darkness, a bow hanging loose at his side. He wobbled slightly as he stood there and when he spoke, his words slurred together with drunkenness.

"You're Galvanor," the vampire grinned as he pointed an unsteady finger at the telepath. "Lyrca talks about you nonstop. If she wasn't so valuable, I'd rip her tongue out and shove it up her ass. And you –"

Bewildered, Matakyli could only stare in silence as he turned to her. She had anticipated everything from a powerful attack to a cunning defense to a baiting of words, but never in her wildest dreams had the demoness envisioned he would be drunk off his feet when he tried to kill her.

"You're..." Sebastian slurred as his eyes narrowed in contemplation. "You're...that... Who are you?"

Out of all the things he could've said, that enraged her the most. Thirteen fucking years she'd flipped him the bird. She had kidnapped his mistress right out of the bed they'd shared. And yet the bastard didn't even know her name?

*The insult! I'm going to claw his eyes out and play hacky sack with them! I'm going to feast on his innards and throw his intestines around my neck like a scarf! I'm going to –*

*Matakyli, this is not the time to be offended.*

*Don't tell me what to do!* she snapped. *The bastard doesn't even know who I am!*

"Ah, wait," Sebastian muttered as he peered off into the distance. "You're that girl who kidnapped Lucille. The one with the fantastic sixth sense. I hunted you for days, you know, but you always kept vanishing every time I got close. What was your name, again? Started with an L..."

*That is it! I'm going to kill him!* But though she shook with the desire to lunge, her body wouldn't listen to her demands. *Let me move, dammit!*

*You will not die tonight.*

As if those words were a signal, the ground started to shake. A series of howls erupted all too close and for one glorious moment, Sebastian's face held a trace of fear.

But then with a cruel light in his eyes, the vampire started to laugh. "I wondered how you would get out of this, Elv've'Nor."

He slipped a finger under the collar at his neck and Matakyli's eyes narrowed in recognition. She knew that band of metal, had used it on her lifemate only days ago. But why was he in possession of it?

"Like the new modifications?" Sebastian purred as he tossed the bow to the ground. "It took us all of five minutes to figure out how to make it protect its wearer from telepathy instead of restricting it. Of course, it would've been impossible without the aid of Ola."

Matakyli's eyes narrowed. Now where did she know that name?

*'Tell me you killed them."*

*"All but one."*

The memory hit her like a freight train. Galvanor stood inside her dream, his eyes tormented by the trauma of his childhood. Guilt and shame had twisted his face – not because of what Ola had done to him but because of what he had become. As if he was to blame for being used as an Amazon seeder. As if he was to blame for his scars and tormented mind.

She was going to kill them all.

"Matakyli, no!"

"You hear that?" Lamia asked as an agonized scream rang out in the distance. "That's your saviors dying at the hand of my brother." She advanced with a smile, her nails raking the stone wall. "So be a good girl and go back to your lab."

Immobilized by fear, Charlie couldn't move even if she wanted to. It didn't matter that she hadn't succeeded in getting more than a few paces outside her lab. It didn't matter that she hadn't actually escaped. She had tried and that would be justification enough for Sebastian to rip into her child.

Tightening her grip on her boy, Charlie did the only thing she could.

"I've seen the way he treats you," she announced strongly. Despite her terror, her words came out without falter. They were sure and honest and she prayed to every god alive that they were good enough to bait the bitch. "You're older than him, aren't you? More powerful. Why be the underling to a bastard?"

With a quirk of the brow, Lamia teased, "You really think a few simple words can get me to help you? Bitch, please. I've been around for millennia. I know all the tricks and you, my dear, have very few left to use."

"Oh yeah?" Charlie asked as she took the smallest of steps back. "You want to share what exactly those are? Preferably starting with the one most likely to work?"

A soft chuckle floated through the air. "You know, in another life we might well have been friends." A hapless shrug. "But we're in this one and your time's up."

As if summoned, a blood-curdling scream erupted from outside the thick walls of the castle. It wasn't one of pain nor terror but one of success. Sebastian had killed those planning to help her. Charlie knew it in her bones. She wasn't going to escape tonight, not ever.

Still, she refused to give up so easily. Pushing out with her mind, she tried to contact the man who had reached out to her earlier. But there was nothing. Once again she was completely alone.

Swallowing hard, Charlie took another step back. It was then she spotted the window. She might not be able to escape the castle, but maybe death was just as good of an option.

"That's it," Lamia cooed, oblivious to Charlie's true thoughts. "Be a good little girl and go back to your lab."

But just when all seemed lost, the mysterious voice returned.

*Jump out the window. Now!*

Like a puppet on a string, Charlie did exactly as he'd commanded. She twisted before impact, breaking the window with her shoulder. Instinctively, she curled her body around her boy, desperate to protect him from the glass.

Bending her head to his, she tried to offer as much comfort as possible. When their skin touched, however, Charlie's gut twisted with nauseating horror.

He wasn't moving. He wasn't crying. He wasn't even gripping her in terror. He was simply still in her arms, a lump of empty flesh. As she peered into frozen, lifeless eyes, her heart stopped with all the force of a train wreck.

*No. God. Please no.*

Faced with this harsh reality, Charlie was in too much pain to scream. Her despair choked her. Her sorrow drowned her. And as Tony disappeared from her arms, vanishing like the illusion he was, her heart stuttered to a stop.

"*Nooo!*"

Dear god, she'd abandoned him. She'd left him like a sacrificial lamb in the hands of a vengeful god.

"*Noooooooo!*"

As her soul escaped on the ragged screams of a broken heart, Charlie twisted in the air. Desperately, she reached for Lamia's outstretched hand. But just as their fingers touched, she was yanked backward by the talons of a massive bird.

"*Stop! Let me go! Tonyyy!*" She thrashed and screamed

like a mamma bear, raking at the talons as best she could. She hit and she pulled, but she was only human.

Her flails did nothing to release her.

Her cries did nothing to save her.

Changing tactics, Charlie took a deep breath and screamed, "*Sebastiaaaaan!*"

As much as she hated the bastard, she would make a deal with the devil himself in order to keep her child safe. For if she escaped, through her own will or not, Sebastian would take his rage out on Tony. She couldn't bare the thought of that, the thought of her sweet little boy once again at the sick, twisted hands of evil itself.

Desperate to catch a glimpse of her dark savior, Charlie scanned the castle's grounds. She needed him to be here. He simply had to come. She had not done everything she had only to fail Tony now. With angry tears staining her face, Charlie begged again.

"*Sebastian!*" she repeated at the top of her lungs, using every ounce of her strength to summon the evil bastard.

She waited a tense second, hopeful he would come, that he would phase in at the last second and save her from this bastard of an eagle. But they were rising above the treetops now. Soon, she feared they would be too high for him to spot. If he couldn't see them, he couldn't teleport to them. And if he couldn't teleport to them...

She would not fail Tony. Not now.

With a sob of frustration, Charlie gripped the talons holding her by her shoulders. She curled her fingers around the middle toe as one would the straps of a rucksack, then swung her legs forward, then back.

Her many years as a pole dancer had gifted her with an amazingly strong core. Swinging her legs forward once more, she curled up sharply at the waist and slammed her feet into the belly of the bird.

A terrible caw pierced the air on impact.

With adrenaline burning hot through her veins, Charlie shoved her feet against the feathered mass. She tightened her fingers around each middle claw, experiencing a split second of hesitation when she looked down.

But then Tony's sweet, innocent face flashed into her mind.

She might not be able to save him, but damn if she wouldn't do all she could in order to make his death a quick one.

Resolved, Charlie took a deep breath.

And then yanked the talons up, forcing him to release her.

Closing her eyes, she fell with silent tears burning her cheeks.

# NINE

*Save her.*

Jack cursed at the sudden demand of the *thing*. For fifteen thousands years it had been content to watch people die. Fated to bring about the destruction of every man, woman, and child, the *thing* had little interest in others. The massacre of Tulaonin hadn't stirred it. The annihilation of Atlantis had only made it yawn. Hell, it hadn't even batted an eye when he had found his lifemate and that chick was one crazy bitch; the two would have gotten along perfectly.

So for it to be all dewy eyed over this one?

She must be one hell of a danger.

But unfortunately, as much as Jack was tempted to let her die, he couldn't. The *thing* wouldn't allow it. With a sudden show of power, it forced him into a dive. As the trees rushed up to meet him, their thick greedy branches waving with the promise of pain, Jack cursed like a drunken sailor.

He stretched out with his talons, trying desperately to

grab her before impact. The *thing* roared its frustration. The wind rushed through his ears. He gritted his beak and with one final push Jack managed to grab her by the shoulders. His relief, however, was short lived.

Twisting onto his back, Jack hurriedly swung her up onto his breast. He barely had the time to wrap his wings around her before the first branch hit him hard. As it slammed into him, he heard the unmistakable cracking of ribs.

Gritting his beak, Jack bounced between the branches like a rag doll. Bones broke left and right; bruises grew under every feather. By the time he finally crashed into the ground, he resembled a crushed pinata.

Seething, he transed while still under his target. As his feathers morphed into freckled flesh and the breaks in his bones mended, Jack rolled the woman beneath him. Jumping to his feet, he then yanked her up beside him.

"You are a fucking idiot," he growled.

*Is she hurt?*

*Not yet she isn't.*

The *thing* slammed into his ribs with a snarl and Jack clenched his teeth on a swear. Reluctantly, he checked her over with a brief sweep of his eyes. He took in her tattered shoes and grubby clothing, the few scrapes and bruises on her body. Even though he was only doing a visual check and not the physical one the *thing* wanted, it still irritated the hell of him that he was bothering.

When the *thing* was finally satisfied that she wasn't suffering too badly, Jack raised his eyes to her face. The sudden flash of recognition hit him like a punch to the kidneys. By the gods, he knew her.

Relief drowned out his annoyance as he took in the bold challenge of her eyes, the stubborn set of her jaw. With a surge of heat, Jack recalled their short time in

Merlin's Dimensio.

She'd been crushed up against his body, his lips on her skin, his tongue on her neck. The rot of the cell had been all around them, the danger of the vampires right above, and still she had stood there in brave silence. No fear had shown in her eyes. There had been nothing but a fierce challenge that had nearly stopped him in his tracks.

The urge to reenact that scene, with their bodies flush up against each other, was damn well overpowering. The *thing* purred its pleasure. His cock twitched with interest. Jack leaned forward ever so slightly. And then Charlie spat right in his face.

"Correction," he said dryly as he wiped the spittle off, his mood now ruined. "You are a right pain in my ass."

"Yeah, well, wait until I stick a knife in it, you piece of shit!" She launched herself at him then, her fingers going straight for his eyes. Jack snagged her wrists and pinned them to her sides, but what the little hellcat couldn't do with her hands, she was content to try with her knees. With a vicious jerk of her leg, she nailed him right where it hurt the most.

"Godsdammit, woman!" he swore as he manhandled her against a tree. "I'm here to save you. Do you know what that means?"

Dodging the violent swings of her head, Jack forced her arms between them.

"*Save,*" he stressed in irritation. "Save. S. A. V. – Oh, for fuck's sake, stop biting me!"

Jack gripped the back of her head and shoved his arm deep into her mouth. As soon as Charlie tried to jerk backward, he yanked her away by the hair. But that only stopped her from biting him, and the imp immediately changed tactics to try to slam her knee into his balls.

Cursing, Jack blocked her with a subtle twist of his

hips. How had he ever thought, even for a second, that they'd had a connection? She was a freaking *kultara,* a thorn in his side, and that was putting it politely. Oh, how he was tempted to strangle her until she fell unconscious.

No sooner had the thought formed than a fierce pain wrapped around Jack's heart. He collapsed to his knees. His grip on Charlie relaxed just enough for her to rip free. He tried to grab her again, but when the pain intensified, he could barely recall how to breathe. His hands clutched at his chest. His vision clouded on a wave of agony, and his eyes rolled back into his head. Then, as clear as day, an image flashed through his mind.

The *thing* had its fucking teeth around his heart!

"You traitorous bastard," Jack wheezed once he was finally released. "You bit me. You fucking bit me."

"I'm going to do more than that, you jackass!" the woman screamed.

At the sound of angry, advancing footsteps, Jack tried to focus. He managed just in time to spot Charlie raising a thick branch above her head.

Growling, the trickster called upon his magic. He had barely managed to tap into it when the *thing* bit his heart again. With a pathetic groan, Jack fell to the ground. Though if he hoped his submissive state would stop her from swinging at him, he was wrong.

Charlie slammed the branch across his back and then cracked it over his head. Though she had hit him hard enough to create stars, that was nothing compared to the trauma of being bitten by the *thing.*

It had attacked him before, slamming into his ribcage to express its displeasure, but never had it created this much torment. What the fuck had pissed it off?

It answered him in a low snarl, its eyes flashing a demonic red. *Don't. Hurt. My. Mate.*

*Oh, hell no,* Jack groaned. There was no way he was going to be shackled to this...this *kultara* for life. He enjoyed bachelorhood, thrived in it actually. The only way he would accept her as his mate was if he had the right to kill her immediately after.

A sharp nip on his heart had him coughing blood even as he wheezed at his own joke. *Kidding,* he said, but of course the *thing* didn't believe him. However, when the woman dropped the branch and turned tail, Jack was released in an instant.

*If you hurt her –*

*Yeah, yeah,* Jack wheezed as he crawled to his feet. *I won't harm a single hair on her pretty little head.* At least, not until he talked to his father and figured out a way to kill the *thing.* Then all bets would be off.

Scowling, Jack stumbled the first few steps, his body too weak from the pain. Despite his target disappearing off into the distance, he allowed himself a few moments to lean against a tree and regain his strength. It wasn't like she could get far anyway.

As he stepped away from the tree, his irritation turned into sudden excitement. The thrill of the hunt had always called to him, but this was something more. Every inch of him was craving this chase. Craving her. An image of Charlie's tight little ass running through the trees had him nearly salivating with desire.

*Chase!* the *thing* demanded. Or had that been his own command?

Instantly, Jack pulled on the magic inside him. With a harsh snap, his spine popped out of his skin. Like a gruesome wave, it rippled from his coccyx up to his neck. His jaw snapped in half and his cheeks were quick to follow. As he dropped to all fours, his face elongated and newfound muscles ripped into existence all across his body. Razor sharp claws replaced his nails and every tooth sharpened into a miniature dagger. His canines stretched long past his lips, and with a fearsome bare of his teeth, Jack stood up on his hind legs.

The moon called to him like an addiction, but neither Jack nor the *thing* was interested. He took a deep breath and singled out the scent of his prey.

And by the gods, did his mate smell good!

The solid punch of desire had him dropping down onto all fours. As soon as his paws touched the ground, he catapulted into action. Within a minute he'd caught up to her.

On a howl of excitement, Jack barreled into her legs. She fell with a scream. Twisting in the air, she then proceeded to beat him with her fists. Her attack might have annoyed him in his human form. As a werewolf it didn't even register.

Jack simply lounged on top of her, engulfing her small form with his massive size. He shoved his muzzle into the lovely dip of her neck. A little yap of appreciation escaped automatically as he inhaled her sweet scent.

Damn, she smelled good. Like really fucking good. She didn't smell of roses nor of any other added flower. She wasn't perfumed by the sweet scent of honey nor the warm tang of vanilla. She was simply unencumbered, her scent one hundred percent hers. One hundred percent a woman's.

One hundred percent his.

*Godsdammit!* Jack screamed as he wrestled the *thing* for control. It had always been stronger when he was a wolf, but never had he had to fight it this hard before. Normally, he'd always been able to subdue it without too much effort, making the added benefits of a werewolf well worth the risk. But now that the *thing* had decided this woman was its mate, it was being quite the fucking asshole.

With a growl, Jack finally managed to shove it back down. The woman squirmed beneath him as he transed, but he still managed to keep her trapped. He was much bigger than her, much stronger, and much, much more pissed off at her continued theatrics.

"Enough!" he hollered, but of course, she flat out ignored his command. Swearing, Jack forced her arms between them. He trapped them with his weight, pressed a hand hard over her mouth, and shoved her head to the ground.

"I said enough!"

Her eyes, a bright blue of seething anger, told him to go to hell.

*Joke's on you,* he thought dryly. *I'm already there.*

"Now I realize you're probably on your period, but I need you to chill the fuck out."

She mumbled viciously beneath his hand. Though he couldn't hear the word, Jack was experienced enough in reading lips against his palm to know what she had called him.

He cocked his head to the side because he knew it would infuriate her. "Nah, I'm definitely not a bastard. Not sure what you'd call my birth though."

Glowering, her lips moved again.

He blinked once, twice. Then he erupted into laughter. She'd replied, 'a mistake.' He had chased her down as a werewolf, one of the most ferocious beings in the Myth, and she still had the balls to call his birth a mistake.

By the gods, he was in love. Too bad she was the most impossible person in the whole bloody universe.

Shaking his head, Jack dismissed his bizarre thoughts. Then he sent a telepathic message to his team.

*We landed about three miles in the woods. Able to retrieve?*

*Negative.*

Rogan didn't give a reason and Jack didn't ask. The vampire hadn't shown up to save his most precious and it didn't take a genius to know why. If Sebastian and Liz now fought side by side, his teammates would need every ounce of concentration just to stay alive.

Which meant Jack was on his own with the target, who wasn't just an infuriating kultara, but also the desired mate to his *thing*.

Thor's balls, why did the gods continue to curse him? First, he was shackled with a monster inside him. Then he was given the biggest bitch of a lifemate. And now this? Maybe he should give up running and finally let his cousin come and kill him. Death had to be easier than this.

Fighting the urge to do just that, Jack glared at the seething woman beneath him.

"Look, I realize this isn't ideal for you, but the full moon is in two nights and we're three days away from our rendezvous point. Do you know what that means?" He didn't give her the chance to answer. "In two nights this entire plane is going to go on fucking lockdown as every werewolf falls under the Craving. Then not even your big, bad buddy Sebastian is going to venture out here to save you, so all you're going to have is me. Do you understand?"

Of course she didn't. She was too freaking crazed to listen as she thrashed beneath his hand. Seriously though, what was her fucking problem? He'd saved her from the most sadistic person alive and instead of being grateful, she –

*Oh. Oh, yeah.*

But damn, using her son had seemed like a bloody good plan at the time. Of course, she should have been passed off to Rogan already instead of being stuck with him in the middle of the fucking woods, but hey, that was all on her. If she hadn't jumped out of his bloody grip, then they wouldn't be here, now would they?

"Look," he snapped. "You can either walk with me looking for every possibility to escape back to that castle or I can knock you out right now and you lose all of those precious chances."

She kept glaring at him, but at least she'd finally stopped squirming. Realizing he was actually close to getting her to calm down, he quickly added, "I will have to sleep eventually, you know." Of course, 'eventually' was in three days from now when they were on another plane, but she didn't need to know that.

"Good," Jack said when she exhaled strongly and flicked her eyes away from his face. It wasn't a clear affirmative, but he suspected it was the closest thing he was going to get. He released the pressure slightly on her mouth.

"Now I'm going to release my hand, but I swear on my cousin's balls, if you try to bite me again or scream for help, I will shove a gag so far down your throat, you'll be shitting it out for a week."

The sharp nip on his heart caused him to wince, but he kept the steel in his eyes. She needed to know he wasn't messing around or he'd have to end up hurting her for her compliance. And despite the thoughts in his head, Jack didn't really want to do that. He would because it was his job, but he wouldn't like it.

Hearing that, the *thing* released him, then sulked away. It didn't sit back down, but it seemed to trust him enough not to hover around his heart anymore. Thank the bloody gods for that.

"I mean it, Charlie. One scream or bite and that's it. I don't deal in second chances. Now nod your head if you understand."

She glared at him for a few seconds before finally giving a sharp nod.

With a secret sigh of relief, Jack removed his hand and jumped up to his feet. He tensed in preparation to grab her when she scrambled up beside him.

"What's your name?"

Her demand instantly reminded Jack of a TV show Hunter loved to watch. On it there was a little girl with a list of people she wanted to kill. Every night before bed she would say the names almost like a vow. As Jack gazed into the pure hatred in Charlie's eyes, he was certain she was creating such a list.

Flashing a mocking smile, he teased, "Fenrir. I don't have a last name."

Her glare didn't waver, but her eyes did narrow. Still, she didn't argue with him.

"Okay then, *Fenrir,*" she said, stressing his name so he knew how dumb she thought his joke was. "Show me the way."

Ha! As if he was stupid enough to go first. Raising a brow, Jack gestured in the opposite direction of the castle. He crossed his arms as he sneered, "I'd say ladies first, but clearly you're no such thing."

Her eyes narrowed and her lips pursed. Jack wasn't a telepath, but he could almost hear the sickening 'thud' of his skull as she imagined smashing it in with a rock.

Note to self, he thought as he matched her glare, sleep somewhere without rocks. Or thick branches, he added dryly.

Finally, with a huff of frustration, Charlie turned on her

heels and stomped further into the forest.

Raising his eyes to the heavens, Jack prayed for the strength to not strangle her.

"Three days," he muttered to himself as he followed. All he would have to survive was three bloody days.

*An eternity,* the *thing* quickly amended. *She is my mate and I will not leave her.*

*Well, shit.*

# TEN

They'd been hiking for hours. It had been a grueling march uphill that Charlie had been forced to undergo without rest or water. Her legs burned. Her shoulders ached. Her tongue stuck to the roof of her mouth, too parched to move. She could barely see past her haze of exhaustion. The only time Fenrir had spoken was to bark a command. The only time Charlie had was to tell him to go fuck himself.

Of course, all that had led to was him increasing the pace, but for that split second of satisfaction, it was well worth it.

Besides, Charlie knew what he was doing. He was trying to wear her down so he could carry her away in his talons and she was determined to show him that wasn't possible. He might think she was near the breaking point because of her time with Sebastian, but actually? Fenrir didn't know the half of it.

She'd been born into a broken home with two abusive parents and neighbors who'd rather look the other way.

She'd had to walk three miles to school every morning and afternoon just to get an education. Oh sure, there had been a bus, but if she'd gotten on it, there would've been hell to pay when she'd returned home. She'd had to cook her own meals, steal her own clothes, and fight her own battles.

'Mother' and 'father' were words that had only existed in the dictionary, right next to 'love' and 'kindness.'

She had survived sixteen grueling years of physical, mental, and emotional abuse. The only plus side to her childhood had been that by the time her father had attempted to sexually assault her, she'd been pushed so far, she'd actually fought back. Charlie had run away that night. With nowhere to go and no friends to rely on, she had fallen on desperate times. Pushed to the edge of suicide, lost in the paradise of drugs and alcohol, she had momentarily admitted defeat.

But that had been and would always be, the only time.

Charlie had suffered the loss of light itself with the death of Eddy, Tony's father, and hadn't spiraled. She had been forced to give up her dreams of an education and hadn't shed a tear. She had spent night after night terrified of how she would raise a child all on her own, determined to do a better job than her parents, but not knowing how. And just when everything had seemed to be getting better, just when she'd spotted the light at the end of a very dark, very lonesome tunnel, Sebastian had appeared like a demon in the night.

So no, nothing Fenrir could do would break her.

She would march nonstop at whatever ridiculous pace he wanted. She would fight the pain threatening to bring her to her knees. She would ignore her hunger pangs and her desperate want for water. Charlie would look for every chance to escape, staying up all night if she needed to. Because she was not going to leave her son.

Tony was the only saving grace in her world and she would give up everything, do anything, to save him.

As Charlie pushed her way through the bush, her grip lingered on a particularly pliable branch. Red hot anger surged through her, with pain and frustration quick on its heels. She might not be able to fight back or escape right now, but to hell if she was going to sit back and play the perfect kidnapee. Fenrir had no idea what he had gotten himself into, but he was about to find out.

She waited until he passed the base of the branch she was holding, then let go with a smile. It snapped back like a whip, landing with a satisfying crack against his flesh. Fenrir's hiss of pain was music to her ears, but Charlie fought the temptation to do it again.

She wanted to annoy the hell out of him, but not so much he decided it would be easier to knock her out.

At the thought of that happening, her heart lurched in fear. Already Charlie had been gone for hours. Sebastian would be getting impatient and soon he would take his anger out on Tony. She couldn't imagine what he would do if she was gone for days.

The mere thought of it was killing her. With a rough shake of her head, she blinked back the tears threatening to fall. She didn't have time to be afraid. Later, when this was all over, she'd curl up and cry herself to sleep. But right now, she had to keep going.

She had to be brave.

Tony was counting on her.

Exhaling the last of her fears away, Charlie called over her shoulder, "So what are you?"

She asked more to distract herself than from curiosity, but as soon as the question came out, everything inside her wanted to know. After all, the more she knew about him, the easier he would be to fight.

"Annoyed, irritated, infuriated? Take your pick."

Before she could flip him the bird, a massive snake dropped down in front of her. It lunged in one elegant strike, its fangs aiming straight for her heart. Terrified, Charlie jerked backward with a scream. Her heel hit something as she retreated and in a jumbled mess of flailing arms and legs, she tumbled to the ground.

Her teeth jarred on impact. Her breath hissed out on a wave of pain and fear. Frantic, Charlie scrambled for a rock or stick, anything she could use to fight with. The snake reared back for a second strike, having missed her only because of her fall.

Its eyes glistened with hungry intelligence. Its mouth gaped in salivating desire. With a hiss of triumph, it lunged again.

This time it nailed her right in the chest. Her feeble blows did nothing to stop it.

She screamed in agony. White hot torment rolled through her veins like molten metal. Whatever poison it had injected her with burned like a thousand suns. Her limbs spasmed from the pain as her eyes rolled back in her head. She was barely aware of the foam rushing out of her mouth or the thick coil of the snake as it wrapped around her.

She was simply lost in the agony of hell.

And then, just like that, it was gone.

Her body still shook from the ordeal, but there was no actual pain anymore. No snake either. Just a jackass standing over her with a sneer of satisfaction on his slapable face.

Angry, but too stunned to move, Charlie settled for a glare. Like her blows with the snake, however, it did nothing to phase him.

"Don't hit me again," he ordered.

He pierced her with his own stare then. Hot and dangerous, it ignited a part of her that spread all the way down to her toes.

Seething with anger, to hell with the consequences, Charlie grabbed a handful of soil and threw it at him. She nailed him right in his mother fucking face.

His jaw clenched, his fingers twitched at his side, and then she screamed.

The ground shifted below her and, for one brief second, Fenrir didn't look at her with frustration or anger. Honest-to-god fear blinked across his face, telling her that this time, the pain would be real.

She reached for him just as he lunged for her. His long fingers wrapped strongly around her wrist. The ground opened up. The birds shot off like an explosion, cawing fearfully as they took to the skies. Her gut clenched in horrible anticipation as she felt herself sinking.

Charlie knew better than to look down. That to do so might very well use up the precious second she had to move. But like a bimbo in a horror movie, she simply couldn't help it. She needed to look.

Her regret was instant.

The earth crumbled beneath her feet, sucked into the mouth of whatever lurked below. All she could see of it were two rows of teeth and they were opening wide in preparation for its dinner.

Fenrir's grip loosened.

Her focus snapping back to him, Charlie watched in horror as he let go. She tried to jump forward, but the dirt suddenly vanished beneath her feet. It had been sucked into the gaping mouth and she was now to follow.

Shouting a curse, Charlie fell about fifteen feet beneath the surface. She landed with a hard thud on the pile of dirt. Something shifted beneath it, jolting her into a roll.

"Stay in the middle!" Fenrir yelled from above.

Scrambling back into the middle of the mound, Charlie fought her desire to flick him off.

The bastard had let go. He'd actually fucking let go when he could've pulled her to safety instead. Every part of her screamed for her to save herself, to not wait for a rescue that was never coming. Every part but one.

Somewhere in the idiotic section of her brain, the same part that had once told her it was a great idea to hide her parents' drugs and alcohol, was clambering for her to trust him. Him, the asshole who had let go.

Before Charlie could realize how idiotic that was, the monster beneath demanded her attention. She jerked her gaze to its teeth and froze. Surely it hadn't just –

*Oh hell no!*

The dirt shifted beneath her again, a vast majority of it disappearing into nothingness as the teeth inched closer. Unbalanced, she dropped to her knees and swore. It wasn't vanishing; it was being swallowed!

As the mouth began to close, Charlie scrambled back to her feet. She cursed Fenrir to every level of hell as she berated herself for trusting him in the first place.

Who the fuck trusted someone who'd just dropped them?

Desperately, Charlie eyed the closing teeth. If she could grab hold of one, then maybe she could use it to climb out. Her chance of success was slimmer than impossible, but she didn't care. She had to try.

Just as she reached out a hand, however, something coiled around her waist. Unable to help herself, Charlie looked down and immediately closed her eyes in relief.

With a jerk, the bald tail hoisted her into the air. She barely missed skimming the tips of the teeth, her feet barely missed being bitten off. A frustrated growl rumbled beneath her and Charlie answered it with a hysterical laugh.

She was deposited on the branch of a tree and she instantly wrapped all of her limbs around it. There was no way in hell she was going to accidentally fall off.

"What the fuck was that?" she asked. "What the fuck are you?"

The monkey-like beast eyed her dryly. His expression said it all. Charlie was a right bitch for not thanking him when he'd just saved her life.

Gaze narrowing, Charlie seethed, "Fuck you; you let go."

She would've flipped him the bird had she the courage to let go of the branch. As it was, she was still shaking with adrenaline.

"It was that or join you down there," Fenrir scoffed once he shifted back to his ginger self. "You're the moron who hesitated. Who even does that?"

"Well, sorry for being fucking human."

He snorted with derision and crossed his arms. "I doubt you have ever been sorry in your life, kultara."

"Well, at least I'm not a jackass bastard!"

"By the gods!" he roared. "What is the matter with you? I've saved you from certain agonizing death and this is the thanks I get?"

Infuriated, Charlie pulled off a chunk of bark and threw it at him. He dodged it easily and that pissed her off even more. "You didn't *save* me," she snapped. "You *kidnapped* me. You kidnapped me and left my boy to die. So screw you, you over-sized piece of shit!"

"Trust me," he mocked as he crossed his lean arms. "Screwing you is the last thing on my mind."

Out of all the quips he could've come back with, why

did he have to respond like a child? Charlie could have handled an angry retort. An insult or a threat would have bounced right off her thick skin. But his childish sting cut straight to her heart.

It was a harsh reminder that she would never see Tony grow up. She would never hear him make such stupid remarks. This bastard had robbed her of the rest of her motherhood and now he was rubbing it in her face.

Dear God, she had never been so tempted to beat a man to death in her life. Sebastian she wanted to torture for everything he'd done, but this guy? She just wanted him gone. Dead and six feet under so his body could match his rotten soul.

"Go to Hell."

Deadpanned, he replied, "Given anywhere you are is Hell, it looks like I'm already here."

God, if looks could kill, Charlie would've looked away just so she could have the pleasure of strangling him with her bare hands. She toyed with the idea of scooting over to him so she could push him off, but her legs absolutely refused to budge. Even loosening them an inch scared the crap out of her.

So she settled for a glare, and Fenrir matched it with one of his own. The seconds passed with neither looking away. Their emotions silently clashed together, warring in a vicious, heated brawl that made her skin tingle. God, she hated him with every fiber of her being and it was obvious he did too. She could see the same amount of rage and irritation reflected in his eyes.

But there was also something else.

Something in the very bottom of his soul that caused her heart to flutter and her face to fill with heat.

Ashamed, Charlie was the first to look away. So he'd saved her, whoopie fucking do. If it hadn't been for him, she wouldn't have needed saving from that mouth thing in the first place.

But despite what she told herself, Charlie was unable to smother her feelings of shame. He had been genuinely scared for her; she'd seen that truth right there in his eyes.

And how had she thanked him?

By pretty much spitting in his face and calling him a bastard.

God, she was a jerk.

But before she could let go of enough pride to thank him, Fenrir dropped from the tree.

Her stomach twisted in nervous anticipation. Her eyes locked onto the ground as she waited for it to open back up and eat him.

"It's safe," Fenrir said as he looked at her. "Charybdis can't move. If you drop in front of me, you'll be fine."

Charlie swallowed hard. She didn't want to go. Down there, monsters appeared out of nowhere. Down there, she would be forced to march further away from Tony. And down there, Fenrir, with his piercing looks and infuriating attitude, was waiting.

But she couldn't stay up here forever.

Reluctantly, Charlie unwrapped her arms from around the branch. Sitting up, she eyed the ground nervously. Then in one smooth motion, she swung a leg over and dropped down.

She stayed frozen in a crouch for a long second. Her eyes skirted over everything as she searched for the smallest of vibrations. Seeing nothing, she eventually rose to her feet.

Grudgingly accepting Fenrir deserved a thank you at the very least, Charlie turned to face him. But whatever concern she thought she'd seen in his eyes was now completely hidden under a wall of scorn.

With a disgusted shake of his head, he shoved past her, knocking into her shoulder with a muttered, "Kultara."

Anger surging through her, Charlie clenched her fists. *Well, screw him and his fucking thank you.* She'd tried twice now and wasn't dumb enough to try a third.

As she watched Fenrir slip silently through the woods, she toyed with the idea of running the other way. Of course, she wouldn't get far, but it would piss him off and that just might be worth it.

Then again, she could always hit him with a rock.

Smirking, Charlie bent down for a stone. She eyed the back of his head, pulled her arm back, and let it fly. It smacked him right in the middle of his thick skull.

*Ah, sweet music to my ears.*

# ELEVEN

By the gods, Jack had never been more scared in his life. Fifteen minutes later and his chest had yet to loosen, his hands had yet to stop shaking. All he could think about was the fear in her eyes. All he could hear was her scream of terror. It was utterly ridiculous.

He barely knew her. Hades' fire, Jack didn't even like her. She was an annoying, ungrateful, violent little brat he wished he'd never rescued. And yet, letting her go had been the hardest thing he'd ever done. He'd watched her plummet inside that gaping mouth and his heart had dropped along with her. It still sat heavily in his gut, too shocked and stunned to move.

Thor's fucking balls, this was not good.

Jack had been watching his friends die for millennia. They'd been great friends too, much better than her, and he'd been fine. In fact, he'd encouraged them to make reckless, dangerous decisions quite often. He'd even found his lifemate, the literal other half of his soul, and now she did nothing for him. Not a damn little thing anymore. Of course, she was a right bitch and he would definitely celebrate her death rather than mourn it, but still. She was his lifemate, whereas Charlie wasn't even a wanted acquaintance.

*She is our mate.*

Running a hand through his hair, Jack ignored that. Charlie wasn't anything to him. Otherwise, he'd care that the wounds on her shoulders had opened up again, but he didn't. Nor did he care that he could hear her stomach growling every so often or that she was in desperate need of a rest. He was completely immune to her desires and realizing all that caused him to relax a little.

*She's falling.*

Heart in his throat, Jack spun around. He'd covered three steps before he realized that she was fine. Though obviously exhausted, Charlie wasn't in any danger of collapsing. Confused by his sudden actions, she eyed him warily.

The *thing* laughed.

Jack muttered a curse.

Frustrated at himself, he crossed the little distance between them and grabbed her by the arm. "You can either hurry up or I can knock you out and carry you. What's it going to be, kultara?"

Ignoring the sharp teeth on his heart and the guilt on his shoulders, Jack met Charlie's withering glare with feigned indifference.

He didn't want this. He didn't need this. And he sure as hell wasn't going to accept this.

She jerked her arm, but she didn't have the energy to pull it loose. He released her anyway, her bare skin having burned him with a heat he didn't want. His hand still itched with her awareness, and he wiped it on his leg in an attempt to stop it. But all that did was make him think of her touching him there.

The smooth skin of her hand trailing up his thigh. The dance of her fingers as she moved to grip his cock. The heat of her eyes. The burning of her lips. The budding of her nipples as he –

"Don't get on to me," she spat. "You're the idiot in front; I'm just following your pace."

With a rough shake of his head, Jack snapped himself out of his lunacy. Eyes hot with contempt, he spoke as if addressing a child. "I've slowed my pace so I don't lose you, kultara, so speed the fuck up."

She shoved past him with a snarl. "I'll go in front then!" As she marched off with a stream of curses, Jack glowered after her.

Godsdammit! He should be happy she'd been so easily played. He needed her fuming with hatred and cursing his fucking name. If he didn't have the strength to fight his unwanted feelings for her, then he sure as hell would make sure she fought well enough for the both of them.

And yet despite his easy win, Jack still felt less like a victor and more like an ass. Swearing, he ran a hand through his hair. He tried to resist the urge to run after her, but he barely lasted a second. Muttering a string of profanities that would make the toughest of sailors proud, Jack hurried to catch up to her.

He reached for her arm, then hesitated. What did he even want to say?

Frustrated, Jack let his hand fall.

*You could try apologizing,* the *thing* offered dryly.

*You could try apologizing,* Jack mimicked in a high-pitched voice. As if he even wanted to. It's not like he felt guilty over not letting Charlie rest for the last five hours. Or treating her like an imbecile. Or yelling at her for not watching out for things she most likely didn't even know existed. Or using her child to lure her out while leaving said child to a fate worse than death...

Oh for fuck's sake! Fifteen thousand years Jack had gone without feeling guilt, and now he was questioning everything he bloody did.

*It's called fa-*

*Don't you fucking say it.*

The *thing* shrugged. *You'll realize it in time.*

*As if it'll matter,* Jack sneered with a shake of his head. *We pretty much killed her child and you seriously think she'll forgive us for that?*

Another shrug. *Her kind is fickle. You just have to offer her chocolate and flowers. Look, there. Those are nice.*

Jack glanced over before he could help it. At the sight of the blood roses, he smirked like the devil. Solid black in color and with stems completely covered in two inch long thorns, they looked more like a symbol for death rather than forgiveness.

*The only reason she would accept those would be to make a garrote from their stems.*

*Maybe if you explained the definition of kultara –*

*Look, if you want to waste your energy pining for a woman who doesn't even know you exist, then fine, but don't drag me into it. And I use kultara as an insult, not as an endearment.*

The *thing* rolled its eyes in exasperation. *Fifteen thousand years old and you're still so stupid.*

*Says the idiot still stuck in a cage.*

It laughed in amusement, but didn't say anything – not that it needed to.

For as much as Jack wanted to deny it, he did feel something for this woman. He'd been intrigued by her from the moment she'd spoken up for him in Merlin's Dimensio. Her defiant nature, her don't-mess-with-me attitude. Even as a prisoner, she had acted as if she was running the place. It was admirable. She was admirable – even if she was currently being a pain in the ass.

Then again, who wouldn't be given what she was going through?

Uncomfortable with his thoughts, Jack attempted to distract himself by scanning his surroundings. All he could focus on though were the blood roses to his left. Flowers. Women liked flowers.

Shaking his head, Jack tried to snap himself out of his lunacy. This was crazy. He didn't even like her.

Besides, there was a reason, a very good reason, he always avoided such complicated relationships. He wasn't about to forget all of that now, especially not for her – a woman he barely even liked.

And even if he did like her, Jack reasoned, it's not like he could ever have her. Hunted for fifteen thousand years and almost killed as many times, Jack's life was not an easy one. It required completely starting over at the drop of a hat. Abandoning friends, lovers, and acquaintances like a ghost. Changing his name, his face, everything. Jack had learned early on it wasn't worth getting attached to anything, not even a pet wolf. Trying anything with Charlie would kill him. Kill her too.

But even when faced with all that logic, his eyes still drifted back to the flowers.

Thor's balls, he was screwed.

With a sigh that sounded more like a growl, Jack grabbed Charlie's arm and pulled her to a stop.

"I went back for you."

"What?"

"In Merlin's Dimensio, you stopped a woman getting drained by two vampires. That was me. I went back for you but you were already gone."

She jerked her arm, but this time Jack didn't let go. His stomach was a tormented mess and his mind was all over the place. If revealing a few things meant he'd find some peace again, then she was damn well going to listen.

"Do you like the color black?"

"What?"

"The color black. It's a very dark shade –"

"I know what black is," she rudely interrupted. "I mean what the fuck are you doing?"

Strenuously holding onto his patience, Jack pressed, "I just wanted you to know that I went back for you."

"And?"

Irritated, he growled, "And I'm apologizing so just bloody accept it, you stubborn woman."

*Smooth,* the *thing* snorted.

*Fuck you,* Jack replied.

"*Fuck you!*" Charlie exploded as she yanked her arm free. "You are the most ignorant, dick-headed fucktard, massive dildo-faced, piss-shiting bastard in the entire fucking universe! Whoopie fucking do, you went back for me. You used my *child* against me. Do you understand that, you braindead moron? You used an image of him to lure me out here while leaving the real him back there to rot! I will never forgive you for that!"

*Offer her chocolate and flowers,* the *thing* frantically urged.

"What if I –"

"Jesus Christ!" Charlie shoved him in the chest, then hit him again with her fists. "You used the image of my child to kidnap me while leaving him there and you think a heartless apology is going to change my fucking opinion of you? This is not a fucking romance novel! I will *never* forgive you. *Never.* It doesn't matter what you fucking do."

Spinning away, Charlie marched off like a machine. She shoved her way through the bush with muttered curses. Her footsteps echoed through the forest like an angry stampede.

Left behind in a state of confusion and frustration, Jack ran a hand through his hair. Bloody hell, what had just happened?

*You should've opened with the chocolate and flowers.*

*Yeah, well, hindsight's a bitch, isn't it?*

Annoyed, Jack kicked a small rock before setting off. He caught up to Charlie in no time. Even as angry as she was, she was still ridiculously exhausted. The trek hadn't been easy in any sense of the word, and unlike Jack, she didn't have a powerful being to pull energy from. By the time they made it to the halfway point, she was near dead on her feet.

*You should let her rest.*

Still irritated over what she'd said, Jack refused. *She doesn't want anything from us, remember?*

Besides, what was the point of being nice if it didn't get him anything in return? And though Jack was back to lying to himself about not wanting anything from her anyway, least of all having her as a mate, he was still upset over the fact that she'd refused his apology. He'd never made one before, and she'd thrown it in his face like he hadn't even tried. Heartless apology, his ass.

*She still needs a rest.*

Jack ignored it as if it hadn't spoken.

Fifteen thousand years, he'd been alive. Not once had he felt the need to apologize and he'd done some damn awful shit. He was his father's son after all.

*There's a river up ahead,* the *thing* tried again. *At least let her have a drink.*

But Jack ignored that too. Or at least he tried to. One

quick glance at Charlie, however, and he found himself agreeing.

Not because he cared, he quickly assured himself. Only because if she didn't get some sort of refreshment, she wasn't going to make it to Aurora's Castle, let alone the portal. And though it would be far easier to carry her when she was too dehydrated to argue, Jack was pretty certain she was stubborn enough to die first.

"Turn left," he ordered. "There's a river up ahead and we could both use something to drink."

When she made no sign of hearing him, Jack rolled his eyes and continued straight ahead. Fuck it. If she wanted to ignore him and miss her chance of a rest, then that was on her.

He'd taken one step before stopping and clenching his jaw. Hades' fire, why couldn't he keep walking?

Growling with frustration, Jack grabbed her by the arm and dragged her to the left. She went stiffly, but he didn't care. He was going to get her something to drink even if he had to pour it down her bloody throat.

He might not want these feelings for her, but they were here and he just had to deal with them. As much as Jack wanted to put them off for a tomorrow that never came, this wasn't exactly something he could run away from. The *thing* was as stubborn as Charlie, and now that it had her scent, it would never stop looking for her.

On the plus side, she wouldn't live long enough for him to need to change any of his habits. A hundred years was nothing, a blimp on his existence that he probably would not even remember.

His chest tightened uncontrollably. Glancing at the stubborn kultara beside him, Jack knew Charlie could vanish in this instant and he would never forget her.

Still, she hated him. He couldn't be with her even if he

wanted to. If she was going to be in his life, it would have to be at a distance. His uncle wouldn't hesitate to kill her, and to be killed by a god was to never see the afterlife. Nothing needed to change.

And yet, it already was.

Looking up at the sky, Jack breathed out slowly. "I'm sorry for the pace, okay? But if we don't get to Aurora's Castle before the moon hits its zenith, you won't live to see it set."

Still giving him the silent treatment, Charlie didn't say a word.

"Fun fact," he said and then immediately wanted to smack himself. 'Fun fact' was never used right before someone said an actual fun fact. Unable to take it back, however, Jack was forced to continue. "Aurora's tale is one of the stories that crossed over into your realm. I believe you call it *Sleeping Beauty*?"

He looked at her then. Though there was obvious curiosity in her eyes, she still didn't speak.

Starting to get a bit frustrated, Jack ran a hand through his hair. It was only when he used his left one that he realized he still had hold of her. Abruptly, he released her arm. Immediately, he wished he hadn't.

"There were a few changes," Jack rambled on as they walked. "You guys turned her into a damsel who needed rescuing when in reality she was a monstrous cu- uh, person, who killed people in their dreams. So more of a Freddy Kruger than a Sleeping Beauty. Though, to be fair, she was a beauty and she did sleep a lot."

*Yep, what a fun fact that all was. Way to go, Jack.*

Thankfully, they were near the river now and he could use its roar as an excuse to stop talking.

Pushing ahead of her, Jack went to check the water's edge. Gindylows and other nefarious creatures often lurked beneath the surface. As exhausted and as human as Charlie was, she'd make a mighty fine morsel.

But as Jack neared the river, he realized his check was unneeded. With a curse, he peered over the edge of the cliff and to the river below. It was about fifty feet down a sketchy, overhanging path. One slip and they'd fall into lethal rapids, hit their heads, and drown.

Looking upstream, Jack calculated it would be about another thirty minutes hike before they found somewhere they could reach the water. He turned to tell Charlie that, but his brain melted as soon as he saw her. Time slowed. His heart stopped. The *thing* screamed.

As much as Jack wanted to move, to jump forward and grab her, his limbs were too frozen to do so. Mouth agape, eyes wide, all he could do was watch as his mate rushed for the edge. Without a falter in her steps, Charlie flicked him the bird and flung herself off the cliff.

# TWELVE

Charlie slammed into the river feet first, hand over her mouth. She fought the urge to gasp as the cold stabbed deeper than flesh, deeper than bone. It pierced her right to her soul. The frigid temperature robbed her of every memory of warmth. The rapid current attacked her like an angry mob. It pulled and it pushed and it crushed her under its waves.

She spun head over heels, tossed from side to side. Her lungs screamed with their need for air. Her skin burned from the freezing cold. Desperately, she clawed for the surface, only she wasn't sure which way was up anymore.

Swivelling her head around, she searched for the warm glow of the moon. When she found it below her, Charlie nearly cried out with relief. Kicking hard, she turned around and fought to reach it. But every stroke of her arms was offset by the rapids. Every kick of her legs lost power due to the cold. Her lungs were nearly depleted now. Her strength nearly gone.

Then, with a final push, Charlie broke free. She gasped

as soon as her head breached the water. It was a deep inhale of desperation and relief, but it was one that was very short lived. Pulled back under, she was shaken like a bunny in the mouth of a wolf.

Her head snapped to one side and then the next. Her body twisted in ways it never should. Her chest burned from the deprivation of oxygen and her heart screamed from the lack of hope. And just when she thought it couldn't get any worse, Charlie was slammed into a rock. Her shoulder split from the impact and she opened her mouth to scream.

Somehow she caught herself just in time. With a force of will that belonged in a hall of glory, Charlie pulled on what little energy she had left. She swam again for the surface, and again she was swept under. Over and over, she repeated the cycle. A gasp for air. A frantic tumble. A desperate fight for her life.

As much as the water coaxed her to give up, though, as much as the river laughed at her attempts to survive, Charlie refused to listen. Her boy was counting on her, and this time she would not fail him.

When next she breached, Charlie took a deep breath and screamed, "*Sebastian!*"

But even she couldn't hear it over the roar of the rapids. Sobbing, Charlie fought back defeated tears. She had hoped that he was out here already, searching for his prize. That all she would need to do was get far enough away from Fenrir so he couldn't stop her from leaving. Then Sebastian would phase to her and Tony would be safe.

"*Sebastian!*"

Refusing to give up, Charlie aimed desperately for the shore. She knew she didn't have much time left. Either Fenrir would find her or she'd be dead of hypothermia.

Neither outcome was acceptable.

As Charlie dragged herself onto the riverbank, her shoulder screamed in protest. Sharp pebbles dug into her hands and knees, but she was too cold and tired to feel them.

"Sebastian," she feebly called. Gasping like a fish on land, Charlie collapsed in sheer exhaustion. Her heart thudded slowly. Her teeth chattered violently. She wanted to close her eyes so badly, so desperately, that for a moment, she couldn't remember why she was fighting at all.

Her eyes drifted half-way shut. Her breathing slowed precariously. But just when Charlie was about to fall into a dangerous sleep, a form appeared like a demon in the night.

"Sebastian..."

Had Jack not been an immortal, he would have died of a heart attack. Watching Charlie get caught by the charybdis had scared the living daylights out of him, but this was even worse.

His chest tightened until he could barely breathe. His skin grew clammy and pale. His eyes burned in his need to find her. But there was nothing. No sign of life, no –

*There!*

A mountain of relief rose up inside him as he watched Charlie breach the surface. In an instant, however, it was crushed under an avalanche of fear as he watched her get swept back under. Poised on the edge of sanity, Jack could only wait with bated breath for her to claw her way back to the surface.

As soon as he spotted her again, he tried to get a hold of her with his magic. If he could transform Charlie into a mermaid, everything would be fine. He'd be able to breathe again and she wouldn't drown before he could get to her.

But it'd been too long since Jack had transformed another. By the time he managed to wrap her in his magic, she was far enough away that he hesitated. He had such a feeble hold on her that something could easily go wrong. Fatally wrong.

Knowing he couldn't help her up here, Jack's heart stuttered to a stop. Mouth dry, he drank in the sight of her bobbing down the river. He wanted to keep her in his sights, needed to see that she kept her head out of the water. Every inch of him screamed that this was the right course of action, but to do so was to lose her forever.

With a deep breath, Jack forced himself to turn away. He fought the urge to jump off the cliff and transform into a marine creature on the way down. Even with fins, he would be lucky to make it out of those rapids alive; it was nothing short of a damn miracle that Charlie hadn't hit her head and drowned.

No, a werewolf was the safer option. He'd be fast enough to get down there within a minute. He'd be strong enough to pull her out of the water if need be. And in the terrifying possibility that he lost sight of her for real, he'd be able to track her despite her cleansing from the river.

Wasting no time, Jack dropped to all fours and transed. He ate up the ground like a madman, crashing through bushes and bounding over rocks. When he reached the end of her scent trail, he veered hard to the left. The trees opened up to reveal the river, and without a thought to the cold, Jack leaped as if his life depended on it.

He hit the water hard. The cold rushed past his thick fur and burned him with its touch. He wouldn't last fifteen minutes in here, so how long would a human?

Fighting his panic, Jack methodically scanned the river. When he caught sight of her curled up on the other side of the bank, so much like a corpse, he instantly forgot how to swim. His head went under. His legs stopped moving. The *thing* howled in mourning, and Jack nearly gave up then and there. But the need to hold her in his arms one last time...

With powerful strokes, Jack propelled himself toward the shore. As soon as he was free of the river, he shook off what water he could and then transed. He collapsed beside Charlie's cold and still form. His heart was in his throat. The *thing* was shaking with concern.

It was only when he went to turn her onto her back that he realized she was alive. Shivering and bruised to hell, but alive.

"By the gods, woman! Are you insane? You could have died!"

The words rushed out before Jack realized he was even thinking them. Overwhelmed with fear and concern and a million other emotions he couldn't name, he started to shake.

Crushing Charlie to his chest, Jack took a moment to breathe her in. She jerked in his arms with a muffled moan, and he instantly held her away at arm's length. Looking her over, he cursed at the sight of her left shoulder. Her shirt was ripped open, and he could see the bruised and bloodied flesh underneath. He'd bet his ass that she'd broken it.

"Dammit, kultara." Jack fought the urge to pull her close again. Instead, his fingers went to the hem of her shirt. He'd lifted it an inch before she smacked him with her good arm.

Instant rage filled him, not because she'd hit him – he could barely feel that – but because he hadn't thought to explain what he was doing. "Calm down. I'm not going to rape you. I'm making a sling for your shoulder."

Her eyes called him a fucking liar and oddly enough, Jack rejoiced at that. If she still had this much fire, surely she was going to be okay?

"As i-i-i-if I'm go-go-going to f-f-all for –"

Jack suddenly pressed his hand over her mouth. When she twisted her head to free herself, he grabbed the back of her head with his other hand and held her still.

"Be quiet," he hissed as his ears strained for the noise he thought he'd heard.

The wind shuffled the leaves overhead. The insects chirped underfoot. The birds continued to sing their eerie songs, not one quieted in fear of a predator. Everything seemed normal, but then he heard it again and this time, the howls were unmistakable.

"Fuck." That had to be at least twelve of them.

Jerking Charlie to her feet, Jack dragged her over to a tree he hoped would be far enough away. He pushed her back down to the ground and covered her in a cloaking spell.

After only a second of hesitation, Jack removed her wet clothing with a flex of his fingers. Then he conjured up a thick blanket and wrapped it around her. Later, he would worry about the consequence of his actions, but right now, all he was thinking about was her survival.

"You stay here and you'll live to see your son. As long as you don't move, they won't be able to see, hear, or smell you. Do you understand me, Charlie?"

She nodded numbly, but it was clear she was barely conscious now. Her blue lips shivered uncontrollably and Jack pulled the blanket tighter around her. He wanted to stay beside her, to keep her warm and awake, but the howls were getting closer and he didn't have the time.

Cursing, Jack rose to his feet and turned away. As he made his way back to the river, he twirled his fingers in the air. Bright green light filled his palm and when it disappeared, it left *Sannurthogn* in its wake.

Curling Odin's device around his ear, Jack called his father. Though he'd expected a recording, it still pissed him off to hear it. Enraged, it took every bit of control he had not to jerk the thing off and toss it.

Growling, Jack left a voicemail that was more a threat than a request. Then he sent the device back to Odin's vault, cracked his neck, and transed.

He dropped to his knees with a snarl. His skin tore. His bones popped and then a blinding burst of light exploded inside his skull.

Suddenly, Jack stood outside of the *thing's* cage. The beast looked at him with its blood red eyes, its mouth foaming with the desire to kill, to protect. For the first time in his life, Jack wasn't afraid of it. He was desperate for its power.

*Release me.*

Without a single thought of caution, Jack shoved his hand inside the cage. As soon as the two touched, there was an explosion of energy. The bars disintegrated, the *thing* howled with triumph, and Jack fell to his knees on a scream.

Back in the real world, the trickster clawed at the earth in his agony. The *thing's* power burned through his veins with a vengeance. It was as if he was being consumed by a thousand suns, hit by a thousand bolts of lightning. His eyes rolled back in his head and then popped out during his trans. Bones cracked and splintered. Muscles tore and regrew. His skin gave way to smoldering fur that mimicked the ashes of a fire. His mouth erupted with a row of razor sharp teeth. His hands sprouted fearsome claws, and his eyes burned with literal fire. When he finally stood up after his trans was complete, it wasn't on two legs like he'd expected; it was on four.

He towered nearly twenty feet tall and when he looked across the raging river, he knew he could cross it in one leap. This wasn't any creature he'd ever changed into before. It wasn't even one he'd ever seen. But Jack didn't have time to reflect on the beast he now was.

With a feral howl, he answered the call of the wolves.

Suddenly, there was a change in the air. The excited musk of the pack now turned sickly with concern. The werewolves it seemed, were hesitant.

With a smile that would've scared even the gods, Jack charged through the woods. He had no desire of letting them get away. The werewolves had decided his mate was to be their next meal and for that, they would not survive. Besides, the *thing* was hungry and it did so love fresh meat.

He tracked them by their scent, pinpointing their exact location long before he spotted them. The first two werewolves never saw him coming. One moment they were running through the woods. The next, they were lying with their heads decapitated and their innards hanging from the trees like tinsel.

The others circled Jack in wary anticipation. Eleven pair of eyes assessed him shrewdly. A few looked to their alpha in concern, but not one of them was backing down.

With a low growl, Jack flattened his ears and lowered his back half to the ground. Tucking his tail in between his legs, he waited for the first idiot to attack. It didn't take long.

Tricked by Jack's submissive display of defense, the werewolf aimed for his neck. Jack dodged its teeth with a jerk of his head. Though he could kill it with a single swipe of his claws, he didn't. He needed them to throw caution to the wind, to think he was more growl than bite. Otherwise, Charlie would be dead before this fight was over.

Keeping his body low to the ground, the trickster slowly backed up. He deliberately stepped within biting range of the wolves behind him. As their teeth scraped his skin, Jack jumped up with a yelp.

He growled again in warning, but this time it fell on deaf ears. His blood was in the air. His body language said he was kill-able prey. With blinding bloodlust in their eyes, the werewolves charged as one.

Claws ripped into his flesh. Teeth sank into his bones. They flung themselves at him from every direction, and within seconds, they managed to push him onto his back. Jack whipped his head from side to side as he shoved against the werewolves aiming for his stomach. To them it looked like he was trying to defend his neck, but in reality he was searching for the alpha.

As soon as he found him, Jack faced the other way. His exposed neck was too much of a temptation. The alpha lunged for it with a snarl, but it never got to taste its sweet warmth.

With a vicious snap of his neck, Jack clamped his jaws around the werewolf and tore him in half. He swallowed the part he had hold of and then vanished in a cloud of smoke. The others didn't even know he'd gone. Lost in the illusion of his spell, they attacked the ground in his absence.

Reappearing behind them, Jack quickly eliminated them with cold efficiency. He tore into throats. He severed spines. He wrapped them in an illusion so thick, that only one of them even sensed something was wrong. Not that it mattered. Nothing was faster than a werewolf, but to

Jack, they moved like a babe.

In under a minute, all the werewolves were dead. Jack, with his fur of embers and his eyes of fire, his mouth dripping in blood and his claws covered in intestines, looked like a gruesome guardian of the forest. With a howl of triumph, he sprinted back to Charlie. But like the alpha that had gone for his neck, Jack never made it to his destination.

A crack of lightning whipped down from the sky. It nailed him right in the back, hitting with the force equivalent to an atomic bomb. The ground burned to a crisp in a forty foot radius. Cooked flesh filled the air. Jack was tossed by the blast, and when he hit a nearby tree, it burst into flames, so scorched was his skin.

He landed on his back with a growl. Rolling to his feet, Jack shook his massive bulk. His burnt flesh flicked off like drops of water. That blast would have killed him five minutes ago, but with the full power of the *thing* finally free, Jack rejuvenated in the blink of an eye.

Glaring at the sky, he turned into embers in the wind. He moved like a shadow, crossing over the river and solidifying on the other side. As much as he wanted to stand guard over Charlie, to check if she was okay, Jack didn't dare. No human could stand up to a god. Even a being as old as he would struggle to stay alive for long.

Another bolt of lightning rained down from the sky. It exploded in a flash of light. Jack closed his eyes and turned his head, but it still managed to blind him. It was the weapon of a god and its power was near infinite. But even so, Jack refused to back down.

Sniffing past the burnt trees and cooked flesh, Jack pinpointed the god with ease. He'd know that scent anywhere, had spent the last fifteen thousand years running from it. But no longer. Tonight, it all ended.

With a snarl of rage, Jack attacked like a man with nothing left to lose.

# THIRTEEN

He rammed into him like a freight train, tossing them both down the mountain. Snapping and snarling, Jack aimed for the god's hands, his arms, his neck. Anything he could reach, he wanted. Blood splattered. Skin ripped. Teeth went flying. Bones cracked and tendons tore.

A thick, sinewy arm wrapped around his neck and tightened. Growling, Jack kicked out with every limb. He clawed deep into flesh, severed right through bone. Before the arm could squeeze any harder, the trickster vanished in a cloud of smoke. He materialized directly above like a god of vengeance.

Dropping on top of his target, Jack bit deep into his vein. A bellow of pain and anger cracked the air. A roar of thunder soon followed. The god slammed an angry fist into his face, but though Jack's head flew sideways, he refused to slacken his jaw. He wasn't just fighting for his survival this time. He was fighting for his mate's.

With a deafening growl, Jack jerked his head to the side. He ripped out flesh and muscle. He bathed in the spurt of blood. As he prepared to strike again, his vision finally returned.

His eyes immediately latched onto his target. The remaining part of the god's neck glistened like a beacon. Jack might not have the powers of a godslayer, but by decapitating his opponent, he would buy himself some time. It wouldn't be much, an hour max, but it would be enough for him to grab Charlie and find his father.

But as Jack lowered his head for a final bite, his sixth sense blared like a fire alarm. Despite the *thing* urging him to end this already, Jack couldn't help but hesitate. Something was off. Something serious.

Before he could figure out what, the god tossed him like a rag doll. He smacked into a tree and went through it like it wasn't there. The fourth one finally caught him and Jack dropped to the ground with a snarl.

*Finish this!* the *thing* screamed.

But still he hesitated.

Narrowing his eyes, Jack desperately tried to pinpoint what it was that was bothering him. He took in the god's iconic red hair and beard, the lightning that crackled all around him. He inhaled the strong, musky scent and the crisp smell of an oncoming storm. He felt the power of the hammer and the insane strength that emitted from it. Everything about him screamed that this was really his cousin, Thor, the Aesir God of Thunder and great son to Odin. From the hatred in his eyes to his frustratingly good looks, nothing seemed out of place.

And yet, Jack still hesitated.

As he wracked his brain, a bolt of lightning slammed into the ground ahead of him. Though it was a good few feet off, it still gave him the chills. He would've been there had he not hesitated.

But it wasn't the near hit that worried him. It was the

fact that Thor wasn't clever enough to predict his actions. The god fought only what he could see when he could see it. He was quick and he was brutal, but he was never this intelligent. He didn't think multiple moves ahead. He simply came in with his hammer –

*Oh, for fuck's sake!*

Jack's Eureka moment came just as a blast of lightning speared him in the chest. His fur dissipated in a pile of ash. His muscles charred to a burnt crisp. His eyes enlarged until they finally exploded from the pressure of the heat. With a mental curse, he turned into a cloud of smoke before any more damage could be done. He waited until he was healed before materializing again. Then, ignoring the shrieks of the *thing*, Jack dropped to his belly and whined.

It was as if he'd cast a spell. The lightning in Thor's hand sizzled out completely. His face went from scary determination to shaky relief. His jaw slackened. His eyes misted. He had such a heart-wrenching look of hope on his face that Jack almost forgot to be pissed at him.

Almost.

The bastard had tried to kill him. No 'Hey, how are you, son? Want to talk? Maybe revert back to your old self so I know you haven't gone batshit insane?' Oh, hell no. Instead, his dad had fucking come in cloaked as his nemesis, his moron cousin who had been hunting him for fifteen thousand years, and then had thrown a lightning bolt at him! Worse, he'd done it when his mate was in danger.

Eyes narrowing, Jack gave a low growl. His father or not, he was going to deal out some hefty revenge – later.

Right now, Charlie needed him and he would not be away from her for a second longer.

Shooting the god a glare that would've made his mate

proud, Jack shifted into smoke. He tried to ignore the thoughts of her corpse waiting for him as he raced up the mountain. The pale blue of her skin as if she'd died in the cold of the night. Heart pounding, chest heaving, Jack poured everything he had into his run. But it wasn't enough.

He couldn't sense her. He couldn't hear her. All Jack could smell was death. It had seeped into the earth, consumed by the trees and flowers until the whole forest reeked of it. The *thing* howled like a monster and Jack's chest tightened with the desire to do the same.

Staggering back into human form, he collapsed by the tree he'd left her at. It'd been beautiful and green when he'd gone. Now it was ugly and black and the worst thing he'd ever seen. But Jack knew that if he just looked down, that if he stared at the burnt ground where Charlie used to lie, that he'd easily find something worse. With a feral scream, he slammed his fist into the tree. The thing creaked as if it was releasing its last dying breath and then it toppled to the ground.

Jack squeezed his eyes shut, but it didn't stop the tears.

A hand touched his shoulder and squeezed. And with that simple action, fifteen thousand years of love and trust was smothered away by anger. His father had killed her. How dare he try to apologize at the site of her grave.

Jumping to his feet, Jack slammed his fist into the god's jaw. His dad staggered back, but before Jack could get in another blow, he mumbled, "Imover."

Jack's fist froze by the side of his head, but he didn't drop it. "What?" he demanded.

His father worked his jaw, then tried again. "Before I hit you with the lightning, I moved her."

"Where?" he seethed.

"I healed her as well."

*Fuck him and his brownie points.*

For once, he and the *thing* wholeheartedly agreed.

Grabbing his father by the shirt, Jack hauled him within biting distance. "Where."

When his dad rolled his eyes, Jack had to fight the urge to rip out the remaining part of his neck. Finally realizing his son wasn't in the mood to joke around, the god sighed. "Aurora's Castle. It's the only safe place around."

Then, before Jack could order him to do anything, his father grabbed his wrist and phased. They landed inside a cave. A thousand crystals sprouted from its floor, its ceiling, its walls. They glistened with bright pink light and varied from two inches to fifteen feet in height. But even as beautiful as the crystals were, Jack didn't see a single one. His sole attention was on the majestic bed in the middle of the floor.

*She's alive.*

His chest squeezed at that. Shakily, Jack crossed over to his mate's side. He pressed a hand to Charlie's forehead, breathing a sigh of relief when he felt a bit of warmth. Once he was certain she was going to recover, Jack turned to face his father.

"Fucking change already."

With a snarky grin, the god did as commanded. The red hair he'd sported was now blacker than death. His chin, once bearded, was now clean shaven. The blue eyes that had glared at Jack from the depths of Niflhel were now a bright green full of love and mischief.

This was his father, all right. Loki, the Trickster God of the Aesir, and a right pain in his ass. Thor's balls, Jack should've known it was him from the first blast of lightning. His dad was able to use the magic and power of anything he changed into, including the gods, but he didn't have the strength to wield Thor's hammer. Nor did he have the ability to see through Odin's Eye nor throw the Bolt of Zeus.

"So it's really you?" his father asked. There was still a gleam of mischief in his eyes, but true concern and hesitation lurked beneath. Though Loki had never failed to protect him from the others, even he feared the release of the *thing* and the prophecy it would bring.

Reminded of it all, the last of Jack's anger faded away. He ran a hand through his hair, then conjured up a pair of chairs. Neither of them felt like sitting.

"Yeah, it's me," Jack said as he started to pace. Now that the adrenaline was gone from his veins and Charlie laid safely beside him, the enormity of what he'd done came crashing down like a sledgehammer. Holy fucking shit, he'd released the *thing*. He'd damned the whole world to chaos and death and for what? A woman he –

But whatever excuse he was about to give, he knew it didn't matter. Not really. Not when, if given the choice, Jack would make the same decision all over again.

Seeing the resolve on his son's face, Loki sighed and finally took a seat. "Tell me about her. How'd you two meet? Planning any kids yet? She know how to cook? I would kill for a lasagna right now."

Jack rolled his eyes as he took the remaining chair. "She's out cold; she's not about to jump up and make you a lasagna." The thought of her doing so, though, filled him with longing. To experience something so simple, so carefree as that – it was a dream Jack never even knew he wanted.

Leaning back in his chair with a sigh, Loki patted his stomach hungrily. "A shame. A properly made one is so much better than a summoned one."

Shaking his thoughts away, Jack focused on the now. "Then summon one from someone's oven," he said.

"What a great idea." Without even a flourish of magic, a table appeared in front of them. On it sat a freshly baked lasagna with a portion of it already missing.

Jack shook his head in feigned disapproval. "That poor family."

"Eh, I wouldn't worry about them. I paid them with a chimera. Those things are rare, you know."

This time, Jack's shake was one of amusement. "No, they're not."

"This one is. Only one I know called Schizmo." With a smug grin, Loki shoveled some lasagna into his mouth.

"Delentia is going to kill you." That fury was one crazy psycho on the best of days. Steal her beloved pet and even Jack, with his love for chaos, didn't want to see what she'd do. Especially since he already knew of a demon who was being punished for all eternity for simply having run over her vegetable patch. Her wilting, rotten vegetable patch. When he was a kid. Which was nearly seven hundred years ago now.

Loki shrugged without concern. "Maybe, but it won't be until after she kills that family, and they had like nine children so... We're fine for a while."

Jack pinched the bridge of his nose as he fought back a roar of laughter.

Loki smiled. "So was that enough small talk or do you still need a bit more time?" He scooped another bite of lasagna onto his fork. Looking at his son, he then picked up more and more of it, trying to gauge how much he needed to shove into his mouth. Did his son need thirty more seconds to gain his courage? A whole minute? Seven?

Once his father had managed to scoop up the whole lot, Jack finally shook his head with a laugh. Slowly, all of his concerns started to slip away.

He looked over at Charlie. "She's the *thing's* mate," he said quietly. "Our mate," he quickly corrected. "She...calms it."

"Really? Funny. Those werewolves would probably beg to differ."

Looking back at his father, Jack growled, "Those monsters deserved it. They were going to kill her. And if you think –"

"Easy there, son," he said holding up his hands. "You're going to want to check that. Those red eyes are a dead giveaway."

A mirror appeared before Jack. Glaring back at him weren't the bright green eyes he'd inherited from his father. Rather, they were the burning red of the *thing*.

Shaking his head, Jack forced the beast back down. It didn't go quietly, but it went much easier than normal.

"Why'd you come as him?" Jack asked to change the subject. He didn't dare say his cousin's name. He might use it as a profanity when thinking, but he'd never say it out loud. To voice a god's name was to allow them to eavesdrop on your conversation and from there, it was all too easy for them to find out where you were.

For once, Loki's carefree demeanor slipped away. His eyes softened, then focused entirely on his forkful of lasagna. Shoving the whole thing into his mouth, he spent the next half hour chewing. As annoying as it was to wait, Jack didn't bother glaring at him. It was only fair that he offered his father the same patience he had received. With a final swallow, Loki met his son's eyes.

"Because if you killed me tonight, I did not want my death on your conscience. And though you would've figured it out eventually...if I could save you from even a second of pain, I would."

There was a moment of comfortable silence. Then Loki

brought up the elephant in the room and Jack's chest squeezed harder than if a giant had gripped it.

"You do know it would be best to leave her, though. To stay with her is to –" The god cut himself off, but Jack wasn't an idiot. He'd already come to the realization that he could never be with her. The gods would never stop coming for him, and the last time they'd hunted on the mortal realm, they'd wiped out an entire species.

*Or did they? It was a long shot, but if it was true...*

Learning forward, Jack suddenly asked, "What if she was an atlantean?"

Loki sat back in surprise. His cunning eyes widened, then drifted over to Charlie. "Is she?" he breathed.

"Could be. Never met one before."

"But you have your suspicions?"

Jack tightened his lips. As much as he wanted to claim he was a hundred percent certain she was a member of the lost race, his father would see right through it. "I doubt she's a purebred, but she could be part. I only have her because she's suspected to have read and retained the knowledge of the *Scrolls*."

Loki's eyes grew calculating. "Then you might as well keep her beside you and well hidden. If word gets out, she'll be hunted regardless of what side she's on. Prometheus damned her whole race with that trick of his. Purebred or halfling, the gods won't care. But –" At this, he turned to face his son. "If she isn't, you would've damned her to a fate worse than death. Killed by a god, Charlie will never find peace in the afterlife. Her soul will burn for all eternity, never to be reborn, never to exist outside the Abyss of Nothingness. So don't claim this lightly, son. You won't live with yourself if you're wrong."

With a hard swallow, Jack shifted uneasily. Honestly, he had no idea if Charlie had the *Scrolls* inside her head or not. Galvanor had claimed she did, but the whole setup had been a trap. Maybe Sebastian had found a way to fake that too. Or maybe Charlie was the decoy for the real atlantean who was still trapped inside his castle. Either way, was Jack really willing to risk her life for his own selfish desires?

"Is there a way we can be sure?"

"Well, yeah. Get her to read the *Scrolls*. Last I heard, they were still in Edinburgh." Loki's eyes narrowed at the sudden amusement on his son's face. "Spill."

"You really should pick up your bloody phone when I call. Then I wouldn't have anything *to* spill."

"Stop being such an ass and tell me. Don't you know children are supposed to respect their parents?"

Jack snorted as he leaned back and crossed his arms. "That only counts for parents that didn't leave their newborn child to go on a seventy-five year fishing trip."

The god rolled his eyes. "Are you really still bringing that up? You're such a freaking drama queen."

"Learned from the best," Jack said dryly.

Loki beamed as if that hadn't been an insult in the slightest. "So you did. Now, spill."

Dropping his chair back down, Jack filled his father in on all that had happened in the past few weeks. When he mentioned Sebastian stealing the *Scrolls*, he got a look of sly approval. When he informed him that the vampire had created hybrid angels, his father snickered with mischief. But when Jack told him that he still had Charlie's child, all signs of amusement vanished.

"So let me get this straight," Loki said as he leaned forward. "Sebastian managed to steal the *Scrolls* by taking advantage of a descendant's curse, which he should have never have known about in the first place. Then he found an atlantean, a race that was supposedly wiped out by us gods multiple millennia ago, to read them. She starts building him an army, which attacks Hel's Exit, where a member of your team just happens to be. Then a vampire there, who hasn't seen Sebastian in years, tells you where he was hiding so you can 'steal this atlantean' from him. A woman, who's not just your mate, but also happens to have a child still under his control?"

The chill that had been slowly creeping down Jack's spine suddenly shattered to every inch of his body. He knew with absolute certainty where this was heading and he didn't like it. Not one bloody bit.

Jumping to his feet, Jack ran both hands through his hair. As he started to pace, Loki stood up and grabbed his arm. Looking him in the eye, the god pressed, "Son, has it occurred to you that this might be a trap? That she's meant to trick you into going somewhere stupid?"

"No," he said with a shake of his head. "You're wrong. Cousin –"

"I'm not talking about your idiot cousin," Loki cut in sharply. "I'm talking about my brother."

Odin, chief of the Aesirs. Great god who sees all and a bloodthirsty bastard who would stop at nothing to make sure Jack's prophecy never came to light. He wouldn't have any problems using a child as an assassin. He sure as hell wouldn't lose any sleep over using one as bait.

*She wouldn't do that.*

"If you're right..." Jack trailed off, his eyes flicking to the bed in longing. He didn't like her, he told himself. He didn't even want her. And she sure as hell didn't want him.

*She is our mate.*

"If you're right..." he tried again, but when he trailed off a second time, his father clapped him on the shoulder. A gentle squeeze demanded his attention and Jack looked to him like a lifeline.

"I can't lose you," Loki said.

With a sharp nod, Jack worked his throat. Breathing deeply, his resolve hardened. His father was right; there were simply too many coincidences for him to ignore. As he looked back at Charlie, Jack ignored the growls of the *thing*, and let his heart grow hard.

"If she's with uncle," he vowed, "then I'll kill the bitch myself."

# FOURTEEN

*No!*

Snapping awake, Charlie blinked frantically at her surroundings. The humidity, the color, the bright light – they were all wrong. It shouldn't be muggy from the heat nor bathed in a harsh pink glow. It should be cold and silver and blue and crawling with things she couldn't see, haunted by things she couldn't sense. The illuminating crystals sprouting from the floor, the walls, the ceiling – they might as well have been flashing neon signs.

'You're not in the woods anymore,' they screamed.

'You're not back at Sebastian's lab, either.'

'You're somewhere new, somewhere far away. You will never see your son again.'

Panic burned a ragged hole in her heart. She tried to sit up, but a thin golden chain around her wrist stopped her from going far. It was wrapped around the headboard, and no matter how hard Charlie tugged, it never weakened.

Growling with frustration, she looked around the room. She tried to spot something she could use to smash the chains apart or break the headboard so she could slip free. Had it a lock, she would've searched for something to pick it.

Seeing nothing, Charlie yanked once more on the chain, then sat there seething. Refusing to admit total defeat, she looked around the room again. This time, she didn't search for an object, but simply tried to discern where she was.

On Earth, Charlie would've assumed she was in a cave, but she knew nothing about the world these supernaturals inhabited. This could be someone's house. After all, it had a bed, a massive fucking bed plated in gold with four posters towering over her head. It looked like something out of a goddamn fairytale. At that thought, Charlie's eyes narrowed.

She racked her memory for something Fenrir had said moments before she'd jumped.

*"If we don't make it to Aurora's Castle..."*

*Fuck!*

Fenrir must have found her when she was unconscious and brought her here. He might have saved her from hypothermia, but he'd damned her to hell. If she was in his team's stronghold, her chance of escape, of saving Tony, had plummeted to its death.

With a primal growl, Charlie wrapped both hands around her binding. She twisted and she pulled and she spat and she swore. She even tried praying again, but it was all to no avail. Even though the chain looked like it would snap from a sick child's tug, some horrible, twisted magic kept it strong.

By the time she finally gave up, little rivers of blood ran down her wrist and pooled on the sheets below. Charlie stared at the stains on her skin, her chest heaving, her heart racing. If she couldn't break the chains, then she'd have to escape the other way. Her stomach twisted in unease, but her resolve was strong.

Tony wasn't just her little boy. He was her life, her entire reason for living. She would not give up on him.

Breathing deep, Charlie looked around the room again. After making sure there was no one to stop her, she eyed her bound hand. Ignoring the nauseous roll of her stomach, Charlie put her thumb in her mouth. She closed her eyes.

Her heart pounded faster and faster until she could no longer discern one beat from the next.

Sweat beaded down her neck.

Her hands grew clammy.

Her brain screamed at her to leave her thumb attached.

But her soul begged her to escape through whatever means necessary.

Swallowing hard, Charlie imagined her thumb was a carrot. She took a deep breath, convinced herself there was no other option, and bit.

"By the gods, woman!"

Yanked up by her hair, Charlie's teeth closed uselessly on the air. Part relieved, part frustrated by the save, she wasn't sure whether to curse Fenrir or thank him, so she settled for a glare.

"You are fucking insane." He bit out each word as if it was its own sentence. "I'm not surprised uncle chose you." When her eyes widened in shock, Fenrir sneered, "That's right, kultara. I know all about your mission."

He said it with such loathing conviction that even Charlie almost believed him. Then she shook her head and shoved his craziness away. "What are you talking about?" she demanded. "I don't know *you* and I sure as hell don't know your uncle."

"So stubborn, even in the end."

The way he murmured it, soft and almost admirably, made her skin crawl. She didn't like the look in his eyes, the hard steel that made him look like a stranger. And though Charlie hadn't really known him to start with, her gut had trusted him out there in the woods. It didn't now and that frightened her.

"Are you even an atlantean or was that just a ploy?"

"What are you talking about?" She tried to pull back from him, but he refused to let go of her hair.

"Of course you're not. Even uncle wouldn't have spared you if you were. So how'd you do it?"

"Do what?"

"Create the angel hybrids that attacked us."

Charlie hadn't been able to make head or tails of his accusations, but this, she thankfully understood. "I infused subjects with the blood of an angel. Sebastian had litres of the stuff."

Angry, Fenrir shoved her down on the bed. "There's no need to lie anymore. Your game's up; you're caught."

"I'm not lying!" she proclaimed. Scrambling to her knees, Charlie pressed, "The blood was dull, not glowing like it should've been. But it was all from one angel, I swear! Why would I lie? Sebastian has my *son*. I will freely give you whatever information I have!"

"One angel?"

"Yes!"

"How many did you make?"

"Twenty-three." Charlie's throat tightened, but she forced her next words out. "I tried more times than that, but not every subject took to the transfusion. Of those that did, nearly half had severe reactions and died within twenty-four hours. The others, I don't think would've lasted the week."

He took her depressing news as if she'd been talking

about the weather. Not one flash of sorrow flitted across his angry face, and that lack of humanity punched her hard in the stomach. Whatever he was accusing her of, it was serious.

Crossing his arms, Fenrir demanded, "How did you know how to do it?"

She knew he wouldn't believe her even as she said it. "A book. Sebastian called it the *Scrolls of Atlantis.*"

"You lie. That book would have told you how to do it with zero casualties."

"You've read it?" she asked in surprise. His jaw ticked and she fought the urge to throw a pillow at his stubborn face. She wasn't surprised because he could call her out and pick apart all her lies, as he so obviously thought. She was surprised because Sebastian had only been forcing humans to try to read it and she'd assumed supernatural beings couldn't, hence his need for her kind.

Before he could accuse her of anything else, Charlie rushed, "I didn't finish reading the whole thing."

"Of course you didn't," he sneered. "How convenient for you."

Eyes glaring, Charlie fumed. "It's the truth."

"Then what am I?"

"What?"

"You said you read the *Scrolls*. My species is in there. What am I?"

"Other than a bastard, you mean?"

His jaw ticked in outrage, but his eyes lit in −

"Yes," Fenrir drawled, his eyes now hard as diamond. "Other than that."

Swallowing down a harsh retort, Charlie scrunched up her eyes in thought. She went over everything she knew about him, crossing off species as she went. He wasn't a telepath because one, that hadn't been his voice inside her head, and two, he could shapeshift. But he also couldn't be a shifter. Most of them could only turn into one other form and none of them could create illusions.

"Well?"

Ignoring him, Charlie closed her eyes and envisioned herself flipping through the *Scrolls*. "You're a trickster," she finally said.

He stared at her for a long moment and then sneered. "Well done. You can spot one of the main species of the Myth."

His sarcasm was grating. His hostility was pissing her off. What the hell had she done to make him so freaking paranoid?

"What is your problem?" she yelled as she tugged on the chain again. "You kidnapped me, remember?"

"And now I'm rectifying my mistake."

He waved his hand and a long knife appeared out of nowhere.

"Seriously?" she shouted, too angry to be afraid. "You kidnap me, drag me up a fucking mountain, and chain me to a bed. You went through all that just to kill me now. Really? Well, fuck you!"

His eyes hardened. A second ago, Charlie would've thought that impossible, certain he was already at the end of the hatred spectrum and nothing she could do would piss him off more. Oh, how wrong she'd been.

"Tricksters can't conjure actual items, only illusions. You would've known that had you read the *Scrolls*."

Charlie stared at him in disbelief. Of all the dickish moves to pull, testing her like that was topping the nine-tiered cake. No one in their right fucking mind would be able to think logically after being dragged into an alien world and then threatened with a knife.

"But you know I'm not a real trickster, don't you?"

Fenrir said it slowly, dangerously, and for the first time in his presence, Charlie truly felt fear. He was going to kill her. She could see it in his eyes. Whatever he thought she was, whatever mission he thought she was on, it was enough for him to justify her death.

"Really, that's your ace in the hole?" Charlie shouted, desperate to get him to see reason. "That I, a freaking human who's just been dropped into an alien world, didn't know a *stranger's* identity? What job did I do then, huh?"

"What?"

Her sudden question clearly threw him. Or maybe it was her exponential rage. Either way, she wasn't giving him any time to think.

"My job. On Earth. What was it?"

"How should I know?"

"You expected me to know what you are," she pointed out.

"That's not the same thing."

"Why not?"

"Because," he growled.

"Because why?" she pushed.

Frustrated, he ran a hand through his hair. "Because... because you're the one trying to kill me, not the other way around."

Her jaw dropped. "That's what this is all about? You think I'm trying to kill you?" Though honestly, had she the strength, Charlie would've strangled him then and there if she could. Ignoring her mounting frustration, however, she tried to think logically. "I am a human and trickster or no, you are still a hell of a lot stronger than me. What was I gonna do? Hit you with a stick? Kick you out of the air? Drag you into the sudden mouth of a charybdis?"

"You did try all of those things..."

*Wow, he's thick*. Holding hard onto her patience, she said slowly, "And did one of them even come close to succeeding?"

Fenrir looked away irritably. "Well, no, but –"

"But *nothing*. I'm a human and you're a transforming, illusion casting whatever it is you are."

He was silent for a second, and Charlie prayed he wasn't nearly as thick as he was currently making himself out to be. When he finally looked at her again, she about sighed in relief. Thank God that seed of doubt had finally been planted.

"So you're saying it's just a coincidence that you're my mate?" he asked uncertainly.

"Yes!" Charlie exclaimed, certain that he had finally gotten what she was saying. But then his words clicked, and her jaw dropped faster than a golddigger's bottoms.

"Say what now?"

"That you didn't allow yourself to be kidnapped or –"

"Hold on a second," Charlie loudly interrupted. Only when he stopped and looked at her with his undivided attention, did she continue. "You said I was your mate?"

"Yes."

He said it so casually, so flippantly that she wanted to claw his eyes out. "Well, unmate me," she demanded.

"Why?" Fenrir wondered. "So you can find it easier to stab me in the back?"

"No, because it's creepy, you paranoid fuck! I don't even know you and you're saying I'm your mate? Who even does that?"

"Look, I'm not exactly pleased about this either." But though his voice was irritable, there was an unmistakable glint of pleasure in his eyes.

Her blood chilled and she shook her head in denial. "What do you mean, you're not pleased? You picked me as your mate, right? So just un-pick me."

"It doesn't work like that. It's...instinctive."

"Bullshit!" Heart beating too fast to think, Charlie couldn't find the words she wanted to say. She could only stare dumbly, wanting so badly to scream.

Had she not already gone through enough? First with her shithole of a childhood, then with the death of Tony's father. Not to mention Sebastian's kidnapping, Tony's torture, and her multiple near death experiences in the last few hours. How could life be so cruel as to pair her with a man like him? Especially after she'd already tasted paradise, had already experienced what a real love could be like?

As if uncomfortable with her silent judgment, Fenrir ran a hand through his hair. He disheveled it in a way that expressed her own frustration and then with a heavy sigh, he twirled the fingers on his other hand.

The golden chain that bound her vanished in the blink of an eye. Charlie rubbed at her wrist, wincing in pain.

"Let me see it."

She eyed his outstretched hand, holding her arm closer to her chest.

"Look, I've saved your life three times already, sixteen if you counted each werewolf I killed while you were unconscious. If I wanted to hurt you, I would've done so already."

"You were going to kill me earlier, though, weren't you? When you accused me of not knowing what you were?"

He looked away briefly. "I thought you were sent by my uncle to kill me," he said. "The bastard's been trying to for years, and it wouldn't be the first time he thought to use a woman."

"And now?" she asked.

"Now, I don't know what to believe."

Almost absentmindedly, he tugged her hurt arm free. His thumb caressed the back of her hand as he looked into her eyes. "But know this, Charlie. If you're lying, as much as it would pain me, I will kill you. It won't be quick and it won't be painless."

A bandage appeared in his hand and he wrapped it around her wrist. Pulling it tight, he continued, "But if you are as you say you are, then I will do everything in my power to please you. You want Sebastian dead? You want me to devote my life to protecting you and your son? Just say the word."

Warily, Charlie smothered the hope rising inside her chest. Things were never this simple. There was always a price.

Looking into Fenrir's eyes, the green windows of his soul, Charlie knew exactly what price he was charging. He was showing her everything and was only asking for something simple, something impossible, in return.

"But first you have to trust me?" she hedged.

A slow nod. "But first I have to trust you."

# FIFTEEN

Reluctantly, Jack dropped Charlie's hand and took a step back. His fingers itched to hold her again, so he crossed his arms. His eyes, desperate to look down at her naked breasts, stayed hard and focused on her face. He needed a clear head and the mere touch of her skin was fucking with his brain. The gods only knew what would happen if he gave in and glanced through the illusions he'd covered her in.

Well, the gods and his cock. Already, it was half-way hard and growing harder by the second. It yearned for a stroke of her hand, a brush of her lips, a parting of her thighs. It wanted him to crawl onto the bed and trail his mouth down her neck and breasts. It begged him to gather her in his arms as he slid inside her and pump in and out until the both of them forgot they hated each other.

One look was all it would take for him to lose his control. One kiss and he would forget she was probably trying to stab him in the back. There were worse ways to go, his cock pointed out, and Jack was forced to agree.

Slowly, his eyes drifted down to her lips.

Scowling, he jerked them back up again and took another step back.

"Do you know where we are?" he asked abruptly. Propping his shoulder against the cold stone of a crystal stalagmite, Jack eyed her warmly.

Her eyes narrowed in suspicion, but he made certain she couldn't see the gears grinding away in his head. He would have one shot at this, one chance to convince her he was worth trusting. If she passed his test, she'd live. If not, he would have to kill her. Worse, he would be forced to do it in such a way that Odin would never attempt such foolishness again.

The *thing* growled. Jack ignored it. It bit him. He smothered an angry curse, but refused to be swayed. He couldn't. Not yet.

For fifteen thousand years, Jack had survived. Not because he'd been clever enough to avoid his cousin, but because he'd been capable of abandoning absolutely everything as soon as his cover was blown. He didn't get close to anyone, didn't try to know those he couldn't leave at the drop of a hat. To trust another, to love another, was to die. Not once had Jack been tempted to bend his number one rule in years...not until Charlie.

So if Odin really was capable of finding people who could call to the *thing*, to make him yearn for a life better than what he had...

"Do you?" he asked again.

Warily, she shook her head.

"It's Aurora's Castle and that bed" —he nodded at it— "was where she slept."

Charlie looked down with a touch of feigned curiosity and Jack couldn't help but smile.

"But you already knew that, didn't you?"

Her head shot up. There was a flash of surprise and a tinge of fear in her gorgeous green eyes. Then she hid it under a challenging stare. "I had a guess."

"Based on?"

"You mentioning it earlier."

He cocked his head as if to give her a friendly point. Their tension, however, didn't dissipate. She sat poised on the bed, her eyes wary, her heart shielded. The *thing* asked him why she would be so hostile if she was tasked with winning him over.

Shifting his weight, Jack never took his eyes off her. "So tell me about yourself."

Her lips tightened. "What do you want to know?"

"Tell me about Tony."

"No."

*See? If she was a traitor, she'd be gushing with answers.*

"Why not?" Jack pressed.

An impenetrable shutter closed over her face. "I said no."

Jack's lips pursed, but he didn't press. "Fine. Tell me about Tony's father. Where is he?" His words came out harsher than he'd wanted them to, and he took a deep breath to regain his control.

"Dead."

*Good. It means I don't have to kill him.*

Jack nearly smiled at the *thing's* jealousy before he caught himself. Somehow, he doubted Charlie would find it as amusing as he did, and though Jack truly didn't care what people thought about his dark humor, he found that her opinion mattered to him.

Shifting uncomfortably, Jack asked, "Sebastian?"

"No."

"Then how?"

"My favorite movie is *The Princess Bride*."

Jack blinked at the sudden change of subject. Then a slow smile curved his lips. "It's a damn good movie."

Her smile was fleeting and hesitant, but at least it was something. There was a moment of awkward silence and then, "What's your real name?"

"My name," he said before pausing dramatically. "Is Inigo Montoya. You killed my father. Prepare –"

Jack dodged the frilly pillow with a laugh.

"Trust works both ways, you know."

He tried to see deeper than the frustration on Charlie's face. Did she really not know?

*Why would she? Our mate doesn't work for Odin.* The *thing* paused so Jack could agree, then snarled when he didn't. *Fine. You don't believe me? Then tell her. You will see.*

Holding Charlie's gaze, Jack murmured, "I wasn't lying. My name's Fenrir."

She snorted as she rolled her eyes. "Yeah, and mine's Gullible. I knew this would be a fucking waste of time."

"I'm not joking."

She must have heard the honesty in his voice because her following snort trailed off into silence. Her eyes focused on his face, hard and sharp and full of nervous uncertainty.

"Bullshit."

When he merely shrugged, she shook her head with a cruel laugh. "Your parents must have had one sick twist of humor."

He cocked an eyebrow in surprise. "You know the tale?"

"Of Fenrir? Who doesn't? He's the one that will kill Od–"

Jack was on her in an instant. His hand was pressed

over her mouth, his eyes were deadly, and the knife from earlier was shoved against her neck.

Charlie's eyes widened. Her shock surfaced for only a moment before it was buried under a mountain of furious, reckless challenge. With a curse, Jack dropped the knife. It wasn't Charlie's fear or anger that made him release it; it was her genuine surprise.

*Told you,* the *thing* said smugly. Jack didn't bother to point out that he'd felt its sharp pain for the second it had thought its mate had actually betrayed them. Instead, his attention was fully on the woman beneath him.

"You can't say a god's name, kultara. Not ever. Now nod if you understand."

She waited a second before giving a rough jerk.

Easing off her, Jack crouched on the bed beside her. Warily, Charlie pushed herself up into a sitting position. He hated that he was the reason she was afraid, hated it more that there was nothing he could do to set her at ease.

"Everyone calls me Jack though," he supplied, hoping they could put the last few seconds behind them. "No one even knows my birth name."

There was a moment of heavy silence, but Jack didn't try to break it. He could see Charlie trying to unravel his mysteries and discover the truth beneath his actions. He'd been both hostile and kind, swapping between antagonist and hero like the flip of a switch. He wasn't surprised she needed a bit of time to adjust; he needed some himself.

In less than a day, Jack's entire life had been tossed upside down, squashed into a pulp, and then set on fire. He'd experienced more emotions in a handful of hours than he had in the last three years. Of course, he'd tried to ignore them, to convince himself that he could walk away from her just like he had with his lifemate. He might've succeeded too had she not fallen into the charybdis. Faced with her potential death, Jack's instincts had won out and he'd been unable to go back to pretending like he didn't care.

*So really,* Jack thought with annoyance, *this is all her fault.* If Charlie had only watched where she was going, then none of this would have happened. But nooo, she had to go jump into a river and cause him to lose his mother fucking mind.

Swallowing hard, he recalled those frantic moments he'd waited for her to resurface. Even now, when he could see that she was safe, his chest tightened like a vice. He couldn't leave her, couldn't pretend she meant nothing to him. Her life was tied to his. Her soul belonged to him. She was his mate and there was nothing either of them could do about it.

Thor's balls, all Jack had to do was look inside himself to know the truth. By the fucking gods, he'd released the *thing* for her! He'd actually damned the whole universe because he was feeling territorial. He could have tricked the werewolves into going the wrong way, but he hadn't. He'd changed for the sole desire of punishing those who had dared to even think about harming his mate.

And he would do it again.

"I really am sorry about taking you from your son."

She looked away, her mouth tight, her eyes gleaming with unshed tears. His heart twisted in agony. His hands clenched with overwhelming frustration. But what did he say to a woman he cared for but couldn't trust? To a woman he respected but didn't actually like? What did he say to a mother whose child he had more than likely killed? A mother who doubled as his mate?

He wanted to laugh and cry at the same time. The *thing* paced restlessly, and Jack surged to his feet to do the same. Turning away from her, he ran a hand through his hair.

"What do you want from me?" Her words were bitter and tired, and Jack's heart twisted again.

Without turning to look at her, he answered. "Proof I can trust you."

"And how am I supposed to give you that? I've told you the truth and you don't believe me. Be honest, Fenrir, there's nothing I can say that'll make you believe me, is there?"

He ran another hand through his hair.

"Probably not," he said honestly because Jack wasn't waiting for the right words. He was waiting for a single action, one that would give him no doubt as to where her loyalties lied.

Turning around, Jack opened his mouth to ask her another question. Instead, his lips stayed frozen, gaping in shock as his eyes widened over the pain lancing through his chest. Surly an innocent civilian wouldn't have been able to do what she'd just done.

Charlie had moved with all the sound of a cat's feet and when she'd attacked, it had been so swift he'd never had the chance to defend himself. Him – a fifteen thousands year old immortal that was able to outwit even the gods.

Jack flicked his gaze down to the knife protruding from his chest. He knew with absolute certainty his death was imminent. Regardless of whether she worked for Odin or if she'd honestly read the *Scrolls*, either way, she'd know how to kill him. All it would take was a few twists of the blade in his heart.

Jack tried to take a step back, but she instantly went with him. Throwing her whole weight behind it, Charlie forced the blade all the way to the hilt. When she felt it pierce his vital organ, she gave it a ferocious twist. As he stared down at her in shock, she twisted it again.

Horror filled her eyes for only a second. Then it was replaced by sorrow and guilt, and finally, by cold-hearted determination. Tears burned in her eyes and Jack had the strongest desire to wipe them away. But his arms wouldn't move and his legs had suddenly collapsed.

Tearing away from him, Charlie watched as he fell to the floor. Her lips wavered. Her hands shook. Her steel, however, remained.

Toppling backward, Jack's head hit the floor with a solid whack. The crystals' glow faded into blackness. The cave grew cold, and Charlie took off, leaving him on his own as death closed in.

He didn't bother trying to fight it. With his last breath, Jack let out a demented laugh, and then he died.

# SIXTEEN

Charlie dashed through the cave, her heart racing, her feet flying. She ducked under an overhang, scrambled through a tight crevice. Cuts and scrapes decorated her body. Thick mud mangled her fine hair. She closed her eyes for a brief second, her mind a horrid mess of guilt and regret.

She'd killed him.

Fenrir. Her...mate. Dead by her own two hands.

Nauseous, Charlie swallowed hard. *I don't even like him*, she reminded herself. *Don't care for him at all.* He'd kidnapped her, tricked her into abandoning her child, and forced her on a death march. He'd tied her to a bed and waved a knife in her face. Hell, he'd actually threatened to kill her.

The bastard deserved to die.

Goddammit, he did.

But despite her constant reassurances, her heart never believed them. It didn't merely ache; it was a crippling mess of agonized mourning.

Her breaths came out ragged and uncertain. Her eyes burned with the need to cry. Depression tightened her chest, squeezing it in a merciless grip. Weighed down by guilt, Charlie staggered through the tunnels of the cave, then collapsed against a tall crystal.

She'd killed him.

Her stomach cried out in a sudden heave. Had there been anything in it, it would have certainly been sprayed all over her shoes.

Or rather, her feet, Charlie suddenly realized. She was no longer wearing her trainers. No longer clothed at all. Her heart wrenched and she heaved again.

He was dead. He was truly dead and with his death, his illusions had faded.

Closing her eyes, Charlie fought hard to find her focus, but all she could see were the memories of her jump.

The icy water. The panic of death. The struggle to the riverbank. Then there was Fenrir gently gathering her in his arms.

His mien had been one of tenderness and pain. His touch had been that of an uncertain child. He had rocked her in his lap – once, twice before suddenly exploding in a wave of anger. No, not anger, Charlie admitted with a wince. But concern. He'd been terrified for her safety as he had with the charybdis. He –

*Stop!*

Charlie pressed her head in her hands, desperate to silence the memories and emotions riding her hard. She should be pissed, frustrated that he'd taken her clothes. She should be relieved, happy that she'd broken free from her kidnapper and could now run on back to Tony.

Because Tony was all that mattered. Was all that ever mattered.

Shoving away from the crystal, Charlie wiped an arm

across her face. She ignored the new pain in her feet and the cold on her skin. She might now be naked, but she was no longer vulnerable. Fenrir had deserved to die and as long as Tony lived...

She could live with that.

She had to.

Taking a deep breath, Charlie pushed on.

"And you say I'm dramatic." Loki rolled his eyes as he stood over his dead son. With an exasperated sigh, he threw his hands in the air. "I leave you for one minute. One bloody minute. With a *human*, for my kind's sake. How stupid are you to not be able to handle one measly human? Even if she is an atlantean, it's not like they are known for their strength."

Their cleverness maybe, but Loki hadn't raised any of his children to be stupid. Reckless, thoughtless, and unconcerned about their consequences? Most certainly. But stupid? Not a bloody one.

Annoyed that Jack still hadn't replied, the god booted him in the shin. When that didn't work, he summoned a bucket of water.

"Last chance," he said as he raised it over Jack's head.

He looked for any sign of movement. A twitch of the finger, a flutter of the eyelids, a subtle rise of the chest. Jack would never stay dead for long, and as soon as his nostrils flared, his rebirth would come quickly.

Loki waited until his son took a ragged breath and then grinning, he threw the whole bucket at his face.

Jack woke with a curse, frustrated beyond all hell. It wasn't the cold water in his face that irritated him nor the metal bucket that soon followed. It was the bloody knife sticking out of his chest. The one his father hadn't bothered to remove. The one Charlie had so generously placed there. Thor's balls, she'd stabbed him! She'd freaking stabbed him.

Her. His mate.

*Our mate.*

*Your mate,* Jack spat. He didn't want her anymore. He hoped she'd fall down a hole and break her neck. Better yet, he prayed she'd get ripped apart like a rabbit by the svein. Anything to get her crazy, infuriating ass out of his life.

The stack of lies burned a hole in his chest, but Jack ignored the discomfort. Besides, it was probably the bloody knife he was feeling anyway. The one she had freaking used to stab him, to twist into his heart and kill him.

Scowling, Jack sat up and wrapped a hand around the hilt. His father snickered in anticipation. Jack glowered in return. Then with a deep breath, he tightened his grip and pulled.

*"Mother. Fucker!"*

A further hiss of profanities erupted like a volcano. Toppling backward, Jack clutched at his chest. Blood seeped through his fingers, gushing with a force that nearly had him dying all over again.

*Damn the woman!*

*Fuck the woman,* the *thing* instantly corrected, but for some reason, Jack wasn't quite convinced they were on the same page. Probably because of its smug smile and blatant 'I told you so' eyes. Shooting it a dirty look, Jack crawled to his knees on a groan.

"Where is she?"

Loki shrugged. "How would I know? I arrived after

she'd already taken off." Holding out a hand, the god hauled his son to his feet. "But no worries. The hunt is normally better than the kill anyway."

He said it lightly, almost as a joke, but that didn't stop the *thing* from growling in warning. It didn't stop Jack from wanting to shove his father against the wall and threaten to cut off his balls inch by precious inch.

It was infuriating how much he still wanted her. She'd actually stabbed him in the chest, had twisted the knife until he'd died. He shouldn't be partially relieved at her betrayal; he should be completely pissed. And yet, here he was, still filled with an overwhelming desire to go after her. To claim her. To have her as his own.

Scowling, Jack stumbled down the cave. His father walked effortlessly beside him, and that pissed him the hell off.

"You could've taken out the fucking knife," he spat.

Loki shrugged. "I figured it served you right. Getting stabbed like that. She didn't even come at you from the back! So what did she do? Show you her boobs?"

When Jack looked away, the god chuckled. "Did you at least get to second base?" At his son's tic of the jaw, Loki howled with laughter, then slapped him on the back. "You are pathetic. Absolutely freaking pathetic."

"Just shut up and go after her kid."

Still laughing, Loki nodded. "Of course. Is there any particular way you want me to kill it? Or shall I bring it back for you to do yourself?"

In an instant, the *thing* ripped free. It shoved its nose inches from the god's face. Eyes burning with the fires of damnation, it bared its teeth with a snarl.

*He is not to be harmed.*

Though it spoke telepathically, the entire cave shook with its demand.

*But his mother –*

*Is. Our. Mate.*

With each word, its eyes blazed and it emitted a low growl. Seeing the stubbornness in its gaze, Loki sighed and held up his hands.

*Fine, but if you go after her like that, she'll die of a heart attack.*

The *thing* snorted. *Scared of me, father?*

It didn't need the god to answer to know the truth. There wasn't a single deity alive that didn't fear him. Ignoring the sudden pang of loneliness, the *thing* stepped aside so Jack could take back control. Now was not the time for its own issues. Their mate was out there, alone and afraid. She needed them whether she realized it or not.

"Bring him back here," Jack commanded as soon as he'd formed. "His name's Tony. Looks like this." He shifted into the boy, then back again. "Oh, and grab his finger too, will you? It's framed. Last seen on the western side, third floor, fifth window from the front."

His father rolled his eyes. "You do recall she stabbed you?" he said. "In the heart. Killed you actually."

"Really? I had no idea. It's not like I have a gaping bleeding hole in my chest or anything."

"Wow, someone's risen from the wrong side of life."

With a roll of his eyes, Jack turned to face his father. When Loki didn't stop beside him, he grabbed his arm with an exasperated grunt.

"She didn't call my cousin," he explained.

"And?" his father stressed.

"And that means she's not working with them. Otherwise, she would've known, this" –he waved at his wound– "wouldn't have killed me. Well, not for good anyway. "

Loki raised an eye. "And that's why you're so happy jolly?"

"Yes. No. Fuck, I don't know."

He ran a hand through his hair, trying hard to discern what was at the heart of his raging emotions. For fifteen thousand years, Jack had been alone. He had basked in his bachelorhood with no intention of ever leaving it. Now all of a sudden, within a few measly hours, he was committed to a person who hated him.

Thor's balls, he wanted everything back to how it was. Nothing but a simple existence where everything was easy...and empty.

"All I know is I want to try. Like you did with the crow lady."

"You do remember how that ended?" Loki said. But beneath his teasing tone was a fleeting glimpse of pain and regret. Morrighan had been his father's one true love...and his greatest hate.

"Yeah, but I also know you don't regret the small time you had with her."

For a moment, his father's permanent grin faded. The spark of mischief died from Loki's eyes. His shoulders, always so light and airy, now sagged with emotions too heavy to carry.

"I'll save the boy." Forcing a smile back onto his lips, Loki punched his son in the shoulder. "In the meantime, try not to get killed. Again."

"Yeah," Jack said dryly. "I'm hoping for a better outcome this time."

"You'll get it." Loki pulled him into a hug, patted his back, and then added, "If only because you can't do any worse than dying."

With a roar of laughter, the god vanished.

Shaking his head, Jack called out anyway. "It's really

freaking lame to laugh at your own jokes!"

He waited a second even though he knew he wouldn't get a reply. The pause gave him the time he needed to settle his frantic nerves. Rubbing at his chest, Jack took a deep breath and blew it out again.

Thor's balls, he had to be the biggest idiot alive.

What made him think he could possibly convince Charlie to spend her life with him – her very short life – after he had kidnapped her and left her child to die?

Mouth dry, Jack ran a hand through his hair. He wasn't surprised it was shaking. His whole body was. Adrenaline and worry poured out of his every pore, making his stress levels rocket to new heights.

By the gods, this was insane.

*Relax*, the *thing* said confidently. *Charlie is our mate. She'll forgive us.*

A heavy pause.

*But just in case, why don't you summon some flowers and chocolate?*

# SEVENTEEN

"For fuck's sake!" Charlie screamed as she crawled back onto her feet. She'd been running for nearly an hour now, scrambling through tight holes and forcing herself to trudge through waist deep water. The memory of her nearly drowning and the fear of new monsters – neither had been easy to overcome.

But she'd ignored her scrapes and bruises and the flickering forms that were more than just shadows. She'd ignored the mini earthquake from a few minutes before, terrified that the cave was going to crash down around her. She had persevered for one reason and one reason only: stubborn hope. But now...

As Charlie stared at the same intersection she'd passed through five times already, she let loose a ragged scream.

*Fuck!* She was stuck in this blasted cave.

She was never going to see her son.

She had murdered for nothing.

Her mate's death had been for nothing.

Clamping down on her rising hysteria, Charlie tried to

build the cave system in her mind. But even with her photographic memory, she couldn't make heads or tails of this place. There were too many turns she hadn't yet taken, too many unknown options and routes she couldn't see. She was going to die in here. There were no ifs, ands, or buts about it.

Releasing a strangled cry that was halfway between a scream and a sob, Charlie hung her head in defeat. Tears glistened behind her eyes, but even as exhausted and fed up as she was, she refused to let them fall. There had to be a way out of here. There just had to be.

"Charlie?"

Closing her eyes, she bit back a groan. Great, now she was hallucinating. Could life not give her a break? One measly break? Out of all the people she could have imagined, why did it have to be him?

Her heart twisted with guilt. Her stomach lurched with nausea as she remembered the feel of the knife as it had slipped through his skin. It had gone in so easily. The only resistance had been when she'd scraped bone.

Swallowing, Charlie steeled herself to deal with her manifested guilt. Her hands curled for strength. With a deep breath, she turned to face her hallucination.

"I'm sorry, okay? But you asked for the impossible. I didn't have time to get you to trust me and I – Are those flowers?"

He smiled as he held them out. "Yes. Do you like them?"

Charlie stared at the bouquet in disbelief. Why would she imagine this? Him she understood because of her guilt, but him with flowers? There were so many different colors, shapes, and sizes that her head spun. Mouth dry, she realized she couldn't name a single bud. Hell, the majority of them, she'd never even seen before. *Why the hell does he have flowers?*

"Why the fuck do you have flowers?"

Fenrir blinked once, opened his mouth, then closed it again. With a huff of irritation, he chucked the bouquet on the ground. He mumbled something she didn't catch, then paused as if waiting for a reply.

Slowly, Charlie inched backward. She did not have the time to deal with this right now. Later, when she got out of this damn cave and saved Tony, she'd face her guilt. But right now, she just needed to get out of here. Feeling desperate, Charlie spun on her heels and slipped down a random passage.

"Wait!"

She ignored him. He wasn't even real. He was dead. She'd killed him. She'd plunged a knife into his chest and twisted it until he'd died. There was no way he was real.

So when his hand closed around her, Charlie did the only reasonable thing. She spun around and punched him in the face.

He stumbled back with a curse. Her fist dropped to her side. Her mouth fell open. Terror, surprise, disbelief – they crashed through her system like a million bolts of lightning.

Holy fucking shit. She'd hit him. She'd...hit...him. Her fist had crashed into his mouth, bruising her knuckles as she'd split his bottom lip. But that wasn't possible. She'd stabbed him in the heart, had twisted the knife until he died. Her hands shook as she remembered the feel of the blade and the horror in his eyes as she'd slammed it home.

Shaking her head, Charlie backed up a small step. He wasn't real. He couldn't be. She'd killed him. She'd –

"By the gods, kultara!" Fenrir's eyes twisted in pain and anger.

She took another step back, her heart beating wildly.

"How?"

But she didn't need him to answer; understanding dawned in an instant. The bastard had tricked her. The knife hadn't been real. Or he hadn't. Or hell, maybe neither of them had. Whatever had happened, he wasn't dead. He was pissed and he was coming for her and Charlie was an idiot for still standing here.

Lurching, she twisted around and ran for her life. She'd made it two steps, three, before he'd tackled her from behind. She kicked out with her legs, flailed at him with her arms, but none of it mattered. His grip never loosened and she knew she was going to die.

They hit the ground hard. A small crystal rammed into her shoulder. The pain flared to her elbow, but it was quickly forgotten as Fenrir crashed on top of her. She gritted her teeth as his weight crushed the air from her lungs. He muttered something beneath his breath. She didn't quite catch it, but his tone said that was probably for the best.

Throwing her head back, Charlie slammed it into his face. Before she could even think of doing anything else, he placed his forearm against her neck and pinned her to the ground.

His words barked harshly in her ear. "Godsdammit, kultara! For once in your life, stop being so fucking difficult!"

She tried to squirm free, but it was utterly hopeless. He had her completely pinned, completely at his mercy. She shook with the frustration and fear of it, but what could she do? Even if she managed to escape, he had the ability to chase her wherever she went. No hole would be too small for him, no distance too far. She was as good as dead, and there was nothing she could say or do that would change that. She might as well accept it and try to die with a bit of dignity.

"Thank you," he said.

"Fuck you," she replied.

He laughed harshly, then muttered something in a foreign tongue.

"If you're going to curse me, at least have the courage to do it in a language I understand," she spat. She wasn't quite sure what had pushed her into goading him, but to hell if she'd take it back.

He laughed again and then shifted his weight off her. Before she could scramble free, he flipped her over onto her back. His eyes danced with mischief as he lowered his head to hers.

Breath hitching, Charlie could only stare in silence. One inch and their lips would touch. One small shift and his mouth would feather across her skin like silk. His eyes burned her soul as a heated smile curved his lips.

"Do you really want to know what I said?"

She swallowed, barely registering he'd spoken. All she could think about was that he was on top of her. She could feel him everywhere and by God, she wanted to touch him. She wanted to run her hands down his back, wanted to learn every hard plane of his body. She wanted to grab his ass as she lifted her hips and wrapped her legs around him. The fact that she wanted him inside her, wanted his name screaming across her lips, caused her freeze. *What the fuck is wrong with me?*

The bond.

The mating bond was making her act like an idiot.

She tried to resist, but then he sucked in a sharp breath and her eyes focused on his lips. She could almost feel them pressing down on hers, rough and careless as he took her with an urgency that mirrored her own. Her breath escaped on quick exhales of excitement. Her lips parted in silent surrender.

Jack's nostrils flared. She could feel his cock swelling against her stomach, and a moan nearly escaped her then and there. His eyes fastened on her mouth, darkening with a need that left her trembling.

Mouth suddenly dry, Charlie instinctively darted her tongue out to wet her lips. It was only when he groaned that she realized her mistake. Her eyes widened at the intimate touch of his mouth. And then they drifted closed as Fenrir moved the scant distance he needed to fully claim her.

This was madness.

This was insanity.

And yet, this was utter perfection.

Fireworks had nothing on the hot electricity shooting through her. It spread from his mouth to every inch of her sensitive body. The feel of his clothes as they brushed against her breasts might as well have been his hands. She felt him everywhere...and yet not nearly everywhere enough.

In an attempt to deepen the kiss, Charlie lifted her chin ever so slightly. He hesitated for the barest of moments, his body as tense as steel. Then with a shattering of his control, Fenrir kissed her with a desperation she felt all the way down to her toes.

His tongue slid inside her mouth, ravaging the very depths of her soul. His hands slid up her sides, slowly learning the curves of her hips and the undersides of her breasts. The stark contrast between the touch of his hands and his mouth was an assault on her senses. His hands were exquisite, but his mouth was pure damnation.

Arching up on a moan, Charlie threaded her fingers through his hair. Her lips moved as feverishly as his did. Her tongue danced just as wickedly. For one glorious moment, she forgot all about the horrors of her life and simply *lived*.

His lips moved to her cheek, her ear, her neck. As she held him close, Fenrir worshiped her with his tongue and teeth and a desire that neither of them could deny.

But just as his hands moved up to cup her breasts. Just as his mouth whispered down past her collar bone. Just as he shifted his hips and tossed her into heaven, Fenrir cursed and rolled off her.

He didn't give her time to adjust before yanking her to her feet and tossing a pile of clothes at her. "Put these on."

She stared at him blankly, her mind still very much on cloud nine. Swearing, Fenrir grabbed the shirt off the pile and shoved it over her head.

With a gasp of horror, Charlie swatted his hands aside and stumbled back. She yanked down the shirt as shame flooded her cheeks. Dropping frantically, she reached for the underwear and hurriedly shoved them on.

Her hands shook as she did up the button on the pants, but it was nothing compared to the tremors racking her brain. What the fuck had just happened? He was the reason Tony had been left behind with a monster, the sole reason her heart was in a constant state of agony. He was the enemy, but one touch of his lips and she'd gone up in flames. Hell, she'd actually kissed him back!

"Charlie –"

She cut him off with a shake of the head. "I hate you."

"Godsdammit, Charlie, look at me."

Her hands fisted as she closed her eyes. She struggled to get her breathing back under control, then dutifully did as he'd requested. After all, he still held all the cards.

Fenrir looked at her for a heated second, then swore. He ran a hand through his hair, pacing first one way and then the other. "Shit," he said. "This is not how I wanted to tell you."

Tossing his head back, he looked up to the ceiling as if for guidance. He exhaled strongly, pinched the bridge of his nose, and then turned around to face her. "Look, I know trust is an issue between us, but I need you to trust me right now."

"Go to Hell."

"Great, glad we got that settled," he said dryly. Then before she could say anything else, he blurted, "I have your son. Or I will soon. My father–"

"*You what?*"

He winced at her sudden shriek, then held up both hands for patience. It was only due to sheer desperation that she obeyed.

"I don't have time to explain as we're about to have visitors, but I swear to you, Charlie, I will bring him back to you."

Swallowing the hope threatening to rise, Charlie shook her head. "But I tried to kill you. Why would you help me?"

His eyes softened. "I'm helping you, kultara, because you killed me. If you had really been working for my uncle, then you would've called my cousin after that first twist of the knife. Instead, you ran."

"I don't understand."

"I know." He smiled. "That's how I know I can trust you." The smile faded as he cocked his head to the left. Hearing something she couldn't, Fenrir muttered beneath his breath and then crossed the distance between them. He reached for her, but when she flinched away, he let his hands drop in frustration.

"I'm not going to hurt you, Charlie. I trust you're not working for my uncle and I meant what I said. I will give you whatever you want, but right now I need you to do something for me. Deal?"

She nodded jerkily, her throat too tight to speak.

He exhaled in relief. "Good. Now pay attention; we only have a few minutes to spare. My name is Jack. You didn't jump into the river and I never pulled you out of it. I have only transed twice this entire time. Once as an illyra eagle and again as a cercope when I saved you from the charybdis. I can't conjure up actual items and you didn't stab me with a knife. And I definitely, definitely did not come back to life. Do you understand?"

He swore in another tongue at her silence. "Dammit, Charlie, please. I need you to tell me you understand."

She blinked dumbly. "I stabbed you?"

He gritted his teeth. "Yes," he finally said.

"But how –"

"I swear I'll explain later, kultara, but right now I need you to trust me. Now can you repeat everything I said?"

When she only blinked again, he pressed, "What's my name, Charlie?"

Faintly, the sound of voices rose up in the distance.

No, not voices she realized with horror. Screams.

As terror gripped her heart, Charlie stepped back and shook her head.

"Dammit, kultara, this is for Tony. He needs you to pull yourself together."

She shook her head again, but this time in an attempt to focus. "Jack," she breathed. "Your name's Jack."

By the time Charlie repeated all the lies he wanted her to tell, her breathing was back under control. Her mind was still a whirlwind of confusion, but through it all one thought reigned.

He was going to save Tony.

And for that, she'd do anything.

# EIGHTEEN

The *thing* growled deep in Jack's chest. Low and feral, it was aimed at the mouth of the cave. Though neither it nor Jack could see the approaching men and women, the *thing* still knew exactly who was about to enter.

Crouching low in preparation to strike, its fur stood high up on end as it released another growl. The idea of anyone trespassing into its haven was enough to make it territorial. The lethal group running their way, though, they were enough to make it feral. Lunging, the *thing* vowed, *I'll kill them all.*

Gritting his teeth, Jack barely managed to keep the beast from rising. Even so, his eyes blazed with the fires of Niflhel and his face half-twisted into the burning ethereal of the *thing's* form. Luckily, Charlie was staring in the direction of the faint screams, too distracted to notice.

As soon as he managed to shove it back down, Jack pinned it with a scowl. *Behave. If she sees you, she'll run screaming and you know it. Mate or not, no one looks at you without fear.*

There was a flash of pain, so alien to the normal anger of the *thing,* that Jack nearly apologized for being harsh. He didn't though. If he gave it any leeway, it would slaughter his teammates one by one. It didn't matter that Jack had fought side by side with them for decades; all the *thing* saw were potential threats to its mate.

After all, Rogan was tasked with bringing Charlie in for interrogation. Matakyli was a reckless demoness who had it out for Jack and wouldn't mind using his mate to hurt him. The third, Aisla, was a lady with a temper who could match even the gods' and right now, she was pissed. The fourth, Cariad, was a smoking hot incubus who could melt even an icy kultara, and the fifth –

Jack snorted. *So there's the real reason.* He would have laughed had the *thing* not been serious about killing them all for it.

Shaking his head, he turned his attention to Charlie. "Come on."

When he grabbed her hand, his eyes heated at the spark of electricity. He knew she felt it too with the way her lips parted with desire. He wanted so badly to pull her into his arms and finish what they'd started, but the slight panic in her gaze held him off.

Her body might crave him, but it seemed her mind had yet to agree. Irritated, Jack dragged her along a bit faster than she could walk.

When they made it to the mouth of the cave, Charlie made a noise deep in her throat. It was a sound of sheer frustration, Jack knew, but that didn't stop him from recalling the softer moans she had been making earlier.

"How?" she wondered, a bit breathless.

Jack nearly pulled her back into his arms before he realized his folly. Charlie was asking about how they had managed to get here so quickly, not how her moans were throwing his mind into the gutter. And her breathless wonder hadn't been out of desire for his kisses, but because she'd had to jog all this time to keep up with him.

Smiling innocently despite her suspicious glare, Jack pretended as if he hadn't been about to kiss her.

"Aurora's Castle was designed to lose people," he cheerfully explained. "Only those that can see through its illusions can navigate its tunnels."

Her eyes blazed with understanding. "You wanted me to stab you. You didn't conjure up that knife to threaten me with it. You did it as an excuse so I wouldn't think it was a trap when you dropped it beside me. Holy shit, it was all a fucking test, wasn't it?"

His grin widened. "And damned if I'm not happy you passed."

"Do you always come back from the dead? Even with a beheading?"

Jack laughed, well aware of what she was thinking. "Been eaten, crushed, and yes, beheaded. Always come back, love." This time he did kiss her. It was just a peck on the lips, but it was enough to make her sputter.

Gods, she was cute when she was angry.

"So is that the trade?" she seethed. "Sex for my son?"

Jack's humor faded in an instant. His eyes flashed dangerously as he leaned in. Eyes widening, Charlie took a hurried step back. Her throat worked nervously as she darted her gaze left and right to see if she could escape. *Not fucking likely*, Jack thought.

Advancing with all the deadliness of a predator, Jack forced her up against a wall. He placed a hand beside her head and smiled wickedly when her breath hitched in response. Ever so slowly, he placed his other hand on the wall.

Her breaths were coming rapidly now. Her heart was

beating so hard he could nearly hear it. He let his eyes drift to the pulse at her neck before lifting them back up to hers. He didn't have to speak to convey his point, but he did it anyway, wanting to see the acknowledgment in her eyes.

He leaned in, his lips a bear whisper away from hers. "We both know this has nothing to do with your son, don't we, kultara? Or are you too much of a coward to admit you enjoyed it? That you enjoyed my tongue in your mouth and my hands on your —"

She reached up to slap him, but he grabbed her wrist before it could land. He tugged it to his mouth. His lips feathered across her palm before moving up and sucking on one of her fingers.

Her eyes dilated in arousal. He might have mistaken it for anger had her body not betrayed her in the most natural of ways. Her hips bucked ever so slightly, and that was all the encouragement Jack needed.

The first kiss had been one of hesitate passion, an exploration of her body and its desires. This one was the complete opposite. It was sinful and it was wicked and it was heavenly bliss. His tongue pushed inside her mouth, not asking this time, but taking.

He pressed his body into hers. He dragged her hand down to the ridge of his pants and rubbed it against his erection. He hissed with pleasure, and she made a little noise in the back of her throat.

Moving his hands from the wall, Jack palmed both of her breasts. He barely bit back a curse at the feel of her shirt, having much preferred her naked flesh from before. Growling, he yanked up the material and thanked his good sense not to have given her a bra. When he teased her nipples, she arched her hips on a moan and her hand tightened around his cock in pure bliss.

Desperate to feel her everywhere, Jack trailed a hand down her stomach. He hesitated at the top of her pants, but when she made no move to stop him, he slipped a finger under the waistband. His whole body tensed with that single act. If she pushed him away now, he'd need every ounce of his strength to listen.

Her hips bucked, lifting toward him and nearly making him feral. Ripping at her button, he pulled down her zipper, then dropped to his knees and kissed her. She jerked against his mouth, and Jack cursed that he hadn't thought to remove her panties first.

He wanted her taste inside him. His tongue, his fingers, his —

*Oh, for fuck's sake!*

Swearing at the feral scream in the distance, Jack closed his eyes with great regret. Though it had sounded well outside of the cave and its hundred foot deep wall of thorns, the cry was still close enough to be a problem.

As another shout sounded, Jack reminded himself that that was his team out there. Nevertheless, he was more than tempted to throw up an illusion so he could continue on as if he hadn't heard. For not only were his balls so blue they were in threat of falling off, but he also feared that if he let her go now, she would do everything she could to stay out of his reach.

She wouldn't even have to try that hard. Once they got back to base, Tegan would want them separated: her for questioning and him for debriefing. Then he'd be back out on another mission, no doubt, and she'd be on her own, locked away for her own good.

The *thing* growled at the idea of her being held by anyone and once again Jack had to fight it from rising.

Swearing for the umpteenth time that day, he rose to his feet and kissed Charlie soundly on the mouth. When he pulled away, it was with great reluctance but no less commitment to do so. He might be fine with leaving his teammates at the drop of a hat, but to hell if he was going to sit by while they died a brutal death.

Even if sitting by felt really fucking good.

Scowling, Jack pulled her over to the thorn guarded entrance. He didn't wait for her eyes to refocus from being kissed senseless. There wasn't any time for that. Instead, he jumped right into it, shoving his hand into the thorns until one drew blood. Instantly, he jumped back and pulled Charlie with him.

She screamed when a black tentacle whipped out of nowhere, greedily seeking their flesh. With a hiss of outrage, the creature sucked up the few drops of his blood and then disappeared back into its home of thorns.

"Right, so now you know," Jack said. "Don't go into the thorns."

And with that he transed into a field mouse and scurried into the thorns.

# NINETEEN

Rogan leaped at his target. His arms wrapped around her waist as he propelled them both to the ground. A twist in the air had him landing on his side, and he quickly rolled her beneath him. Her eyes burned with a demonic hatred, but she didn't dare move. She might've suddenly been thrust into the role of captain on her team, but he still outranked her by several tiers.

"Doona make Mauvali's sacrifice meaningless," he ordered roughly.

Aisla bared her teeth as she struggled with her rage. Her and Mauvali had been as close as sisters. Some rumors even claimed that they would've been lovers had they not worked on the same Elv've'Norc team.

Rogan wasn't one for idle gossip, but as he stared into Aisla's eyes, he knew that that one at least had been true.

"Aisla," he snapped with clear command. "We are to stand up and run. Do ye understand?"

Fierce pain pinched her features as she struggled with her decision. Then she gave a sharp nod, and he was off her immediately, dragging her to her feet beside him. As Mauvali's screams merged with the frenzied howls of excitement behind them, Rogan pulled Aisla forward with ruthless determination.

Later, when he was back in the arms of his lifemate, the water elementalist would mourn the loss of the two comrades who had died tonight. But until then he had to keep it together or no one was going to make it out of here alive.

Galvanor was once again infected with the Plague. He had to resist using his powers in order to stop the deadly disease from spreading past the point of recovery. Kyli was missing an arm, it having been torn off by the claws of a wolf. She would have died had it not been for Mauvali's team arriving at exactly the right time...and the wrong.

Elizabeth's power had grabbed hold of them as soon as they'd landed, and it'd been a mindless slaughter ever since. The four werewolves Galvanor had brought in to fight Sebastian had turned on Rico, the werewolf on the other team. He was an alpha like no other, powerful enough to defy a full blood moon even in the face of serious temptation. But one push of Elizabeth's power and he'd dropped to his knees and changed. As he'd taken on the werewolves to force their submission, Sebastian had turned his full attention to Matakyli.

He'd phased to rip out her neck, but Dominix had flashed there just in time. She was an echidna, a direct descendant of the Mother of Monsters and her retaliation had been brutal. Under the power of Elizabeth, Matakyli had grabbed Galvanor and run, unwilling to risk his life when he was no longer able to protect himself. They hadn't stopped running since, and Rogan was glad for it. He was absolutely certain that they would have died had they stayed.

For a moment, it looked like they might have had a chance to retreat without casualties. The five werewolves were all occupied with each other. Mauvali, a strong telepath and captain of the other team, was also infected, but she was still willing to use her powers. As it was her first time in contact with the disease, she had a healthier immune system in which to fight it. For there was no building up an immunity to the Deusychosis Plague; each run in with it would only weaken one's defenses.

The persapic had forced Lamia to her knees as Aisla, a young fae, had sprinted over to finish the vampire with her blades. She had moved with wicked speed, but Rico had moved faster. He'd forced the four werewolves into submission within seconds, and now had them turning upon whoever was closest. Unfortunately, Ruthnor, their teleporter, had been unlucky enough to be that someone.

Within a second, Mauvali had turned her attention to controlling the wolves. Lamia had attacked Aisla with her claws and fangs, tearing deep into her side. Cariad had rushed to Aisla's aid, barely managing to save her from certain death. Rico had turned on Dominix as the other wolves were forced upon Sebastian. The vampire killed two of the pups and then Elizabeth...Elizabeth had changed the game.

Rogan's lips tightened at the memory, and he dragged Aisla through the woods at a greater speed. He would not lose anyone else tonight. Mauvali's sacrifice would not mean nothing. On this, he swore.

But as the persapic's cries finally stopped and the howls increased tenfold, Rogan doubted he'd be able to see his promise through. The wolves that chased them would not stop no matter how many times their hearts were stabbed or their limbs were ripped from their bodies.

Death simply could not claim a body twice.

Jack knew he was about to enter a war zone. The screams he'd heard had been those of agonized pain and loss, of furious anger and vengeance. He could smell the sickly sweetness of the blood roses as their pollen erupted into the air. Their roots had finally claimed there was enough iron in the ground for them to grow well, and the frantic races between prey and predator would allow their pollen to go far. The overwhelming sweetness of it clogged Jack's nose, and he almost missed the underlying scent of death.

He paused in his race through the thorns. The beast shifted inside him as it too thought the smell was wrong.

His sixth sense tightening in horror, Jack sprinted as fast as he could. He quickly found the svein lair and pursed his lips at the size of it. Dominix would only be able to phase one person in at a time. He only hoped it would be enough.

After marking the area with his scent, Jack raced out of the thorns and transed back into himself. Even though a vampire would have given him increased speed, power, and agility, the werewolves had been created solely for hunting bloodsuckers. Their bite was made poisonous to them. The vampire's scent drove them mad, increasing their testosterone and adrenaline until they were near impossible for one to defeat. And though shifting into a dragon or echidna would have been a much more effective choice, Jack wasn't supposed to have enough power left to do that.

These might be his comrades' lives on the line, but he would not give up Charlie's safety for theirs. Already, Odin would have sensed the release of the *thing*. He had an all-seeing eye and was most likely already searching the area for the new face of his hated nephew. Loki had assured Jack he'd cloaked the area, but it was only a matter of time before Odin discovered who was to blame. Jack couldn't risk giving him anymore clues than he already had.

"We are to stand up and run. Do ye understand?"

As Rogan's voice drifted out from under the screams of the night, Jack turned his attention in its direction. He strained his eyes for the slightest of movements, his body pumping with adrenaline as the *thing* moved restlessly inside him. It didn't like being away from its mate with the smell of death so near, but nor did it want to leave anything alive that could hurt her.

With the coldness of a killer, Jack watched as the first shape came into view. Matakyli raced straight at him in full demon mode. Her right arm was missing, torn off at the shoulder to reveal a ragged mess of flesh and muscle. Her other arm was pinned to her chest, and it was only upon closer inspection that Jack realized why. She was carrying her lifemate, Galvanor, who was unconscious and bleeding from every orifice in his face.

Coldly, Jack moved his attention past them, seeking out the woman that could save them all. He spotted her at the back of the group. Though she was a good hundred yards away and mostly hidden by trees and shadows, her monstrous form was unmistakable.

Towering on six limbs, she stood as tall as a giraffe. The back four looked like tarantula legs and carried the whole of her weight. In contrast, her front two were sharp and curved like scythes. They were twice as long and forced her back to permanently arch so she stood like a praying mantis. Large poisonous fangs protruded from her mouth and eighteen eyes sat on her bulbous head.

Leaping into action, Jack hurried into the woods. He almost faltered when he passed Aisla and Rogan. She had swollen eyes and dried tears on her face, whereas he had the look of someone who would be forever haunted by the choices he'd made.

Pushing on, Jack sniffed the air for the scents of the other people who should have been here. When he caught Mauvali's trail so entwined with death, he knew the truth. His heart twisted, then tightened like a vice when he couldn't find a trace of Ruthnor nor Rico.

With a burst of speed, Jack made it to Dominix. She looked at him with one of her eyes as the others stayed scanning the trees surrounding them. She was on high alert and one of her back legs was bent at a useless angle.

Cariad stood beside her. The golden haired incubus shouldn't have been here though. He'd been forced to take leave after the massacre at Xi'aghn. Jack, however, was glad that he was. They could use any amount of help they could get.

"Do you have it?" Cariad snapped as soon as the trickster got close. The *thing* bristled at the anger in the man's voice, not liking any hint of a threat where its mate was concerned.

Jack didn't either, but he knew the anger came from stress and not a desire to harm her.

"Yes," he said as he turned to Dominix. "Phase the wounded to my scent. There's only room to take one at a time, and you have to be spot on and quick with your phasing." He didn't bother explaining that if the thorns didn't rip them to shreds, then the svein would. He'd marked right in the middle of their lair, it being the only clearing in the thorns. Echidnas couldn't phase long distances. Rather, they were only able to jump in short bursts. Jack just hoped that the distance he'd marked was one she could make.

As soon as Dominix phased to Galvanor, Jack returned his attention to Cariad.

"What are they?" he demanded and the incubus' face turned grim.

"Zombies."

Jack's eyes narrowed. Zombies didn't exist even in their worlds. But then he remembered the memophoric photos he'd been given about the attack on Xi'aghn. Elizabeth had raised the dead and it was with them that she had annihilated Cariad's team.

"Shit. How many?"

Before he could reply, a bulking form barreled into Jack's chest. It was all snapping teeth and slicing claws, and he only barely managed to keep it from ripping off his head. He transed underneath it, turning into a fly, before reverting back into himself behind it.

He threw up cover around him and Cariad even as he distracted the wolf with the illusion of a vampire. The lycan jumped on it without hesitation, and soon, three more barreled into the fray.

Jack went to hack at the wolves while they were distracted, but Cariad roughly pulled him back.

"It won't matter. Their hearts are gone and one's even missing its fucking head."

Jack stared in horror as he realized the incubus was right. The werewolf's head was completely gone and yet it still sliced at the illusion before it.

*Let me out!*

*You can't kill them.*

Desperate to protect their mate, the *thing* burst free with a surge of power. Jack barely managed to throw up an illusion before Cariad could witness its demonic form. The *thing* ripped into the wolves with such ferocity that their bodies soon resembled confetti. And yet the pieces still moved, twitching on the ground like bloody worms. It was enough to make even Jack feel sick and he'd seen it all.

He took one last look at the slaughter and then chased after Cariad, who was already running toward the rest of the team. The incubus thought Jack was right alongside him thanks to the illusion, and the trickster slyly stepped into its place as he waved his magic away.

Galvanor and Matakyli were already gone, and Jack dared to breathe a sigh of relief. Hopefully that meant the phasing was going well enough. As if summoned by his thoughts, the echidna reappeared before them.

Her entire body was covered in fist-sized wounds. It was as if she'd been skinned by a cookie cutter. Cariad, Aisla, and Rogan looked at her with confusion, but Jack knew what had done this to her. The svein must have managed to grab hold of her as she'd entered their lair. With their lines of mouths on the underside of their tentacles, they'd sucked off neat circles of her flesh.

Ignoring the questioning stares, Dominix spread out her two blade-like arms. The majority of her eyes looked at Aisla as she expected her to step inside her embrace. The fae did so without hesitation, completely trusting that the echidna wouldn't accidentally behead her with her arms. They closed around her like a cocoon and then the two were gone. In another four seconds, Dominix was back with more holes in her flesh.

Once the two men had stepped into her arms, Jack transed back into a field mouse and raced through the thorns. He could feel the tension in the air as the svein moved restlessly around him. They had already fed a great deal tonight, but their gluttony urged them on.

Darting under their tentacles, careful to keep himself

hidden under his magic, Jack finally made it out the other side. He shifted as soon as he was through, and his eyes hardened considerably. He threw up a cloaking spell over his face, certain his eyes were now a blazing red. His mate's scent was in the air; rich and heady, it signaled her readiness to mate.

Except it wasn't because of him.

As Charlie watched the incubus with clear lust in her eyes, Jack was overcome by a fierce flare of jealousy. The *thing* bared its teeth and he almost did the same. It was only Charlie's sudden glower at the man that stopped him from doing something foolish.

"Cut it out," she snapped. Cariad raised an eyebrow but did as she'd requested. The incubus' power didn't vanish completely, but it did ebb enough that Charlie's heat was no longer flooding the place.

"What happened?" Jack asked to distract the both of them. "Where's Ruthnor and Rico?"

He'd held a glimmer of hope that the two were alive, but at the increased tension in the cave, that hope died a sudden, painful death.

"Rico's still alive," Aisla snarled. Her hands bunched at her sides as she pierced everyone with a fierce glare. Even though no one made to argue, she pressed on all the same. "He is!" she shouted. "He's survived numerous moons before and he'll do it again! He's alive, so stop mourning him like he isn't!"

Her eyes burned with tears, and she whirled on her heels so they couldn't see them fall. A fae did not cry, especially not a royal like her.

Jack turned to Rogan. The elementalist looked as if he'd aged a century in the last few hours. His eyes were beyond tired and his shoulders stooped with a weight too heavy to carry.

"How's Galvanor?" Rogan asked Matakyli. Despite his fatigue, his voice was still strong. Rogan would not crack under the weight of his responsibility until everyone was safe...or no longer able to be saved.

"The bleeding won't stop." In contrast, the demoness' voice was choked and raspy. It was the very definition of desperate.

"What's wrong with him?" Jack asked.

"He has the bloody Plague," Cariad bit out. Thick, heavy tension rolled off his shoulders as he stood with his arms crossed and his feet a shoulder width apart. It was obvious he had not yet recovered from his teammates' deaths at Xi'aghn and tonight was taking its toll.

Jack shifted uneasily as his thoughts turned to concern for his father. There were only a handful of things that could kill a god and the Deusychosis Plague was one of them. It was why the deities had sided with Sebastian all those years ago – right up until the moment the vampire had destroyed Perspic and trapped the plague inside it. No longer of any use, they'd swiftly abandoned him to his own devices.

Jack should have remembered to tell his father about the plague's reappearance, but with everything else that had happened, he'd simply forgotten. Throat tight, the trickster cloaked himself from his comrades and conjured *Sannurthogn* into his hands. He curled the device around his ear and waited anxiously for the call to go through.

But as always, his father didn't answer.

# TWENTY

The table crashed into the ground. The chair slammed into the wall. Sebastian phased to the other side of the study and grabbed his bloodkin by the throat. He squeezed the air from Lamia's lungs, delighting in the discoloration of her face.

"You knew better than to fail me," he seethed.

Lamia didn't bother to mouth an apology. She merely stared at him with her cold, dead eyes. As much as he wanted to watch her beg, Sebastian knew she never would. Their parents had seen to that within her first few years of life. Locked in a cell, her body sold for every twisted pleasure, Lamia had learned in the cruelest of ways that weakness was never to be shown.

Snarling, Sebastian tossed her into a wall. Then he turned sharply to his left and smiled at the trembling woman in the corner. Now she was much more fun. Not as good as Charlie had been whenever he'd dangled her son in her face, but Elizabeth was better than his useless bloodkin.

His dimples flashing, Sebastian crooked a finger in her direction. She made a delightful whimpering sound as she scurried to his side. He liked to think that even without the curse forcing her to obey his every command, she was now so broken that she would obey him regardless. The thought lifted his spirits a little.

But then Sophina had to go and ruin it. "*Don't do this,*" she pleaded on Elizabeth's behalf. "*You're a good man.*"

The sound of her voice was as desired as it was hated. Sophina's conscience had disappeared from his drunken thoughts during the fighting, but now she'd blissfully – frustratingly returned.

Furious at the turmoil she was causing him, Sebastian grabbed the new stump that was Liz's arm and squeezed. Her scream was euphonious. Enthralled, he increased the pressure until she fell to her knees.

It was funny really. When Sebastian had watched the echidna cut off his descendant's arm, he'd been furious. Now he almost felt in her debt. Of course that wouldn't save the echidna from dying by his hand, but maybe he'd only keep her alive for a year instead of decades.

The thought of revenge made him smile.

If only he didn't have to wait so long.

Frustrated, Sebastian kicked Elizabeth in the gaping wound in her side. She didn't even scream when his foot got caught under her rib cage.

*What a waste of good effort.* He scowled.

"*You used to sing when you chased lightning bugs and every time you watched a romantic play, you'd cry. So how can this be the man you've become?*"

Sophina's voice was full of pained sorrow. He could almost see her heart breaking, and his chest tightened in response. It had always killed him when she'd become this upset.

First, her lips would purse, tightening with the refusal to wobble. Then, her eyes would fill with tears she tried so hard not to let fall. And when she was truly close to breaking, she would look off into the distance, unable to bear even seeing the thing that had hurt her. He'd never managed to last long after that.

And now, as if nothing had changed between them, Sebastian's heart wrenched in agony.

*I'm sorry, Soph. Help me, please.*

Jerking back, the vampire shook his head with a growl. Those weren't his thoughts. He believed in what he was doing, had come to terms with his sacrifices millennia ago. He would be the savior of the helpless and the damned. He would be the god who listened to the cries of the desperate. He would be strong for those who were weak. It was what he had sworn.

*Don't you see?* Sophina sighed sadly. *You've become the very monster you swore to eradicate.*

"Enough!"

Elizabeth flinched at his feet. Even Lamia looked at him nervously. Their fear should have been heavenly to witness, but instead, it made his stomach twist and his shoulders feel weighted by lead.

Baring his fangs, Sebastian battled for the control he knew he was losing. His fists tightened as he stalked toward the door. His eyes burned with pure malice as he refused to buckle under Sophina's strain.

"Find her," he seethed as he yanked open the door. Then he turned to face Lamia with hatred in his eyes. "Do not fail me again."

She inclined her head. By the time she lifted it, he was gone.

If only Sophina would leave so easily.

Loki smirked as he watched the vampire battle with what he'd assumed were his own drunken creations. Sebastian might be one of the most ruthless mortals alive, but it seemed even he was susceptible to the power of guilt and all the flaws that came with it. Had he not been consumed by his personal demons, the bloodsucker might have realized those voices inside his head, the ones he thought were there because he'd had a bit too much to drink, were actually the creations of a telepath. And a telepath within this very castle as well.

Loki's grin widened. It had been decades since he'd witnessed such underhanded mischief. Had his eldest son not been going through a midlife crisis, he would have been tempted to hang around and watch as the chaos unfolded. After all, he wasn't the Trickster God of the Aesir for nothing.

*Then again*, Loki reasoned as he watched Sebastian fall further under the telepath's tricks, *Jack is being a tad ungrateful...*

Ordering him about, snapping at him for not removing a measly knife. Telling him his jokes were lame. *Calling me all the bloody time,* the god dryly added as his phone rang for the umpteenth time. He promptly sent it to voicemail.

*Really.* He huffed. *He should show me more respect.* Especially since Loki had never given in to his temptation of selling him to Poseidon. That transaction would have gifted him with some serious good coin. Not to mention, favors. Loki loved being owed favors.

Granted, Loki was the whole reason his son was wanted by the Graecian god in the first place. Then again, Jack *had* been a fully grown adult when he'd stolen the

Trident, so...

With that issue now nicely cleared up, he summoned a bucket of caramel popcorn and a magical chaise. He laid down with a smile, threw a handful of the salty sweetness into his mouth, and watched gleefully as Sebastian got played like a fiddle.

*Do you remember us at all?* she asked mournfully. *Do you ever think about me?*

*How can I not?* the vampire growled as he strolled drunkenly through the castle. *You won't go away.*

His chest tightened and his breaths came out hard. The thought of Sophina leaving him again was as painful as it was ecstatic.

*I didn't mean here, right now when you've had too much to drink in this haunted place. I mean when you're out there, all on your own. Do you ever think about us?*

*Why would I?* he snapped. *You're dead.*

He waited expectantly for a reply, then started to panic when none came. *What could I possibly gain from that? I lived with my guilt for centuries. You think it didn't kill me that I couldn't save them? That Erin died in my hands, and you –*

He cut himself off with a strangled cry. He didn't notice the tears running down his face, too lost in his past to be aware of the present. Nor did he notice the direction his feet were taking him. Perhaps if he had, he might have stopped. Then again, perhaps not. As much as he hated being harassed by Sophina's memory, he also yearned for her voice. For the first time in millennia, he could listen to her without hearing her screams.

His tears fell quicker now.

*When I what?* Sophina pressed. Her voice held an

element of ice to it. Sebastian closed his eyes in shame.

*We both know what happened.*

*I want to hear you say it.*

*Why?*

But whatever reason she gave, Sebastian didn't hear it. His entire attention was on the door now in front of him. It filled his thoughts, poisoned his heart with shame, and pounded loudly in his ears until he couldn't hear anything else. The tempo rose, his mouth ran dry, and his throat closed in pain. Falling to his knees, Sebastian let loose a ragged scream.

And somewhere in the dark, watching with vivid eyes, a soul smiled cruelly. After all of these long hard years, they would finally have their justice.

If only they hadn't had to wait so long.

Sebastian didn't know how many hours had passed as he sat there crumbled on the floor. All he knew was that by the time he rose, his voice was gone and his eyes were dry. He had no more tears left inside him. No more pain.

Hollow, he crawled to his feet and reached out a shaky hand. He hesitated a long moment before turning the handle and stepping into the half decorated room.

The walls were a pale blue. The skirting boards were a warm gray. There was a bespoke rocking chair in the corner, so ancient that Sebastian feared a single push would break it. But it was the dusty crate in the corner that grabbed his attention.

Sophina had used it as a placement piece while she'd waited for him to finish the real thing. On top of it, laid a hoop with seven delicately carved ravens hanging from it on silver ribbons. Tentatively, Sebastian picked it up and held it close.

*This was supposed to be our starting over,* he accused. *Why didn't you stay?*

He waited, but Sophina didn't answer. His drunken memories of her had quieted long ago. All he was left with now was the black heart in his chest, the first (and last) mobile he'd ever carved, and the haunted memories of a child he had killed. His child. Sophina's child.

It seemed there were tears still left inside him after all.

# TWENTY-ONE

Charlie eyed the newcomers, trying to discern what species everyone was. In addition to the obvious drazic demoness, she had already identified the incubus and echidna. The latter had shifted into her human form and now resembled a short Asian woman with long black hair that reached her knees. Her eyes were a dark brown and as hard as the rock they mimicked.

The dark haired man beside her, however, was harder to identify. He pierced Charlie with an unsettling gaze, but she forced herself to meet it without flinching. He had the most electric blue eyes she'd ever seen and there was only one species with eyes that blue. He had to be a water elementalist.

Flicking her eyes at the woman who had stormed away, Charlie's brow furrowed. She was tall and thin and walked with a grace any lady would envy. Even with how furious she was, the woman still moved as if she was gliding.

"Tell us what you know about Sebastian's plans," the incubus demanded.

Steeling herself, Charlie turned to face him.

She'd planned on not telling them anything until they went back for Tony, but had since decided it would be best to tease them with a bit of information instead. After all, if she could get them to trust her, then surely she'd have a better chance at using them.

"He wants to raise the dead," she said evenly.

"No shit!" the tall woman roared even as the demoness snorted, "No fucking duh!"

Charlie's eyes narrowed. "Will you be interrupting me this whole time? Because if so, I'd rather do this after I've had a rest and something to eat."

The incubus reached into a pocket and pulled out a nutrient bar. He handed it to her with softer eyes. "It's not the tastiest, but it's substance."

The smile Fenrir – Jack had been struggling to hide when Charlie had snapped at everyone now turned into a scowl. Annoyed at how his jealousy made her feel, she smiled sweetly at the incubus. "Thank you," she said.

Jack's eyes narrowed.

"Sebastian wanted us to raise the dead with their memories intact. Elizabeth can only bring them back as mindless, vicious drones, so it was my job to make them human-ish again," she said between bites.

"How?"

The elementalist cut in before she could answer. "Ye will be informed on our return."

"Fuck that!" the tall woman snapped. "We lost two of our teammates and there's no knowing if Rico has joined them! So don't pull that clearance level shit, Rogan! We risked our lives for this bitch and I want to know why!"

The elementalist didn't move a muscle, but there was some change in his mien that caused the tension in the cave to skyrocket. Charlie glanced nervously at Jack and then scowled at herself for turning to him for assurance in the first place.

His smirk told her he'd noticed. Her scowl deepened. His smile only widened.

"And ye will, Aisla. When we return."

Aisla's fists clenched, but she eventually spun on her heels with a curse.

"I understand there are protocols, Rogan, but she's right. We deserve to know."

The elementalist turned to the incubus with steel in his eyes. "Aye, ye do, Cariad. *When we return*. But we have more pressing matters. We're stuck here until the blood moon goes and the full moon wanes." He turned to the demoness. "Unless ye have a way to reach your brothers, Matakyli?"

She shook her head. "I've never been off plane before, but if H-"

Jack was on her in an instant, his eyes hard. One hand flew over her mouth, the other over her open wound. Her words turned into a sharp gasp as she collapsed to her knees in agony.

It was over and done with within a second, far too quick and surprising for any of the others to have reacted.

"No one can say a god's name," Jack said as he turned to face the group. He avoided his mate's eyes, however, not liking the raw horror he saw there.

"You know that they can listen in on any conversation when their name is spoken. If even one of them learns we have someone whi can read the *Scrolls*, we'll all be killed. And do you know what happens if you're killed by a god?"

The silence was deafening. Even Aisla bit her tongue.

"What do the gods want with her?"

"It's best you don't know," Jack murmured. But though

his words were soft, there was no denying the warning beneath. Aisla shifted uncomfortably. Rogan and Cariad held Jack's gaze with steel in their eyes, but neither man said anything.

"Why not let them have her then?" Matakyli snapped. "If she's dead, she's no good to Sebastian and no worry to us."

"Because they won't stop at her. We mean nothing to the gods. They will kill everyone Charlie has ever met, regardless of whether they know the truth or not."

"So then we kill her," the demoness growled as she stood back up. She wobbled from the pain, but her mien was one of stubborn determination.

Charlie looked back at Jack. He wasn't looking at her, but she knew he sensed her growing panic all the same. She could see the lethal shift in his shoulders, a silent dare for anyone to be stupid enough to try.

"I will say this once," he said calmly. "You will not speak a god's name around her or when talking about her. You will not harm her. Anyone that does any of these things, I will kill myself." There was a heavy pause as he looked at everyone individually. "And in case you think I can't take you because of previous brawls" —his eyes flashed a hellish, brutal red that had them all tensing with unease— "think again."

Jack's gaze caught hers and Charlie swallowed hard. Her heart thudded loudly beneath the knot in her throat and she struggled to keep her breathing even. His eyes, looked like the very fires of damnation. They should have terrified her with how hot they burned, but all she felt was a deep connection, like coming home. Uncomfortable, she looked away.

"And in case it wasn't clear," he added as he stalked over to her side. "She's mine."

He pulled her against him with one swift tug of his arm. His lips crushed down on hers, rough with emotions neither of them could understand. His tongue stole inside her mouth and robbed her of every thought of resistance.

When he finally released her, they were both breathing heavily. His eyes were back to a startling green and as she stared into them with wonder, he kissed her again.

And then it clicked.

"You bastard!" Charlie shoved him away with all her might. She wiped at her mouth with the back of her hand just to piss him off. She was delighted with how easily that worked.

"Don't you dare touch me!" she seethed when his hands rose toward her. "You have the power to kill Sebastian, don't you? *Don't you?*"

Her chest heaved with frustration and she wanted so badly to wrap her arms around herself lest she fall apart. But she also wanted to wrap her hands around his throat, and scream as he died beneath her rage. The reminder that he'd come back again infuriated the hell out of her.

"Answer me, dammit!"

He ran a hand through his hair. "Yes." He'd said it so quietly that she almost missed it.

Her mouth moved wordlessly as her anger gave way to pain. "And yet, you didn't. You left my son to die by his hands while you ran away like a coward."

He didn't deny it.

Shaking her head, Charlie took a small step back. Her heart felt like it was breaking all over again.

"I can't change the past," Jack said quietly. "But I am trying to rectify my mistake."

"You mean your father is," she spat, refusing to give him anything. Tony could be dead now because of him. Or worse. A broken sound cracked from the deepest part of

Charlie's soul and she raised a hand to her mouth as if that could stop the rest of her sobs from escaping.

Pain twisted Jack's face. "I'm sorry, Charlie. I really am, but I didn't even sense Tony there. And yes, I do admit it would not have mattered if I had – not then." His eyes held her with a stark honesty that ripped through her defenses. "Which means Sebastian has managed to hide Tony in ancient magic. As able as I am to rip that bastard apart, I'm not strong enough to find your son. So I sent my dad."

She didn't want to believe in him. She didn't want to trust him. She didn't even want to look at him. But she didn't have a choice. He was all she had, and Charlie would make a deal with the devil himself to get her child back. "How long do you think it will take him?"

Jack opened his mouth, then closed it again. He offered her a hopeful smile, but she'd already seen the flash of worry in his eyes.

"He should have been back by now?" she asked, her throat raw.

He hesitated, but that was enough for her to know the truth. Seeing that, Jack sighed and ran a hand through his hair. "There's a chance he might've died."

She stared at him in shock. Her heart broke for him as much as it did for her.

"The disease Galvanor has" –the trickster nodded to the unconscious man on the ground– "can only infect certain people."

"You mean persapics," she said, having read about it in the *Scrolls*. "But a persapic can't give birth to your kind."

His silence caused her heart to slam in her chest. He couldn't possibly be hinting at that.

"You don't mean..." She swallowed. "Who?"

But she didn't need him to answer to know who his

father was nor to know who – or rather, what – Jack was either. He'd already told her.

Her eyes went wide as she scrambled back in fear. She bumped solidly into Rogan, but he didn't react to her at all. Looking up at his blank features, Charlie's fear turned into terror. Jack could kill her right now and no one would know. He'd cloaked them in an illusion. He'd made it so no one could hear her scream.

"Holy fucking shit." She trembled as he approached. He moved slowly, as if stalking skittish prey.

"I don't believe you," Charlie whispered hoarsely, but neither of them believed that lie. "You can't be," she tried again, but that wasn't convincing either.

"I know this is a shock–"

"A shock!" she exploded. "You're – you're – I thought you'd *lied* about that! You let me believe you were named after him! Not –" She broke off with a shake of her head. This was all too much.

"I thought you would be happy to have a god in your corner," he said bitterly.

She heard his pain and winced. She knew what it was like to not be accepted simply because of what you were.

But then, there was a huge difference between being a stripper and the monster that was to bring about the end of the fucking world!

"Wait. God? As in singular?" Sometimes Charlie hated her curiosity.

"Yes. My father is. I'm not."

"But you're – you're *Fenrir!* The giant wolf god and god eater. The one tasked with killing – Holy fucking shit! You're going to get me killed!"

He winced with guilt in his eyes. "Uncle has been trying to kill me for fifteen thousand years and hasn't succeeded," he said confidently, as if that was supposed to make her feel better.

Her mouth dropped open. Then she snapped it closed again. "I can't fucking believe Tony and I were actually safer with Sebastian!"

His eyes hardened as if he'd been slapped. Oh, how she wished he had been.

"I will protect you, kultara," he growled. "Besides, if anyone's going to kill you, it's going to be me. You're a bloody nightmare!"

"Great!" she yelled. "Then leave me alone!"

"I can't!" he snapped viciously as he grabbed her by the shoulders. "Can't you see that I've been trying! But I can't leave you. I just can't."

He crushed her to him, ignoring her struggles as usual. Funny though, that she didn't knee him in the crotch. As much as she hated him, her body craved the comfort and feeling of safety he gave her.

The irony made her choke on a laugh.

"By the gods, you're going to be the end of me. Take her."

He shoved her back then and Charlie realized he'd pushed her out of the illusion. Everyone was looking at her warily now, but it was the demoness she was focused on.

Matakyli had Galvanor slung over a shoulder and was walking toward her with hatred in her eyes. The fact that Jack wasn't pushing between them, however, told Charlie that it had been the demoness who he'd ordered to take her.

Eyes narrowing, Charlie rolled onto the balls of her feet. "I'm not going anywhere without my son."

"You've not been given a choice," Matakyli growled.

Charlie leaped for Jack. She snagged his arm hard enough to bruise. "Then you'll have to make it for me. I know you can't take the three of us, not with how weak you are. So if you take me, you take Jack and Galvanor stays to die."

It was one of the biggest bluffs she had ever made. Drazic demons couldn't phase according to the *Scrolls*, so if this one could, Charlie had no idea how powerful she was. She just hoped Matakyli's obvious concern for the man in her arms was enough for her not to risk it.

The demoness gnashed her teeth as she stopped in her approach, and Charlie nearly sighed in relief. But then the woman smiled. It was cruel with a knowledge she didn't understand. "You grabbed the wrong Jack," she sneered.

Before Charlie could make sense of those words, the demoness grabbed her arm and phased.

# TWENTY-TWO

Charlie collapsed to her hands and knees, the world spinning wildly around her. Her stomach heaved in protest, but it was so empty the only thing that came up was acid. She coughed as it burned her throat, then wiped at her mouth with the back of her hand.

Goddammit! She was going to kill Jack the next time she saw him. The bastard had tricked her. Again! The demoness' words of her grabbing the wrong Jack finally made sense. He had to have thrown an illusion in his place while he stepped out of reach. The bastard! How dare he trick her into leaving her son a second time!

Furious, Charlie opened her eyes. She tried to look around for Matakyli so she could demand to be taken back, but the world was still spinning too fast for her to focus. Ever so slowly, everything began to settle and she was able to gather her bearings.

She knelt inside another large cavern. The air was hot and sticky on her skin. The rocks were bathed in a bright green light. Unlike the warm light of the other cave, this one flickered and waved as if it were alive. Her stomach twisted and she heaved again.

"By the gods, Matakyli! What happened?"

The yells came from behind her. Charlie's head spun with the volume of them, and she tenderly pressed her fingers to her temples in an attempt to soothe away the pain. It didn't help.

"Sebastian was there and – What in the Niflhel is *she* doing here?"

"I thought it would be funny." Charlie could almost hear the shrug in that masculine voice.

"Rahu, you ass. If Rogan finds out, he'll kill you."

"I'd like to see him try. Could you imagine what they'll sing about me if I kill Rogan the Undammable Current?"

"Knock it off, Rahu," another male said. "He brought her for her powers. Adriel's still out and we needed –"

A shrill ring cut him off, and the light in the cavern flickered from green to blue. Charlie's back prickled in awareness, and for one stupid second, she wished Jack was beside her. Shaking her silly thoughts away, Charlie slowly turned around. As her eyes widened, her jaw dropped in utter amazement.

Three towering demons stood in front of her. The two men were easily twice her height and were built as thick as rugby players. Their muscles bulged under their dark red skin, flexing as they turned their backs to her. Two balls of black fire appeared in the hands of one demon. The other held what looked like a pair of steel whips.

Matakyli stood between them, also fully demonic. She wasn't as tall as them, but she looked just as intimidating, just as lethal. Even with her missing arm, she looked capable of kicking some serious ass.

But it wasn't the three demons who had caused her jaw to drop. It was the floor-to-ceiling wall of fire behind them. It crackled as if it were alive, flickering from one color to the next in a beautiful array of colors. The blue changed to purple to yellow and back to green.

"Fuck me. What in Niflhel is going on?" Matakyli growled as numerous dark shapes started to form inside the flames.

"Now you know why he brought Emma," the demon with the whips said grimly. "We barely survived the last call."

"There were this many only a few hours ago?" she asked, clearly taken aback.

"More," the other demon snorted as his fires burst with restless energy.

Charlie swallowed hard as the dark shapes began growing clearer with their advancement. The forty or so forms quickly morphed into eighty. Six of them were as tall as a three story house. Though the others were all smaller, many were still taller than the demons.

"Emma..." the fire demon pressed. "Now would be a bloody good time for you to get to it."

"I – I –"

Charlie blinked in surprise. She'd been so focused on the fire wall and the demons that she hadn't noticed the small woman in front of her.

She crouched beside Galvanor, her eyes wide with fear. Her mouth moved with more words, but not one of them came out. Charlie blinked again.

"Holy shit. You're Elizabeth's twin."

The woman flinched as if she'd been smacked. Then she rounded on her in an instant, her already wide eyes growing wider.

"Y-you know Liz?" she breathed.

Charlie flicked a worried glance at the flames. Fifteen of the things behind it now had faces. Some had horns.

Others had fangs. Most of them had dried out bodies that had shriveled in the heat. The one thing they all had in common, however, were blazing eyes of fear. They were like wild animals backed into a corner, willing to fight to the death in order to escape.

Charlie swallowed hard as she struggled to keep her wits about her. The woman tugged on her arm again, this time a bit desperately.

"You know Liz?" she repeated.

"Yes," Charlie replied, her mind whirling back to their first conversation. "She said you had enough power to control Sebastian?"

The woman looked away. "Yes. No. Not quite. I mean – It's – I can –" She took a deep breath, then tried again. "Rogan calls it pulsing."

Charlie nodded in understanding, having read about that too. When a supernatural hit puberty, they would undergo what they called an 'ascension.' Their powers would develop. Their bodies would start to heal. And for the stronger races, they would begin to pulse. Their powers would lash out uncontrollably at random intervals, and for a short time after, they would become vulnerable.

"How often does it happen?"

"About every –"

Emma was cut off by hellish screams. The first fifteen forms had finally split from the flames, and they now charged like a pack of wolves. Charlie lurched toward Galvanor, her hands groping his pockets for any kind of weapon. He would have had one at the start of their mission, and she prayed that he hadn't lost it somewhere in the woods.

With grim relief, she dug a knife out of his left boot. She turned it over once in her hands before rising on shaky legs. She might die within seconds of a fight, but to hell if she was going down without one.

Instinctively, Charlie stepped in front of Galvanor and Emma. Although she was the least powerful, she was the only one currently capable of defending them. Galvanor was still out cold and Emma was too shaken to be of any use.

Charlie gripped the knife harder. Then with a deep breath, she forced her fingers to relax. She was already tired, nauseous, starving, dehydrated, and fighting a killer migraine. There was no point in wasting what little energy she had on a death grip.

With weary eyes, Charlie waited for the first wave to arrive. It didn't take them long.

As their challenging war cries rocked the cavern, the demons erupted in a blur of motion. A whip slashed out at a levitating woman in black. It cut clean through her neck before wrapping around the man behind her. A fireball sailed through the air, hitting a man with four arms. The flames exploded in an instant, covering every inch of the thing's flesh.

Matakyli rushed past her brothers with a yell. She tossed her knife in the heart of an enemy and catapulted over him as he fell. She grabbed her blade back in mid air, dropped into a crouch on landing, and then swiped a leg into another man. He went down with a scream that promised retribution, but he was dead by the time he hit the ground.

Another man advanced. With one jerk of Matakyli's head, the blade in her hair sliced across his midsection. As his intestines spewed across the floor, the demoness lunged at him, her other knife leading. It slashed across his neck, severing it completely.

Within three seconds, the first wave was dead. Within three more, another one had arrived.

The first giant came with the fourth.

Charlie rolled onto her feet as her heartbeat turned erratic. Though the demons were still fighting with an uncanny ferocity, it was obvious they were tiring. The demoness had already lost a lot of blood beforehand, and now she was starting to feel its effects. She stayed in between the other two, wise enough to know she needed their protection.

"It's not closing!" the demon with the whips shouted.

"Fuck!"

"I'm going to have to force it!" the other male roared. He released four fireballs in quick succession, each one slamming into a different opponent with enough accuracy to kill.

"No!" Matakyli screamed.

"That'll be suicide!"

"It's either that or we all die!"

As if to emphasize his point, the giant advanced with a ground-shaking roar.

"I'll go!"

"And leave me to be king? Over my dead body!"

With a maniacal laugh, Rahu advanced. He blazed through half a dozen bodies before he was kicked aside by the giant. The foot had barely grazed his side, but it was enough to send him flying.

He slammed into the people unlucky enough to be in his way and then jumped to his feet with a roar. His fire blazed out in a ring around him, incinerating the two dozen foes nearby. Leaving behind a circle of ash, he conjured up more fire in his hands and formed them into lethal whips.

As a shrill scream split the air, Charlie jerked her attention away from him. Matakyli was now dropped to one knee, and there was a long blade protruding from her back. The other end shot out of her chest, only a few inches to the left of her heart.

The two male demons roared like wounded animals. Simultaneously, they conjured up four balls of fire and launched them at the echidna responsible. Each one hit the top of its blade-like arm, burning it into a crisp faster than Charlie could gasp. The male closest then dropped into a crouch to pick up the whips he'd released. He spun low, cracking one weapon out to hit the smoldered flesh of his target. The arm severed so cleanly that it didn't move those precious inches into Matakyli's heart.

The other whip shot out. The monster's head went flying, and another scream ripped through the air. This one came from Emma as she curled up on the ground with her head in her hands.

Charlie looked for the threat approaching, and stepped back when she saw the seven foot tall man heading her way. She nearly sagged in relief when his head went flying.

But then a woman in white appeared in front of her. She'd come from nowhere, forming out of the shadows themselves. A harsh smile split her lips as she lunged with crazy eyes. Charlie's gut urged her to run, but her motherly instincts demanded she stay and fight.

Rolling onto the balls of her feet, Charlie swiped her knife. The blade missed. Her hand was knocked to the side. The weapon went flying, and the next thing Charlie knew, her feet were dangling in the air and she was struggling to breathe.

The woman cocked her head to the side. Her smile was now one of cruel satisfaction. Charlie kicked out with her feet and watched with wide eyes as they went straight through her torso with no resistance. It was like she was kicking air.

As the seconds passed, Charlie's vision started to narrow. Her flails began to weaken and tears rolled down her cheeks. Memories of Tony flashed past her eyes like a movie reel. She relived the moment she'd learned she was pregnant, his first walk, his first word. Then there was Jack with his infuriating smile and his slap-able –

Suddenly she was on the ground again, gasping for air as she clutched her throat.

It was only when her raspy coughs sounded loud in her ears, that Charlie realized the overwhelming quiet.

The screams had stopped.

The sound of flying body parts had stopped.

Even the ground was still, the hoard of footsteps having disappeared in a single breath.

Chills raced down Charlie's spine, and with tentative slowness, she looked up at the scene before her.

"Holy fucking shit." Her mouth dropped in wonder.

Every single foe they'd been fighting was now frozen. Mid-step, mid-punch, mid-scream, it didn't matter. They didn't move even to blink.

"About fucking time," the fire demon growled. He ran a hand over his face as he flicked his eyes to the other demons. Matakyli shot him a shaky grin that he didn't bother returning. With weary steps, he then made his way through the crowd.

"Wait!" Emma shouted. Her voice was strained, but there was no mistaking the command beneath. As soon as the demon paused, she took a deep breath and stood on shaky legs.

Charlie's skin crawled with the sudden flare of power. She glanced around nervously, trying to pinpoint what was happening, but she needn't have bothered.

All around them, their enemies began to move. Charlie lurched for the knife she'd dropped, but when she stood back up, it clattered to the ground once more.

"Holy fucking shit," she breathed.

It was a sentiment the demons seemed to share as they watched in open-mouthed silence. The dead shuffled back to the flames, and the wall accepted them with open arms. As soon as the last one passed through its fire, Emma collapsed with a groan.

With a disbelieving shake of his head, Rahu continued on his way. He created a ball of green fire spanning both his hands and then held it up to the flames.

Charlie screamed as the wall shot toward him with greedy fingers. The fire consumed him in an instant and an agonized roar erupted from its depths. Just as quickly as he'd been taken, the demon was released, and he crashed to the ground with a sickening thud. His entire body was charred to a crisp, but his chest still rose and fell.

Matakyli made a pained noise as she rushed to his side. Laying one hand on his shoulder, she vanished them both.

Suddenly exhausted, Charlie collapsed to the ground. Her body shook as she came off her high of adrenaline. As the remaining demon approached them, she tried to steel herself for the strenuous journey she knew was coming.

But her stomach was already twitching in agitation and her eyes were quickly drooping. By the time she was thrown over a shoulder, Charlie had already embraced the darkness.

# TWENTY-THREE

To say that the control room in Heldron Castle was in an uproar would've been like saying Poseidon was only slightly upset with the beautiful woman who had stolen his Trident. Whereas in truth, the Graecian Sea God was consumed with rage and the castle was in utter chaos bridging on the point of war.

Pyro was nearly in full demon mode. His eyes burned red as he roared at Hunter, who was stationed behind Xeno. She stood on the balls of her feet, knives in her hands and a lethal warning in her eyes. A little more than a decade ago, she could've taken the demon on without so much as a sweat. Ever since her decline into a fallen angel, however, her strength and powers had slowly been waning. She could barely knock out a human with her light, and though it would still burn the soul of any demon it touched, Jack doubted her power was strong enough to take down a furious, seven hundred year old Heldron.

"Pyro, enough!" Matakyli ordered as she pulled on his arm. The tug did nothing. Maybe if she'd had both of her hands and was in perfect health, she could've moved him. Given the rage on the demon's face, though, Jack didn't think so.

"I'm not letting that, that *thing* into this castle!" he roared as his horns grew ever taller, warning them he was seconds away from a change.

Losing control himself, Tegan slammed his fist onto a side table and cracked it in two. As the pieces crashed to the ground, there was a sudden descent of strained silence. Everyone turned to the berserker nervously, their aggressive feuds momentarily forgotten.

Jack's fingers flared with a magic he was supposed to be too depleted to use. The *thing* shifted with a growl. If Tegan went into a Rage, Charlie would be in danger, and the beast wasn't about to let that happen.

"I am *done* with these negotiations," Tegan growled as he struggled to keep his anger at bay. "That 'thing' is coming down here and you *will* show him respect. This is *your* bed that you made, and by the gods, you're going to lie in it!"

When the berserker pierced his red eyes at the demon, Pyro snarled in challenge. Matakyli tensed. Xeno's hands burned with light. Hunter unclipped his gun. Rogan pulled water from the vials in his jacket. Dominix shimmered as she waited halfway through her change. Aisla and Cariad both raised their hands in fighting poses. Kasem and Kaide, the twin teleporters who had retrieved them from Aurora's Castle, unsheathed their swords. Jack pulsed with power and the *thing* rose to just beneath the surface.

The next second would determine the fate of the entire Heldron Kingdom.

With a final gnashing of his teeth, Pyro turned away. Tegan lowered his head, and the whole room breathed again in relief.

Once Jack was confident a fight wasn't about to erupt, he asked, "So what was that all about?"

He and the others had only arrived mere minutes ago. A few hours after Matakyli had left, the two teleporters had appeared and whisked them to Heldron Castle. They hadn't even finished materializing when they'd heard the commotion upstairs. Kasem and Kaide had immediately phased to the control room, and the rest had followed as soon as they were able.

"Adriel needs an archangel if he's to recover," Hunter said. His eyes flicked nervously to Pyro, but his voice stayed strong. "Earlier, when we were heading to the dungeons, I realized that the reason he wasn't healing properly was because the grenade had been infused with angel blood. I thought Xeno would be able to heal him because —" He cut himself off abruptly as he cleared his throat. "With the addition of the Plague outbreak and the Heldrons' current conditions —"

Matakyli and Pyro both growled at the subtle insult.

"I suggested that Gabriel come down," he finished weakly.

Jack's brows furrowed. If Hunter was championing Gabriel, then it was serious. The archangel was a sore spot for the human given Hunter was in love with Xeno and Gabriel was her ex. Her very powerful, way out of Hunter's league, smoking hot, angelic ex who had spent over a millennium by her side. And though Hunter would never act on his feelings for their comrade, it didn't stop him from disliking the man who had hurt his love so deeply.

"And he will be," Tegan confirmed. "With Rahu and Adriel unable to defend Hel's Exit, this would've become an angel matter anyway."

"We could've handled it," Pyro snarled. His eyes were

back to their usual black, but there was still fury raging inside them. "Leshi is already on her way and Emma has proven she is strong enough to take on forty of the dead on her own. We would've only had to –"

"And how did she prove herself?" Rogan asked, his voice deadly quiet.

Pyro met his stare unflinchingly. "She joined us. It took her awhile to be of any use, but she proved herself in the end. We owe her our lives, Rogan. Not just Matakyli, Rahu, and I, but all of us. The dead would have escaped tonight if she hadn't been there, and I would take her with us again."

"Rogan," Hunter said softly. "I've talked to Emma and she's glad she went. She needs to feel like she's helping. Let her do this."

The elementalist stiffened at Hunter's words.

"If it is truly her choice, then I will not stop her."

The *thing* called him a fool. Rogan had the power to force Emma to do his bidding thanks to her curse; if the beast had that kind of magic, it wouldn't hesitate to use it to keep Charlie safe – regardless of her own wishes.

Jack silently voiced his agreement. That woman was going to be the death of him. She never listened to a thing he said, and the thought of her doing so was intoxicating. There would be no more arguments every time he opened his mouth. No more heart attacks from watching her nearly kill herself. It would be pure bliss. The *thing* was right. Rogan was being a fool.

"Gabriel will be here within the hour," Tegan said before turning to glower at the elementalist. "In the meantime, I want to know everything that happened and why in the gods' name you made a decision that killed two of our people and left one behind."

He then turned to Jack. "And concerning the package

Matakyli brought back, you better give me a damn good reason for it to stay."

For the second time in as many days, Charlie jerked upright upon awakening. She came up swinging, her sleep-fogged brain having not yet identified the man who had grabbed her. Strong hands pinned her down and soothing reassurances were murmured against her hair.

Groaning, Charlie faced away. "You can get off me now, Fe– Jack. I'm not going to hit you."

When he didn't move after a few seconds, Charlie turned back to face him. She sucked in a breath over how close he was. She swallowed with sudden desire. His nostrils flared with an intense need as his eyes focused on her mouth. His head lowered. Her body trembled. He hesitated only a fraction away.

She reminded herself that she was still angry with him. He had forced her away from her child twice now. He couldn't be trusted and kissing him would only be setting her up for more betrayal. But she hadn't been with a man for years, not since Eddy had died, and already she was lifting that final distance.

Their lips touched. His tongue slipped inside. One of them moaned or maybe it had been both. All she knew was the feel of his mouth and the weight of his body as he crawled on top of her. Something prodded her thigh and she sucked in a breath at the feel of it. He wasn't big; he was bloody massive.

Jack shifted his hips and she sucked in another breath. His cock was so close to her entrance now. One more shift and he'd be there. Even though their clothes and the covers were still between them, Charlie felt sinfully naked. Her body clenched as a flood of heat pulsed between her legs.

Just one more shift. One more rocking of his hips. Instead of inching closer, though, Jack lifted his body off her completely. She started to protest, but his mouth was still fused to hers and every sound she made was swept up by his greedy tongue. And then he was pushing back down on her, the covers no longer between them.

She moaned when his cock once again brushed her thigh. She arched with a cry when it trailed a bit further to the left. It rested right on the edge of her pussy, and she was desperate to feel it truly. She wiggled her hips and his hands were there in an instant, holding her down so she couldn't move. He sucked in a harsh breath after he stopped kissing her.

She looked up to see his eyes opened to reveal a fiery red. She almost flinched, but his clear desire had her quaking instead.

Ever so slowly, his head bent to look at his cock. Unable to help herself, Charlie looked too.

She nearly came undone at the sight greeting her. Their clothes were gone, vanished by magic and an impatient need. His cock, large in every sense of the word, stood at stiff attention, pointing at the curls covering her entrance. His hips rocked forwards. Hers rocked up. With a hiss of desire, the tip of his cock entered her slick opening.

Her fingers weaved through his hair, pulling his head to hers. His mouth claimed her as he pushed himself in another inch. She screamed his name. He jerked forward and sheathed himself completely.

Her whole body hummed with pleasure and she –

"Having a nice dream?"

Eyes opening wide, Charlie jerked awake for real. Jack stood above her, the cockiest of smiles on his handsome face. His eyes twinkled with mischief, then burned with lust as they traveled down her body.

Her cheeks burned, but she refused to cower beneath his gaze. "What do you want?" she snapped.

"The question I want to know is what do you want?" he asked in a smoky timber.

Charlie shivered as she remembered the feel of him in her dream. A few more seconds and she would have orgasmed. Her cheeks flushed brighter.

"Would you like to show instead of tell?" He'd tried for light, but the words came out gruff. The knowledge that he was suffering as much as she was empowered her.

She leaned forward, her words a mere whisper. "You came in seconds."

She had expected him to recoil at that, his manly pride hurt enough he would give her some much needed space. Instead, Jack rocked forward with hunger in his eyes. "Inside you?" he breathed.

Her lips parted. Her cheeks burst into flames and Jack closed his eyes on a moan. "By the gods, woman, you're going to be the death of me."

He yanked her to the edge of the bed before she could scramble away. Though if Charlie was being honest with herself, she wouldn't have moved even if he'd given her all the time in the world. Her eyes latched onto his lips, then fluttered closed as he took her mouth just like he had in her dream. The kiss was desperate and promising, but over way too quickly.

His eyes burned with a feral desire as he released her and stepped away. "If we didn't have a meeting in half an hour, I wouldn't have stopped."

Her body said to skip the meeting. Her brain said to stop being crazy. Breathless she asked, "What meeting?"

His eyes closed briefly. "My father never came back."

Her face paled at the reminder of who his father was. If

Loki, an actual god, hadn't been able to retrieve Tony, then who could?

"So I scheduled a meeting with an Amazon. They're mercenaries and for the right coin, they'll do anything."

She nodded, but she wasn't hopeful. Sensing that, Jack took her hands in his and knelt down in front of her.

"We will save him, Charlie. Sebastian can't stand up to me, not when −" He cut himself off, his eyes guarded. "I only need the Amazons to find him and they will. They have wolves and witches in their ranks. Whatever magic Sebastian used to hide Tony, they'll find it and then break him out. I promise. But you need to shower and get dressed first. The woman we're meeting won't see anyone who doesn't dress like royalty."

"She's good enough to be that choosy?"

"Yes."

His clipped answer gave her hope. Nodding, Charlie threw the covers off her and stood. Jack had risen with her, and now he handed her a pile of clothes. She couldn't see what they looked like since they were neatly folded, but it was obvious that they were expensive. The fabric felt like heaven itself.

"The shower's in there." He hesitated as if he wanted to say more, then turned briskly on his heels.

As the bedroom door shut behind him, Charlie entered the ensuite.

Minutes later, she stood in front of the floor-length mirror, her wet hair curled up in a towel. As she stared at her reflection, a mixture of annoyance and excitement warred inside her. The former because she was dressed in such a way that a man couldn't help but wonder what was underneath her garments. The latter because Jack was going to be that man.

Reminding herself she was still angry with him helped

about as much as it had in her dream. Her body didn't care that she found him despicable, especially since she wasn't sure if she saw him that way at all anymore. Yes, he'd kidnapped her, treated her like an ass, and had threatened to kill her. But he'd also saved her more times than she could count and had promised to rescue her son even at the risk of his own secret getting out. Not to mention, the man kissed like a god.

Jack seemed to be taking this mating thing seriously. Would it really hurt if she did the same?

She bit her lip.

He was strong – almost a god, if not quite. He could protect them from whatever monsters lurked in the dark, and Charlie wasn't a fool. She knew damn well that if anyone else realized she could read the *Scrolls of Atlantis*, they'd want her with as much ferocity as Sebastian had. So it made sense for her to want to stay with someone who could protect her and Tony.

Not to mention, the man kissed like a god.

A knock on the door caused her to jump out of her musings. Her heart began to hammer at the idea of Jack seeing her dressed like this. Suddenly nervous, Charlie stole one last look in the mirror. She uncoiled the towel from her hair and ran her hands down her skirts. Then with a deep breath, she opened the door with her eyes on her feet.

"Is this how it's supposed to go?" she asked as she played with her skirts. "I wasn't quite sure with all the layers."

She scowled at the crack in her voice and the nervous twitch of her hands. Bloody hell, she was acting like a schoolgirl with a crush and not a mature woman who needed to stay on her toes. Annoyed, Charlie forced herself to look him in the eye.

Her mouth parted with desire the second she did. If she thought her clothes were provocative, his were downright foreplay!

The tailored suit fit him to perfection. Tight black pants hugged the hard planes of his thighs before dipping into black leather boots. An equally dark shirt spread across his chest, so tight she could see the buds of his nipples. Her mouth watered at the sight of his chest as it peaked through the open buttons of his shirt. And if that wasn't enough to make her ready in an instant, his parted tailcoat matched the sultry red and gold of her outfit, making it crystal clear they were supposed to be an item.

Jack's eyes heated under her stare. They dropped first to her cleavage and then trailed slowly down her legs. As his gaze seared back up her body, he took a step forward, and she had to clench her toes so she wouldn't do the same. They probably only had ten minutes left to get ready and that wasn't nearly enough time for what she suddenly had in mind.

"You keep looking at me like that, kultara, and I'm going to have to reschedule this meeting."

She tried to take a step back, but his hands were on her waist, holding her still. His eyes dipped to her lips. His fingers tightened on her hips, and Charlie was certain he was going to kiss her.

Her mouth parted in invitation. His nostrils flared. His head lowered, but then he gritted his teeth and cursed in a language she didn't understand.

His quick step back, however, told her what his words had not. There would be no kissing. She tried to ignore her disappointment at that, but then his hands were on her stomach and all thought fled her.

With hot efficiency, Jack tugged at the thin scrap of fabric she'd used as a belt. The skirts hadn't seemed able to stay up without it, and her breath hitched when he undid the knot. She clutched at the fabric so it didn't fall down, but her hands trembled with a raw need to release them.

"It goes like this," he murmured. He let the belt drop to the floor as he took the top of the skirt in his hands. Slowly, she let go. There was a heated moment while he warred with his desire to do the same. Then he cleared his throat, and with deft movements, he shifted the layers of her skirt until they alternated between the red patterned fabric and the pale translucent gold. He secured it with the buttons she hadn't known what to do with and then bent down to pick up the belt.

His eyes drifted up her legs as he rose, the skirt doing very little to hinder his view. The layers were narrow and the amount they overlapped wasn't much. With any shift of her legs, a bit of flesh would blaze through and offer a teasing display of what lurked underneath. It didn't show everything at once, but more than enough to keep a man looking in his hope to see more. And as Jack rose to his feet, Charlie couldn't help but fidget.

He tied the belt back around her waist, using a knot that was far more complicated and beautiful than the one she had used. It sat right below her belly button and its whole purpose seemed to be drawing people's attention to her sex. Her clenching, wet, aching sex.

"And the top?" she asked breathlessly. "Did I do that right?"

He didn't even look. "No."

His hands moved up to the knot between her breasts. It was undone within a second. He froze with the two ends in his hands. They trembled as he cursed.

"We don't have time," he said hoarsely. Redoing the knot, he moved the translucent fabric she'd thought was a shawl so it only draped over one shoulder. He fastened the front of it to the knot between her breasts and the back to the middle of her skirt. After a last tie that bound it to her shoulder strap, he gave a satisfactory nod and stepped back.

"Thank you," Charlie blurted out before he could turn away. "For fixing my attire, saving my life, and...and for rescuing me."

His eyes pierced her with heated determination. "I didn't rescue you, kultara. I kidnapped you," he said, parroting back her earlier words. "But I promise you I'm going to make up for that. Now come. Lycra is not a woman you want to keep waiting."

He held out his hand. It was a simple extending of his arm, but they both knew it was more than that. It was a silent question of whether she trusted him, whether she desired him, and most importantly, whether Charlie was finally ready to accept that she was his mate.

After a brief hesitation, Charlie slid her hand in his.

# TWENTY-FOUR

It took Jack a moment to pull her along. As soon as Charlie's fingers had slipped through his, all he could think about was jerking her into his arms and kissing her senseless. His cock was hard and ready, painfully erect from his altering of her clothes. He'd wanted to strip them off her, to push aside the layers of her skirt and bury himself deep inside her.

Had he simply given in, Jack could've been sucking her breasts by now, his fingers tight between her legs. She would've gripped him, arched for him, moaned for him. She would've been screaming his name as he came in a matter of minutes. Hell, seconds. Already his balls were pulled tight with the need for release.

One simple tug and Jack could have the fantasy that was rolling through his mind. Charlie's mouth beneath his. Her tongue swept up and claimed. Her legs wrapped around his waist as she took his cock with the same fervor he had to give. She would wind her hands through his hair as she arched those perfect breasts –

Swallowing hard, Jack jerked his gaze back up to her face. He allowed his eyes to linger for only a second before looking away.

"You're not going as yourself to this meeting," he said roughly as he finally, *finally* managed to pull her toward the door. "You'll be representing a client interested in Tony's welfare." He flicked his eyes to her, trying hard not to dip them back down to her breasts. "That means you cannot show any emotional interest in his wellbeing, Charlie. No one can know you're really his mother."

She paled, the pain in her eyes finally jerking his mind clean out of the gutter. He hated that he had to ask this of her, but Lycra could not know who she really was.

Charlie swallowed and gave a sharp nod. "I can do that."

"Good," Jack said, his voice cold from the detachment he needed. "Because the woman we're meeting is the one who gifted Tony to Sebastian."

With a gasp, Charlie ground to a halt. She yanked her hand from his. She glared at him in disgust and horror, and he had to bite his cheek to stop himself from telling her he had lied.

Though there was a good chance Lycra was involved in Tony's kidnapping, Jack didn't know for certain. But he couldn't tell Charlie that. He needed to know she wasn't going to break cover regardless of what she learned.

Otherwise, Lycra would inform every power-grabbing psychopath she knew given the opportunistic business-bitch that she was.

"And you're going to pay her to get him back?" Charlie seethed. "I'm not going to let that bitch profit twice from my son!"

"There's no one else we can ask."

"There has to be other mercenaries! What about any

men?"

"There are some but none with her reach." Jack didn't bother explaining that the Amazons constantly targeted their competition. Any guilds holding more than twenty people were permanently disbanded.

"I'm not paying her," Charlie spat as she stubbornly crossed her arms.

"Then Tony dies."

She recoiled as if she'd been slapped. He bit his cheek and dug his nails into his palms. If he had to be cruel to protect her, then so be it. He would not risk her life when a few harsh words would save it.

"If you'd prefer to stay behind –".

"Fuck that. I'm going, and that bitch is going to tell me everything." Her eyes hardened with wicked pleasure. "And then after we save Tony, I'm going to kill her."

Jack shook his head. "You can't be planning her death at this meeting, Charlie. She'll pick up on it and think you're planning a trap. Like it or not, we need her help."

There was a tense silence as Charlie bared her teeth. Anger burned bright in her eyes, seeping out from the very depths of her soul. Then with a shuddering breath, it was gone. Everything was gone.

Filled with unease, Jack's eyes narrowed. He knew he should be applauding Charlie's sudden change. Her ability to become the cold representative she needed to be would aid her in this, in life. But all he felt was a hard knot of frustration.

He didn't like the woman now standing in front of him. Charlie had blocked off her emotions and the world along with them. Her eyes had emptied of all feeling. Her mouth had hardened like the wall around her heart. It physically hurt him to see her like this. Jack wanted her fire and passion back. He wanted to see inside her soul and feel that connection between them. But now he was closed off along with everyone else. It bothered him. A lot.

Growling, Jack yanked Charlie to his chest. He took her mouth, hungrily, feverishly, desperately. He ran a hand up her side, cupped a breast. His tongue stole past her lips and demanded she open for him. When she didn't, he nipped her and let loose another growl.

He was desperate to know he hadn't been lumped in with everyone else. That those she was keeping at a distance, even for the short amount of time she'd be playing this role, didn't include him. He needed that knowledge like he needed his next breath of air.

His need mounting, Jack rolled her nipple between his fingers. He kissed her deeply, searingly, possessively before turning his lips to her neck. She exhaled sharply, and a feeling of pure satisfaction uncoiled deep in his chest. The *thing* purred.

Focusing his tongue on the crook of her neck, Jack was rewarded with another gasp. So he did it again, this time sucking and nipping until she was gasping in pleasure. Her wall was now broken, her ice melted. Jack should have stopped there, but he didn't. Couldn't.

His lips trailed down her collar bone as he continued to work her nipple mercilessly in his fingers. He needed her.

*Claim her.*

His mate's hands weaved through his hair, guiding him down to her breasts. After quickly untying her knot, Jack pushed aside the two ends as well as the translucent half shawl that draped over her shoulder. His mouth took the fullness of a breast as a rumble of pleasure erupted from deep inside him. He licked and sucked until she cried his name. Then he moved on to the next one, planning to ravish her until she came. But the mere sight of it caused him to freeze.

His vision narrowed. The *thing* howled in agony and outrage. Jack was aware his eyes had now changed for the entire world was painted red with his need for blood. His face twisted into the ethereal smoke and ash of the beast.

"I will kill him slowly," he vowed, but his voice was no longer his. It was the deep baritone of the *thing*. Its power was unmistakable, as was its fury.

Trembling, Charlie tried to cover the ugly red branding on her chest. He shoved her hands aside as he glared at the imprint of the key. The *thing* screamed for vengeance and then with a burst of power, magic exploded from Jack's hands.

A flash of brilliant green light filled the room. Caught off guard, Charlie jerked away, but she quickly stilled under the heat of his eyes. The *thing* growled at the need to kill, to harm, to hunt. Sebastian would die by their hands. Ripped to pieces over and over again every time he was reborn. They would make it their mission to find him, in this life and the next.

Snarling, Jack focused on Charlie's chest. As soon as his magic faded from her skin, he stepped back with a surprised nod. Satisfaction filled his eyes as he stared at the healed flesh of his mate.

He'd never treated another before, his powers having always been used for death and destruction, but the *thing* had been adamant it would work. That an ancient magic was woven into the core of who they really were, gifted to them by their father, who in turn had received it from his father. It was the power of the gods, of life itself, and though Jack was not a god, it seemed he still possessed a trickling of their magic.

A sudden rap at the door cut off the questions Charlie clearly wanted to ask. Jack quickly stepped in front of his mate's nakedness as the door opened. He could hear the rustling of her clothes behind him, and his eyes narrowed as Hunter poked his head inside.

"The car's here," the man said as he swept his eyes between them. A knowing smile lit his face. Jack bared his teeth, daring him to comment.

"Want me to buy you a bit of time?" Hunter drawled. "What do you need? Ten, six? Seconds."

Jack tossed a summoned knife. It slammed into the closing door, burying down to the hilt. Laughter echoed from the other side, then carried on down the hall.

"We should go." Charlie rushed past him. Her face was awash with guilt.

Jack's heart twisted as he found himself once again on the wrong side of her walls. He'd learned enough about her over these last few hours to know what she was thinking. Her son was still in the hands of a sadistic vampire and here she was kissing the very man she held responsible.

"Charlie..."

She shook her head, a silent demand for him to drop it. His jaw clenched. He didn't want to let it go, to let her go. He wanted her to want him, to trust him enough to lean on. He hated the stiffness of her shoulders and the brave front she always hid behind. He yearned to hear her laughter, to see even the smallest of her smiles.

Did it make him an ass if he wanted those things before he retrieved Tony? Before he could never know whether she smiled because of him or because of what he'd done for her?

Jack's desire to know left his legs frozen. Lycra wouldn't see her if Charlie showed up alone. It was only because of him that they had gotten this meeting so quickly. He could come up with an excuse he couldn't go and then Charlie couldn't go and then he would have more time to win her over and then –

The *thing* whined. It knew she would never forgive them if they held off on saving her son. Jack did too; he just wanted to pretend he didn't. With a defeated sigh, he followed his kultara in silence.

TWENTY-FIVE

# TWENTY-FIVE

Charlie shook with too many emotions to process. Guilt clashed with feverish desire. Hot anger mixed with cold indifference. Elation was buried under a touch of fury. Jack sat beside her in the backseat of the luxury car, quiet and aloof. A thousand more emotions slammed into her because of him and none of them were nice.

Her body still burned from his kisses. Her breasts still ached from his touch. All Charlie wanted was for him to pull her onto his lap and make her forget all the troubles and fears suffocating her.

And of course, that only crushed her with more guilt. How dare she enjoy herself while her son was still in the hands of a sadistic vampire. What kind of mother was she?

Tears clogged her throat, but Charlie refused to give them a voice. She needed to be strong for this meeting. Cold and professional, that is what Jack had said. Tony was counting on her and she would not fail him again.

Subconsciously, Charlie rubbed at the healed brand on

her chest. Even though she had watched Jack's magic at work, she still couldn't believe Sebastian's claim on her was actually gone. Her fingers trembled as she stroked the smooth skin of her breast. A single tear rolled down her cheek.

For the first time since she'd been kidnapped, Charlie felt a genuine flare of hope. Not only could Jack save her son, but he could heal him too. Maybe he could even give Tony his finger back.

A broken sound escaped her and Charlie covered her mouth in shame. She was stronger than this. She had to be.

"Charlie..." The way he said her name made her ache. Laced with pain and frustration, it was as if Jack was hurting simply because she was.

Her eyes closed. As much as she wanted to fall into his arms and let Jack take care of her, she couldn't. It wouldn't be fair to Tony and she had already betrayed him enough.

When Jack reached for her hand, she jerked away. "I'm fine," she assured him.

She knew she hadn't been convincing, but he didn't push and for that she was grateful. Jack's tenderness wrecked her defenses, and she couldn't afford to be weak right now.

Taking a deep breath, she closed her heart and mind. In an instant she fell inside herself, into that closed off shell that had been her haven for most of her childhood. Her mother and father hadn't been able to hurt her here and neither would Lycra. For here, Charlie felt nothing. She simply existed, a soulless capsule that waited for the peacefulness of death.

"Tell me about her," she said. Charlie might not be able to plan Lycra's death at this meeting, but to hell if she'd go into it blind.

"How much do you know about Amazons?"

"Enough to know I wouldn't cry over one's death regardless of her age."

"Even a four year old?"

Charlie nodded. "I've read some killed as young as two."

The way Jack looked at her, hard and searching, made Charlie want to squirm. It should have been impossible. Nothing ever reached her here. She had perfected this internal shelter long ago. Its base had been constructed out of a substance harder than her father's hands. Its walls had been construed from the tough sinews of a mamma bear. There were no windows, no gaps for any feelings to squeeze through. Not even Eddy, Tony's father and the love of her life, had been able to reach her inside these walls.

And yet, one look from Jack and all of her defenses crumbled.

Now ashamed by her answer, Charlie looked away. She knew that the Amazons who killed that young were victims just as much as those whose lives they'd taken. The *Scrolls* hadn't been written in bias. It explained the ways of this world as simple fact, however harsh they might be.

Amazons normally recruited girls from off the streets. Abandoned teens. The babies of prostitutes. The kids wanted dead by someone rich enough to hire a hitman. But sometimes they were taken from families. They had to be loving ones with two parents and the daughter could not be more than four. Any older and their minds would be too broken after their initiation.

A week after they were taken, the toddlers would be placed in a room with a glass wall down the middle. On their side there would be nothing. On the other there would be two chain-link walls running perpendicular to the glass, dividing the space in three. A wild animal would be in the section on the left, having been beaten and starved until it was completely feral.

Then the girl's parents would be led in. One would be placed in the middle section and the other in the right. A device with two buttons would be handed to the child. They could only be pushed in order and there had to be a minimum of two days between each push. The first one would lower the wall on the left. The second, the one on the right.

To make sure the parents didn't kill the animal, they would be told that if their daughter failed in this, then she'd be used as a pillar. If she refused to press the second button, having learned what it did, then again, she'd be used as a pillar.

And the life of a pillar was worse than death. They were the flesh and blood versions of fighting dummies. They were hit and cut, skinned and burned. Their every waking moment was one of unfathomable agony. It was even said that by the time they died, their souls were so broken that they could never be reborn. Instead, they would forever wander the afterlife as empty shells.

Charlie hung her head in shame. "I can't lose him."

Jack squeezed her hand. "I know. But I need to know in no uncertain terms what you want from me, Charlie. I don't want you to –"

He cut himself off and pulled his hand away.

She knew what he'd been about to say though and her stomach twisted. He had wanted her to tell him where to draw the line so he didn't accidentally cross it and cause her to hate him. Then he'd realized she'd hate him either way. If he killed any kids to save her son, she'd forever be wracked with guilt. If he didn't and Tony died...

"Would you really –" She cut herself off as abruptly as he'd just done. That wasn't an answer she wanted to hear, especially since she was pretty certain she knew what he would say. Jack would kill whoever she wanted him to, regardless of their innocence.

And the thing was? Charlie didn't want to tell him not to. Not when there was any chance, however slight, that he would be forced to kill kids in order to save her own.

As the luxury car pulled out of the garage, an awkward silence hung between them.

"Have you killed any children before?" Charlie finally asked. She winced at how accusatory that sounded. She had only meant to find out how killing a child would affect him, if it would at all. She winced again.

Jack turned to her in the heavy silence. His face was so guarded that it might as well have been carved from stone.

"Not deliberately," he said emotionless. Still, there was something in his tone that gave her pause.

Swallowing hard, Charlie looked away. She didn't want to see the pain in his eyes. She didn't want to know that going so far to save her son would impact Jack so strongly. She wanted him to rescue Tony regardless of the consequences. After all, that was the whole reason she had agreed to be his mate. He said he'd do anything for her, she reminded herself. Anything at all. Well, this was anything. She had no reason to feel guilty.

Ignoring the burning of her soul, Charlie looked out the window.

She startled at the view of towering demons, squat dwarves, and every supernatural species in between. She recognized the blue skin of the lizoras, the bulking masses of ogres, and the tattooed flesh of sorcerers. They crowded the sidewalks and spilled into the streets like dropped bags of rice. It was a miracle that none of them were hit.

Charlie couldn't see the car's speedometer due to the divider being up. Still, she would bet her child's life that it wasn't anywhere close to twenty. It felt more like sixty. Or seventy.

Instinctively, Charlie groped around for her seat belt. The things outside might survive being hit by a massive car going eighty miles an hour, but she sure as hell wouldn't. Dread pooling in her gut, Charlie looked to Jack. "Where's my seat belt?"

"Same place as the crumble zone," he said with a wry grin. "They don't exist off Earth."

Charlie paled as white as snow. "Please tell me our chauffeur is a street racer with decades of experience."

"He hasn't been alive for decades," Jack mumbled.

Realizing she'd heard him, Jack took her hand. She suspected he thought that was a comforting gesture. It was not.

"Lycra is a shadow walker," Jack suddenly said.

It was obvious what he was doing. One side of her brain said not to listen to him. Rather, she should be panicking and demanding to get out of the car right this second. The other side grabbed onto his words like a lifeline, completely content with being blinded to her imminent doom.

"Why couldn't we have teleported there again?" she asked even though she knew the answer. Her vomiting all over the Amazons wouldn't exactly have given them a good first impression. Not to mention it also would've poked a major hole in her story considering Charlie was pretending to be a seasoned representative. No human other than a green recruit would agree to be phased to an important meeting.

"I could distract you with a kiss if you'd rather?"

Charlie glared at him even as her libido nodded an enthusiastic yes. "What's a shadow walker?" she asked.

He sighed, clearly having preferred if she'd chosen the second option. Faced with his boyish charm, Charlie was wracked again with guilt. Would she be killing this side of him with her request? Forever robbing him of the ability to smile, to laugh, to make jokes and flirt?

*He's killed thousands*, she reminded herself. *Probably anyway*. Really, what difference would it make to him if he killed a child? An Amazon child at that?

"Talk to me," Jack murmured as he took her hand. His eyes pleaded with her to lean on him. She was tempted to more than he'd ever know. But she couldn't, not when Tony was all on his own. Not when she was asking Jack to kill for her simply by refusing to tell him not to.

Swallowing hard, Charlie shook her head. "What's a shadow walker?" she repeated.

He stayed silent for a tense moment, then sighed. His hand never left hers though and for that she was glad.

"They can control and travel through shadows," he explained.

"I'm guessing they can kill with one too?" Everything in this world was dangerous according to the *Scrolls*. Even the cute little fairies would just as rather feast on your eyeballs than shake your hand. Or finger, as the case may be.

"No," Jack said. "But they can kill by consuming one. Your shadow is attached to your soul. It's why creatures born under the power of the Craving don't have one."

"So how do I defend myself is she decides to attack?"

Jack's face was grim. "You pray she kills you with a knife because having your shadow taken" –he shivered as he unconsciously rubbed a hand over his heart– "hurts like a mother fucker."

Charlie's jaw clenched in frustration. She started to ask him something else when she noticed he was still rubbing at his chest. Before she realized she'd moved, her hand was over his. Jack stilled beneath her. The air crackled with electricity. She wet her lips and then made the mistake of looking up at him.

His eyes were wide with shock. It was as if he'd never had anyone care for him before and didn't know how to react to her empathy.

Charlie's heart broke for him. How could she ask one so troubled to take on yet more pain? Even if he'd killed thousands, even if he was hardened to their deaths, he still had a soul. He was still good deep down and killing a child could change all that.

Her stomach twisted. Her throat burned.

She wanted to tell him to not kill any kids to save her son, but she couldn't. Tony meant the world to her. They and Jack did not.

"What happens when you die?" she asked. It was a coward's way of ignoring her guilt, but it was all she had. If she let it fester, she'd ask him to do something she'd later hate him for.

Jack swallowed as if fighting the urge to kiss her. His eyes dipped to her lips. This time Charlie didn't wait for him to close the distance.

Her mouth claimed his. It was tender and sweet, so very different from the lust filled craze that usually overtook them. Jack pulled her onto his lap. She tried to get back off, but he wrapped his arms around her and held her close. His embrace was needy, almost desperate in his desire to have her stay. He wanted her, not just sexually, but emotionally and that knowledge floored her.

Charlie deepened the kiss. He moaned. But though she

could feel the tremors raking his body as he fought the urge to take her faster, harder, more feverishly, Jack stayed gentle beneath her caress. Where she was kissing only to soothe his pain and to hide her own guilt, he was kissing as a lover.

Shakily, Charlie pulled away. He squeezed her tight, pressed another peck to her lips, and smiled lightly. He knew she wasn't ready, but the look he gave her told her he was willing to wait.

Her heart twisted with yet more guilt. She started to say something, but their chauffeur cut in before she could make a sound.

"We're here." His voice was high-pitched and young.

Charlie's eyes widened in horror. "Has he even finished puberty?"

Jack laughed. Then he kissed her again and climbed out of the car. Charlie didn't fail to notice he hadn't answered. Still, what could she do? They were already here.

Her nerves intensified as she remembered where 'here' was. The Amazon compound. The home of the bitch who had sold her son.

Anger rose viciously inside her. Taking a deep breath, Charlie fell back into her internal haven. Then she took Jack's outstretched hand and rose to face her demons.

# TWENTY-SIX

There was only one way into the Amazon compound. A hundred foot tunnel barely a car width wide cut under the front of the building. It ended in the middle of their practice yard, so as Jack stepped out of the vehicle, he was instantly surrounded by a nightmare of activity. Knives and arrows whizzed through the air. Swords and shields clashed with vicious intent. The idea of wooden practice weapons was foreign here and every so often a shrill scream would emphasize that.

The *thing* shifted with unease. It didn't like that its mate would have to traverse through so much danger. But though Jack shared its concerns, he held out a hand for her anyway. As Charlie rose behind him, she sucked in a breath of disbelief. It seemed nothing she'd read about in the *Scrolls* had prepared her for the harsh reality of an Amazon upbringing.

"They're so young..." Her words were quieter than a whisper. Her eyes were wide in shock and horror.

Jack's stomach twisted, not because of the atrocities

happening around them but because of his ties to this place. If Charlie ever found out how deep they ran, every bridge that had been built between them would burn in a matter of seconds. Every time she looked at him, it would be with the horror she barely concealed now. Every time he touched her, she'd flinch in memory of this place. The knowledge made him bitter. It wasn't fair.

"They're older than two," he grunted. When Charlie's hand went stiff in his, Jack gritted his teeth. He knew he was being an ass. His nerves were getting to him, but it was also more than that.

There weren't many things that could hurt him these days. He'd seen too much to be bothered by the pain and struggle of everyday life. But Charlie seemed to find every chink in his armor and then had no issue driving a knife through the holes and twisting.

She'd made him feel terror and sheer helplessness by endangering herself. Anger and embarrassment had filled him after she'd dismissed the first apology he'd ever made. And now she was stuffing him with bitterness and self-loathing.

He wanted to matter to her. He wanted a future with his mate, a connection that went two ways instead of one. But because of who he was he might never have that, and it was eating at him like acid.

Jack knew she was using him only to save her son. Her motivation couldn't be more obvious. Charlie didn't feel the deep connection that he felt for her. By the gods, all he had to remember was the feel of the blade as she'd plunged it into his chest and twisted. She'd killed him without any regret. And now she was asking for him to trade what little he had left of his soul for her own selfish reasons. It bothered him. A lot.

Here he was willing to give up the entire world for her,

and she wouldn't even ask him not to kill a child.

The *thing* pointed out that by giving up the world, he'd effectively be killing billions of kids anyway. Although true, its logic only served to irritate Jack further.

He just wanted to matter to her. Was that really too much to ask?

A terrified scream cut through his thoughts and caused Charlie to lurch closer against his side. Even with all the bitterness he was feeling, Jack instinctively wrapped an arm around her. Although Lycra wouldn't allow any of the Amazons to harm them, she'd do nothing to protect them from the horrors of her world.

"Keep your eyes straight ahead," he ordered.

The screams were originating from a teenage boy on their left. Jack didn't have to look to know what was causing him pain. Males here were only ever used as a pillar or a seeder. If the boy was out here, then he wasn't chained to a bed and having his semen harnessed for the next generation of killers. So whatever was happening would involve the spilling of blood. It would scar the boy both physically and mentally. With luck, it would kill him.

Charlie's grip tightened. He could feel the tremors racking her body. The *thing* slammed into his ribcage, urging him to save the kid and become a hero in Charlie's eyes. But even as the cries intensified, she never once asked him to intervene. And so he did not. Charlie had made her choice. Her son was worth them dealing with the Amazons, and so he would do nothing to jeopardize that.

"Lycra asked me to meet you." A young girl with a lollipop in her mouth materialized in front of them. She wasn't old enough to have gone through her ascension. Rather, her sudden appearance was a display of the skills she'd learned here.

At the girl's bright smile, Jack instinctively pushed his mate behind him. Anyone that could feel joy in this hellhole had to be a devil in disguise. And any child that asked for a lollipop as a reward had to be certifiably insane. Rewards like that didn't around come often, and they were the only way one could escape a day of torturous training. Which meant the child didn't merely survive here; she loved it and that made her dangerous.

The girl's smile brightened as she caught his reaction. Then she turned on her heels and guided them through the rest of the courtyard. Since the building was built as a square with the practice yard in the middle, it wasn't long before they were inside.

The door closed behind them, the young Amazon showed them up the stairs, and then all too soon, they were standing outside Lycra's door. A quick rap on the stone announced their presence a second before they were ushered inside.

Instantly, Jack's skin tingled with awareness. His eyes landed on Lycra as she sat behind the large desk. A bolt of electricity passed between them, sharp and undeniable. Nevertheless, Jack ignored it as did she.

Rising, Lycra stood tall. Her shoulders were pulled back. Her chin was held high. It was a regal stance that belied her trashy upbringing. Jack felt Charlie stiffen beside him, and he squeezed her hand to tell her to relax.

"Thank you for agreeing to meet with me," Charlie said as she nodded politely. Her words were calm, too calm, and that made Jack still with unease. She had pulled back into that emotionless hole inside herself, cutting him off along with everyone else. The urge to pull her back out was crippling, so Jack forced himself to let go of her hand. Charlie would never forgive him if he messed this up.

Lycra nodded as she sat back down and gestured to the

two seats across from her.

"Jack told me it was urgent, and given what he pays..." She trailed off with a shrug and a secret smile that spoke of an unfathomable payment.

Jack's eyes narrowed. He'd made it clear when he'd contacted her that his usual form of payment was off the table. He should've known better than to accept Lycra's agreement without the binding of coin. But then he'd heard Charlie moan his name in her sleep, and he hadn't been able to disconnect the call fast enough.

By the gods, he was going to pay for that now. If Lycra realized how desperate they were, there was no way she'd accept his coin. She'd demand payment in the old way, and he'd be forced to give it. Charlie wouldn't even ask him not to.

Bitterness filled his mouth.

"We will speak of payment later," he said coldly. "She might decide you're not qualified for the job."

Lycra's smile turned to one of amusement. He wasn't fooled for an instant that it was real. An Amazon didn't have the capability to feel smugness or any other genuine emotion. She grinned only as an attempt at intimidation. She knew there was no one else as qualified for the job as her women. This was simply her way of calling his bluff.

"Let's get started then, shall we?" Charlie prompted as she leaned back in her chair. "What do you know about Sebastian?"

"Which one?" Lycra challenged.

Charlie's silence would've been damning had she not pinned the Amazon with a look of pure annoyance. His mate was playing her role to perfection and Jack couldn't help but feel a burst of pride.

He had worried about bringing her here. It hadn't been because he thought he wouldn't be able to protect her.

Jack might not be a god, but he was damn close. No, it was because he feared she would hate herself for blowing her cover and putting the whole operation at risk. It seemed his worries had been for nothing.

"I know of him," Lycra said.

"Let's cut the shit. You've worked for him. Recently too. You helped him locate a child."

"I might have."

Charlie pierced her with another stare, but Lycra was not a princess of the Amazons for nothing. She gave as good as she got and this time, it was Charlie who backed down first.

"My client isn't interested in maybes. If you're going to waste her time, then this meeting is through." Charlie rose. "I thank you for seeing us on such short notice."

Jack stood up quickly. He hoped Charlie understood she couldn't linger. His mate flicked him a glance, then held out a hand. As soon as he took it, she turned toward the door.

To all appearances she was steadfast in her decision to leave, but Jack could feel the clamminess of her palm. He knew she was terrified she was making the wrong choice. Unable to soothe her without Lycra seeing, he tried to project utter confidence in his walk and prayed that Charlie saw it. For the thought of her hurting, even for a few seconds, made him ache. The *thing* gnashed its teeth as it demanded Lycra's head for daring to cause her discomfort.

Charlie opened the door before the Amazon called them back. "I did procure a child for him. I am surprised how you knew about it given I took the contract myself and merely passed over the boy's whereabouts. I'd be interested in trading information."

Charlie's knuckles turned white as she gripped the door

handle. Suddenly, she released it and turned back around with a cool smile.

Jack stilled with a sharp understanding. Charlie hadn't been shutting down in order to put distance between them. She'd been trying to protect herself from the pain she knew was coming. And with the amount of ease in which she did it, his mate was well practiced. There was no way she'd learned to do this during her short time with the vampire. Something traumatic had happened to her before then, something so bad she'd shut down in order to survive. The *thing* shifted and for a moment, his eyes blazed red.

He would kill whomever had harmed his mate. There would be no mercy, only pain.

With the *thing* appeased by his vow, his eyes slowly turned back to green. Causally, Jack turned around. As he made his way to his chair, he tried to ignore the Amazon studying him.

But as Lycra followed him with blatant interest, his entire body burned with awareness. Disgusted by his reaction, Jack dropped a hand on Charlie's shoulder and squeezed. He drew strength from his mate, but he was also showing Lycra he was no longer available.

Not that the Amazon wasn't already aware. She had known for years he wasn't interested in her anymore. It was why she demanded payment in the sick, degrading way she did. Still, that didn't stop her from trying to get him back. To get him to submit and act as her pet once more.

By the gods, how had he ever been desperate enough to think they were a good match?

Of course, he knew the reason. After fifteen thousand years of watching everyone die, Jack had been overcome with loneliness. He'd yearned to find someone he could share his life with. So when he had come across Lycra, he'd foolishly let himself believe she was the one.

After all, their connection had been explosive and instant. Their darkness was eighty percent compatible. Jack had been confident he could change her with time, that he could heal the wounds her childhood had inflicted, but instead, she'd changed him. She'd sucked him further into the darkness, and it had taken the death of a child to pull him back out.

He would never forgive her for that. But even as much as he hated her, Jack always found a way back to her. He told himself it was for the missions, but deep down he knew the truth.

It was no wonder Lycra believed he'd return to her.

As if picking up on their connection, Charlie flicked him a glance. Then she turned back to Lycra, seemingly without suspicion, but he wasn't fooled. His kultara was too smart for her own good. It was only because she was more concerned with something else that she didn't delve into what she'd learned.

"Do you know where the child is now?" Charlie asked.

"Yes."

"Good. My client wants him back. She's willing to offer ten million if he's alive. Half that if he's dead. And twice that if he's back by this time tomorrow. If you find him and can't get to him, get in touch. If we manage to bring him back alive, you get seven mil. If he's dead, you get five."

Lycra sat back with a cold smile. "Is that all? You must not care for him that much."

Charlie stiffened. "My client," she stressed, "is very interested. Name your price then."

Jack stilled. His gut twisted. Charlie had no idea what she'd just offered. Lycra leaned forward like a predator about to pounce.

"How did you know Sebastian came to me?"

Charlie pursed her lips. She looked like she was debating whether or not to answer rather than scrambling to think of something to say. Just when Jack thought she had come up empty, she spoke.

"Let's just say a little bird told us."

Thor's fucking balls. That answer would have been clever in different circumstances. Charlie had thought only to create discord among Sebastian's ranks, to get him to search for a mole who didn't exist. Unfortunately, she didn't know that mole was very real and had been helping them for months.

How could he possibly salvage this?

He couldn't. He would have to inform Tegan and hope for the best. But they didn't have a way of contacting the person inside. They didn't even know his identity.

Godsdammit, Charlie was going to hate herself when she found out.

*We could never tell her...*

Jack hesitated. The *thing* had a point, but he didn't like the idea of lying to his mate. He lied to so many and wanted something different with her. Something real.

So somehow, by some bloody miracle, he was going to have to fix this.

"Does this bird have a name?" Lycra asked without expression.

Charlie smiled. "Do you want this job or not?"

"I am curious as to why you've come to me instead of your bird."

His mate didn't even hesitate. "My client's in it for the long run. If she can't get the boy, it won't ruin her plans."

"And yet, she'd pay five million for him dead."

"She is a mysterious woman."

Lycra stared at her in silence. She was attempting to unsettle her, Jack knew, but Charlie never wavered. Not even a little.

Eventually, the Amazon leaned forward with a nod. "I take half my payment upfront."

"For expenses, of course. But you'll only be getting two and a half million. There's every chance you'll bring him back dead."

The Amazon nodded.

Rising gracefully, Charlie shot Jack a look. It was a bidding to come, but it was also more than that. She was asking how she did. If Lycra was being honest about taking the job. If she was about to see her son again.

Jack flashed a warm smile as he rose. Her expression didn't change, but he could see relief now hidden behind her cold professionalism. The sight warmed him. Even as closed off as she was, Charlie was still letting a small part of him through.

"Jack."

He stilled. His smile vanished in an instant. He knew damn well what Lycra was calling him back for.

"I told you over the phone it wasn't going to happen," he said as he turned to glare at her.

"Then the boy returns dead."

Lycra's face was expressionless, entirely without the glee that would have alighted anyone else's. Charlie shook beside him. It was the first chink in her armor, and Jack knew that if he didn't get her out of here quickly, her walls were going to come crashing down in one glorious fell.

"My client –"

"Is willing to pay five million for him dead."

Lycra stared at her as if daring her to claim otherwise. Charlie couldn't though, not without revealing this was personal for her. And his mate was smart enough to know that if Lycra knew how invested she was in the boy, she'd request a hell of a lot more than ten million and the moneyless payment from Jack.

Knowing there was only one move he could make, Jack cut in before Charlie could say anything else. "Wait for me outside, kultara. I'll be along shortly."

Lycra smiled. His stomach churned. He didn't like paying her like this. He liked it even less that Charlie would be right outside and able to hear everything. He could cloak the room, hide the noises they were about to make, but he'd rather have her listen than jump to her own conclusions. Maybe she'd hear his self loathing and hatred. Maybe then she wouldn't judge him as harshly as he did himself. He knew that was a fat chance, but what choice did he have?

He would not be the reason Lycra killed Tony. She never made a statement she wasn't willing to carry out.

"What's the payment?" Charlie demanded.

"Nothing you can pay. Now go."

She hesitated. Concern filled her eyes. It was the first show of emotion she'd revealed since the meeting. And it was because of him. For him.

Jack's chest felt as if it was about to burst. He wanted to pull Charlie into his arms and kiss her senseless. He wanted to crush her against his chest and show her how much he loved her.

Dear gods, it was true. He loved her. He wanted to spend the rest of his life with her, learning her, teasing her, conversing with her. He wanted to peel back her layers and snuggle inside her walls. He wanted to see her smile, hear her laugh. He wanted a million lifetimes with her and then a million more.

But it didn't matter what he wanted. Not yet. Because

Jack would not taint the beauty of his kultara with the ugliness of his ex. And he damn well wouldn't gift Lycra with any piece of his mate.

"Go," he repeated softly.

Slowly, she nodded and then headed for the door. He waited for it to click shut before turning to Lycra.

"I will kill you," he vowed.

Her lips curled into a smile. "You say that every time and yet..."

He never did. But this time was different. This time he had a mate to take Lycra's place. Smiling fiendishly, Jack closed the distance between them.

# TWENTY-SEVEN

Charlie stared at the door, torn between two desires. One half of her wanted to leave them to it so that when she saw her son, Tony would be alive. The other half wanted to barge in and stop Jack from paying the bitch. Charlie wasn't stupid nor naive. She knew what kind of payment the Amazon was after.

It was obvious the two had shared a history. It was even more obvious Lycra wanted him back. As soon as they'd entered, Charlie had been pierced with 'the look.' The one women had been eyeing each other with since the dawn of time. That quick assessing stare to see if someone was worth worrying about. And given the hostile gaze Lycra had pinned her with immediately afterward, Charlie had known she'd be fighting for Jack before the meeting was through.

She simply hadn't expected him not to, and Jack's lack of resistance irritated the hell out of her. Yeah, he was doing it for her and Tony. She got that, she really did, hence her hesitation. But bloody hell, did he have to accept Lycra's demands so willingly? He hadn't even tried to think of something else to pay her with! Not a single thought; just 'go away, Charlie, so I can fuck this stupidly hot Amazon.'

And seriously, what was with how hot Lycra was? She looked like a freaking goddess instead of a mere mortal. Lovely bronze skin. Eyes of the most startling violet. Thick straight black hair that complimented the high angles of her face like a piece of art. Bloody hell, Charlie wanted to punch her in the face just to see if she was real.

But even as starstruck beautiful as Lycra was, surely Jack knew she was crazy? Even a blind forty-year-old virgin could see that. So what was it about her that still called to Jack? Was Lycra that wicked in bed?

As if pulled from her thoughts, a moan crept through the door. Charlie's vision turned red. Jealousy festered inside her. It burned so hot not even her internal void could smother its flames. Glowering, she reached for the door handle. Jack was hers, dammit. Lycra had no right to claim him.

"I wouldn't do that if I were you."

Charlie swirled around at the familiar voice. She fought to keep her face expressionless as she stared at Lollipop Girl. The girl was leaning against the wall, her nose wrinkled in childlike disgust. A new lollipop poked out of her mouth.

"I did that last time, and I walked in on something I can never unsee, you know what I mean?"

She pulled the lollipop out of her mouth with a wet plop. Holding up her other hand, she made a circle with her thumb and forefinger. Eyes wide, she shoved the sweet through the hole and pulled it back out again. In and out. In and out. The girl shuddered.

"And when was the last time?" Charlie couldn't help

but ask.

She reminded herself that it had been anger on Jack's face and not arousal when Lycra had called his name. She also recalled he was doing this for her and if she stopped them, Tony would come back dead. But dammit, the idea of him with that bitch right now, just on the other side of the door...

"I don't know?" Lollipop Girl shrugged. "A week or so ago? Yeah, that's right because I got my hand stabbed to the floor. I remember being kept awake by their grunts and moans for two nights. I was so tired I picked a fight with Yanet, and she was three years older than me. Dumb as a post though. Stabbed my hand to the floor and then turned her back on me, thinking I'd stand down."

She rolled her eyes. "You should've seen the look on her face when my sword sliced into her chest." Chuckling, Lollipop Girl pulled the sweet out of her mouth. "So what's it with Jack and you anyway? He your boyfriend or something?"

"He's my mate," Charlie growled. Had it not been Tony's life at stake, she would have barged through the door on those words.

"No shit. The bastard's got two?"

"What do you mean two?"

"Don't you know? Lycra's his lifemate. You know two halves of one soul and all that. Or three I guess with you." She popped the lollipop back in with a shrug. "Is it weird being a part of a three instead of two? Ah, shucks. You gonna be joining them in there, lady? Cuz they go at it long enough already. Sometimes it's a full week before any of us get a lick of sleep when he comes calling. At least tell me you ain't a screamer like she is?"

Whatever else she said, Charlie didn't hear it. She was still stuck on the news that Jack was Lycra's lifemate.

They weren't merely exes like she had thought. They weren't even just soulmates. They were *lifemates*. They were two parts of the same soul, which meant whatever Lycra had done, Jack would have done it too. Under the right circumstances, he would have sold her son to a monster. The knowledge made her sick.

Swirling around, Charlie reached blindly for the door handle. She needed to speak to Jack. She needed to hear him say –

What? What could he possibly say that would make this okay?

"Hey, lady. You listening? I said I got a message for you from Kevin."

Charlie almost snapped she didn't know a Kevin when chills suddenly raced down her spine. Her anger was doused in an instant, replaced by a stomach-clenching horror that left her breathless and shaky. She did know a man by that name. Or had known him. Briefly. Right before Sebastian had ripped him up off the ground and sunk his fangs into his neck.

Charlie tried to tell herself it was just a coincidence. That the girl was speaking of a different Kevin. There had to be hundreds or thousands of men by that name. But her gut refused to relax and Charlie had long learned to trust her instincts.

Slowly, she released the handle and turned around. "What is it?"

"Don't know. Didn't open it." The girl tossed a small box at her, and Charlie caught it automatically.

Her heart thudded something awful.

The box was wrapped like a gift. Pitch black paper with a crimson red ribbon tied around it. There was a tag attached to the bow.

With shaky hands, Charlie flipped it over to read.

*'Next ones are his, love.'*

She sucked in a breath. There was only one person who called her that. Nauseously, Charlie undid the ribbon and tore at the paper. The box inside was closed with a magnetic clasp. Ears ringing, she slowly opened it. Her throat clogged with the contents of her stomach. Her eyes burned as her body was racked with trembles she tried so hard to contain.

"Who gave you this?" she demanded. Surprisingly, her voice wasn't shaking. Her heart was beating so hard.

"Not part of the message, lady."

Charlie gripped the box tightly. She wanted to look up and demand Lollipop tell her, but she couldn't. Her eyes were glued to the set inside the box. The small morbid eyes that looked so similar to Tony's. Her heart lurched.

There was a piece of paper folded against the side. With shaky hands, she pulled it out. Her eyes widened as she read it. Dread settled deep in her gut. The tremors were uncontrollable now.

"No." It was a whisper. A plea. A begging to gods who would not listen. She read it again and again, but it was no use. The words did not change.

A bang sounded behind her. She jumped. Shoving the note back inside the box, she closed it and handed it to the girl. She was terrified Jack was about to exit and see their transaction. He would never let her do what needed to be done in order to save her son.

But the door didn't open. The bang simply sounded again. And again. And again. Lollipop Girl groaned.

"Oh, sleep, I miss your touch already," she wailed dramatically. With a shake of her head, she tucked the box inside a pocket and vanished.

Left alone, Charlie sagged against the wall and closed her eyes. She wanted to give up on life, to curl into a ball and cry herself to sleep. The rhythmic banging behind her caused her stomach to churn, but not even anger nor disgust could penetrate her deep sorrow.

Sebastian had sent the note. He knew where she was. No, it was worse than that. He'd sent the note days ago. He'd known where she would be.

She struggled past the flood of despair threatening to drown her. She needed to think logically. She needed to figure this out. Tony was counting on her and she would not be the reason he lost his eyes.

But bloody hell, what could she possibly do?

Sebastian was three moves ahead of them all. He'd set everything up, had thought of every possible outcome. He'd explained it all in his note to show her exactly what he was capable of. To let her know that even so far out of his reach, she was precisely where he wanted her to be.

He'd attacked Heldron Castle to bring the Elv've'Norc to it. He had deliberately left a loophole in Elizabeth's orders, knowing she would release Nivan. And with the demon infected, Tegan's resources would be divided. The plague would be his top priority. It had the potential to kill millions in the space of weeks. Sebastian did not. Yet.

And then Sebastian had sent Elizabeth to Lucille, knowing that even after all this time, she would be loyal. She loved him obsessively and there was nothing he could do to her that would make her turn on him. She'd led Rogan and his team straight into a trap. Only its purpose hadn't been to kill the Elv've'Norc. It'd been to get Charlie out. To get her right where she was, exactly where he wanted her to be.

Because the plague could only be contained by angels. It was why Sebastian had chosen the Underground in which to release Nivan. If any angels descended, they would create a plane-wide war. Tegan's hands would be tied. He'd be desperate. It was the perfect situation for Charlie to offer her special services.

She could read the *Scrolls*. Save Halzaja. Save her son. All she had to do was learn what Sebastian wanted.

There was no other option.

The door suddenly opened behind her. She jumped and turned around, careful to keep her despair hidden. It wasn't hard.

As soon as she saw Jack, all she felt was rage. He was shirtless, his pant's waistline askew. Lycra sat on the desk behind him, her breasts free. Her hair was a mess and the look in her eyes was that of a woman who had the upper hand. Gnashing her teeth, Charlie swirled on her heels and stomped away.

"Kultara, wait."

Jack grabbed her arm. She tried to yank it free, but his grip was too strong. "Let me go," she seethed.

"It's not what you think."

"Oh?" She spun on him then, her eyes blazing. Angry and hurt, she jabbed him in the chest. "Are you saying you didn't fuck the woman that sol-" She stopped abruptly, horrified over what she'd almost revealed.

"I've cloaked us," Jack said softly. "You can speak freely."

His eyes were torn, but she didn't care. Charlie exploded in an instant. "She sold my son, you bastard! And you - And you, you *slept* with her!"

Tears burned in her eyes. Out of all the things she had to be upset about, that shouldn't have mattered the most. But it did. Dear God, it did. It felt like he'd betrayed her in the worst of ways.

She'd been ready to deal with the fact that Lycra was his lifemate. It wouldn't have been easy, but she would have accepted it eventually - as long as Jack was willing to sever all ties with Lycra. But he'd gone and slept with the bitch, or if not that, he had at least kissed her. He had at least removed Lycra's shirt so he could see her breasts. The thought of him touching them made her sick.

She *needed* him, but instead of being able to turn to him, all she could see was him with Lycra. She hated her. Hated Jack and everything he made her feel.

Shoving him with everything she had, she screamed, "I know! I know how deep down you're the same as she is! She's your *lifemate*, isn't she? You share the same soul, the same fucked up evil! You're both monsters! Just admit it already! You would have sold my son too, you bastard!"

As soon as the words were flung out of her mouth, she was desperate to take them back. The agony on Jack's face, the shock and horror in his eyes – they were nothing compared to the self-loathing twisting his lips. He hated himself and his ties to Lycra. Charlie saw that as clear as day, and her heart cracked into a million pieces. She wanted to soothe him and tell him she was sorry, that she hadn't meant what she'd said, but she couldn't. Her throat had stopped working. Crushed under her flow of emotions, Charlie could only stare in deafening silence as she waited for him to reply.

The tension built between them. Jack's self loathing vanished as if it had never been. His eyes now sparked with anger, warning her of the storm to come. Charlie tried to take a step back to diffuse the explosion that was about to happen, but he still held her arm. His fingers tightened around her hard enough to bruise. With a fierce scowl, he yanked her to him.

She stumbled into his chest. Heat spread all the way to her toes at the touch of his bare skin. His muscles were hard and defined. Her breasts were sensitive and wanting. With a catch in her throat, Charlie looked up into his dark green eyes. They swarmed with the fires of his anger and burned with the depth of his pain.

"You're right," Jack growled. "I'm exactly like she is. I just take what I want."

And with that he crushed his mouth to hers.

# TWENTY-EIGHT

Jack's kiss was entirely primal. He ravaged her mouth with possessive sweeps of his tongue. He grabbed her ass with both hands and pulled her against his rising erection. She mumbled something against his lips. Her hands pressed against his chest, but there wasn't any power in her push. Charlie's brain might be saying no, but her body sure as hell wasn't. Her body was saying take me on this goddamn floor and Jack was almost enraged enough to listen.

Never had he been more furious in his life. After everything he'd done for her, how could his mate still think the worst of him?

He hadn't kissed Lycra. He'd needed to be in the room to control the illusion, had needed to leave his shirt behind to tether his magic to so it stayed after he left, but he hadn't touched Lycra in any sexual way. Not this time, not in the last three years. Not since she'd tricked him into killing a child, and for Charlie to claim otherwise, that...that *hurt*.

Everything he hated about himself was manifested in his lifemate, and Jack tried his damnedest to be better than that. And yet, all Charlie could see was that they were one and the same.

It infuriated him. It *killed* him.

His anger mounting, Jack squeezed her ass and then spanked her with a loud whack. Charlie jumped against him. Her hands pushed the barest amount. She turned her head away, but it was a moan that escaped her lips and not the one word that would stop him in his tracks.

For as much as Jack craved her punishment and the release of his own frustration, he would stop if she told him to. He only prayed she didn't because there would be no future for them if she did.

If Charlie couldn't trust him, if she couldn't feel the truth in his touch...

Panicking, Jack jerked Charlie's mouth back to his. He swept her tongue up with a growl. She shuddered against him, kissing him as deeply as he kissed her.

Grabbing her breast, he gave it a hard squeeze. He bit her lip, and when Charlie gasped, he shoved his tongue back down her throat with an animalistic hunger. He trailed his lips down her neck, sucking and licking as she quivered in his arms. Heat surged through him as he yanked the strap of her shirt aside. The fabric tore; he didn't notice. All Jack was focused on was lifting her breast free and claiming it as his own.

She arched into his mouth. He spanked her to tell her to stay still. The pleasure was his to take and give as he so desired. He was not hers to use, not anymore.

Growling, Jack bit her nipple. Charlie cried out in a mixture of pain and desire, but she didn't arch this time. Pleased, he sucked her harder. He twirled his tongue around her areola. He pulled her nipple further into his mouth and bit again.

"Jack!"

Her fingers wove through his hair. Her hips arched with need. She was on the verge of coming, but he was not ready to allow Charlie her release. She'd hurt him too many times. She had cut his heart too deeply. She deserved to be punished.

Ruthlessly, Jack tore away from her delicious breast. He spun her around and pinned her arms behind her back. He pushed his cock into her palms and closed her fingers around it.

He hissed as she struggled to find the opening in his pants. He had half a thought to stop her, but none of the energy. Moaning, he rocked his hips. Her fingers closed around his bare shaft and squeezed. He gripped her hand and forced her to hold him tighter.

Crazed, Jack bit her neck. She jerked beneath him and his cock followed suit. He pinched her nipple, not for her pleasure but for his own. In this moment she was his to use, his to own, his to punish.

Slamming his hips forward, he pushed into the tight hole of her hand. He moaned. He bit. He squeezed. She wiggled her ass against him and Jack nearly saw stars.

"Are you wet for me?" he hissed.

"Yes. Jack, I –"

He cut her off with a jerk of her chin and a claiming of her lips. He stroked his tongue inside her. He rocked his hips faster. When he was seconds away from coming, he trailed a hand down her stomach and parted the folds of her skirt.

She hissed in a breath. Shoving her thong aside, he feathered a finger across her slick opening. The wet feel of her desire sent him straight over the edge. With a shout of possession, Jack shoved three fingers inside her and ejaculated all over her bare back.

He collapsed against her and withdrew his hand. She tried to turn around, but he bit her neck to keep her still. He wasn't done punishing her, not yet.

"Run to the car, kultara."

"Jack –"

He didn't let her finish. He spanked her hard on the ass and shoved her forward. When she spun to face him, he let his eyes flash red.

"Run, kultara, or I'll take you right here, right now."

Scared and excited, his mate fled.

The chase was on.

Sprinting behind her, Jack eyed the lush curve of her ass. It was a masterpiece of perfection and his hands fisted with the urge to grab it, to knead it with his fingers before spreading it for his tongue. He'd eat her ass as he fingered her clit and he wouldn't stop until she couldn't remember how to speak. She'd give him nothing but screams and moans. No accusing eyes, no sharp remarks that hit him harder than any hammer.

Dear gods, how could love hurt this much?

Chest tightening, Jack shot forward and grabbed her around the waist. He needed her in his arms. He needed to feel the comfort of her skin and know that some part of her at least still wanted him. Still craved him as he did her despite his ties to Lycra.

Spinning his mate around, Jack claimed her mouth. She parted her lips in open invitation. Her hands were in his hair. Her hips arched against his cock as she let loose the most delicious moan. He was hard in an instant.

Cupping her ass, Jack lifted her off the ground. She wrapped her legs around him and they both hissed as his cock pressed against the slick opening of her vagina. She wiggled and it took everything he had not to surge inside her. No one could see them. They were still cloaked. He could have her without anymore waiting.

But Jack didn't want to take her here. As much as he wanted Lycra to hear Charlie's screams of ecstasy and know she was no longer on his mind, Jack didn't want to use his mate in that way. Charlie was not a pawn. She was a queen. She was his queen and furious with her or not, Jack would give her the respect she deserved.

Growling, he set her back down, spun her around, and pushed her toward the car. Then just because he could, he spanked her ass to jolt her forward.

Racing through the compound, Charlie reached the outside in a few minutes. The practice yard was still crammed with Amazons, and she turned her head to look at him. That simple show of trust rocked Jack to his core. His anger abated, but only slightly.

"Jack, I –"

He cut her off with a solid spanking. He didn't want to hear anymore of her accusations. He didn't want to listen to any reasons why fucking her right now might not be a good idea. He simply wanted her as a man, as her mate, as an aching heart only she could soothe.

"You have one minute before I'm inside you," he warned.

Eyes widening, she took off like a rabbit and he chased her like prey. Jack burned with the need to grab her, to sink his teeth into her flesh until the whole world knew she was his. He wanted her screaming his name. He wanted her gripping his cock with the understanding that there would never be another. Not for him and definitely not for her.

She was his mate, godsdammit, and he wasn't waiting any longer to claim her.

She ripped open the car door when he lunged for her.

Tackling Charlie inside, he landed on top of her exquisite body. He shoved the pieces of her shirt aside and clamped his lips around her breast. She arched into his mouth. She ground her hips against his leg. He bit down on her nipple and she collapsed back against the seat.

"Don't move," he commanded.

She whimpered with need, but that was her only protest. Pleased, Jack pulled the door shut behind them, then quickly went back to sucking on her beautiful flesh. He wrapped one of her hands around his cock and the other around his balls.

Pumping slowly into her fist, he worshiped her like a sex starved addict. He wasn't slow. He wasn't gentle. His tongue was quick, his lips were hard, and his teeth clamped and scraped against her nipples. She screamed his name, her hand clenching around his cock as she teetered on the edge of orgasm.

"Not yet," he growled. Tearing his mouth from her sensitive buds, he bit her neck. She jerked beneath him, but he held her hips down, refusing to let her rub against him like she so desperately wanted.

"Jack, please..."

"No." He held her tighter. "You'll come with me or not at all."

She whimpered, but he lapped up her protest with a practiced tongue. He claimed her every moan and ragged breath. His fingers dug into her hips. His cock pressed into her stomach. She writhed beneath him, her breaths coming in hard pants as she gripped his cock even tighter.

Swearing, Jack jerked her hands away. A few more pumps and she would have had him exploding all over her stomach. Forcing Charlie's arms above her head, he conjured up a silken rope. After quickly tying her wrists together, he attached the tail to the grab handle. Charlie jerked against the binds, but they held strong.

With a carnal smile, Jack ran his hands down her body. He was going to take his time with his mate; he was going to punish her in the most primal way possible. Fondling her breasts, he trailed his lips down her neck. She shivered. He lowered his attention, his fingers and mouth brushing a sensitive path to her skirts.

"Jack!"

She jerked when he touched her thighs. Her wrists twisted in the binds. Her body arched with need. His cock jumped in response, but he wouldn't enter her, not yet.

Pushing her legs apart, Jack started at her knee and ran his tongue up her leg. She moaned, then positively screamed when he licked the inside of her thigh. Writhing as Jack sucked on the sensitive flesh, Charlie tried to line up her pussy with his lips. The orgasm inside her was building to a crescendo, and one touch would catapult her into heaven.

"Jack!"

His mate's frustrated cry made Jack's cock surge with need. He gripped her hips harder, forcing her to stay still. Ruthlessly, Jack turned his attention to her other knee. Licking his way back up to her center, he stopped so close and yet still so far away.

Again and again, he teased her, kissing everywhere but that one spot she wanted to feel him most. Charlie panted with frustrated desire. Her legs were soaked with the evidence of her need. Her bound wrists were raw from her twisting and still Jack teased her.

"Jack, please..."

"Please what?" he rasped as he moved up her body. His cock trailed the length of her leg until it pressed against the slick lips of her entrance.

She squirmed on a whimper, but his hands were firm

against her hips. She couldn't move, couldn't push upon his cock like she wanted to do.

"Jack, please..."

"Please what?" he repeated as his lips dropped to her neck. She shivered against him. Her hands strained to touch a part of him, any part of him, but her ties were too short. She could only lie with her hands over her head, the rope and Jack's body effectively pinning her down.

"Please what?" he demanded again, his teeth sinking into her shoulder.

She arched beneath him. Her eyes closed on a wave of bliss. Panting, she opened them again, searching for his bright green eyes.

He sucked in a breath. His eyes heated, and he knew there was nothing he would deny her. He might be punishing her in this moment, might be taking his anger and frustration out on her body, but he would never be cruel to her. He wanted something, needed something from her that he blindly thought this would give him. His chest tightened as he waited for her anser.

"Please take me," she whispered. "Make me yours."

Jack's face twisted. His anger melted. Then with a primal groan, he slammed his cock inside her. Stars exploded in his vision. His body clenched with delicious torment. He wasn't going to last long, not anymore. Not after she'd just asked him to claim her.

Dear gods, she actually wanted him and not just with her body, but with her heart and mind. She wanted him to claim her. She wanted him to make her his. It was all Jack could think about when he slowly pulled his cock out and reentered just the tip.

With a moan of protest, Charlie writhed beneath him. She arched her back, pushing her breasts against his chest as she wrapped her legs around him. His breath caught with the strength of his restraint. His muscles rippled with the refusal to slide his cock any deeper.

"Look at us, kultara," he ordered right before he kissed her senseless. His cock jerked at the feel of her tongue against his, and he almost fell back inside her. But the desire to have her watch as he entered her, to have her eyes fasten on his cock with an undeniable hunger, to have her breaths come out hard and fast in anticipation of seeing him disappear in the depths of her soaked flesh...

"By the gods, kultara, look at us."

He lowered his head to their joining, his cock jerking again when she did the same. He looked back up, his eyes turning feral at the sight of her hunger. Her mouth was open; her eyes were wide. Her cheeks were flushed with desire, a desire that was all his.

Groaning, Jack pushed inside her as she watched. She fell back with a scream, her eyes closed in pure ecstasy. Her nails dug possessively into him. Her pussy clenched tightly around his cock.

"Not yet, kultara," he groaned. She whimpered and the fact that she was trying to fight it jerked him to the edge. His chest tightened. His eyes burned. With a fierce need, Jack captured her lips. It was sweet where the previous ones had been bitter. Loving where the rest had been angry.

He stayed still on top of her, his lack of movement allowing the both of them to step back from the edge of orgasm. He nibbled on her lip as he stroked his tongue slowly across her own. Charlie's hands strained against the binds above her, and desperate to feel them on him, Jack reached up and untied them.

Her fingers were through his hair in an instant. They ran up and down his back, then cupped his ass in an urgency for him to move. Slowly, Jack rocked his hips. She closed her eyes on a moan. He hissed in a shaky breath.

"Jack..." she gasped when he refused to pick up the pace. He wasn't angry with her anymore. He didn't want to take her in a fit of rage. He wanted this to be special, for her to feel the love in his heart and know he would never leave her, never betray her.

"Look at us, kultara."

As she peered down at his cock, watching as it slid in and out of her, glistening from her desire, Jack pressed a hand to her clit. Her fingers dug into his ass. He stroked her pussy as his cock slowly picked up the pace. Within seconds they were both panting, their bodies moving in a dance of ecstasy.

"Now, kultara," he urged, his breath ragged and harsh. "Come for me now."

With a scream of ecstasy, Charlie shattered beneath him. Her pussy gripped him, milking him, and with a primal groan, Jack shot his seed inside her. Utterly spent, he collapsed on top of her. Only, her shudders kept him hard. The scent of her arousal kept him wanting.

A slave to his desire, Jack began moving again. She hitched in a tired breath, but her hips lifted with each thrust of his own.

Shifting, Jack wrapped his arms around her and sat up. She came with him, sluggish still from her recent orgasm. He kissed her lips, her neck, her shoulder before easing her back so he could reach her breasts. Charlie cried out as he captured her nipple in between his teeth. One of his hands stole between her thighs as the other toyed with her other breast.

The noises she made drove him crazy, and with a sharp thrust, Jack sheathed himself back inside her. Charlie took him to the hilt with a gasp. Her hands wove into his hair. Her thighs tensed, squeezing him as she sat on his lap, fully penetrated, fully claimed.

Jack brought his lips up to her mouth and she took them hungrily. He grabbed her hips, lifting her up and slamming her back down in sync with his thrusts. She moaned. So did he, and together they flew apart once more.

Gasping, Charlie slumped in his arms. Her head rested on his chest, feeling the rapid beat of his heart. He held her tightly, his cock still hard, his body still wanting. The thought of having her every minute of the car ride back was exhilarating.

They had about three hours left and Jack was planning on using every second of it. But first he had to tell her about Lycra. He had to make her understand just how much he hated the bitch so his mate would never have to worry.

With a reluctant sigh, Jack kissed Charlie's forehead and lifted her off him.

She looked at him, flushed and smiling. His heart twisted. How was he going to get through this?

*We don't have to tell her now,* the *thing* attempted.

But he did. If there was to be trust between them, Charlie had to know – everything.

"I had a son once," he said abruptly. When she looked at him in surprise, his throat tightened. Somehow though, he managed the next words.

The words that made her look at him like a monster.

"But I killed him before he could scream."

# TWENTY-NINE

Charlie recoiled in shock. Her stomach revolted. Her skin crawled. Holy hell, she'd just let this monster inside her. She'd let him touch her, kiss her, claim her. She itched to rub at her skin, desperate to erase the memory of him from her body.

Her eyes flicked to a door handle. She wanted out. She couldn't stay in here with him. It was too confined. She was too trapped. Her lungs staggered to a stop.

Bloody hell, why would he tell her this? Why would Jack wait until now before revealing something so vile? Dear God, did he actually think she would forgive him? That she would be so –

Charlie stopped. She tore her gaze away from the handle and looked Jack in the eyes.

*"Have you killed any children before?"*

*"Not deliberately."*

Her face twisted in shame. She shouldn't have jumped to conclusions. She should have realized that though Jack was an ass at times, he wasn't a monster. The pain in his eyes when they'd talked about him killing a child on the way over should have convinced her of that. Hell, it had convinced her at the time. But after learning about his ties to Lycra, it had been all too easy for Charlie to see the worst in him.

Wetting her lips, Charlie asked, "What happened?"

Jack stared at her in silence. It was obvious he'd expected her to yell at him, and the shame on Charlie's shoulders grew. Tentatively, she reached for his hand. "You said you didn't kill him deliberately, so it was an accident, right?"

His lips moved, but no sound came out. Then with a shake of his head, he pulled his hand away. "No. I meant to do what I did."

"I don't understand."

The silence stretched painfully. Then ever so softly, he said, "Lycra told me about a drug they gave to Amazon children. She said it would allow them to heal before their ascension and grow into their powers faster. I asked her to use it on our son...but she said he wasn't worthy because he was a boy."

Charlie's heart clenched with horror. She knew where this was going. She reached for his hand again. When he tried to pull away, she simply wrapped her arms around him. She would not let him go through this memory, this nightmare alone.

"I should have listened to her." He spoke so softly, Charlie had to strain to hear him. "I thought she was just being a bitch. I didn't know..." He closed his eyes. "I killed him. He wasn't even alive a minute before he −" He stopped abruptly. Clenching his teeth, Jack's face tightened with pain.

She tried to think of something to say, anything to ease his guilt, but what was there? Charlie would never forgive herself if Sebastian killed Tony. To be the one actually responsible for his death... She couldn't fathom it.

"I later learned Lycra knew what I had been planning. She had manipulated me from the start, using me to kill my own son so she wouldn't have to raise a boy."

Charlie's mouth dropped open. She squeezed him tighter.

"She played me like a fiddle and I was dumb enough to do everything she predicted."

"You didn't know," Charlie said softly.

"I didn't check!" Jack shouted, raw and angry. Moisture glistened in his eyes, but in one blink it was gone. He'd pulled his pain back inside himself to a place she couldn't reach.

Charlie looked at him in shocked silence.

"I'm sorry." Jack took a deep breath. "I should not have shouted at you."

Numbly, she shook her head. She didn't care that he'd lost his temper. She was horrified over what he'd gone through.

"What was his name?" she asked.

Just when she thought he wouldn't answer, he said, "Canis."

"That's a lovely name." It sounded hollow even to herself. Frustrated she was saying all the wrong things, Charlie let loose a sigh. She gave Jack a tight squeeze before releasing him. Sitting up, she looked him in the eye.

"I'm so sorry, Jack. I'm sorry you lost Canis and I'm sorry I don't know what to say. But I do care and I can't fathom what you're going through. To lose your son like that..." Her eyes widened in more pain as a terrible suspicion gripped her. "No one knows, do they?"

He shook his head.

"You never grieved."

"And why should I have that luxury?" he snapped. "I killed him, Charlie. I killed my own son!"

"No!" She gripped his face in her hands, desperate to get through to him. "You wanted your son to be stronger so he could survive when your cousin attacked, didn't you? Didn't you!"

Jack nodded, albeit reluctantly. He clearly didn't want to be relieved of any guilt. He thought he didn't deserve that – not after what he'd done. Charlie knew that feeling well.

But she wouldn't let this go. She couldn't bear seeing him in so much pain. Fiercely, she pushed, "So if you want to blame someone, you blame him. God, I will help you kill Od– your bastard of an uncle when the time comes. He's hunted you for how long? And for what? A prophecy that might not even come true? You are a good person, Jack. You might have made a mistake, but you were manipulated by a heartless bitch. It wasn't your fault. You tried to give Canis the best life possible."

She froze as a memory popped into her head. It was a fragment of the *Scrolls*, a bit of information about the Amazon way of life. Her stomach revolted, but her mind raced. If Jack knew, would it make it better or worse for him? Slowly, she asked, "Was Lycra a princess when she gave birth?"

He nodded and Charlie took a deep breath.

"And you thought you were getting through to her, right? Changing her way of thinking?" Though she'd made them out to be questions, she was confident she was right. Jack wouldn't have risked a child with Lycra if he didn't believe she could change.

He nodded and her face twisted in empathy.

"Jack...I think Lycra might have thought she was doing

a mercy."

He twisted out of her touch. Horror, disgust, and denial flashed across his face. "You're –"

"Wait, just let me speak! If an Amazon gives birth to a son, they're killed. But if that Amazon is a princess, then she must use him as a pillar. She has to prove she's still worthy of her position, and it's sick, Jack, what they require her to do to him. I think –" She took a deep breath. "I think, in her own twisted way, Lycra cared. And she still does. I saw how she looks at you –"

"Get off me."

He shoved her, not giving her the chance to move. Charlie fell onto the floor and scrambled to her knees. She tried to reach for him, but he dodged her hand.

"No, she wouldn't have done that. She's an Amazon. She doesn't have feelings. Not for me and not for her son. He was a boy, Charlie. Do you know how Amazons feel about us males?" He was screaming now, his voice ragged and raw. The only thing that had gotten him through his pain was his hatred for Lycra, and now Charlie had taken that away. He couldn't believe it. He wouldn't. She could see the battle in his eyes. She could feel it inside of her.

She'd felt the same when Tony's father had died. She'd wanted to be mad at the people who had killed them. She'd needed to be mad. And when she'd found out the truth, that it had been an undeniable accident, a simple oven fire that had spread across the apartment complex, it had nearly broken her all over again.

"She wanted him to die!" Jack shouted. "She wanted me to kill him so I wouldn't blame her for doing it herself. But I do! I hate her fucking guts! Every time I see her, I want to kill her! So you see, Charlie, you never have to worry. That bitch might be my lifemate, but damn if I ever accept it."

Tears filled Charlie's eyes. She'd done this to him. Jack was reliving his pain all for her. All because she had accused him of being the same as Lycra. She felt sick. A hand flew to her mouth. She needed to make this right. She needed to help him. There was so much agony inside him and all because of her.

"Do you know what she makes me do?" he raged. "What payment I have to give? Because if you did, you wouldn't say she cares about me or anyone else! She's a heartless bitch. Or don't you care? As long as I save your son, you'll happily offer my soul. Is that it?"

Charlie winced, but she had no refute. Had she known the pain Lycra inflicted on him, she would have refused to let him pay – but only if she wasn't being honest with herself. For as much as she cared about Jack, he wasn't her son. She didn't love him.

"I tried to tell you not to, but you said –"

"I did what needed to be done so you wouldn't hate me! What Lycra does is nothing compared to the thought of losing you. Not after I've –" He broke off abruptly, but she could see what he'd been about to say in his eyes. In the way they pleaded with her, worshiped her, begged her not to hurt him anymore. He loved her.

Swallowing hard, Charlie forced herself to hold his gaze. Everything inside her wanted to look away. She was used to running. Was honed for it. But her mate was hurting and all because of her. She couldn't hurt him anymore.

"Jack, I'm so sorry. I –"

"Don't. You don't even know what you're sorry for."

She winced, but still didn't look away. Taking a deep breath, she said, "I know exactly what I'm apologizing for because I've been where you are. I know what it's like to give up my body in exchange for –"

"What?" Pure fury radiated off him. For a moment Charlie thought she saw shadows flickering beneath his skin.

Nervously, she rushed, "When I was living on the streets, I needed certain things." She winced at her word choice. "I wanted certain things," she corrected. "And the only way I could pay for them was to –"

"Who?"

"What?"

"Who asked that of you?"

She was terrified by the ferocity of Jack's words. He was planning on killing the men. She knew that without a doubt. Swallowing, she squeaked, "It doesn't matter. My point –"

"It doesn't matter! By the gods, woman!" He yanked her up off the floor and onto his lap. "It matters more than anything. I'll kill him."

"Th-he's already dead," she blurted. "The cops went to arrest th-him and he resisted. He died on the way to the hospital." It was a lie, but she didn't want Jack to learn what kind of men they were or how many she'd been willing to please in order to get the drugs they had been offering. She wasn't that girl anymore and she wanted to keep that past behind her.

Cupping his face in her hands, Charlie said, "I am sorry I asked you to pay Lycra, Jack. I thought you wanted to be alone with her. You pretty much ordered me out."

"I –"

"Let me finish." She took a deep breath. Her body trembled with emotions she wasn't yet ready to face. She was used to being alone, and the thought of letting another person into her life terrified her. Charlie had been completely destroyed when she'd lost Eddy. If she lost Jack too...

Closing her eyes, Charlie whispered, "I nearly went back in."

In the following silence, she glanced up. She wanted him to know the weight of that statement. That she'd nearly put him above her son. That she cared about him. That maybe she was nearly on the verge of loving him back.

"I didn't have sex with her," he blurted. "I swear to you. She tried to seduce me, but I –"

"It's okay, Jack," she said as she opened her eyes. "I believe you."

"You do?" His eyes widened.

She smiled softly. Leaning forward, Charlie kissed his lips. Tenderly, lovingly.

"Yes. Because you would never hurt me like that," Charlie whispered.

"And that would have hurt you?" he breathed.

Charlie nodded. "Very much so. Because you're mine Jack and I do not share."

Leaning forward, he kissed her. He ran his hands up and down her back. She pressed herself into him, staying instead of running away. Fighting for him instead of retreating like a coward.

Breaking the kiss, Jack squeezed her hips. He leaned his forehead against hers. Their breaths mingled in soft exhales of passion.

"I need to be inside you." Jack looked into her eyes. Kissed her again. "Guide me in."

Never breaking his gaze, Charlie reached for his cock. She rubbed it against her slick opening, her pants coming faster. Jack sucked in a breath as he watched her react to the feel of his shaft. Her eyes became half hooded. Her lips parted in silent surrender.

Deftly, Jack maneuvered her onto her back. She

stretched out across the seats, and he pressed on top of her. Every inch of her skin was claimed by his. Every place they touched felt like bliss.

Charlie shifted beneath him. She cupped his ass as she lifted her hips to take him deeper. Moaning, her head fell back. Her perfect breasts arched against him and he palmed one greedily.

"*Unn þú mér*," Jack murmured as he pressed his lips against her neck. "*Ann ek þér.*"

Charlie's heart clenched. She had no idea what he was saying, but the way he said it – as if he was cherishing each word like the most golden of treasures – told her all the same. Eyes glistening, Charlie held him tightly as he moved inside her. She pressed little kisses all over his forehead and when he lifted his head, she kissed his face.

"*Óst min, kyss mik.*"

He smiled. Her breath caught. Then he was capturing her lips and stealing every ounce of her air. His cock moved inside her with such reverence. His hands held her with such tenderness. The build up was so slow and exquisite that when they finally toppled over the edge, they each found a bit of heaven.

"*Unn þú mér. Unn þú mér, ann ek þér.*"

# THIRTY

*Dear gods, what have I done?*

Hidden inside his illusion, Jack paced like a man about to be hanged. His nostrils flared. His jaw clenched. His hands flexed at his sides, then ran raggedly through his hair. He was an idiot. A complete fucking, brain-dead idiot.

By the gods, he'd made love to Charlie. He'd taken his sweet time with her, had used up every minute in their car ride back. He had worshiped her, cherished her, showed her in no uncertain terms he was in love with her.

Which meant Odin, with his all-seeing eye, would now know Jack had a weakness he would die for. Jack had put his mate in danger and all because he'd become a bit too distracted, been a bit too *stupid* to remember his uncle was always watching.

*Fuck!* Growling, the trickster slammed his fist into the wall of the Heldron study being used as an Elv've'Norc control room. The dark stone cracked beneath his assault, splitting in six foot long tendrils that did little to appease his anger.

"This is turning into a nightmare..."

*No shit*, Jack thought. Everything was falling apart around him. He'd released the *thing*. Odin would have honed in on that excess of energy as if it was the last item in a Black Friday sale. The Aesir king was undoubtedly locked away, shifting through his billions upon billions of visions even now. It would've taken his uncle months to pinpoint the one soul who had disappeared the moment the *thing* had been released. Now it would only take him weeks, days maybe because Jack had been too stupid to control his emotions.

All Odin would have to see was the *thing* slithering across his skin and he'd know. And once he did, Odin would see their shared moment in the car.

That vision would flash like a neon sign. *The great god eater finally has a weakness*, it would scream. *The one prophesied to kill you can now be easily baited and destroyed.* All it would take was a threat to his mate...or her son.

By the gods, if Odin found Tony before Lycra did...

Thor's balls! Jack needed his father. Loki had always fixed –

Jack stopped on a hard swallow. Pain laced his heart at the thought of never seeing his dad again. By the gods, he'd been fucking up left and right these last few days.

*Look on the bright side*, the *thing* said. *Our situation can't get much worse.*

Jack smiled weakly. Loki would have said something similar... Right before making his life much worse.

As if his father had to get in one last trick even from beyond the grave, the door opened ominously. The man who entered made Jack's hairs rise for he had the power to make Jack's life a hell of a lot worse. And given the way things were currently going for him...

"Gabriel," Tegan greeted with a nod. "How's Rahu?"

Jack swore, then leaned against the wall and dismissed his illusion. It wouldn't have done him any good to stay behind it anyway as archangels had the annoying ability to see through them.

As Gabriel passed under the threshold, he flicked a glance around the control room. His eyes dismissively swept across Pyro, Rogan, and Aisla before landing on Jack. Fighting the urge to twitch, the trickster met his gaze head on. Angels could detect a lie when spoken, but archangels could detect secrets. The more damning the secret, the easier they were to find and Jack was hiding a bloody gold mine. One slip and Gabriel would be on to him. His heart started to beat a bit faster.

The archangel looked at him a second, an infinity longer before turning to the berserker. "He's healing in his own time. Since he touched the flames of Niflhel, I can do nothing for him. That is a bargain between him and the gods."

Tegan nodded tersely. "And Xeno?"

The archangel didn't move a muscle, but there was a sudden stillness about him. Like a deadly energy that was just dying to be put to use. "She's struggling," he said calmly. "We will need to bring down more angels."

"There will be war."

All eyes flicked to Pyro. He glared at the archangel. His eyes were a demonic red, his thick arms crossed. His stance was defensive but not threatening.

"Our people will not tolerate your kind down here whatever the reason. I'd suggest forcing every persapic to the surface."

"No," Tegan sighed. "They'll just panic and go into hiding."

"How are you not causing a panic now?" Aisla asked. "Doesn't Gabriel need to touch them in order for them to heal?"

Pyro grinned wickedly. "Yeah, but we issue a royal invite." No one, not even a hunted convict, would dare refuse an official summoning. To do so would lead to a fate worse than death – for them and their family.

"When they arrive, we offer them a drink of our best whiskey, which by the way, we are claiming back on expenses," he said pointedly to Tegan. His eyes widened. "As well as fixing the bloody wall! What in He-ck's name, Jack!"

Jack shrugged innocently. The demon stared at him in reverence, a look the others didn't share. Tegan, Rogan, and Aisla looked guarded, as if they were all wondering when they'd have to put him down. Their stares hurt, but he refused to let it show. Gabriel gave off nothing but an air of indifference.

Shaking his head, Pyro turned back to Aisla. "Then we, uh, we wait for the drugs to kick in because heck if we're going to waste anymore than we need to. By the time they wake up, viola, the disease is gone."

"And how do you get them to stay?" Aisla asked curiously. She knew full well that if they let them go before the disease was contained, they'd just have to capture them all over again.

The demon's grin widened. "We offer them a position at our castle. It's all very honorable."

Her eyes narrowed. "By offer you mean threaten and by a position you mean as a slave?" Her words dripped with venom. To a fae slavery was worse than death.

Pyro shrugged. "Tomato tomato."

Aisla looked like she was ready to lunge. Rogan shot her a glare to keep her in place. Seething, the fae turned away.

"Ye lass," the elementalist said to Jack. "'Tis true she can read the *Scrolls*?"

Jack forced himself to stay relaxed as his eyes flew to Gabriel. The archangels might claim neutrality, but he didn't doubt for one second they would hesitate to kill Charlie in order to stop the gods from ripping apart the planes in their attempts to find her.

"I don't know." Gabriel looked at him, but it wasn't a lie. Jack could draw as many conclusions as he wanted, but in truth, he didn't know a damn thing for certain.

"You don't know?" Tegan asked very carefully. His skin rippled beneath the surface. The room stretched taut with violence. "Mere hours ago, you assured me she was worth the lives of two of our own and the loss of another. And now you're telling me. You. Don't. Know?"

"Oh, he knows. He just doesn't want me to."

Jack's eyes snapped to Gabriel. His own skin rippled with power as the *thing* clawed just beneath the surface.

"She's no threat from me," the angel assured him.

*He lies! Let's kill him!*

Jack barely managed to rein the *thing* back before it ripped out the man's throat. An angel couldn't lie. Regardless of how small the fib might be or if it would stop a war from raging and claiming millions of lives, an angel could not voice it.

"She claims she can." Each word was pulled from Jack with a pair of pliers. He might've believed Gabriel when he said he wasn't a threat to his mate, but he still didn't like voicing a secret that could easily get her killed.

*Odin could be watching.*

*As if I need the reminder,* he scoffed.

Had Sebastian not had Tony, Jack would have ferried Charlie away in a heartbeat. But there was no way she would leave her son, which meant they were sitting ducks until Lycra found the boy. And unfortunately, this was the best place they could wait. His comrades would stand little chance against the gods, but not even Odin would risk damaging Hel's Exit in order to kill an atlantean. For if the dead escaped, Jack wouldn't be the one bringing about the end of the world.

"Well, there's a sure way to find out," the demon said impatiently. "Give it to her and see if she can read it."

"She's sleeping."

"Oh, I'm sorry. I didn't know her shuteye time was more important than the whole fucking world."

Jack bristled. The demon's glare turned challenging. Before either of them could do anything stupid, Gabriel cut into the silence.

"Let her sleep," he said. "Xeno and I can hold for a couple more hours. Besides, it would not be wise for the *Scrolls* to be read without a clear mind, and I am certain her trip was not an easy one."

Pyro didn't look happy, but he didn't argue the point either. He was thickheaded, not stupid.

Nodding, Tegan dismissed them. Jack couldn't get out of the room quick enough. He needed to get to Charlie and make sure she was alright. With luck she would have read about a way to keep herself cloaked so strongly that not even Odin's magical eye could spot her.

"Jack."

Swearing mentally, Jack stopped to face his captain. Rogan eyed him warily, as one might a wolf he'd backed into a corner. A sharp pain pinched Jack's chest. The trust between them had been broken and he might never be able to get it back.

"Are ye –"

A sudden shrill cut the elementalist off. His lips

321

pinched in a grim line. Hel's Exit was calling and his lifemate was about to greet it.

Jack nodded at Rogan. "Talk later?"

"Aye."

Swirling on his heels, Rogan grabbed Pyro's arm. In another second they were gone. Jack would have been relieved at that near miss had it not meant he was now alone with Gabriel, Aisla having already vanished down the hall.

"I know the girl is not sleeping. Take me to her. We three need to talk." When Jack didn't acknowledge him in any way, the angel merely shrugged. He turned with a wave. "Suit yourself, but I could have saved you a lot of worry about a certain uncle of yours."

Jack lunged for his arm, but Gabriel's stupid wings were in the way. He didn't know what to grab. "Wait!"

"Yes?"

It was a battle to get the words out. "She's this way."

With a sharp turn, Jack led the angel to his mate. He hesitated at the door. He was about to tear her world apart even further than it already was and he wanted to give her as much time as possible before that happened.

"You haven't told her?"

Gabriel's intuition was bloody infuriating at times.

"I didn't have time," he snapped. Twisting the handle, he shoved the door open. And then he slammed it shut again with a curse.

"Jack!" Charlie shouted, the door doing little to muffle her surprise.

He closed his eyes, then opened them again and glared at Gabriel. "If you saw anything –"

"I was right behind you. How could I have?"

Jack's eyes narrowed. The archangel was a good six inches taller than him. He could've easily fucking seen.

Everything. The *thing* wanted to kill him for it, but he decided to accept the olive branch Gabriel had offered instead. Plus, the angel had hinted at having information Jack was desperate to hear.

Gritting his teeth, he called through the door. "Are you dressed yet?"

"In what? The scraps of this dress you've left me? They barely cover me anymore! Though I'm sure the big hunk behind you wouldn't mind."

*That's it. Kill him.*

"Kultara..."

"Well, are you going to summon me more clothes or not?"

Gritting his teeth, Jack did just that.

"Seriously!" A moment later she yanked open the door dressed in a wolf onesie. Jack stared in horror at the perky ears on her head and the way the black fur hugged her body. By the gods, she was not supposed to be attractive in this. She was supposed to look ridiculous and stupid. Instead, she looked cute.

Utterly adorable.

Entirely enchanting.

"Holy fucking shit, are those wings?"

Snapping out of his budding fantasy, Jack pushed into the room. He grabbed her by the arm, pulling her far away from the big hunk behind him. Unsatisfied with the distance, he crushed her to his side. Unsatisfied with how she was still looking at Gabriel with her jaw on the floor, Jack tilted her chin and kissed the living daylights out of her.

She leaned into him with a sigh. Her mouth opened greedily, and Jack possessed it with his tongue. Finally satisfied, he pulled away with a smug smile. "You look cute."

Her eyes narrowed. "I am so getting you back for this."

"Oh?"

She blinked, then smacked him on the chest. "Not like that! I'm going to pour honey down your –"

She stopped.

Gabriel coughed. "What's your name?"

"Charlie. What's yours?"

"Gabriel. I'm an archangel."

She lunged for him. Caught entirely off guard, Jack didn't have the chance to stop her before she landed her fist into Gabriel's jaw.

"You bastard!" Charlie screeched. "Where were you when I prayed all those times? Where were you when I begged you to save Tony? You let my son stay in the hands of that monster! Just what kind of angel are you!"

Jack's humorous grin vanished at the sight of her tears. He pulled her into his arms, sheltering her from the pain Gabriel wrought with only the knowledge that angels were real. That they'd ignored her screams for help and left her trapped in a nightmare with no way to help her son.

"You're no angel." She rubbed angrily at her tears, replacing her pain with fury. "You're as demonic as the bastard who kidnapped me."

A heavy silence descended between them. Gabriel wouldn't strike her down for speaking her mind, but he might very well take that as his cue to leave. The *thing* wasn't about to let that happen, not without hearing what he had to say.

But it seemed its power was unneeded. With a curt nod, Gabriel accepted Charlie's accusations. Then he turned to Jack, dismissing them so easily.

Only the threat of Odin finding his mate held Jack's tongue. His grip on Charlie tightened.

"Your uncle cannot see her. Prometheus spelled the book when he learned he was caught. Any who can read it are cloaked in the magic of Dolos, Lugh, and Loki."

Jack tensed at the mention of the gods. Prometheus might be chained to a rock far away from the reaches of society, but the other two weren't. Dolos and Lugh were trickster gods like his father and answered to their own courts. They couldn't be trusted not to turn Charlie in for their own amusement.

"They cannot hear when I speak their names," Gabriel assured him. He didn't explain and Jack didn't press.

"Why would Pro-guy spell the book?" Charlie asked.

"Because he's the one who created your kind."

Jack felt her stiffen. His throat tightened. "Charlie," he murmured. The news had to come from him. After all he had put her through, he owed her that much. "There's only one race that can read the *Scrolls of Atlantis.*"

"You lie."

She struggled in his grip, but he refused to let her go. Turning her to face him, he looked her in the eye. "I wish I was."

"But Sebastian had a whole dungeon full of us. Of humans!"

"But none of them could read it, could they?"

She shook her head in a panic. "No. No, they could. All of them could!"

"They could see the words, but they couldn't read it," Gabriel corrected.

Jack shot him a glare. It did nothing to stop the angel.

"Humans evolved from your kind. Their power is minuscule. Only a purebred or half-blood can read the *Scrolls of Atlantis,* and given the power inside you, Charlie, you're not the latter."

"Jack..." Her eyes pleaded with him.

"I'm sorry. What he says is true. Prometheus created a race that held curiosity above everything. They were weak of body, but had the strongest of minds. He called them atlanteans."

She laughed nervously. "Like the lost city?"

He shook his head. "The city was named after them and the people who founded it weren't atlanteans. Not the real ones. They were simply innovative humans, too smart for their own good."

She paled. "Does that mean Anthony..." Now she turned completely ashen. She sagged against him, horror alight all over her face. "Dear God, that means Sebastian can..."

"Sebastian can what?"

Charlie started to tremble. Tears flooded her cheeks. "Before you took me, Sebastian said there was a way to take my power, but it would leave me in a coma-like state... If he knew I was...if I... He'll know Tony..." Her mouth worked uselessly. Her eyes pleaded with him to tell her that this had all been a joke. Tell her that and she'd forgive him.

His heart broke. "Tony's powers won't come until his ascension at puberty."

It was a lie, but what else could he say? She was already so close to breaking. If she knew there were ways to steal powers even without the *Scrolls*. If she knew atlanteans were born with their gifts and not gifted them at puberty. She would break. He knew it like he knew the sun would never rise on Blódyrió. As much as he didn't want to lie to his mate, he couldn't tell her the truth. If Sebastian hadn't merely been bluffing and in fact had known what she was, what Tony was... the boy was most likely dead.

Jack looked helplessly at Gabriel.

"That's not the end of the story, Charlie," the angel murmured.

"It's enough for now."

"Not if you want her to live. She needs to know."

Charlie gripped Jack's shirt in her hands. She sniffled against him and then used the cloth to wipe her eyes. "Tell me."

"The gods declared your race an abomination. If they learn what you are, your body will be destroyed and your soul annihilated, never to be reborn. If you want to live, you and Jack need to go into hiding. Forever."

"Not without Tony."

Gabriel didn't reply.

"Of course not without him," Jack assured her. Dead or alive, he would bring Tony back to her.

She took in a shaky breath. "So what do we do now?"

Her cheeks were red, her eyes swollen. Her courage, however, was unmistakable. Jack had never been more floored, never felt more proud.

"You read the *Scrolls*." Gabriel looked at Jack as he spoke, his eyes piercing and knowing. "And you pray you find a way to bind a god."

# THIRTY-ONE

*A god's power is not as infinite as they wish to believe. Odin may be able to see everything, having dived under the roots of Yggdrasil where he sacrificed his eye and endured days of suffering as he hanged from the Tree of Life, all to gain the sight of Wisdom from the Well of Mimir itself; but fear not, young child of mine, for even his Wisdom knows bounds he does not wish to admit. His strength is also his weakness, growing as the worlds grow. The Aesir King may see all, but he sees everything all at once, his visions coming in crippling, blinding flashes of inescapability that neither he nor anyone can decipher in the time the deeds are done. Likewise, Poseidon is the strongest of us all, though Thor Odinson of the Aesirs will undoubtedly dispute that quite heavily for his mind is small and strength is all he has, but as I know and so do you, my child, that strength is not the solution to, nay even beneficial to everything that is of the worlds around us. For despite his strength, Poseidon has a weakness like few others, a punishment his father inflicted in fear of his* son's rising power and the prophecy that would see to the loss of the kingdom beneath his high seat. To speak of it is to go the way of Kronus, who is buried in a hole high above the stars and the moons and the suns. But alas, my time nears and I must leave for the sins that I have been said to have committed and in honest heart, I have seen to the crimes accused, of which was gifting you this book, the Scrolls of Atlantis which are written with the waters of Mímisbrunnr, where I did not sacrifice as Odin once did to gain admission to drink its Wisdom in the proper accords, a crime against balance which will lead to an eternity of punishment you will be forced to also endure if caught by the gods I once called friends and allies, and so I shall tell you of Poseidon's curse. His power lies within his trident; own it away from him and he cannot control the seas as his power is bound to it through the power of Gleipnir, an ancient magic no god can break. And so my child, I give you the knowledge on how to bind a god in such a way that Kronus bound his second son, in hopes that we shall never meet.

A collection of six ingredients must be held before you can begin: the spittle of a bird, the beard of a woman, the breath of a fish, the sinews of a bear, the sounds of a cat's feet, and the roots of a mountain. Impossible some of these may seem in the world of existence, but I assure you, my child, that they are merely hidden from eyes unable to see the truth...

"So what's it say?"

Charlie gritted her teeth as someone pushed in a bit too close. His head blocked out half of the book; his shadow blocked out the rest. The urge to snap the *Scrolls* shut on his nose was almost too tempting to resist.

"Leave her alone, Hunter. How can she read with your thick head in the way?" A friendly shove pushed the man out of her vision. Charlie was about to mumble a thank you when an even bigger head blocked her view.

"So is there anything in here about phasing? I figure I have a head start since I can already do it when Helelopi calls."

"Helelopi?" Hunter asked, bemused.

The demon shrugged. "It was all I could think of to change her name to. So anything in here about phasing?" He flicked through a few pages even though he couldn't see a word of its secrets. "Maybe here?"

He pointed to a section about how to rid yourself of lenchitis, which were worms that only entered through the anus.

If Charlie wasn't so frustrated, she might have laughed. "Do you want a cure for the Plague or not?" she snapped as she pushed on his shoulder. He was as solid as a rock though and didn't so much as acknowledge her attempt to move him.

"Pyro."

The demon snapped to immediate attention. Turning on his heels, he faced the doorway. Curious as to who could command such a large creature, Charlie turned to look as well.

She rolled her eyes. Of course it would be a bigger, scarier demon. Grabbing the book, Charlie tried to sneak off with it, but a massive red hand pinned it to the table.

"Is there anything in here about forcing obedience?" the new demon asked. "I'm open to chains if there's nothing about mind persuasion."

"I'm supposed to be working," Charlie growled.

He flicked her a glance; she nearly jumped at how feral it was.

"So I've heard," the demon murmured. He smiled and it looked like death itself was about to come calling.

Skin crawling, Charlie took a step back. Challenging Sebastian to do his worst might have saved her with him, but that tactic wouldn't work here, not with a demon. He would see it as a challenge, and according to the *Scrolls*, one should avoid such situations if they wanted to live.

Just to be certain, Charlie took another step back. The demon's smile stretched. His eyes grew predatory.

"Or you could tell me about the angle who helped you make those grenades." He took a step toward her. Her breath caught.

"Cut it out, Adriel. We need her to find a cure."

He didn't even look at Hunter. He was a lion entirely focused on the final moments of his hunt. "The angel you used must have been partly fallen seeing how I'm not dead."

Charlie took another step back; he followed.

"Was that your doing too or was it simply luck on my end?"

"I never saw it."

"No?"

Charlie shook her head. "Sebastian had containers of its blood. It was dull. I can give you the angel's DNA sequence?"

Smiling charmingly, Adriel stepped back and gave her space. She sucked in a breath as she flicked a glance at Hunter. The man was pale. A hand lingered on his gun. She swallowed hard, aware of just how badly that could have turned.

"You do that for me." The demon winked at her and then turned to Pyro. "I'd like to see Rahu now."

As the two disappeared down the hall, Hunter crossed to her side. He placed a reassuring hand on her shoulder. "I won't tell anyone if you make a few more of those grenades…"

He'd said it humorously, but Charlie had a suspicious feeling he wasn't joking.

"Is he always so intense?"

Hunter shrugged. "That's the first time I've properly met him. By the time we arrived, he was already blasted to smithereens and struggling to recover. He only woke up about half an hour ago when Gabriel came down to heal him."

Charlie's mouth tasted bitter. So the archangel would answer some prayers, just not hers. God, she hated him.

"We should get to work." The sooner she could get Gabriel to leave, the better.

After sending Hunter off to gather supplies, Charlie settled back down at the table. She flipped through the *Scrolls* until she found the passage she was looking for.

She had only seven days to learn how to give the dead back their memories. Seven days in which to arm herself to the teeth before she confronted Sebastian. For though Lycra had been paid to find her son and Jack had assured her that Tony wouldn't be in any more danger until he hit puberty, to hell if she was just going to sit back and wait.

Determined, Charlie began to read.

*Sunlight, in the soft form of dusk and dawn, will not harm a born vampire's flesh anymore than moonlight will harm yours, but in the strength of the noonday sun, their eyes and skin will burn a glorious red, blinding and weakening them enough for one of lesser power to claim their life.*

*To build a solar grenade, you will need...*

# THIRTY-TWO

Jack stared out the window, his eyes hard. It had been five days since they'd visited the Amazons. Five days of them not hearing a word. Lycra should've found him by now. The fact that she hadn't gotten in touch was making him worry.

For if there was one thing Jack had learned about Charlie in this past week, it was that she was impatient. And stubborn. And with the knowledge of the *Scrolls* at her fingertips, Jack feared what she would do should she give up hope on Lyrca.

Frustrated, Jack turned from the window.

"Sup."

Screaming a curse, Jack jerked backward. He hit the glass behind him, and it cracked beneath his weight. Loki stood in front of him with a cheeky smile. He wiggled his brows with a growing smirk.

"By the gods!" Jack roared as pushed himself off the glass before it gave way. "I thought you were dead! You couldn't find the time to tell me you were okay?"

"Not really." Loki flicked some nonexistent lint off his shoulder. "First, I had to hide the boy without using my powers, else I'd get infected with the bloody Plague – something you forgot to mention by the way."

"I tried to call," Jack said a bit guilty.

Loki gave him a pointed look. "Yeah, well, next time try harder. Then I had to get to Eir to make absolutely certain I wasn't about to die a most agonizing death because hey, my *son forgot to tell me about the bloody Deusychosis Plague reappearing*."

Jack winced.

"And only after I sat through an *eternity* of her fucking nagging, could I go back and get the boy."

"So you have him?"

He reared back as if offended. "Of course I have him. I'm the bloody god of mischief. If I can't kidnap one measly boy, then what am I even doing with my life?"

"Besides being a right pain in my ass?"

Loki cocked a brow. "Funny. Last I heard you were quite fond of having things up your ass."

Jack shook his head. "You did not just go there."

The god smirked. "Reliving your first time now, are we?"

"Dear gods! Just show me the boy already."

Jack shuddered as his father laughed. Then all of his embarrassment vanished as a little boy appeared. Tony stood with his shoulders hunched. His eyes were red from crying and his lip wobbled with fear.

"Hey," Jack said as he crouched down. "My name's Jack and that's my dad."

The boy started to cry.

Loki rolled his eyes. "See, this is why I left until you grew up a bit."

"You didn't leave me. You completely forgot about my

existence."

Loki shrugged. "Potato potato."

"Well, what do I do to get him to stop?"

"Tape his mouth?"

Dear gods, why had he even asked? Barely stopping from rolling his eyes, Jack tried to offer the kid a reassuring smile.

"You're okay. You're all safe. No one's ever going to hurt you again. I promise."

If anything, that only made Tony cry harder. Jack winced with the slightest bit of panic. He flicked a glance at his father before remembering the god was all but useless.

"Hey, I know. Why don't we go see your mom. Would you like that?"

When the crying turned into sniffles, Jack exhaled in relief. "Come on. I'll take you to her," he said as he rose and held out a hand.

"N-now?" Tony was obviously confused. He looked at Loki beneath his lashes, like he didn't dare begin to hope.

Jack frowned. He shot his father a suspicious glare. Loki looked the very definition of innocent, but Jack wasn't fooled. Scowling, he let his eyes promise future retribution. It was one thing for the god of mischief to be a shitty guardian to him. It was quite another to be one to his mate's child.

"Yep, right now," Jack said as he turned his attention back to Tony.

"She's here?"

Jack nodded. "Yes and she'll be so happy to see you. She's talked about you every day you've been gone."

Tony looked at him all confused again. Then he shot a nervous glance at Loki. Jack's eyes narrowed. A horrible suspicion started gnawing at his stomach.

"Dad," he drawled icily. The boy flinched, and he immediately lightened his tone. "Tell me you didn't do what I think you did."

"I didn't do what you think I did."

His jaw clenched. Standing, Jack said in a voice way too sweet to be nice, "So you're saying that this isn't a random child you stole and made to look like Tony?"

"Yep. I mean nope. Wait, which one means I didn't do that?"

"For fuck's sake! It was one job! I gave you one damn job!" Jack grabbed his father by the throat. His eyes flashed a furious red as the *thing* snarled its own displeasure.

"What? I couldn't find him and then I got the Plague."

His anger deflated just a bit. "You did?"

"Sure, why not."

Jack growled.

Rolling his eyes, Loki held up his hands in surrender. "Okay, okay. I might have gotten distracted and forgot what I was there for until I was halfway around the plane."

"You can phase." Jack's grip tightened and his eyes narrowed.

Loki cocked his head to the side with a smug grin. "Oh yeah." In an instant, the god was behind him with an apple in his hand. He took a bite out of it, completely unfazed by the fury radiating off his son.

"You know," he said around a mouthful of apple. "This isn't really an issue. He looks the same as Tony. He sounds the same. Just tell her his personality change is because the poor boy's been traumatized."

"You ass! Charlie is going to know. She's not a distant parent like you were! She actually *cares* about what her son's going through and will try her hardest to help him. I will *not* let you play with her like this! It isn't funny, you heartless fucking bastard!"

"Unicorn." The apple vanished.

Jack almost asked him what the hell he was talking about, when he stopped. He stuck his tongue against his cheek as he struggled for control. Unicorn had been his safe word during sex a few years back.

"Look, you want to know the truth?" Loki sighed as if the next sentence was going to kill him. "I couldn't find him. I couldn't sense him. I couldn't feel him. To all senses and purposes, Tony wasn't there, and I just didn't want to disappoint you, so yeah, I took another kid and tried to fix it." He gave an apologetic shrug.

Jack's anger disappeared in an instant. He ran a hand through his hair as he took a step back. "I'm sorry. I shouldn't have said those things."

"No, you're right. I was a shitty parent –"

"Yes, you were. But you're not now and I shouldn't have alluded to anything different. I just – She loves him so much. I don't think she could live without him."

Loki frowned. "So what do you want me to do with him?" He waved to the kid staring at them with wide eyes.

"I don't know. Just get rid of him."

His dad conjured up a knife. "No, not by killing him! For fuck's sake! Stop joking around and take him to an orphanage or something."

The knife vanished and Loki raised a brow. "So you don't want me to give him back to the family I stole him from?"

Jack was going to kill him. He really was. Before he could take a step forward though, his dad was gone and so was the kid.

Sighing, Jack ran a hand through his hair. What the

hell was he going to tell Charlie? Loki obviously thought Tony was dead, and honestly, Jack was starting to think that too.

So maybe he'd reacted too hastily? Maybe his dad was right and he should –

No. He couldn't do that to her. Charlie deserved to know the truth even if it killed him.

*Even if it kills her?*

He swallowed.

"Hey, so have you thought about what you're even going to do with a kid?"

Having expected it this time, Jack barely reacted when his dad suddenly appeared and slapped him on the back.

"Did you when you made me?" Jack asked dryly.

"Sure I did."

Jack snorted and flicked his father a glance. "And what, pray tell, were your thoughts?"

"That it would be freaking hilarious to convince that family I was a fertility goddess."

The god grinned. At Jack's roll of the eyes, he let loose a deep belly laugh.

Oddly, Jack found this to be quite comforting. "Well, at least I can't do worse than you and look how I turned out."

A relieved smile graced his lips right before his father destroyed it.

"You mean seriously demented with huge trust issues and the inability to make true friends?"

Jack's heart began to hammer. Thor's balls, Loki was right. What the hell was he thinking? He couldn't be a father. He had no idea where to even begin. Fuck, he hadn't even been able to convince the not-Tony kid to stop crying. He couldn't do this. His breathing became rapid. He started to hyperventilate.

Was it wrong to sort of, maybe, kinda wish Loki was

right in his assumption that Tony was dead? His wince at the mere thought of that said it was.

But bloody hell, what was he going to do!

"Relax," Loki laughed as he slapped him on the back. "You'll be fine."

His heavy, thought-filled pause caused Jack to panic. "What?" he demanded.

"Nothing. I was just remembering the fish you had as a kid. How long did they last again?"

Jack paled. He was going to be sick.

With a roar of laughter, the god vanished. Jack braced his hands on his knees and tried to take deep breaths, but it didn't help.

Charlie, he needed Charlie. He could ask her all of his questions before Tony got here. Yeah, that was it. He could do that. She would know what to do. Slowly, his breathing started to calm.

Standing back up to his full height, Jack took another deep breath and then headed for the library. He opened the door, fully expecting to see her hunched over a pile of books like she had been for the last few days. Her brows would be scrunched up in concentration. A few loose tendrils of hair would be cascading over her face. And her tongue would be peaking out of her mouth as she struggled to make sense of whatever she was reading.

But he didn't see any of that. He didn't see her at all. Frowning, Jack scanned the empty room.

"Charlie?"

He stepped inside. His stomach twisted. The *thing* shifted restlessly. *Where is she?* "Hunter?" he called out.

He rolled his eyes when he didn't get a reply. Moving quickly, he poked his head around the many aisles until he found his comrade sitting on the floor in the middle of a circle of books. He stormed over to him and tapped him on the shoulder.

With a yelp, Hunter jerked to his feet and then nearly tripped over a pile of books. He dropped to the ground to tidy them up before standing to face Jack. "What?" he asked exasperated.

Jack would have smiled had he not been so distracted. "Where's Charlie?" he asked.

Hunter shrugged. "I don't know. She went to take a break some time ago."

"Know where she went?"

He shook his head.

"Know what time she left?"

Another shake of the head. Jack wasn't surprised. Whenever Hunter was reading, he was absolutely dead to the world. Sighing in exasperation, he turned around and made his way to the kitchen.

There were only the two teleporting swordsmen sitting at the table though.

"Hey, have any of you seen Charlie?"

Kasem and Kaide shook their heads.

Frowning, Jack made his way to his bedroom. He couldn't think of anywhere else she could be, but the tightening of his gut told him he would once again fail to find her.

Picking up the pace, Jack ran to his room. He shoved the door open and it slammed so hard into the wall it left a hole. He didn't notice.

"Charlie?" he called out.

A sickening silence was his only answer.

The *thing* whined.

His heart dropping, Jack made his way to the bedside table. There was a hastily scrawled note on it. With a shaky hand, he picked it up.

*Jack –*

*I wish I could have said goodbye in person. I wish I* ~~could have said that I just know that~~ *I wish I had more time with you. You're an ass, but you're a nice ass and I*

*Fuck, if I had more time, I'd throw this away and start over.*

*Just, can you do me a favour? Could you make sure Tony goes to a good family if Sebastian*

*I have to believe he'll keep his word. I'm sorry.*

*I have to go. Take care.*

*Charlie*

Numbly, Jack traced her name with his forefinger. Tears flooded his eyes as a fierce rage filled his heart. She was gone. She hadn't trusted him enough to turn to him. She hadn't even thought enough of him to ask him to look after Tony himself. And she was gone. She hadn't even said goodbye.

Crumbling up the letter, Jack let loose a feral scream. The *thing* roared inside him, and before he knew it, he was the ethereal form of the beast. He charged through the house, ignorant to the screams of terror and surprise coming from his comrades.

A knife sliced his leg and he lashed out with a snarl. The demon went flying. A roar filled the air, but it was quickly drowned out by his own. He bit through an arm. He shoved through another body. The *thing* wanted to kill them, but Jack was oddly hesitant. He wasn't sure why though. They were standing between him and his mate and anyone who did that deserved to die.

*Where is she?* he roared.

*Jack? Can you hear me?*

He paused. A knife sliced into his chest, but he didn't care. *Tell me where she is.*

*Who?*

*My mate.*

Jack growled at the sudden silence. He didn't even notice that the attacks had stopped. All he wanted was to hear what the telepath knew.

*She's not in the castle, and I'm not strong enough yet to find her.*

*You would have heard her thoughts. Where did she go?*

*I'm still recovering. I haven't been able to listen –*

*You lie!*

A torrent of water slammed into his face. Swords sliced into his stomach, his back. They flashed around him, moving so fast and randomly that he couldn't grab them. Snarling, he vanished in a puff of smoke and then landed on top of a raging demon in full form. He tried to bite down on its neck, but a flood of water caused him to choke.

A bright light burned his eyes. It wasn't enough to truly blind him, but it was more than enough to distort his vision. Furious, he lashed out at whatever moved. His paw was caught mid-blow.

"Down, doggie! Down!"

Jack froze. He knew that voice. The *thing* growled, determined to keep him buried. It didn't want Jack's conscious stopping it from doing what it needed to in order to find its mate.

"Don't make me ask again," the sweet voice said.

Slowly, the fog started receding from Jack's mind.

"That's a good boy. You want a treat, huh? Do you? Do you? Well, you're going to have to change for me then because I'm getting way too distracted by how cute you are."

The *thing* drew back in offense. It was a monstrous god eater. It wasn't cute. It was vicious. It was mean. It was – Oh gods, what was she doing? Its back leg jerked on its own accord as a small clawed hand scratched him behind the ears. Its tongue lolled out.

And that blissful distraction was all Jack needed to regain control.

"Delentia?"

"Aw. Change back into a pupper," she pouted. "You were so cute! I wanted to take you home."

The baby chimera beside the winged goddess roared, hissed, and bayed at him. Jack ignored it.

"Do you know where she is?"

"Of course I do! Why do you think I'm here?"

"So tell me," he growled.

"Don't tell me what to do! First, I have to speak to Adriel."

She looked around the room, and Jack winced when he did the same. His comrades were in a fair few pieces and he was quite aware of his hands and teeth being stained with their blood. He tried to say sorry, but none of them would look at him.

Swallowing hard, Jack looked at the ground. He'd try to fix things between them later. Right now he had to get to his mate before she did anything stupid.

"Del–"

"Oh, Adriel, my dear," Delentia cooed. "I'm so hurt. You woke up and didn't even call? What kind of friend are you? Oooh, is that pizza I smell cooking because I would *kill* for one topped with pineapple and fairy wings. Do you know what those bastards did to me? They folded my socks! Worse, they folded them *matching!* Can you believe it? Fucking *bastards.* Almost as bad as this guy over here, am I right?"

She flicked her thumb at Jack. Her eyes narrowed when no one replied.

"Oh, yeah."

"Yes."

"Of course."

"A right bastard."

Delentia smiled sweetly.

"But don't be too mad at him. You see he's −"

"Delentia..." Jack pressed. He knew he was risking death by interrupting her, but he couldn't wait any longer. Charlie was in danger.

The winged goddess turned to him. She stared at him blankly for a long second before giving an exaggerated blink. "What are you still doing here? Don't you have a lifemate on Blódyrió to kill?"

His eyes narrowed. The *thing* clawed at his chest once more and with a strangled cry, Jack shifted into a janua wyrm. He was the size of a large dog and his scales rippled with every color of the rainbow and then some. Fire built in his chest and with a roar, Jack blew a flame of pure energy.

The air rippled around it, bubbling like a pot of boiling water. It seemed the very fabric of the universe was being stretched and pulled apart inside the flame. Then with a sudden hiss, a hole ripped open. Blódyrió shone through from the other side, but the portal was closing fast. With a fierce growl, Jack lunged. The tip of his tail was cut off as it closed around him. His scaly flesh dropped to the floor with a deafening smack.

The room was heavy with silence. Even Delentia was momentarily stunned.

"What in the gods' name is he?" Kasem breathed.

Delentia waved her hand dismissively. "Oh, just the god that's going to bring about the end of the world. Nothing to worry about. Nothing at all."

And with that she headed for the kitchen, all the while singing about dying fairies and the cutest of puppies.

# THIRTY-THREE

Jack slammed into the earth like a comet. His magic sent shock waves throughout the Amazon compound on Blódyrió. He knew it was a reckless move. Showing such a large amount of power would be taken as a blatant middle finger to the gods hunting him, but Jack simply didn't give a damn.

Lycra knew where Sebastian was hiding. She knew where Charlie had run off to. The bitch would tell him where his mate was even if he had to fight Thor and Poseidon to hear it.

With a bellow, Jack conjured a knife into his hand and then launched himself at the closest Amazon. She had been knocked onto her back by his landing and hadn't yet managed to regain her feet. With his knife now slicing through her spinal cord, she'd never get the chance.

Rolling off her, Jack surged back to his feet. Another knife materialized in his other hand. As soon as it appeared, it was gone again, flung into the skull of a rising Amazon twenty feet away.

The *thing* lunged in his chest, ramming into his ribs with such force Jack heard the cracking of a bone. He ducked out of instinct, knowing the *thing* was trying to bring him to his knees.

Immediately, he heard the whistling of an arrow. He watched as it flew directly overhead, just missing his scalp. With a feral growl, Jack spun around on his heels in the direction the attack had come and launched one of his own.

He didn't wait to see if his knife had struck. He knew it had. These women might have been trained to kill since they were children, but so had he. And Jack was a hell of a lot older than all of their ages combined.

"Lycra!" he screamed as he focused his magic on the building to his left. He could conjure objects from half way around the universe and he could take them away just as easily. With a destructive wave of his hands, the building vanished in a puff of green smoke.

No sooner had it gone, than it reappeared directly on top of the building opposite. The roar of crumbling stone drowned out even the feral howl of the *thing* inside him. If Lycra had been ignorant to his arrival, she damn well wasn't now.

Jack's eyes burned in anger as the dust swirled around him. Under its gritty cover, he slipped past near a dozen Amazons like a ghost. The only sign of his passage was the pooling blood around their bodies as they sank to the ground, their heads severed.

Lycra would answer to him without her fucking sisters there to intervene. They wouldn't be able to protect her from his wrath, but they might be able to fend him off until the gods arrived. Jack was determined that wasn't going to happen.

Nothing was going to keep him from finding his mate,

least of all some fucking Amazons.

"Lycra!" he screamed again as soon as he ripped off the door to the main compound. A ball of fire slammed into his chest, sending him flying back off the porch. He hit the ground hard, his brain rattling from the pain. Growling, he arched back onto his feet, sending the flames away with a flick of his hand.

They reappeared at the entrance, shooting out in all directions as the tongues of the fire fed off his magic. The five Amazons who had been standing there waiting for him now all writhed on the ground in agony. But despite being roasted alive, not one of them screamed.

The *thing* chuckled cruelly inside him, its mouth open in a drool of anticipation. Jack was aware his eyes had changed, darkened into that blood red stain of revenge. He could feel the *thing's* power coursing through him. For the first time in his life, the *thing* was content to let him have all the control.

Stalking back to the compound, Jack walked through the flames as if they weren't there. Another nifty trick his father had taught him, turning reality into an illusion. Normally, that was an extremely draining thing to do, but with the *thing's* excess of power, Jack felt like the god he almost was.

Standing in the middle of the engulfed entrance, he lifted his nose to catch the specific scent of his lifemate, but all he could recognize was the thick smell of smoke. Irritated, he doused the flames with a flick of his wrist and then inhaled again.

The *thing* rumbled deep in his chest when he finally found her, and Jack answered with a cruel grin of his own. So she wanted to play games, sitting up there in her room with a glass of wine in her hand?

Fine. Jack was all too willing to play.

Stalking toward the stairs, he glowered at the row of Amazons watching him. Though they stood at regal attention, their fangs bared and their hands full of blades of all kinds, not one of them moved to stop him. Lycra must have given him passage and here, her word was law.

It didn't matter that he had just slaughtered over half of their sisters and destroyed two of their three buildings. It didn't matter that he was here to torture their leader until she told him what he wanted to know. An Amazon did not feel anything, not even loyalty to their fallen sisters. Those that fell were seen as too weak for their group.

Jack's desire to kill them all where they stood, current threat to him or not, tugged at every inch of his soul. It would only take him a minute, one glorious, bloodthirsty minute. But who knew how much time Charlie had left? Did he even have a minute to spare?

Frustrated, Jack settled with pinning them with a deep warning growl as he climbed the stairs they guarded. Not one of them flinched, but they all tightened their hands around their weapons, and that pleased the *thing* enough to stop him from attacking.

Once on the second floor, Jack ignored the guards completely. His attention was focused solely on the room at the end of the hall.

"I knew this day would come," Lycra said as soon as he kicked open her door. She stood beside her desk, a sword held horizontally in her hands. As calm as ever, she picked up the rag beside her and smoothed it down the blade's length. The recently applied oil caused the metal to glisten in the moonlight.

Oh, Jack would find great pleasure in tossing Lycra through the row of picture windows behind her.

With a cruel sneer, he stepped into the room and shut the door behind him. The sharp click of the lock was music to his ears, but Lycra didn't even raise a brow at the blatant threat.

"What do you want, Jack?" she asked as she finished polishing her sword.

"Tell me where Sebastian is," he growled.

Almost as if bored, she replied, "You know I don't reveal client information."

His hands clenched as he took a threatening step toward her. "You will once I'm done with you," he vowed as he called upon his magic. Except, this time, it didn't come.

A flash of fear sliced through him, but he quickly trapped that down before it could show on his face. Besides, he wasn't afraid of facing Lycra without his powers. He was terrified about how he could save Charlie and her son without them.

"No need to panic," Lycra said as if she could read his thoughts. She placed the polished sword on her desk, then picked up the bottle of wine and two empty glasses. She held his gaze as she filled them. A cold smile sat on her face, but it didn't reach her eyes. They never did with Amazons.

Finished, Lycra placed the bottle back on the table and transferred one of the glasses into her empty hand. Taking a sip, she glided toward him without fear.

"Your magic hasn't disappeared," she murmured as she held out a glass. "The room's simply been enchanted so you can't use any of it."

He glared at her for a moment before taking the wine she offered. No sooner had her fingers released it, than Jack threw the red drink in her face and lunged for her.

"Cute, but I don't need any magic to kill you," he growled as they toppled to the floor. He picked up her head in his hands and slammed it back down with a sickening thud. He didn't bother with a second attempt, instead using the time to scramble off her to get back on his feet. Already, she was turning into a shadow and reappearing behind him.

She might be thousands upon thousands of years younger than him, but she still had half his soul, half his power, inside her.

Fighting her was going to waste too much precious time and Jack was already growing desperate.

"I'll pay you!" he growled as the Amazon solidified back in front of him. "Whatever you want, I'll fucking pay it."

She tilted her head to the side as if complementing what he could possibly pay her. He knew it wouldn't be money she demanded, but favors. He only hoped she wasn't smart enough to ask for a lifetime of indenture because Jack was certain he wouldn't even hesitate before agreeing.

His kultara needed him even if she didn't fucking know it. He would not fail her. He couldn't. Charlie was everything to him. Life would be pointless without her.

As the silence stretched, it took everything he had not to drop to his knees and beg her. If he showed his cards before she offered a deal, it would be over. She'd own him completely.

A blank mask fell over her pretty features, and Jack knew she had finally come to a decision. She didn't want to reveal her hand anymore than he did.

"Fuck me."

"What?"

"That's what I demand as payment. Not just once, but whenever I want it. I will call you and you will stop whatever it is you're doing to fuck me."

Jack stared at her in horror, unable to keep his hatred

for her hidden any longer. "I'm an Elv've'Nor. I can't just drop what I'm doing and cross a few planes whenever you're horny," he gritted out.

"Of course you can," she said. "You can make objects phase, why not yourself?"

He started to tell her it didn't work like that, when he realized he'd never actually tried to before. Catching his hesitation, she sauntered over to him with a cold gleam in her eyes.

This wasn't about sex. Jack knew that. Lycra wanted the one thing he had been denying her for the past three years. She wanted complete domination over him again and knew that she would never have it as long as Charlie was a part of his life. The bitch.

She was going to make Charlie hate him forever.

A cold sweat broke out on his skin as she pressed her breasts against his chest. Leaning into him, she purred. "Fuck me and you'll know where she is within the hour."

He wrapped his hands around her throat and growled, "I'd rather cut it out of you."

She didn't panic. She didn't twist away. She simply stood there staring at him, waiting for the touch of his lips.

Staring into her dead eyes, his hands cutting off her air supply, Jack was hit with the undeniable knowledge that she would not break. He could tear off every one of her limbs and she still wouldn't tell him what he wanted to know.

There was only one thing he could do.

*Fuck!*

Cursing, Jack crashed his lips down on hers. His kiss was rough, hard, angry. Disgust rose up inside him like lightning, its sharp blade stabbing deep into his gut. It spread like wildfire up to his heart, making his lungs burn with every harsh inhale.

But despite the torment the kiss was causing, Jack didn't stop. If this was the price he had to pay, then so be it. He'd grovel for Charlie's forgiveness after she was back safe and sound in his arms.

Lycra moaned beneath him and her lips parted with an invite he could not deny. Angrily, Jack shoved his tongue inside, hissing when she bit him hard. He jerked his head backward, his eyes glowering with hatred. She met the grim line of his lips with a smirk, then reached around the back of his neck and yanked him to her.

This time her mouth was already open, demanding that they start exactly where they had left off. With his tongue deep inside her, Jack pushed her backward until he slammed her into the wall. His hands curled with the want to truly hurt her, to bruise and maim her perfect skin. Only the knowledge that she would get off on the violence stopped him – and then, only just.

But after he rescued Charlie and her son, after he killed Sebastian with his own damn hands, Jack would be back. And then Lycra would learn what it really felt like to feel pain.

She writhed beneath him, her back arching so her breasts pressed fully against his chest. There had been a time when her fierce passion had left him breathless, wild, and obsessed. Where he couldn't think of anything other than to be inside her, rocking until they both found release.

But now Jack's body yearned for something different entirely. The only similarity was that he wouldn't wait long until he was sated. Lycra never had appreciated the act of foreplay anyway.

Pulling his head back so he could look at his lifemate, Jack breathed hard. His eyes were hooded with feigned lust, his lips swollen from the kiss. A wicked gleam curved her lips when he pressed a palm to her breast. He squeezed hard, and when she gasped in pleasure, he tightened his grip. He needed her eyes to close, dammit.

Though an Amazon was trained to kill even while riding the throes of an orgasm, Lycra had always lost sense of her surroundings whenever she had been with him. The dreamy shutting of her eyes had been a blaring sign of her complete relaxation; Jack only hoped that telltale hadn't changed.

Forcing himself back to her lips, he kissed her like his life depended on it. And in a way it did. If Charlie died, so would he. He knew that all the way down to his bones. She might not be his lifemate, the other half of his soul, but she was his mate. Her happiness was his happiness. Her sadness was his sadness. Her death was his death.

Finally, Lycra closed her fucking eyes; about goddamn time.

With sharp reflexes, Jack snatched the sword off the desk and shoved it deep into her chest.

Lycra's eyes widened in shock, her lips parted on a silent scream. Agony twisted her face for the barest of seconds before disappearing under a fiery rage.

With a dangerous, devious grin, Jack sneered, "You shouldn't leave sharp tools lying around all willy nilly. Hasn't anyone told you that it's dangerous?"

He jerked the blade in a slight twist, scraping the edge of her heart. She hissed in a breath, her eyes darkening with fury.

Jack leaned in, making sure he put most of his weight on the blade. He stopped a mere breadth away, his eyes as vicious as his smile. "Now tell me where Charlie is, or I'll carve your heart out."

Her nostrils flared, but just when he thought he had the

upper hand, Lycra smiled sweetly. Too sweetly.

A cold sweat broke out on Jack's neck as a solid rock of nausea dropped to the pit of his stomach.

Fucking. Amazons.

"Don't test me, Lyrca. I'll do it."

She cocked her head to the side as if contemplating something other than her imminent death. Turning her saccharine gaze back on him, Lycra leaned forward. She scraped her heart against the sharp blade as if it was nothing but cotton candy.

"Does it look like I'm trying to stop you?"

With a feral scream, Jack jerked the blade up and to the right. He sliced clean through her aorta, but other than a minuscule flinch, she didn't react.

Godsdammit! She hadn't been bluffing.

Now what was he supposed to do?

His chest heaved with frustration as his eyes searched her face. He wasn't quite sure what he was looking for though. Was it pity? Did she want him to beg?

Because he fucking would.

But just when his knees started to buckle and his desperation began to seep into his eyes, Jack spotted it. That telltale sign of jealousy.

Holy shit. Charlie was right. Lycra cared about him.

Grinning like the devil, Jack stepped back and yanked the sword out of her chest. Before she could register his change of heart, he released the sword's hilt only to grab it by the end of its blade. Swinging it around, he shoved it straight into his own chest. He gritted his teeth as he slammed it home, nicking the top margin of his heart.

It hurt like hell, but Lycra's sharp scream of alarm made it all worth it.

*Jack. Fucking. Pot.*

As his heartbeat increased, scraping the edge of the

blade with each pulse, Jack grinned like the devil he was.

"Now tell me where Sebastian is," he sneered. "Or I swear I'll cut out my own heart to get to yours."

# THIRTY-FOUR

The castle wasn't as ominous as she remembered it. Maybe it was because she had hope this time. Or maybe it was because she was now willing to die. Whatever the reason, Charlie didn't hesitate to walk up the steps.

She pushed the heavy door open. It creaked loudly in the silence, announcing her arrival to all inside. She'd barely made it past the threshold before she was yanked forward and slammed against a wall.

"Where's Draven?" Sebastian demanded.

"Who?"

"The man who brought you here."

"I brought myself here." Charlie held up her wrist to show him the teleportation device. He barely spared it a glance before he gripped it in his hand and crushed it. She bit her tongue as the metal pieces cut into her skin. If she hadn't made a backup, she would've been devastated.

"So what other toys did you bring?" Sebastian purred.

She raised her chin. "I want to see Tony first."

His eyes narrowed as he leaned closer. "What other

toys. Did. You. Bring?"

"Tony first."

"Do not test me, love. I've had a killer migraine these last few days and I am reaching the end of my patience. Do you remember what I said I would take from him next?"

Charlie swallowed. "If you hurt him, I will never tell you what you want to know."

He smiled handsomely. "Yes you will because I will drag out his death for weeks, months, years. You will tell me what I want to know, love. The only power you have here is deciding what state your precious son will be in by the end of it."

He released her and turned his back, telling her in no uncertain terms that he didn't believe she was a threat. Charlie slipped a hand into her pocket and curled it around a grenade infused with sunlight. Sebastian might be a born vampire and thus not die from direct rays of the sun, but he would be blinded by it. Hopefully blinded enough for her to slip her blade into his chest and cut out his heart.

"The list of toys, love." Sebastian talked with his back to her, and it took everything Charlie had not to attack him now. She would only have one shot at him and by God, she was going to make it count.

"I have what you want."

At that, he turned and cocked a brow. "You brought me world domination and a cup of Zurali tea?"

Charlie blinked, completely caught off guard by his change of demeanor. She had the instinctive urge to ask if he was okay, then reminded herself she didn't give a shit. Besides, it was probably a tactic he was deploying just to keep her on her toes.

"No," she said slowly. "I bought you a soul stealer."

Releasing the grenade, Charlie pulled a small box out of her pocket. It had runes etched across every inch of its surface. Its carvings had taken her hours to complete in the private confines of a bathroom. In order to not draw suspicion, she'd drunken a ridiculous amount of water every hour which had slowed down the rest of her work considerably. If he crushed this as quickly as he had the transportation device, she was going to kill him.

He looked at it almost as if bored. "You planning on using it on me?"

"I wish." She gestured at him with it. "It's for you."

When he plucked it from her grasp, she added, "You need more than that to give a corpse back its memories, but you can't do it without it. It allows you to –"

"I'm familiar with soul stealers," he murmured. There was a sharp pain in his eyes, quickly gone.

"Anything else?" he purred.

Charlie bit her tongue. Slowly, she shook her head. "I'm desperate, not stupid."

He stared at her, and for a moment, she thought he was going to call her a liar. Then he shrugged, pocketed the soul stealer, and vanished.

She stepped forward with a shout. Fear gripped her heart, but before she could scream his name, Sebastian reappeared holding her son. She stood stock still, daring not even to breathe lest he disappear because of it.

"Mummy!"

She trembled at the sound of her little baby's voice. "Pumpkin? Are – are you okay?"

"He's fine. Though he won't be for long if you don't give me the way to read the *Scrolls*. Of course, that's assuming you haven't come back just to watch him die?"

"No. I figured out a way to share its knowledge."

He removed his hand from Tony's neck.

Swallowing, she looked him in the eye. "You have to drink from me," she blurted. "Only a select few can read the *Scrolls of Atlantis,* and by consuming my blood, you become one of them. The effects won't last for long, but it'll be enough time for me to tell you how to raise the dead."

"That's what you think I went through all this effort for? So I can learn how to bring someone back from the dead?"

His grin twisted her stomach. Her heart hammered in her chest. Dear God, she couldn't be wrong. Tony's life depended on it. Sebastian had to want this. "I –"

"Well, come here then."

Sebastian held out his hand. Her legs shaking, Charlie crossed the few feet between them. She offered her wrist, but he ignored it. Grabbing her by the waist, he crushed her to his chest, and bit her neck.

Biting back a scream, Charlie spasmed against him. The pain was unbearable, but just when she thought her legs would buckle, it vanished. Instant desire surged through her veins, overpowered only by her self loathing.

With a low chuckle, Sebastian released her. Charlie clasped a hand to her neck, glaring at him even as her body begged her to return to his embrace. He licked his lips, his tongue darting out between his fangs.

"Now tell me." He looked pointedly at Tony.

Charlie grabbed Tony's hand and pulled him behind her. He went silently and that worried her more than if he had screamed. She wanted to look at him, to check him over and make sure his mind wasn't shattered, but there wasn't any time. Sebastian was waiting, and if there was one thing that would inflict his rage, it was testing his patience.

"The soul stealer will grab the soul of any recent kill.

You have to –"

"How do I claim the soul of someone long dead?"

Swallowing, Charlie took a step back. She shifted her body slightly so she could sneak a hand into her pocket without him seeing. She gripped Tony's hand harder.

"You have to call the soul to you. You'll need five drops of their blood, the binds of their prison, and the gift of a god."

Taking another step back, Charlie pulled the pin on the grenade. One. "If they were murdered, you will need the heart of their murderer." Two.

"And if their murderer is already dead?" Three.

"Then you'll be joining them in Hell, you son of a bitch." Pulling the grenade out of her pocket, Charlie flung it at Sebastian's face. Swiveling, she dropped to her knees and pressed Tony's head against her chest. She closed her own eyes just in time to miss being dazed by the flood of light.

Sebastian wasn't so lucky. He loosed a feral scream as the sunlight stole his vision. Born to a race who never saw anything brighter than the moon, his eyes couldn't handle the full light of the sun. The tissue in his retinas burned away, leaving him completely blind.

But a blind vampire was still a dangerous one.

Frantic, Charlie reached inside her pocket and pulled out her spare transportation device. She clasped it around Tony's wrist, the coordinates for Heldron Castle already programmed into it. She pushed the button and together, they vanished into thin air.

A moment later they reappeared in Jack's room. She cried out in relief, but it quickly turned into a scream. Sebastian had managed to grab her shirt as they'd phased, and he was now standing behind him.

Footsteps sounded from outside. She tried to shove

Tony in their direction, but he refused to let her go. Tears streamed silently down his face.

By the time Tegan and Xeno burst into the room, the three were gone.

Charlie moaned as she landed back in the ruined castle on Blódyrió. Her stomach heaved, and she vomited all over her son just as he did the same to her. She tried to comfort him, but she was ripped away before she could utter a sound.

Tossed into the wall, Charlie felt something crack in her chest. She tried to crawl to her knees, but a sharp kick kept her down. Feebly, she reached for the knife she had strapped to the inside of her waistband.

Her head reeling from the constant phasing and her introduction to the wall, Charlie didn't react fast enough to the next boot coming her way. Groaning, she dropped back to the ground. She kept hold of the knife, however, and focused all of her attention, not on getting up, but on defending herself from his next attack.

Sebastian didn't even hiss in pain when she sunk the blade into his shin. It embedded into his tibia and as he reared back, he took the knife with him. Knowing her death was imminent, Charlie tried to scream for Tony to press the button on his transportation device. But a grip around her neck cut her off. She was yanked up off the ground, slammed into a wall, and then tossed once more.

Bones cracked in more than one place. Blood flooded her eyes and leaked out of her mouth. Coughing, she tried to clear the blood from her throat so she could scream at Tony to go.

Two feet appeared in front of her, and her heart sank in full terror. Adrenaline surged through her, giving her the strength to finally pull herself up.

"Tony, no!"

But her scream came too late. Sebastian grabbed her son.

She swung for him, but a dismissive backhand knocked her down. Dizzily, she stood back up.

"Leave her alone!"

There was the sound of flailing fists. Little fists that broke her heart even as they did nothing against the vampire they were attacking.

"Sebastian, please..." Charlie didn't believe in miracles. She'd learned there was no point praying to the gods or angels. In her heart, she knew she was going to watch her boy die, ripped apart by a monster she could not defeat.

Tears streamed down her face. She reached for her son, to at least hold some part of him so he wouldn't die alone. She was crying so much, bloodied so much, that she thought she was imaging the look on Sebastian's face.

The horror. The guilt.

Releasing the child, Sebastian stumbled back. His eyes never left the tear-stained face of the boy.

"Erin," Sebastian croaked.

Eyes misting, he vanished.

Charlie stared at the space he'd just occupied in shock. She blinked as she clutched Tony to her chest. Her ribs screamed in protest, but that only made her hug him tighter.

She looked around wildly, certain Sebastian was toying with them, certain he would be back any moment to rip her son from her arms. Frantically, she groped for the transportation device on Tony's wrist. She choked on a sob when she found it broken.

"Mummy."

"I'm so sorry, pumpkin. I'm –"

"*Charlie!*"

She flinched at the sudden scream. Then relief had her

collapsing to the ground as she recognized the voice that had called her name. He'd come. Even after she'd left him without so much as a goodbye, Jack had come to save her.

She was never going to leave him again.

"By the gods, kultara, what were you thinking coming alone! I would've come with you! I could've protected you!"

He gathered her in his arms as carefully as he could.

"Tony..."

"He's right here. I'm not going to let anything hurt him. Hey, stay awake. Keep your eyes open, kultara. Fucking keeping your eyes open!"

Charlie struggled to lift a finger to her lips. She needed him to be quiet. She couldn't sleep with all his yelling. Her eyes closed.

"Mummy!"

Snapping them back open, Charlie tried to stand. She needed her feet on the ground. She needed to defend her son.

"That's it, Tony. Keep talking to her."

"Mummy, I need you."

Her hand fluttered. Reaching for him. Jack guided her hand to Tony's. Gripping her son's hand, Charlie's eyes fluttered closed once more.

"Mummy!"

When Charlie's eyes didn't open this time, Jack held her tighter, wanting so desperately to shake her awake. He turned his head to the skies.

"Loki!" he screamed. "*Gods-fucking-dammit, Loki*!"

The following second took an eternity. But then he felt the power of a god, and Jack closed his eyes in relief. His father would save her.

A crackle of thunder jerked his eyes open. His heart stopped in his chest as a lightning bolt seared the ground in front of them. Tony screamed. Charlie opened her eyes, but soon they would close forever.

For it wasn't Loki that greeted them. It was Thor.

# THIRTY-FIVE

Jack's grip on Charlie tightened. The urge to cloak them and run took every ounce of his will to ignore. They might be able to hide from his cousin, but they wouldn't be able to run fast enough to save Charlie. There was only one option.

Slowly, Jack dropped to his knees. "Kill me later, cousin, but please save her first."

"No one's killing anyone." Loki appeared behind the Aesir God of Thunder, soon followed by Delentia. Tony hid behind Jack at the sight of the winged fury. The boy's trust in him squeezed at his heart.

"Well, isn't this a lovely family reunion?" Delentia cooed. She petted the chimera forever at her side. The lion head gave a low roar.

"Dad?" There was a world of trust in that one word. Loki smiled and stepped forward.

"It's going to be okay, son. Let me have her."

When Loki bent down, Jack was hit with the sudden desire to back away. He didn't want to let Charlie go. But he knew he had to if he wanted her to live. Lycra might be right about him having the ability to phase, but he didn't want his first time to be moving his critically injured mate.

Swallowing, he placed Charlie in his dad's arms. He didn't even have time to blink before they were gone. Tony screamed and Jack turned to comfort him.

"It's okay, Tony. That was my dad just now and he's taken your mom to the hospital. We're going after her. I promise." He shot a challenging look at the two gods before him. Delentia wasn't paying them any attention, but Thor's eyes sparkled with the rage of a storm.

"Come." Thor held out his hand.

Jack hesitated, then slowly rose to his feet. He flicked a glance at Delentia, but she didn't look at him at all. Trusting that she wasn't here just to watch him die (although she'd done that quite a few times over the years, she hadn't recently), Jack grabbed Tony's hand and led him over to his cousin. He conjured a knife in his other hand, hidden by his magic.

Without a word Thor grabbed his arm and phased. They arrived in the great hall of Valhalla. Though Jack had been here only once, many years ago, it was a sight he would never forgot.

Three intricately carved benches stretched the full length of the hall. The designs of the one in the middle told the stories of the gods past and present and future. Loki's time as a female horse was captured in its grain, as was Thor's dalliance in a wedding dress and Odin's trek to the great roots of Yggdrasil. The bench on the right was where prophecies were told. The one on the left held the likeness of every species, man and beast, across the Seven Planes, etched into its surface.

Above, the ceiling was crafted from golden shields and

crossed with weapons of lore. They were to be retrieved on the day Ragnarok arrived. The warriors that filled the hall were to be the ones to wield them.

And at the end of the great hall sat two thrones. They towered above the place on their dais, which was carved with ancient runes no mortal could read. In days long past this was where Odin saw the universe, but he had since moved that magic into his empty eye socket. Now he had an all-seeing eye that was the curse of Jack's existence.

"Fenrir." As Odin spoke the hall grew quiet. "You've grown too bold." There was no missing the threat in his tone.

Jack pushed Tony behind him. "I'm here for my mate, nothing more."

"The atlantean," he growled. Murmurs rippled down the hall. "And is that her child?"

"Please uncle, show them mercy."

"They are an abomination! They are not worthy of mercy!"

The hall shook from Odin's words. Power slammed into Jack's chest and he struggled not to fall to his knees. The *thing* clawed to the surface, giving him strength to stay standing. Murmurs disrupted the hall once more.

"It's free."

Instinctively, Jack dropped into a dive. He grabbed Tony as he rolled. Thor's hammer slammed into the ground, barely missing where he'd just been. Lurching onto his feet, Jack covered himself in magic. He started to concentrate on trying to phase when a small hand gripped his arm.

"Stay, boy. Sit."

Flashing a pointy-toothed smile, Delentia turned to address the hall. "My apologies for being late." She dipped into a bow, first at Odin and then his queen. Thor, she slapped on the ass and gave him a wink. The god grinned back at her and Jack rolled his eyes when she fluttered her lashes in return.

"Delentia."

Running her hands down her bright green tutu, the fury turned her attention to Odin. "Oh yes, where was I? Other than mentally stripping your son I mean? Ah, that's right."

She snapped her fingers.

Loki appeared with Charlie beside him. She was fully healed and Jack ran to her with Tony in his arms. She embraced them and showered her son with kisses. As Jack handed Tony over, he looked at his father. Loki gave him a reassuring smile, though it didn't quite meet his eyes.

"As you're aware, Fenrir's now out of the closet."

"Cage," Jack muttered.

"That too."

To be fair, she wasn't wrong.

"Which means our strongest enchantments have failed to contain him. Rebinding him would be pointless."

She picked at her teeth. "What we need is a stronger chain." Waving dramatically, she pointed at Charlie. "I give you...Gleipnir!"

"Um, what?" At Jack's words, Charlie was pleased to see she wasn't the only one confused. Thor scratched his chin. Odin shared a look with his wife, Freya. The whole hall was silent.

"I don't understand," Charlie said. She set Tony down in case she was suddenly grabbed and turned to Delentia. "Gleipnir is a combination of six ingredients. I read about it in the *Scrolls*."

"You admit you are an atlantean then?" Odin boomed.

Charlie turned to him, her chin high. "That's what I've been told."

"So she –"

"Pickle sauce," Delentia cut in. "Hush kitties and bacon cake. Mmm, I'm making myself hungry." Patting her stomach, she let out a loud belch. A feather floated out. She plucked it from the air and grinned.

"Gleipnir, come forth lass."

Charlie looked at Jack. His lips in a thin line, his fingers twitching at his sides, he gave her a small nod. With slow steps she crossed to the fury's side.

"Tell the great Aesir King what ingredients are needed for Gleipnir. Well, go on, girl, we don't have all day. Between my ramblings and the light of the moon, time's a wasting."

Charlie took a deep breath, knowing that her, Jack's, and Tony's lives might very well depend on her conduct. "Gleipnir needs the sound of a cat's footfall."

"Exhibit A." Delentia turned to Jack. "When she stabbed you in the chest in Aurora's Castle, what was your first thought?"

"Ow."

She narrowed her eyes. "Your defense mechanism is going to get you killed."

Swallowing, Jack thought back to their time in the cave. His eyes widened. "She moved with the sound of a cat's feet."

"Correcto! She's quite a silent lass despite her figure saying otherwise." She ran her eyes down Charlie's body and shook her head in disgust. "Next ingredient!"

A bit taken aback, it took Charlie a second to answer. "Um, the beard of a woman."

"Exhibit B." The fury held up her middle finger. "Another name for someone who carries out a deal on behalf of another in order to conceal their identity is... Drumroll please!"

Loki summoned up a drum and gave her one hell of a drumroll. She shot him a beaming smile. "A beard! And who did you represent, girlie?"

Charlie swallowed, her heart pounding. "Me."

"And would you say you are a woman?"

"Yes."

"I knew it! Shall we carry on?"

Confidence and hope slowly began to build inside her. "You also need the roots of a mountain."

"Ding, ding ding! Exhibit four!" Delentia opened her mouth, closed it. Then she scratched her head. "Argh! I knew I forgot something." Snapping her fingers, the fury swirled to face Charlie. She pointed at her, her little face serious. "You girl are more stubborn than a forest. It's no wonder your roots will birth mountains." Nodding, she smiled. "Next."

"The sinews of a bear."

"And the constructs of your mental haven?"

"Is of a substance harder than my father's hands and of the tough sinews of a mamma bear." It was a phrase Charlie had come up with when she was with Eddy. A reminder that she was stronger than her childhood.

"What was that?"

Charlie flicked a worried glance at Jack. His eyes bore into hers with too much understanding. His father held his arm as if to hold him back. Jerking her gaze to Odin, Charlie blurted, "The next requirement is the breath of a fish."

Delentia turned to Jack. "And after she jumped into the river, you changed her slightly before panicking and giving up. But what was it that you gave her for like half a second?"

Jack swallowed. "Gills."

"Ta da!" She turned back to Charlie. "And the last ingredient."

"The spit of a bird."

Delentia grinned. "Bird's the word for a hot lass in England, is it not? And what did you do when you ran into Jack that second time?"

Charlie's cheeks burned.

"She spat in my face," Jack said bemusedly.

"Exactly! So we have the six ingredients in one lass." Delentia flourished her hands down Charlie's body. "I give you...Gleipnir, the only chain capable of holding Fenrir!"

She stared at Odin expectantly. The gods's eyes were narrowed, but the anger that had radiated off him before was now muted.

"So she is." His eyes turned cruel. "Her son, is not."

"Ah, but without her son, she dies and then no more chain for Fenrir."

Odin's jaw ticked and Charlie feared he was going to take her son regardless. Frantic, she swept him in her arms. Tony buried his head in her shoulder. Jack and Loki both moved beside her in silent support.

"If I may offer an exchange?"

Odin moved his hostile gaze to Jack. After a strained moment, he nodded.

It would kill him not to rip her parents apart himself, but a god's hunt was never a peaceful thing. For that, and for Charlie's and Tony's life, he'd forfeit his right to kill them by his own hand. Raising his voice, Jack addressed the hall. "For the lives of these two atlanteans, I give you the lives of two others." Catching his father's approving eye, he paused, letting the silence linger. The whole crowd shifted forward to hear what he would say. Loki smiled. Jack finally continued, "Her parents are fair game. They're both purebloods."

Hushed murmurs turned into excited whispers. It had been way too long since the gods had had a proper hunt. Bets were already being made, plans already being drawn between friends. As the fever mounted, Odin studied Jack and Charlie with hard eyes.

It took everything he had to hold his uncle's gaze.

"Let's finish this then." The hall became silent in an instant. Odin stood, his power flooding the hall. "Bring the altar. For tonight we hunt!"

Cheers erupted. Feet stomped on the ground. Mugs banged on the tables. Charlie held Tony tighter as she stepped closer against Jack's side.

He wanted to offer her comfort, but the ceremonies of the gods were rarely a pleasant thing. Most involved intense pain; many involved sacrifice. The *thing* rippled beneath his skin, read to burst forth in an instant if it was needed.

His mouth grim, Jack turned to face his father. "What happens in a binding ceremony?"

Loki swallowed. "They will strip you of part of your true self. Just enough that Fenrir, that 'thing' inside you, will no longer be able to rise. That part of yourself will be bound to Charlie and part of her will be bound to you. It's not a pleasant process, made worse by the knowledge that she is to undergo the same agony."

"Then we must stop this."

Loki grabbed his son's shoulder. "No, son. You will want this."

"I would never wish her pain," he growled. His eyes flashed a dangerous red at the sight of Thor and his brother, Baldur, carrying in a bed-sized altar.

"The pain is temporary." Loki tugged on Jack until his son turned to face him. "But the binding of true selves is forever. Jack, this binding goes by another name. It's a ceremony that mortals find joyous and cause for great celebration."

"Holy fucking shit," Charlie breathed. Her eyes grew large as she turned to Jack. "It's a wedding."

"What?"

Charlie looked at the god of mischief. "That's what you're saying, isn't it?"

Loki nodded with a smile.

"Wait, what?" Jack repeated, his heart pounding, his palms growing sweaty.

"Son, you're to be married in the old way."

Jack's eyes flashed to Charlie's. She stared at him in silence, no hint of a smile on her lips. He mouth grew dry. His stomach twisted. He didn't want her married to him by force. He had to stop this. Turning, he –

"Ask me, Jack." Charlie touched his shoulder, halting him in his tracks. "I won't say no."

His fists tightened as the *thing* howled inside him. It didn't care about being bounded. It liked the idea of being a part of Charlie, of living in her, feeling her like Jack could. It wanted this. But it didn't want her by force. And nor did he.

"I won't marry you through coercion. I want –" He stopped abruptly.

She moved in front of him. Tony was no longer in her arms. The fact that she was focused all on him, only him, squeezed his heart with both joy and pain.

As much as Jack wanted to make her his in every way, he didn't want her to later resent him. He didn't want her choices ripped from her through a marriage she didn't want. But by the gods, did he want her to want it.

"I love you," he blurted. "But –"

She put a finger against his lips. A smile softened her face and his heart hammered because of it. She was so beautiful, so radiant. He wanted to cherish her forever.

"Then ask me," Charlie murmured. "I promise that when I answer, it will be because of what I want. Not what your uncle does."

Jack searched her eyes, looking for anything that told him she was lying. That she was only saying this because she had no other options.

But he didn't see sly determination in her eyes. He saw honesty and warmth. He saw a budding love even if she wasn't ready to admit it.

Heart flopping, Jack pulled her into his arms and ravaged her lips. She kissed him back, hungrily, happily. Pulling away, he looked at the source of all his happiness and smiled. "Charlie, whatever your last name is, will you marry me?"

He held his breath even though she'd assured him of her answer. His whole world stopped as he waited for her to speak.

Her lips curled into the brightest of smiles. "Yes, Jack," she said as she gazed up at him in longing. "Yes, I will."

# EPILOGUE

The wedding was like nothing ever experienced in the mortal realms. Every god and goddess of the Aesirs and Vanirs filled the great hall. Their eyes were fastened on the large altar in the middle, each wanting to be a witness to a ceremony that had not taken place for millions of years.

For to bind one's true self to another was a much more serious matter than simply offering up part of your soul. The soul was renewed with each birth; the true self was not. They would be bound together for all eternity, in life and death, and each of its many cycles.

To gods that knew the infinite stretch of life, that was simply too long of a commitment.

But to Jack it was everything he wanted. Charlie's life would be too short even if she lived five thousand years. He wanted forever with her. He didn't want a day of his life spent without her.

So when Freya bound their hands together with a braid of her own hair, Jack couldn't help but shed a few tears.

Happy ecstatic tears that barely spoke of the joy he was feeling.

Charlie smiled at him. She touched her loose hand to his cheek and he turned to kiss her palm.

Freya finished tying their hands and then straightened above them. Power radiated off her, covering Jack and Charlie in a magic that had touched the lives of so many. It was the essence of love itself. The infinite amount of nights many had spent waiting for a lover's return. The gentle squeeze of the hand. The secret smile one gave when they thought their crush wasn't looking. It was every cherished kiss and shared burst of laughter. It was an eternity. It was solid. It was theirs.

Charlie squeezed his hand just as Jack squeezed hers.

"Do you, Fenrir, the Wolf God and son of Loki, the God of Mischief, take Charlie Markson as your lifelong mate?" Freya asked.

"Yes," Jack breathed. Then he blinked, the goddess' name for him having finally registered. "Wait, I'm not –"

"Later, son." Loki winked, then nodded for Freya to continue.

"And do you vow on your blood and the soul of yourself inside her, that you will cherish her, love her, and bring her no harm?"

"Yes."

"Do you vow on your blood and the soul of yourself inside her, to take her pain as your own, her dreams as your own" –Freya looked at Tony– "and her child as your own?"

His throat tightened. He looked at the young boy held in his father's arms. Tony hadn't uttered a word since they'd gotten here. His little fists gripped Loki's shirt. It was as if he believed holding it so tightly would keep him safe.

Jack smiled at him. It wasn't going to be easy raising a child so traumatized and Jack was terrified that he was going to mess him up even more. But by the gods, he would try his hardest to do right by his second son.

"Yes."

"Your life is hers, do you vow this?"

Jack looked lovingly into his mate's eyes. Into his kultara's – the thorn that guarded the rose and made it all the sweater. "Yes."

Her smile grew.

Freya turned to her. "And do you, Charlie Markson, daughter of Prometheus, take Fenrir, the Wolf God and son of Loki, as your lifelong mate?"

Charlie's words were the most beautiful ones Jack had ever heard.

"I do."

### Kultara

A massive pain in the ass.
A thorn in one's side.
Someone you want to kill because of how much they
annoy you...

But a rose is not complete without its thorns.
A kultara is someone who is flawed,
someone who is frustrating and imperfect,
but someone you love all the same.

Want to know what happens to next with Tegan?

Join my newsletter to hear the
latest news about
*Rage for Her*
(chapter one below)

# Sign me up now!
https://mirandagrant.ck.page/0e074e9c (direct)
mirandagrant.co.uk (sign-up form)

# Author's Note

Hello everyone!

Thank you so much for reading *Tricked Into It*. I fell in love with Jack as soon as he'd premiered in *Elemental Claim* and informed me that he was afraid to fly. Like Rogan, I was baffled by this given he can change into a bird on a whim. I cannot express how delighted I was when I learned that he was a child of Loki and was being hunted by Thor the Aesir God of Thunder. Or that he was the one to steal Poseidon's trident, along with his father. That is definitely going to come back to bite him in the ass when he has to explain to Charlie why their future daughter is being hunted by the God of the Sea.

But that book is a long way away as I have the *War of the Myth* series to finish (nine more books!), not to mention all the other interconnecting series.

Many cheers and happy reading,

PS: A special shout-out to the Koala Hospital in Port Macquarie, Australia. It's an absolutely fantastic non-profit that focuses on the conservation of, surprise, koalas. If anyone else can spare any change, please do! https://shop.koalahospital.org.au/

# 5 REASONS TO SIGN UP TO MY NEWSLETTER

1 Have the chance to end up as a character in one of my books!
2 Have the chance to join either my beta/ARC reader team.
3 Download sneak preview chapters.
4 Get all the latest information about upcoming releases.
5 Get free book banners and other cool promo.

## *Sign me up now!*

https://mirandagrant.ck.page/0e074e4e9c (direct)
mirandagrant.co.uk (sign-up form)

# 3 REASONS TO LEAVE A REVIEW

1 They give me the strength and confidence to keep writing. The more reviews, the faster I write.
2 Chance to see your reviews inside one of my books.
3 I will love you forever.

# RAGE FOR HER

**He saved her, slept with her, then left
Hopefully straight to Niflhel**

The bastard. Phoebe doesn't care that Tegan's the head
of the Elv've'Norc and has the weight of the Seven Planes
on his shoulders. He didn't have to be a jerk these last
twenty years, avoiding her calls, ghosting her completely,
restricting her to this castle-like prison. If she doesn't
escape soon, she's going to go into a murderous rage. Or
do something drastic.

Something she is absolutely flippin' certain he isn't
going to like.

**He saved her, slept with her, then left
And every step away was torture.**

Every night, Tegan thinks about calling her. And every
night, he stops. If his enemies find out there's someone he
cares about, they'll torture her to get to him. Just like they
did his first wife.

And so he stays away. Stays focused on protecting the
Seven Planes. With Sebastian gearing up for something
big and the Deusychosis Plague nearly running free in the
Underground, he has a lot to keep him distracted.

Until she calls...
asking to marry another man.

# Death Do Us Part

### Honey, Does This Taste Like Poison to You?

I've never been a fan of murder. The mess, the smell, the whole hiding the body thing after – it always seemed like way too much work. But trust me, when you're married to Richard Morningstar, that "work" starts to feel an awful lot like "play". The man is a snake and king of the fairies.

A barbarian. A war monger. A sex god. Uh, I mean a...an ex pod? Doesn't matter.

The point is, it's either him or me. Because one of us is going to die, and at the moment, it's *my* execution scheduled in three weeks. So I just have to figure out a way to kiss him – *kill* him – before then, take his throne, and turn his whole nightmarish kingdom upside down. Easy right?

Maybe – if he wasn't my lifemate.

And if my panties didn't drop every time he snapped his stupid fingers.

# Burn Baby Burn

## Everything is About to Burn

We all know the story. Cinderella's father remarries. She gets a shitty new family. He dies in a tragic accident and she is forced into a life of servitude.

But what happens when Ella's father is brutally murdered and she's sold to the Romans? What happens when she meets a dark fae who tempts her to embrace the embers in her heart? When he shows her the fire she was born with and coaxes those powers to light? What happens when he tells her that she doesn't need a prince.

She needs a crown.

# The Little Morgen

## She kills without mercy

On her thirteenth birthday, Thalliya watched her entire
family get slaughtered. The humans cut off their fins and
hung their heads from their Viking ships. Left cradling
what few pieces remained of her twin, Thalliya screamed
to the gods for vengeance.

Answered by the Goddess of Love and War, Thalliya now
guards the seas without mercy.

## He fights without fear

Ragnar is hired to take care of the mermaid terrorising the
western seas. With seventeen kills under his belt, he
thinks little of venturing into the Mouth of Hel. It'll be a
quick job with a quick pay...

But when his ship is wrecked and the majority of his crew
is drowned, Ragnar realises that it's not a mermaid he's
hunting. It's a morgen, a dark mermaid, that's hunting
him.

And there's only one way to kill one of those.

You have to get her to fall in love.

# Bjerner and the Beast

## He's Sworn to Protect the Emperor at All Costs

When he was a child, Bjerner sacrificed his eyes to the Goddess of Death. Raised as a warrior, he's now a trusted member of the Varangian guard. As he struggles to keep the emperor alive, Bjerner is forced to take a mission that will either see him killed or see him hailed as a hero.

## She's Tired of Heroes

All they ever want to do is try to kill her. Ever since she was born, Ophidia has been hunted like an animal and all because of what she is: a beast that has the power to turn people into stone.

Forced to hide in a cave her entire life with only the dead heroes for company, Ophidia desperately wants her next visitor to be a little less stabby.

And less inclined to look at her face.

And would it really kill them to just *talk* to her first?

But as the centuries pass, she's starting to lose hope that such a man exists...

# ONE

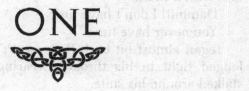

"The hel I am!"

Tegan slammed his glass on the table. The amber liquid splashed over the rim, but he barely felt it soak his hand; the fury inside him boiled too bright. It physically crawled beneath his skin, the slithering Rage a clear sign that he was seconds away from exploding.

Gripping the table's edge, the berserker's eyes flashed a dangerous red.

In two seconds, the room was going to get ripped apart. In six, he'd be going for his agents. And once they were down, there would be nothing to stop him from ravaging the city. He had to get control of himself. And fast.

The table splintered beneath his fingers.

"Look," he growled into his earpiece. "I realize –"

"I'm not talking about this anymore."

Her voice was as lovely as silk as it flitted through his mind. It wrapped around his heart, all delicate and soft – right before baring its teeth with all the venom of a pissed off viper.

Swearing, Tegan released the table. With an ominous creak, it split in two, then crashed to the ground.

His lips pursed. His eyes narrowed. Fighting the urge to release the entirety of his anger, Tegan clenched his fists with a snarl.

"Dammit! I don't have time –"

"You never have time!"

Tegan almost bit back that wasn't true, but the denial lodged tight in his throat. Swearing in frustration, he stalked around his suite.

He glared at the stone walls that made up the castle. They were a dark gray, a perfect match to his current mood. In three hundred years, Tegan hadn't lost control of his Rage outside of a fight, but just hearing Phoebe's voice...

Just hearing what she wanted him to do...

The wall cracked beneath his fist.

To hel if he was going to comply.

"I have to go," he snapped.

"Don't you dare –"

Yanking the earpiece off him, Tegan tossed it on the table. He remembered too late that it was no longer there. Snarling, he snapped the phone back up and threw it at the far wall.

"Godsdammit!"

He hadn't seen Phoebe for nearly twenty years. He'd even fooled himself into believing he'd managed to put her behind him. Placed her in a forgotten box that he'd never have to deal with.

She was much safer that way.

*He* was much safer that way.

And since he was the head of the Elv've'Norc, an organization tasked with protecting the Seven Planes, all the fucking *worlds* were safer that way.

"Fuck!"

Picking up the chair, Tegan slammed it into a wall. The Rage clawed at his heart, demanding he give in to his most primitive desires. He threw the remaining pieces of the chair at the other side of the room, then clenched his fists with a snarl.

Taking a deep breath, Tegan struggled to regain his control. But the stud in his ear demanded his attention, burning with the weight of its significance. He wanted to reach up and touch it, to find comfort in it like he always had. Only this time, he knew it wouldn't bring any peace. Nothing would. Not after Phoebe had requested what she had.

Growling, Tegan exited his suite and stalked into the hall. The polished obsidian walls cast back his reflection, showing that the Berserker Rage still slithered beneath his skin.

It rippled across his broad shoulders, the very soul of temptation. There was nothing more addictive than listening to its call and feeling the power of the gods coursing through his veins. It made him feel unstoppable, invincible, and completely at peace – at least until he came back to his senses.

Then the truth of his destruction, the faces of the dead...

Eyes narrowing, Tegan glared at his reflection. Slowly, his tattooed flesh settled back to normal. The Rage inside him quieted to its normal pounding.

Striding towards the stairs, Tegan lowered his mental guard just enough for Galvanor, one of his telepathic agents, to notice.

*Get everyone to the control room,* Tegan commanded. He frowned when there wasn't an immediate reply.

Galvanor had contracted the Deusychosis Plague a few

days ago and it had nearly killed him. Only the man's quick reactions had stopped the disease from sinking deep into his brain. The angels had cured him within a few hours, but that had still been long enough for the disease to greatly weaken him. And then, as if that wasn't enough, Galvanor had contracted it a second time in less than forty-eight hours. He'd slipped into a coma. It had taken him days to recover.

Galvanor had since assured him that he was fit enough to continue with the mission. And Tegan, wanting to keep the specifics of this operation as secret as possible, hadn't pushed. But maybe he should. If Galvanor was struggling to even read his thoughts, then it was time to –

Tegan slammed into the wall as a monstrous roar ripped through his skull. His head split open in a blinding migraine and he punched the cold stone to combat the pain.

Clenching his teeth, Tegan growled past the sheer agony in his mind. He ignored the blood dripping from his nose. Drawing on his power, he then shoved himself upright and took a heavy step forward.

*Galvanor!* he snapped.

The energy that took, the pain it caused, almost made him collapse back against the wall. *Control yourself!* he shouted as he stalked down the hall.

He'd barely passed the room next to his when a roar and a crash sounded from inside it. A moment later, the door flew across the hall, quickly followed by the body of an enraged demon. The beast hit the wall, smashing out chunks of stone. As Pyro crumbled to the ground, a growl erupted deep from his throat.

Tegan snapped his head to the doorway. His Rage boiled to the surface in preparation for a fight. Even the strongest of beasts would hesitate to cross a berserker in full power.

But the man in the doorway wasn't phased. Gabriel stepped into the hall, his hands down at his sides in complete relaxation. His pitch black hair fell in front of his eyes and with a single toss of his head, he put it back in place. Power rippled from him with the energy of an alpha. Even Pyro, the reckless demon whom Gabriel had just tossed through the air, didn't dare retaliate.

Glowering, Tegan forced his Rage back down.

"You're needed upstairs," Gabriel said nonchalantly. His large black wings ruffled behind him as he turned down the hall. It was a clear dismissal, a warning that they should go quickly despite any questions.

Clenching his teeth, Tegan turned to Pyro. Before he could say anything, another scream ripped through his head. His growl of frustration was lost beneath the roar's ferocity.

*Galvanor!*

But then Tegan realized his folly. The sound wasn't coming from inside his head this time.

The castle walls shook. Dust dropped from the ceiling. Another roar echoed through the hall, coming from the floor above.

They were under attack.

Pyro's gaze crashed with his. Moving as one, the two jumped into action, rushing towards the stairs. Both of their beasts crawled beneath the surface, but only Pyro changed forms as they ran.

His horns elongated. His bulk increased. Each footfall echoed with his anger. When he yanked the stairwell door open, he accidentally ripped it from its hinges. Tossing it behind him with a growl, Pyro rushed inside, taking the stairs four at a time.

Tegan was quick behind him. His skin rippled with his

Rage, but there was a danger to pulling on its power. A Berserker's Rage did not always stop when the threat was over nor did it always discern friend from foe. To use it could destroy more than it saved.

A haunted memory started to rise. Tegan promptly squashed it.

*Galvanor, report,* he commanded. Although he'd find out for himself in a few seconds when he burst onto the next floor, Tegan didn't like going in blind. If there was something he needed to react to immediately upon entry, he'd prefer to be prepared.

*There's a – Matakyli, no!*

Tegan crashed to the ground. Pyro screamed as he fell through the door. Galvanor's power was out of control, ripping through their minds like acid.

Gritting his teeth, Tegan pulled himself up the stairs. Blood dripped from his ears. A single red tear ran down his cheek. When he got to Pyro's limp form, he scanned the room for the threat, but he needn't have bothered.

Standing in the middle of the living room, its back brushing the ceiling, was a monstrous wolf. Its fur was made up of smoke and embers. Its red eyes glinted in a dangerous challenge. Blood soaked its mouth, dripping from canines which were fully bared.

Limp against the wall, her body torn and unmoving, was Matakyli. Galvanor crouched protectively over her, his face twisted in agony. Lowering its head, its black fur rising, the thing let loose a terrible growl.

Tegan rushed forward to meet it. He ran a hand down his bare arm, tracing the intricate tattoo that covered him from his shoulder to his wrist. As soon as his fingers glided off his skin, a ten foot claymore appeared in his hand, the tattoo now gone. The sword sang with power, its hilt embedded with the magic of his people.

The wolf focused on the blade in an instant, a growl erupting deep in its chest. Familiarity flashed in its eyes at the weapon, causing Tegan to bellow in anger.

There was only one species that wielded blades like his, and Tegan's family was it. They were the only berserkers, the only ones with tattooed swords on their bodies. If the beast had harmed any of his sisters...

With a warrior's cry, Tegan swung the claymore at the wolf's head. One cut was all it would take to cleave through anything, regardless of how thick or strong.

Snarling, the wolf dodged with an uncanny speed. It countered even faster, its teeth sinking into Tegan's arm before he could so much as blink. Jerking him off the ground, the wolf tossed him through the air.

Tegan dropped his sword before he crashed down the stairs and impaled himself on it. The tattoo etched itself onto his mangled arm. As soon as he hit the ground and regained his feet, he pulled the claymore back off his skin.

He lunged through the broken door, sword leading, only to quickly dive to the ground. Pyro sailed above him, barely missing taking him down with him.

Jumping to his feet, Tegan's eyes narrowed. The beast was no longer facing him. A knife was stuck in one of its hind legs, thrown by one of the many people who had now arrived on scene. The dagger looked more like a needle in a pincushion than anything damaging though, but it had done its job. The wolf was no longer focused on him. Now all Tegan had to do was sneak up on it and he could kill it in one fell swoop.

Ignoring the cries of his agents as they fought off the creature's snapping jaws, Tegan inched forward.

*Where is she!?* the beast roared.

Tegan froze as the demand ripped through his brain. He knew that voice, the one coming from the wolf. And unfortunately, as much as he wanted to rip the man a new asshole, he wasn't about to kill one of his best agents. Not without knowing why he had attacked them in the first place.

Still, Tegan didn't sheath his sword. And he didn't stay frozen for long, inching forward once more.

*Jack?* Galvanor asked slowly. He'd opened his mind a little, letting everyone listen but no one speak. *Can you hear me?*

*Tell me where she is*, Jack growled.

*Who?*

*My mate.*

Tegan's grip on his sword tightened. If Galvanor didn't know where Charlie, Jack's mate, was, then all hel was about to break loose.

After a strained silence, Galvanor confirmed his fears.

*She's not in the castle and I'm not strong enough yet to find her.*

*You would have heard her thoughts.*

Jack growled. Tegan raised his sword.

*Where did she go?*

*I'm still recovering*, Galvanor said. *I haven't been able to listen –*

*You lie!*

Tegan swung, aiming for a leg. The attack would cut it clean off, but it wouldn't be lethal. With luck, the pain would distract Jack enough that they could bring him down.

But the plan was all for nothing.

The blade missed, swinging through a cloud of smoke and ash. Tegan's eyes widened as the wolf became an ethereal form. Jack was a trickster, capable of physically mimicking various species, but the one thing he couldn't do was take on new powers. No trickster could.

No mortal could.

Tegan's heart rate sped up. But if Jack wasn't a mortal, then why wasn't Gabriel up here? As an archangel it was Gabriel's duty to police the gods.

Before another thought could form, Tegan pivoted to avoid snapping teeth. Claws slashed towards his neck and he met them with his sword. Relief swamped him when the paw went flying, severed as if Tegan had been cutting butter.

Whatever Jack was, they could still fight him. They could still bring him to his knees.

Pivoting, Tegan went in for another swing. The blade sliced through a cloud of embers. Before he could shift his direction, a paw slammed into the side of him. The sword went flying. His tattoo reappeared on his arm as the blade vanished into thin air.

Tucking fluidly, Tegan rolled into the fall. He ended back up on the balls of his feet, sword in his hand. His mangled arm bled profusely. His head pounded with a killer migraine. His chest ached from broken ribs.

Ignoring the pain, his eyes narrowed on Jack. The wolf seemed to be smiling as it lifted a paw to show its claws. Tegan's eyes widened. That was the same limb he'd hacked into; the one whose paw he'd just severed. For Jack to regenerate a whole new part that quickly...

Racking his claws across the ground, the wolf lunged. Tegan raced towards it with a yell. He dove onto his knees as Jack's teeth ripped through the air where he'd just been. Sliding between its legs, Tegan lifted his sword and sliced clean through the wolf's chest. He'd barely cut more than a foot deep before he was engulfed in a cloud of smoke.

A snarl warned him too late that Jack had reappeared in front of him. Bloody teeth filled Tegan's vision. He couldn't stop his slide. The Rage crawled beneath his skin, ready to erupt in a show of glory in order to save his life.

Before Tegan could embrace the Rage, a spout of water whipped past his head. It slammed down Jack's throat, causing him to snap his jowls shut before he could swallow Tegan whole.

Jumping to his feet, the berserker aimed another swing. Rogan aided his attack this time, shooting water at the beast's eyes and mouth so it couldn't fight back. Kasem and Kaide, two teleporting swordsmen, appeared beside him. They vanished just as quickly, phasing in and out just long enough to slice at Jack in a tornado of blades.

Together, the seven of them worked as one. Adriel attacked from the front with Aisla, their blades and arrows tearing into Jack's flesh in a thousand cuts. Pyro, having stormed back up the stairs, now had demon fire pouring out of his palms. The two swordsmen phased high and low, left and right, never lingering long enough to be attacked.

Tegan ducked as a fireball singed his hair. It flew through the cloud of smoke and exited the other end. Aisla barely managed to dodge out of its way, but by avoiding the fire, she'd stepped right into the line of razor sharp claws.

Her scream ruptured the air. A demon's bellow soon followed. As Jack jumped on top of Adriel, Tegan's eyes narrowed. If they didn't finish this soon, they wouldn't be able to.

As if sharing his thoughts, Xeno arrived on scene with her hands burning in a holy light.

*Get back, now!*

Galvanor's command screamed in their heads. All but the two drazic demons obeyed in an instant. When Xeno hesitated because Pyro stepped into her line of vision,

Tegan tackled the demon to the ground. Xeno might be weakened due to her fall, but her light could still burn the soul of a demon. It could still kill one that was already on the verge of collapse.

As they fell to the ground, Pyro went to elbow Tegan in the face. His attack floundered as a blinding beam stole his vision.

Prepared for it, Tegan had already closed his eyes. He tucked his head to protect them further. As soon as the light faded, he jumped to his feet and rushed Jack with his sword.

The way was clear. Jack was momentarily blind. It should have been a done deal with Tegan's blade ending the fight in one fell swoop.

But right as he began his swing, a powerful energy slammed into his chest. He was hurled back, his arms and legs leveling out in front of him. His sword flew wide. A man screamed. And then Tegan crashed through a wall, his temple slamming against the rubble.

Searing pain exploded inside his skull. The world went dark. Instantly, the Rage jumped to the surface, bringing him back to sharp awareness.

With a feral growl, Tegan's eyes snapped open. They glowed a bright red, the color of blood, the color soon to paint these walls. Pushing himself into a sitting position, the berserker shoved his dislocated shoulder back into its socket. He stood, unsheathed his sword, and kicked through the crumbling wall with a warrior's yell.

The wolf's head snapped towards him. Jack growled low, his fur on end, but he didn't move. For standing in the middle of the storm, one hand holding his paw in mid air, was what looked like a child ballerina.

She was dressed in a bright blue tutu, baggy unicorn leggings, and knee high boots. A crop top shirt hung from her shoulders, creased by the elastic bands of her angelic costume. Glittery fabric wings hung limply on her back, an odd contrast to the real ones, leathery and red, peaking above her head.

Lost in his Rage, Tegan didn't register her identity. With a bellow he rushed forward. The ballerina turned to face him. A sincere smile lit her face. Digging a blade out from between her boobs, she tossed it at his face.

He leaned his head to the side, felt the knife whistle past his ear. A sneer of triumph curled his lips. Two steps later though and it was gone.

As a deafening crack split the air, dust rained down on him like hail. He threw his arms up automatically. Tried to dodge out of the way. But as he did so, a piece of loose obsidian slid out from under him. And as the ceiling crashed down upon him, Tegan's roar was lost beneath the rubble.